D1111719

"Reading Lillie Vale's *Wrapped with a Beau* is like stepping into the warmest, coziest Christmas movie you can imagine. I wish I could walk down the streets of Piney Peaks, a town so festive that even the most disastrous meet-cute involves a large candy cane lawn decoration. Even if you aren't in a cold climate, this book will make you feel like you're snuggled under a blanket beside a crackling fire as snow falls outside."

—Kerry Winfrey, author of *Faking Christmas*

"*Wrapped with a Beau* is the gift of the season. Lillie Vale perfectly captures the thrill, beauty, vulnerability, and depth of falling in love—and I *dare* you not to fall scarf over snow boots for Elisha and Ves. Piney Peaks is the cozy, heartwarming, fairy-lit haven you've been dreaming of. This warm embrace of a book begs to be savored by firelight."

—Courtney Kae, author of *In the Event of Love*

"*Wrapped with a Beau* is everything a holiday romance should be: full of heart, heat, and cozy intimacy. Lillie Vale's writing is clever and compulsively page-turning, and the banter-filled chemistry between Elisha and Ves had me melting all the way from their hilarious meet-disaster to their well-earned HEA. The idyllic setting of Piney Peaks felt so real that I wanted to book a flight there as soon as I turned the last page, just to live in Elisha and Ves's sparkling world a little longer. I loved every minute of this absolute gift of a book!"

—Jessica Joyce, author of *You, with a View*

"I'm ready to move to Piney Peaks! I devoured this delicious, opposites-attract holiday rom-com that's as sweet as Ugly Christmas Sweater cookies and as hot as Spicy Grinch cocktails. Lillie Vale's *Wrapped with a Beau* is an utterly heartwarming tribute to found family, small-town charm, and finding magic where you seek it. Bursting with cozy holiday cheer, heartening family dynamics, and sparkling banter, these lovable characters and their instant chemistry will stay with you long after the last snowflake has melted. This book will wrap you up in a big, warm hug—tied with a bow!"

—Lauren Kung Jessen, author of *Lunar Love*

Also by Lillie Vale

The Decoy Girlfriend

The Shaadi Set-Up

Young Adult

Beauty and the Besharam

Small Town Hearts

WRAPPED
with
A BEAU

A NOVEL

LILLIE VALE

G. P. PUTNAM'S SONS

NEW YORK

PUTNAM
— EST. 1838 —
G. P. Putnam's Sons
Publishers Since 1838
An imprint of Penguin Random House LLC
penguinrandomhouse.com

Copyright © 2023 by Lillie Vale

Trade paperback ISBN: 9780593422045
Ebook ISBN: 9780593422052

Printed in the United States of America
1st Printing

BOOK DESIGN BY KATY RIEGEL

Whatever you do,
do it with grace and gumption

CHAPTER ONE

Elisha

There isn't a lot that Elisha Rowe is sure of at this hour, but as she shivers on her parents' snow-dusted porch in fluffy pink slippers and a pom-pom beanie, she's sure of this: someone has broken into her house.

Well, not *her* house. Rather, the green, gabled Victorian across the street. She doesn't own it—could barely afford a square foot of the sprawling place—but until the new owner takes possession, she thinks of it as hers. Mostly because her beloved neighbor, Maeve Hollins, had always made her feel like it was her home away from home.

Maeve and Elisha's grandma Lou, may they both rest in peace, had been lifelong best friends who adored romance, cocktails, and Christmas—not necessarily in that order. As a child, Elisha had always considered Maeve's house their clubhouse: a place to go after school for Maeve's famous hallongrotta, the sweet and crumbly raspberry thumbprint butter cookies that were a staple of Elisha's childhood, and back-to-back romantic movies. Much to Maeve's and Lou's amusement, by age ten, she was mouthing along with the dialogue of her favorite movies, and by twelve, she knew them by heart.

And this was her first Christmas without either of them.

If Maeve's mischievous cats, Thor and Thorin, hadn't woken her up—well-timed swishing tails in the face and headbutts to the kidneys—she would have slept right through the lights flicking on across the street. Before she'd even had the chance to blink the sleep out of her eyes, her protective instinct had kicked in. How *dare* someone break in.

"You've got to be kidding me," Elisha huffs. It's six a.m. and she should still be snuggled into her warm flannel sheets, waiting for the smell of hazelnut coffee to wake her. Instead, she's seriously contemplating violence. "You're a determined thief, I'll give you that."

The figure's blurred shadow moves behind Maeve's living room windows. Elisha can't be sure, but it looks like they're searching for something. Her eyes narrow, her toes curl tight.

It's the first of December, which puts this affront right on schedule. Every December, tourists made the trek to their Poconos mountain town of Piney Peaks for photo ops with Maeve's house, which had become famous for its role in the 1974 classic film *Sleighbells under Starlight*. Elisha is used to seeing total strangers flirt with trespass, but without Maeve here to find it charming and invite them in for hot cocoa and a cozy chat . . .

No one's breaking in on Elisha's watch.

She's already marching over when it occurs to her that it *might* not be the best idea in the world to surprise an intruder empty-handed. Without breaking stride, she snatches one of her mother's giant plastic candy canes lining the driveway. Despite the size, it's flimsier than she expected, weighing almost nothing. Not exactly the most menacing object of self-defense.

She half frowns, then gives it an experimental *whack* against her palm. It stings a bit, but not enough to do any true damage. Okay, so this *definitely* isn't her best idea, but to be fair, she's way better at talking herself into things than talking herself out.

Thank god she's not wearing her winter boots. They would have crunched across the street, announcing her arrival. Instead, her slippers silently sink into last night's snowfall. As the cold bites at the sliver of exposed skin on her ankles, Elisha winces and pretends this is all in the name of stealth rather than rushing in without thinking.

The soggy slippers muffle her ascent up the Victorian's stairs, and she avoids the creaky board one step from the top in the nick of time. Once she's reached the front door, she only stops long enough to scrape off her slippers on the cheeky *Hey There, Pumpkin* welcome mat, still there from when Maeve had decorated for Halloween. The pink toe-bunny on each slipper is crusted with a beard of ice she can't quite manage to shake.

But her gaze snags on the snow already there, not yet melted. A thief with manners who brushed off his feet at the door? Frowning, she tests the door handle. Unlocked, the door silently swings open.

She leaves it open in case she needs to make a quick exit, inching past the wide foyer and into the living room, or as Maeve used to call it, the front parlor. Like every other room, it's an incongruous mishmash of coziness and ostentation that shouldn't work but somehow does.

Immediately, her eyes land on the broad-shouldered back of a man who, despite the generous dimensions of the room, towers over everything in it: the spindly end table teetering with the last books Maeve was shuffling through, the Tiffany torchiere floor lamp lowlighting the hand-painted frieze wrapping around the room. He's the kind of tall that makes Elisha, at five foot seven, feel dainty in comparison.

Her Goliath is mumbling to himself now, shoulders hunched as he scrounges through the drawers. He flips through the stack of papers in his hands quickly, scrutinizing them for just a second or two. Tossing Maeve's treasured memorabilia on the floor—like *trash*—as he goes.

A whole lifetime discarded as if it's nothing.

Elisha bristles, watching the soft flutter of theater programs, movie ticket stubs, and elegant wedding invitations as they scatter on the hardwood floor. Her fingers clutch her impromptu weapon even harder.

"Why couldn't it be money?" the intruder asks, actually tipping his head to the ceiling as if he expects an answer. His sigh is followed by a growl. "This whole place is a fucking fire hazard."

Elisha stifles a laugh at how quickly his despondency turns to irritation. He's seriously criticizing the clutter? Those who break into other people's houses do *not* get to throw stones!

His neck suddenly straightens, shoulders dropping. The move is uncannily similar to the one the cats make when sneaking up on each other, about to pounce.

She must have made a noise, given herself away somehow. The Goliath starts to turn.

Her fight-or-flight kicks in. She raises the candy cane high above her head, ready to bring it down. "I'm armed!" she half warns, half shrieks, leaving off the *dangerous*, because of course she's not.

He doesn't know that, though.

With a startled yelp, he stumbles, almost slipping on the pile of Maeve's precious mementos he had just tossed on the floor.

Elisha can't help it—she shrieks again.

The candy cane swings through the air. It misses the man entirely, but it's too late to stop the force of its arc. The knobby part of her knee catches the brunt of the blow like a doctor testing her reflexes with a tiny hammer. Pain ricochets down her leg, a hundred times worse because it's self-inflicted, and even worse, it's acutely embarrassing.

Immediately, involuntarily, and absolutely inconveniently, her eyes well with tears.

The lawn ornament slips from her fingers, clattering to the floor. Her leg gives out and she collapses in an elegant heap. A jumble of swears erupts from her mouth. If Goliath guesses most of them are aimed at him, he doesn't make a peep. Instead, he crouches.

Through her blurry vision, she can make out two things:

One, he does not look at all pleased to see her. Which is a shame, because two, he's gorgeous.

Even if he is a thief. An exceedingly well-groomed and well-dressed one, if that belted, expensive-looking coat and thick red scarf are anything to go by.

He raises a sharp dark brow, a shocking contrast to his platinum-blond hair. "Are you done?"

She's too busy tentatively massaging her injury and mulling over which adjective would perfectly describe the striking shade of his blue eyes when she realizes he's speaking to her. "What?"

"Whatever tantrum you're throwing," he says. "Are you done?"

"Excuse me?"

Now he's the one to look annoyed. "I'm not repeating myself a third time."

She gapes. "You're not even going to ask me if I'm okay?" She gestures at her knee.

His eyes flick down as if to ascertain it's not serious, then back to her face. There, he holds steady, almost as if he's mapping her for clues. Elisha scowls and juts her jaw out, breathing through her nose.

"I'm not in the habit of inquiring after the well-being of people who break and enter," he drawls finally.

"I didn't 'break' in," she says with finger quotes and a scoff. "I'm protecting this house!"

He bristles at the implication that it needs protecting from *him*, the sharp line of his jaw growing even more taut as he sets his mouth in a grim line. "Ah, yes. The woman dressed like a deranged elf who escaped from the North Pole strikes terror in my heart."

She glances at her slippers and pajamas. *Okay,* rude. *Accurate, but rude.* Not one to let a good tit-for-tat opportunity slip by, she says dryly, "Guess that explains your scream."

He shoots her a dour look. "I did not scream."

She smiles sweetly. "If that's what you need to believe."

His jawline is so rigid that she's surprised she can't hear teeth cracking. "So, either you're part of the neighborhood watch, or you like to play at being a knight and defend unguarded houses."

Well, when he puts it like that, her actions sound childish rather than brave. Now it's her turn to quietly fume. "Something like that."

Goliath plays along. "And that's the best armor you have?"

She rolls her eyes. "What can I say, my chain mail is in the wash."

He nods at the candy cane. "Along with your sword, I'm guessing."

"Bite me."

At that, he almost smiles. Worse, her own lips threaten to curl. She stomps down the urge.

"I don't want to argue with you," he says, even though he's giving a *great* impression otherwise.

"Wow, the view must be awesome from your moral high ground. Last I checked, intruders don't get to act offended when they're caught in the act."

"Know a lot of them, do you?"

Elisha huffs. His voice is silky, with a hint of a New York accent, and manages to sound both amused and taunting at the same time. Mostly taunting. "Yeah, we all hang out in the same bar. You should come to our weekly Intruders Anonymous meeting."

"I guarantee that you'll never see me in any bar *you* frequent." His smile is like a paper cut. "And, as it happens, I'm not an intruder. I own this house."

"Ha. Try again."

With an unrepentant eyebrow raise, he crosses his arms. "And why is that so unbelievable?"

She gives him a derisive sniff. "Because according to her lawyer, Maeve Hollins's great-nephew owns the Christmas House." Then she narrows her eyes, eyeing him up and down.

Expensive shoes. Expensive coat. Even-more-expensive-looking haircut. *He's not . . . There's no way that he could be . . . But what if . . . ?*

"Wait. You're not . . . ?" she asks weakly.

"Maeve's great-nephew, Ves Hollins. And I wish I could say it was a pleasure to meet you, but—"

Elisha's cheeks burn at the way he lets the sentence hang.

He shrugs like he didn't just insult her, getting to his feet without offering her a hand. "So, want to tell me who the hell you are?"

"Elisha Rowe," she croaks.

Her name has never felt more like a tangled ball of scratchy yarn is lodged right in her throat. It worsens when she has to tip her head back to look at him. Ves. He has a name now. A rather sexy one, really. Which makes her shitty first impression all the more of a shame, but she shoos the thought away.

"So, Elisha, now that we've established that you're the only intruder here . . ." Ves's voice is as stony as his jawline. "Care to explain why?"

Her stomach nose-dives like Santa's sleigh crashing through the atmosphere, aiming for a chimney.

Well, Ves, she thinks, *I'm here because I was watching Maeve's cats until I knew whether you wanted to adopt them, and they suck at personal space and letting me sleep in. And sure, go ahead and laugh, but this house is one of my favorite places in the whole world, and I did think I was protecting it, actually.*

But if you want the full story, I'm the film liaison for our Chamber of Commerce and I busted my butt to make sure the fiftieth-anniversary anticipated sequel to Sleighbells under Starlight *will be filming in Piney Peaks this January. Since the house is yours now, I need you to sign the location release because I promised everyone that I would and Elisha Rowe does* not *go back on her word.*

I know we got off on the wrong foot, but feel like helping a girl out?

Nope, can't do it. Asking him for a favor now would be entirely inappropriate and completely pathetic. Her window of opportunity to make a good first impression was just smashed into smithereens thanks to a candy cane and some questionable judgment. Had she really thought her elf pajamas and pink bunny slippers were cute? Why hadn't she thrown on a robe before leaving the house? Or, better yet, changed into something remotely in the realm of adult?

So Elisha sighs and points haphazardly in the direction of home. "I live there. Welcome to the neighborhood."

Ves crosses his arms and arches an eyebrow, clearly unimpressed. "Piney Peaks *really* needs to work on its welcome committee."

CHAPTER TWO

Elisha

I might as well have introduced myself as Elisha Rowe, the biggest fuckup in Piney Peaks history," Elisha says with a groan, sinking her head into her arms on the counter at the Old Stoat pub. Even after an achingly slow Friday at work, her run-in with Ves Hollins hasn't diminished her embarrassment in the slightest. "I keep seeing his face in my mind. Ugh! I can't believe I took a swing at the man who inherited Maeve's house when the one thing I needed to do was to win him over." She heaves a sigh. "What the fuck."

Ves Hollins. The hot man. The *really* hot man. Which shouldn't have even been a thing that she noticed, but now that she has, she decides it's an unhelpful adjective. So no, not the hot man—the *smug* man. That suits him better.

And right now, he's the man who holds the fate of this movie and her sparkling reputation in the palm of his hand.

Elisha's best friend, Solana Pereira, gives her shoulder a sympathetic rub. "It's not that bad, Lisha. I bet he's already forgotten it."

"Would *you* forget a deranged woman in elf pajamas playing

Whac-A-Mole on your head with a giant candy cane? Nothing short of a time machine can undo that epic disaster."

"Heh. Yeah, that was pretty bad."

Elisha groans again.

"But!" cries Solana. "Let me finish! It's not like you actually succeeded in Whac-A-Moleing him. Just be extra nice, redeem your terrible first impression, and make Ves Hollins see how lovely you are, my darling."

Elisha lifts her head. "There's no fixing this, Lana. Literally the second I told him that I was simply a concerned neighbor, he kicked me out. I apologized, but he didn't even let me finish before he slammed the door in my face. Oh, and he kept the candy cane."

"Well, you did try to hit him with it . . ."

Elisha's right eyelid twitches. "Friday happy hour drinks are getting less happy by the minute."

"Sorry, sorry! I'm back to being optimistically supportive BFF." Solana gestures for Adam Lawson, her bartender boyfriend, to bring them both a second fruity Grinch cocktail. "You're good at wooing, so woo. You know how tight my mom is with the annual budgets, but you still managed to convince Madam Mayor to literally create our town's first-ever film liaison position in the Chamber of Commerce."

"You know that's different. Your mom loves *Sleighbells* almost as much as I do, and attracting more productions here is a supersmart way to boost our economy. Plus, she's known me my whole life and knew I'd already wanted to come back home, especially after Grandpa's heart attack." Elisha fixes her with a knowing look. "And you were keeping her updated on the work I was doing in Atlanta."

Lana grins, unrepentant. "What, like I'm not supposed to brag about my best friend?"

"You were doing the groundwork to angle for me to come home, admit it."

"And what, may I ask, is so wrong with that?" Lana waves her hand in the air. "You *should* be using your superpowers for your hometown. Atlanta doesn't need you the way Piney Peaks needs you."

"And we missed you," Adam chimes in, over two decades of friendship packed in his words. "Everyone did. You're the heart and soul of this place."

Elisha's taken aback at the matter-of-fact way he says it. Apparently, by some unspoken understanding, Maeve's mantle has passed on to her. Her heart lodges in her throat and she has to clear it several times before she can speak. "Yes, yes, you all love me. But Ves Hollins is a stranger." She sighs, seeing the disdain on his handsome face with horrifically vivid recall. "Honestly, Lana, I get the feeling he's immune to any wooing from me."

Solana and Adam share disbelieving glances. Their faith in her is flattering, but what strikes her even harder is how their shared expressions just drive home how much Elisha wants that kind of relationship for herself. Where all it takes is a look to communicate. Her friends have it, her parents have it . . . even her grandparents. The last time Elisha did was . . . Her brow furrows. Wait.

Has she *ever*?

"Dunno, Lisha, it's pretty hard to stay mad at you."

Adam hums his agreement, pouring Grinch ingredients into a massive cocktail shaker like he's concocting a potion. A bit of this, a dab of that. His movements are practiced and confident, almost mesmerizing. "And when you tell him how much it meant to Maeve, I'm sure he won't turn you down," he says. "I mean, she left him the home she adored. She must have trusted him to look after it."

But now that Elisha thinks about it, Ves had seemed weirdly indifferent to the history and charm of Maeve's beloved Christmas

House, carelessly tossing mementos to the floor and muttering to himself like this was the last place on earth he wanted to be. Plus, while there had been the odd anecdote or two over the years about a great-nephew who lived in New York, Maeve, who had lived here longer than Elisha's been alive, never had any family come visit. Unlike the other older residents on their street, there were never any vanloads of nieces, nephews, and assorted munchkins. Maeve had been— No, not alone.

She'd had the Rowes: Elisha's parents, Jamie Rowe and Anita Rowe née d'Costa; Grandma Lou, before she passed; and Grandpa Dave, Lou's husband and recent retiree, who always had time to fix a leaky tap or snowblow the driveway for Maeve.

"If wooing fails, you can always try begging," says Solana.

Elisha makes a face. "You can't be serious."

"Whatever works, babes. You've worked so hard to get all your French hens in a row that it would be a shame to tell Hollywood it's a no-go."

Elisha grins at the holly-jollied idiom, then slumps. "And kiss my reputation for coming through in a crisis goodbye? Not to mention Greg will finally have the ammo he's been looking for to *really* be insufferable, compared to the garden-variety sufferable he is right now. I wish it would penetrate his thick skull that my competence is not a threat to him."

Solana snorts. "Competence is always a threat to people who are used to skating by on mediocrity."

"Especially middle-aged white men," Adam quips as he shakes their cocktails, the silver of his cuff bracelet reflecting off the shaker.

"True," says Elisha. That's her boss to a T.

"Is it weird that you saying that kind of turns me on?" Solana crooks her pointer finger into the V of his black tee, tugs him in for a kiss.

Elisha's used to their PDA, even envies them for it a bit. They're a gorgeous couple: Lana with her warm golden skin and cloud of ochre curls, courtesy of her Black mom and Spanish dad, and Adam, who, despite being white, is often tanner than his girlfriend. In summer, when he's not working, he's almost always outdoors, helping out at his family's painting business or going on shirtless runs, showing off his impressive abs and the tattoo sleeve on his left arm.

At the familiar sight of their passionate lip-lock, one of Adam's buddies from high school, sitting farther down the bar with his work friends, wolf whistles. "There goes Adam, kissing the customers again!"

Adam breaks the kiss to scowl. "Only *one* of the customers, asshole!" he calls back, but the laughter drowns him out. With an eye roll, he returns to their drinks. To Elisha, he says quietly, "However you decide to handle things with the new owner, you do need his permission. Not to put too fine a point on it, but literally everything depends on the film crew using Ves's house."

He's right, but the reminder that a stranger holds their fate in his hands makes Elisha groan. It's *Piney Peaks*'s Christmas House. Not his. "I know, I know."

"No pressure or anything," Solana quips, but the levity doesn't quite land. Without the house, there's no movie sequel, but there's more than just Elisha's reputation at stake, and all three of them know it.

Nearly every single mom-and-pop business on Main Street was featured in the 1974 classic *Sleighbells under Starlight*. In the romantic comedy, an English duke from the previous century travels through time in his sleigh, getting caught in a Christmas-week blizzard, only to be saved from hypothermia by a spunky hippie waitress in Piney Peaks. Hijinks ensue when the bewildered and achingly proper duke is mistaken for her respectable—and completely fake—fiancé, who she needs in order to prove she's grown up enough to take over the family diner. It only gets more bonkers from there.

But despite its quirks, it's hilarious and wholesome and, most importantly, sweepingly romantic. There's something about that will-they-or-won't-they energy of the culture-slash-era clash that socks Elisha right in the heart, along with the rest of America. A quintessential Christmas classic, it's one of the few movies so iconic that it hasn't been remade in recent years with a hot new cast and cool CGI effects.

During the original filming, nearly everyone in town was either an extra milling about in the background or knew someone who was. Maeve's dad, Doc Hollins, gave permission for their house to be used as the waitress's family home. Elisha's own grandparents both had speaking roles as owners of the Chocolate Mouse, the local sweetshop where one of the most romantic scenes of the movie took place. The credits are full of familiar, if a little small and fuzzy, last names.

Naturally, when news of plans for a fiftieth-anniversary sequel were announced, everyone in town was delighted to sign new location release forms so their business could be featured again. In Elisha's role as town film liaison, she loved nothing more than going door-to-door to get those signatures, reuniting the town for the movie that meant so much to them.

And, of course, Maeve was the first one to sign for the sequel. But with her death, the existing contract is moot. It's Ves Hollins's signature Elisha needs if she doesn't want the whole town, her boss, *and* half of Hollywood to blame her.

Especially since none of them even know about this little hiccup, and she plans to keep it that way.

"Okay," says Solana. "So getting him to give you filming permission is going to be a teensy bit more difficult. It's not like you're a stranger to a challenge."

Teensy? Elisha blinks incredulously. "You do remember he kicked me out into the cold, let me hobble across the street, and kept my mom's lawn ornament hostage, right? That's a bit more than a 'challenge.'"

"Maybe," admits Solana, smiling her thanks at her boyfriend when the drinks arrive. It's a busy night, so they don't have more than a few seconds to make heart eyes at each other before it's back to business. "I guess it just depends on whether you're up for it or not."

Elisha ponders the answer in the sickly-green reflection of her cocktail. If she wasn't up for a challenge, she would never have left the comfort and safety of her hometown for the opportunities in Atlanta after college. With an established and bustling film office, Elisha often had more work than she could comfortably handle, but she always enjoyed the challenge . . . *and* the satisfaction that came with pulling it off.

More importantly, if she weren't up for it, she would never have come back. She's no stranger to hard work or lost causes—her time away from Piney Peaks proved that. There's nothing she can't achieve if she goes after it with her whole heart. As her grandpa always says, everything is possible with grace and gumption.

She gulps rather than sips her melon-lemon-lime drink. When it comes to men, she's never had to do the chasing before, professionally or otherwise. "Do you really think I can win Ves over? Woo him?"

"You're the best at what you do, babes. You've rolled with worse punches than this and come through victorious." Solana squeezes Elisha's shoulder. "It'll all be . . . Oh, shit. Okay, don't look now, but—*I said don't look!*"

CHAPTER THREE

Elisha

I t's the worst thing Solana could have said; her exclamation has Elisha already swiveling around on the barstool. And a second later, it's too late to pretend not to have seen the couple entering the Old Stoat. Yeah, this is definitely no longer happy hour. It's not even remotely in the vicinity of "getting drunk enough to forget your impending problems with the hot new neighbor that you one hundred percent caused yourself" hour.

Because Bentley, Elisha's ex-fiancé, has just swanned into the pub with a woman's hand tucked into the crook of his flannel-clad elbow, the classic red-and-black plaid Elisha always loved but he refused to wear back when they were dating. The diamond sparkling on the woman's finger almost distracts from the glint of her gold wedding band.

Almost.

The last time she saw him, he was just a face on a screen, flickering in and out on a shitty Wi-Fi connection, breaking her heart. Even now, three years later, she feels the phantom pain of a knife between her shoulder blades.

"Ellie!" Bentley's shout is loud enough that the entire pub turns to gawk. When his wife slips her arm from his, he strides forward with a huge grin. "Talk about a blast from the past!"

His joy at seeing her is as puzzling as the fact that he's here. In her town. In her pub. In her personal space bubble. Her heartbeat spikes as he opens his arms. *Wait, he's not going to—He can't seriously expect—Oh, okay, he is and he does. This is actually happening.*

"Oh, um," she says, words muffled into the front of his chest, angling her knees awkwardly to the side and wondering how quickly she can let go without appearing rude. "Hi?"

Bentley lets her go first, stepping back to rejoin the wife who he still hasn't introduced. "How are you? You look great." And then, in a way that's somewhere between a compliment and an insult, "I should have known you'd never leave Piney Peaks. You're still here after all these years, huh?"

Solana gives him her frostiest smile. "She left Atlanta to come here, actually. She's an amazing film liaison. You know she was a lifesaver for the latest Taft Bamber indie film? Yeah, my girl Lisha here was the one pulling all the strings to make it happen. *She* never gives up."

"You give me way too much credit!" Elisha laughingly protests, flushing. "It was a team effort."

"Hey, if my best friend doesn't toot her own horn, I'm going to do it for her," Solana declares. "You're a badass and Piney Peaks is lucky to have a superstar like you. Quit eating humble pie."

If it were anyone other than Bentley, Solana wouldn't be so hell-bent on making a big deal about Elisha's accomplishments. And with anyone else, Elisha would make much more of an effort to downplay how hard she'd worked to attract and promote commercial filming for the Georgia Film Office.

But the truth was that she'd been damn good at her job; none of the other entry-level hires had gotten the coveted promotion, and before she'd left, anyone who hadn't flamed out had been working under her. So the petty part of her guesses it doesn't hurt that Bentley knows that other people saw her worth, even if he couldn't. After all, humble pie is pretty much the *worst* pie.

"Oh?" He searches Elisha's face like he's looking for confirmation. "Finally cut those apron strings, huh? Good for you, Ellie."

Fuck you wouldn't be a very festive response, so Elisha chooses to ignore that. "Hi," she says, holding out her hand to the woman next to Bentley that he still hasn't thought to introduce. "This is my best friend, Solana"—Solana gives a little wave—"and I'm Elisha Rowe."

She makes a point to use her full name, pointedly staring at Bentley until he frowns. *Lisha* is reserved for Solana, who'd given her the nickname in kindergarten, and Ellie was *never*. It was too sweet to suit her, but Bentley always loved using it even when she told him she wasn't a fan. Once, she'd convinced herself he was affectionate, but now she knows he was actually just being the other A-word: annoying.

"Tori." The woman's handshake is solid, firm. "I've heard a lot about you."

"All good things," Bentley says with a laugh.

It's the kind of small talk old friends make all the time, but it makes Elisha bristle.

Of course *he* has nothing bad to say about her, *she* hadn't done him wrong.

She wasn't the one who proposed in their last semester at Drexel University, three years into their relationship.

She wasn't the one who accepted a job teaching econ and math at Piney Peaks's high school so that his partner could move back to her beloved hometown, only to turn it down a few weeks before the semester started because of a better offer at some fancy-schmancy East Coast prep school.

And she definitely wasn't the one who kept promising to show up and finally move into the cute little apartment they'd rented above the Main Street toy shop, only for *soon, soon, I promise, I'm just tying up some loose ends first* to turn into *oh, by the way, I'm not coming after all. Found some greener grass. I'm just starting my career, I can do better than Piney Peaks. Would you mind sending my great-grandmother's ring back?* Without a shred of shame, much like how he's standing here now.

"So, if everything was so great back in Atlanta, what are you doing back here?" Bentley gestures around the Old Stoat, as if Piney Peaks is somehow the lesser option. Which, Elisha realizes, to him, it probably is. It's enough to set her teeth on edge.

"I could ask you the same question," she parries, keeping her voice light, bright, and, if not merry, then at least casual. Everything she isn't at this exact moment but is trying desperately to convey. "You finally showed up. Three years too late, though, huh?"

His eyes flick to Tori. "Things change."

It's an artful way of dodging the question. Vague, limboing between honest and mysterious.

Elisha can feel Solana's worried gaze. Maybe she shouldn't have jabbed at him like that in front of his wife. She tips her drink in his direction, then throws it back. "Guess they do."

"I'm ready to put down roots." Bentley slips his arm around Tori's waist. "Victoria wanted to get out of New York City and she has family in town, plus I'm familiar with the area, so . . . why *not* here?"

Maybe because a reasonable human being does not deliberately move to the same town as his ex-fiancée unless he's trying to win her back? Which Elisha is pretty sure is not what's happening here, with a wife in tow—who happens to be wearing the same diamond engagement ring Bentley had once slipped on Elisha's finger. She doesn't hold back her scoff. All class, this man.

"So, you're just visiting for Christmas?" Solana asks Tori.

Elisha supposes it makes sense; even though Piney Peaks isn't the vacation destination it used to be, it's one of those chocolate-box villages that get all decked out for the holidays.

"Oh, no." Bentley is the one who answers, shaking his head. "We visited over the summer to start looking at houses when we decided to start trying. You know, for a family." He grins adoringly at Tori, who doesn't seem thrilled with their personal business suddenly being laid out there. "We just got here today to continue the house hunt. We're short-term renting an apartment right now, but we'd like to find a real place before the semester starts."

Elisha suddenly feels the overpowering urge to throw up. And it has nothing to do with the sickly-sweet cocktail she just chugged. "You what?" she rasps, voice as hoarse as if she'd guzzled a glass of something a *lot* stronger.

Solana takes one look at Elisha before quickly leaping in with "Wow! Congratulations!"

Elisha's too nauseated to summon the gratitude for her best friend's swift response.

"I'm actually, uh, going to be teaching economics and AP calculus at the high school starting in the spring semester," says Bentley.

She blinks. That can't be right. "The same job that you turned down before?"

He shrugs as if unapologetic. "Like I said . . ." *Things change* hangs in the subtext between them.

Tori's gaze shifts between the exes, forehead creased. "Am I missing something here?"

In the silent standoff that follows, Elisha feels her right eyelid working its way up to a twitch. It usually only happens when she's stressed at work—sometimes providing logistical support is more drama than it's worth—but it rarely occurs in Piney Peaks.

That it's happening now, in front of Bentley of all people, is unacceptable. One, she doesn't want anyone to think he's successfully gotten under her skin (even though he has). Two, he's not allowed to win their breakup by showing up back here (and she can tell that he totally and mistakenly thinks he is).

It's petty and not very Christmasy of her, she knows, but *come on.*

It was one thing when she knew in the general-existential sense that he was out there somewhere in the world living his life. But not right here, right now, in front of her with his pretty new wife and a flannel shirt that he used to say he'd never be caught dead in. Looking for all the world like he belongs here.

In her town. Where she lives.

Where she could run into him at the grocery store, reaching for the last carton of eggs and go through the whole *no you, no, please, I insist, you* spiel. Be obliged to wave at him across the street instead of hurrying away without making eye contact.

Her stomach lurches. In a town so small, what if nowhere is safe? Maybe they'd even wander into her parents' year-round Christmas emporium, the Chocolate Mouse, for décor and desserts. Coo over how cute the little baby stockings would look on their mantel. Make small talk at the checkout. She'd have to go from pretending he didn't exist to exchanging requisite niceties on a weekly, if not daily, basis.

"Listen," says Bentley, flashing his most charming get-out-of-trouble smile. "We're planning a little holiday soirée soon. We'd love it if you and Solana could come."

"I'm probably going to be busy," says Elisha.

"I didn't even tell you when it was yet."

"And yet I'll still be busy."

He raises an eyebrow. "With?"

"Work. I'm putting this town on the map again. It's why I came home." She tips back her chin in challenge, meeting his gaze. "*Sleighbells under Starlight*."

Down the bar, Adam's friends all whoop in solidarity, raising their glasses to her.

"What?" Bentley scoffs. "Ellie, that movie was old even when you made me watch it in college. Hell, it was old decades before we were even born. You're not seriously still flogging that dead horse?"

Eye twitch. Goddamn it. "It's a classic. Right up there along with *It's a Wonderful Life*."

His tone could almost pass for fond when he replies, "Ellie . . . you're still such a dreamer."

"Maybe I am, but I also follow through when I say I'm going to do something," she says coolly.

His jaw tics.

Solana smirks. "People who underestimate Elisha do so at their own peril."

By now, a small crowd has gathered around them, clearly intrigued by the direction of the conversation. Friends and neighbors are nodding, name-dropping some of the other productions she's matchmaded: the zombie apocalypse web series, the vegan chocolate bar commercial, those shoestring-budget slashers . . .

Their well-meant support warms her, but Elisha's smile is brittle. "The *Sleighbells* sequel is just the start. Big things are happening for Piney Peaks." From the corner of her eye, she catches her best friend shooting her a what-are-you-doing look. "We're just tying up a few loose ends, but it's pretty much all in hand to start filming at the Christmas House."

Bentley frowns. "That old place? Really? We stopped by to take a peek over the summer with Victoria's folks, and it was pretty run-down. Lost its magic, right?"

Okay, fine, maybe the house hasn't been repainted in the last couple of decades and the steps creak and Maeve didn't have the money to fix the blocked chimney and some of the fancy decorative shingles are damaged or missing, but still. The house is *perfect*.

"But we're rooting for you, Elisha," says Tori brightly. A long pause. "Aren't we, Bentley?"

"Absolutely. Well, we better nab a table. Christmas may be the hap-happiest season, but it's also the bus-busiest one." He laughs at his own joke as they turn away. "Don't forget, we definitely want to see you both at our party! And bring your boyfriends! Oops, sorry. 'Dates.'"

Surprised that he corrected to use inclusive language, something she had tried to drum into him while they were dating, Elisha forgets to be mad at him for a second.

"Hey, I forgot to ask—you seeing anyone, Ellie?"

Ha. Nope. Still mad.

"Oh, I'm sure you'll see us around," she says without thinking.

"Victoria and I can't wait to meet them." Bentley winks. "Don't forget that I have ex-boyfriend vote of approval."

He sweeps Tori away before Elisha can point out that *no the fuck he does not*, and it's *ex-fiancé*, if they're being technical about it.

CHAPTER FOUR

Elisha

So," says Solana delicately.

Elisha groans. "Don't say it. Or, if you're going to say it anyway, Grinch me first."

"Hey, Adam, can we get two more Grinches, please? And make them spicy!"

"You got it, beautiful!" he calls back, wisely having stayed away during the conversation with Bentley.

"Grinch acquired," says Solana. "Had no idea this was going to be a three-Grinch-problem kind of night. What the hell was that, Lisha? You didn't have a damn thing to prove to him."

"I know, *I know*."

"You said to me, and I quote, that getting the Christmas House now was 'more than a challenge.' Not a done deal!"

"Lana, I know. I'll figure it out."

"You took a swing at Ves!"

"You remember that I was the one who was actually there, right?"

"Okay, okay. Let's forget about the house for a minute. You magically have a 'boyfriend' now?"

"Nuh-uh," Elisha says triumphantly. "I only vaguely implied it. And it's not like I'm going to show up at their little party, so it's a moot point. I just didn't want Bentley to think I was single."

"But you *are* single."

"When *your* ex shows up in Piney Peaks, you can criticize," Elisha grumbles. "So I showed off a little to look good. So what? I *had* to. I'm twenty-eight years old, back in my hometown, and living with my parents."

"Um, you're back for a good reason, though: your family. It was a strategic decision, Lisha. You could have gone anywhere. Coming home wasn't any port in a storm, it was your destination."

"But he doesn't know that. Look, you saw how he behaved. Not to be a Petty Betty, but he clearly thinks he's 'winning' the breakup." She air-quotes.

"Except he just let it peter out instead of actually making a clean break," says Solana. "Which, as far as I'm concerned, makes him a coward who isn't even in the same league to compete with you. And, anyway, he's back in the same job he once thought wasn't good enough. Isn't that fishy?"

"Very. Then again, he's looking to 'put down roots' in *my* hometown, so clearly good decision making isn't his forte."

Solana snickers. "I mean, he didn't marry you, so what other proof do you need?"

"I fucking love you," Elisha proclaims, giving her best friend a smacking kiss on the cheek. "I probably shouldn't have said anything about the movie, but I couldn't stand the thought of him thinking I was moving backward. I can't look both single *and* unsuccessful."

Solana gives her an incredulous stare. "Um, did you not hear me talking you up? You're the biggest goal-getter I know. Who cares where you're doing it? You're still kicking ass and we're lucky to have you. Also, totally not a suspicious segue at all, but apropos of something, was Ves attractive?"

"What?" Elisha laughs. "What does that even have to do with anything?"

"Hear me out. I was just thinking that if you were up to the challenge, you could easily charm him into being your arm candy during all of Piney Peaks's endless festivities during the Winter Festival."

Elisha doesn't even let herself indulge in the idea, positive that hell would freeze over twice before Ves found her *charming*. "Um, arm candy? So we're just choosing to conveniently ignore the part where I launched a candy cane attack on him?"

Solana waves a hand dismissively. "He'll forgive you. Season of miracles, right? You know, your grandpa Dave asked me about hooking you up with a date for the Chocolate Mouse holiday party. I didn't have the heart to tell him you'd already one-night-standed or flat-out rejected all the eligible men in town."

"Thanks," Elisha says dryly.

Solana keeps going. "But *Ves* just got here, so he's probably sticking around for a while. Maybe you could woo him for his signature *and* rub his hotness in Bentley's face? Two turtledoves, one stone?"

"Is this you being optimistically-supportive-BFF or too-Grinch-drunk-to-think-straight-BFF?"

"Pfft. I can hold my liquor." Solana smirks. "So, hot or not?"

"Ummmmm."

"Hot," Solana decides. "I knew it. Probably drop-dead gorgeous."

"I never said that. I didn't even get a good enough look at him. I was too busy staring at the floor hoping it would swallow me up." Flippantly, Elisha adds, "Maybe he was hideous."

"I know all your tells, my darling. You can't fool me. And your avoidance is delicious, because you're only this cagey when you don't want me to be right."

"Just because you and Adam started a rom-com-worthy love affair last year does not mean you get to scheme up romantic intrigues for me. Deciding to be each other's dates to get through wedding season is *sooooo* not comparable to how much groveling I'll have to do to redeem myself."

"What do you have to lose? You have to charm him for the house, anyway. Might as well get a few dates out of it while you're at it. No one Christmas-parties like Piney Peaks."

That's true, Elisha muses. And if this year is anything like the last, she's going to spend every single party panic-sweating and dodging mistletoe.

But relying on Ves? A stranger? Who she kinda-maybe-sorta tried to clobber?

Elisha wrinkles her nose. "Lana, I don't even know if he's available," she admits. "I mean, maybe he's with someone. But even if he's single, he has zero reason to help me out."

"That you know of. You just need to work out all the angles like you do when you're liaising. Find out what he wants so you know how to get it for him. Then you can have your fruitcake and eat it, too."

Okay, yes, she's undoubtedly attracted to him. Yes, she wants to redeem herself. Yes, she needs to get her mom's Christmas ornament back. It might be a lost cause, but she has the grit and gumption to see this through. She knows it. Like her boss back in Atlanta was fond of saying, Elisha excels under pressure.

She taps her finger against the rim of her glass, thinking. "Not to use 'Ves' and 'perfect' in the same sentence, but I have to admit, Ves would be the *perfect* guy to piss Bentley off. I mean, he owns the house from my favorite Christmas movie of all time. It would be amazing to rub it in Bentley's face after how dismissive he was about it just now. He obviously thinks this town is just a footnote in movie history and that I have no chance in hell."

Her best friend grins delightedly. "I just talked you into doing it, didn't I?"

"If Ves wants a proper Piney Peaks welcome," says Elisha—mind already buzzing with ideas involving festive cellophane wrapping, homemade cookies, and a *much* cuter outfit—"he's going to get one."

CHAPTER FIVE

Ves

As he stands in the living room of his great-aunt's cluttered, cross-stitch-*everywhere* frou-frou house, Ves Hollins thinks this is, quite possibly, the worst day of his life.

Even before he met Elisha Rowe, his morning was off to a bad start. After doing school visits in Chicago and giving away classroom sets of his middle-grade fantasy books, which had been delightful, he'd booked a red-eye flight to Pennsylvania so he could deal with Maeve's estate. That was the first mistake: he should have returned home to New York City instead of coming straight here.

It all started when he'd been forced to spend the night stuck at his departure gate at O'Hare International Airport, waiting out weather delays and nursing overpriced single-malt whisky while halfheartedly thumbing through one of the books he'd picked up at the airport bookstore. And when the plane had eventually taken off, the turbulence was terrible. The child behind him had kept kicking his seat, the mother said nothing even when Ves politely asked her demon spawn to stop—and then, if all that hadn't made him cranky enough, the rental agency had given his car away.

All so that when he finally arrived in Piney Peaks via Uber, nose annoyingly bleeding from the high altitude, a woman broke into his great-aunt's house and attempted to decapitate him with a giant candy cane. Near-death by Christmas ornament. Joy.

On top of that, most of the food in the fridge had spoiled, the kitchen stank of the curdled milk he'd poured down the drain, and the ancient coffee machine looked older than he was, sputtering out liquid that smelled burned and tasted even worse.

And after an absolutely wretched start to the day and a shower in a bathroom that reeked of rose-scented potpourri and set off a pulsing migraine, the latest indignity: an apologetic voicemail from the valuation house canceling his appointment and letting him know that because of family emergencies, backlog, and the holidays, they would reschedule for the new year.

If only he'd known earlier, he would have flown straight to JFK from O'Hare . . .

But it's too late, now. He's here, and his schedule is all fucked.

"It sounds terrible. You should come back home," Arun Iyer says consolingly over the phone when Ves is finished regaling him with the events of his first full day in Piney Peaks. "Spend Christmas with us."

This is why his best friend and literary agent is Ves's favorite person, but third-wheeling on another holiday sticks in his craw. "It's your first Christmas with Cade as a married couple."

"But I literally already hung your stocking on our mantel."

"You didn't."

Arun immediately sends him a pic. "Ye of little faith."

Ves allows himself to bask in the soft glow of warmth in his chest when he sees the bright-red stocking with his name on it. "I'm here now. Might as well get a head start sifting through all the junk in this place. I don't think Maeve or her dad threw out a single thing in the last hundred years."

"Surely that's an exaggeration?" Then, without skipping a beat, Arun asks, "Want me to take a few days off to come down to Pennsylvania?"

Ves flushes. "I wasn't fishing for help, but I appreciate it, anyway. No, I've got it."

"Okay, but the offer stands. So, is everything how you remember it?"

Ves scoffs. "Be real, the last time I was here I was *seven*."

And twenty-three years have passed since then. But to his horror, the truth is that all his repressed old memories are attempting to scale his glacial walls: Being dumped at the doorstep of a great-aunt he'd never met with a suitcase so heavy that the grunting taxi driver had to drag it to the front door himself before taking off without a goodbye. Realizing with a sudden shock exactly how long his one-month "holiday" would really be. Watching the taillights fade into the distance and regretting that he hadn't chased after the taxi and begged to be taken back to the airport. Remembering his father's stern *Behave* and that his mother had forgotten to pack all his favorite things and absolutely none of his comfort-read books.

Thinking that he could run away before anyone came to the door, and *then* his parents would be sorry. *Then* they wouldn't spend all their time with their lawyers, bitterly arguing about who had let the other down the most.

He had been so caught up in imagining his parents' grief and eventual reconciliation that he scarcely noticed the door opening. Buttery light spilled through, along with the sweet scent of what he'd later learn were Aunt Maeve's famous sugared pecans. And when Aunt Maeve smiled at him—like he was wanted, like she couldn't be happier to have him there—he suddenly couldn't remember why he'd been so frightened of her, after all.

He shakes himself out of the memory. He's never liked to linger in the past too long.

"You know what *is* still the same, though? Piney Peaks," Ves muses, brow furrowing. "It's like the place is a magical village suspended in a snow globe. It's weird."

"I think you mean charming." Arun's voice is amused.

"No, I definitely mean weird. Everyone's so friendly. Three people waved at me through the open window. The *window*, Arun. I had to draw the curtains. Someone *mimed* asking me over for coffee."

"Sounds terrifying. Make sure you sleep with one eye open tonight. That is, if you sleep at all . . ."

"Somehow I get the impression you aren't appropriately sympathetic to my plight," Ves drawls.

"*Nooooo*, whatever gave you that idea?"

"You mock, but if you don't hear from me tomorrow it's because the neighbor girl decided to break in—again—and finish what she started."

Arun snort-laughs. "See! Not everyone there is friendly! Maybe she's just as surly as you!"

"Ha. Ha. Ha." Ves rolls his eyes, regretting that he's not on video so Arun can get the full effect. "I'm not surly. I'm inconvenienced."

"Riiiiight," says Arun, tone wry. "And how hot is she exactly?"

Ves jolts. "What? That's not—I didn't even notice—" He stops sputtering to say firmly, "That is irrelevant."

"Not to the person asking the question, it's not," Arun mildly replies. "You only get this irritated when it's someone you begrudgingly like despite yourself. And yes, before you ask, you *are* that predictable. So fess up: You like this girl?"

Ves thinks back, summoning up a memory of short chestnut curls and rich, mossy-brown eyes that turned gold at just the right angle. A pert nose, slightly reddened to match the rosiness on her sun-kissed cheeks. He hesitates before answering, parsing through his conflicting emotions. Does he admit she's gorgeous and risk more teasing? Or gloss over it in hopes Arun will lose interest?

Finally, he settles for a noncommittal, "She's not without her charms. But listen, I don't have the first clue about how to deal with this house, I *really* don't want to involve either of my parents, and I'm going to break out in hives from all the clutter. It's too much."

In the lingering silence that follows, Ves knows Arun gets exactly what he means in the way that only a best friend who has known you from childhood can.

There's no doubt in his mind that sorting through the chaos of someone else's left-behind life is going to be torture. There is just so much *stuff* everywhere: things that are not crap, things that are maybe crap, and things that are definitely crap.

And he feels guilty making a judgment call on any of it. When it comes to his own belongings, it's so much easier to be ruthless. He was Marie Kondo–ing before the rest of the world even knew the method. It's hard to explain, but in most other people's houses, he feels out of control when he's surrounded by so many unnecessary trinkets and knickknacks.

Of all the epithets Ves has accumulated over the years, *sentimental* is not one of them.

Unencumbered? Yup.

Minimalist? Definitely.

Inflexible? Oh, absolutely.

The Christmas House still feels like Aunt Maeve's, not his. Not his to change, not his to decide about, and no lawyer or piece of paper can convince him otherwise. His fingers itch to cull the clutter into something manageable, but at the same time it's so overwhelming that even the idea of getting started feels too uphill to wrap his head around.

"Have you made any headway so far?" asks Arun.

The *yes* is on the tip of Ves's tongue before he takes it back. Looking around the living room, he's disheartened to realize he'd been working all day with so little to show for it. He stares at his three tiny piles and after a quick glance at his watch, officially gives up. The many-headed hydra of mess will have to wait until he gets some dinner and a good night's sleep.

"Why don't you hire one of those cleaning services?" suggests Arun. "Get them to just trash everything and scour the house from top to bottom so you can sell it and be back home in a few days."

If only. Ves sighs. "Dad specifically said *not* to do that. Maeve inherited the house from her father, who was apparently one of those eccentric, wealthy old dudes. Dad remembers a lot of first-edition books and valuable paintings, so I have to get those assessed. But that won't be possible until the new year."

Arun makes a sympathetic sound. "So I guess this wouldn't be the best time to put on my agent hat and tell you the bad news?"

"You heard from Dom?" Immediately, Ves's mind flies to the book proposal for his next middle-grade fantasy he'd delivered to his editor, Dominique Horowitz, in June. "She doesn't want the book?"

"I want to reassure you that she does love it, and if it were just up to her, she'd buy it in a heartbeat, but . . . The long and short of it is the publisher thinks you're treading the same ground all over again. Their market research is telling them that readers are tired of lonely Chosen One narratives with shitty parents who don't care that their kid is plunging themself into danger to save the world from darkness."

"In other words, the exact opposite of my first series," Ves says flatly. "What the hell do I know about positive support systems?"

"*Hello*, you have me, very much *not* chopped liver," Arun says with a note of censure. "Anyway, it's not a definite no. It's more like 'What else is Ves working on that we could take a look at?'"

Which is cagey-masquerading-as-upbeat publishing-speak for no. "At the moment?" Ves furrows his brow. "Nothing that would be a fit for them. Dominique seemed so excited about this one that I thought we were all set."

"Okay, well, no problem. Publishing is already winding down for the holidays, so we have time to come up with something else. Now that we know Carlton House is looking for something more, mmm, heartwarming, we can work with that."

Ves aims for positive, but he's off by a mile as he grumbles, "Sure. Whatever. Okay."

"Is that your pissed 'whatever' or your standard 'whatever'?"

Ves digs his teeth into the meat of his inner cheek. "No, that's my Christmas-spirit 'whatever.'"

"Proud of you for taking this in such stride," Arun says brightly, ignoring Ves's inelegant snort. "Just let your creative genius do its thing so we can wow the socks off them. I'm here for whatever you need. Bouncing ideas, pep talks, pet pics. I mean, not my pet, obviously, since Cade still isn't budging on us getting a corgi or seven. But I'm here for you, day or night. And hey, maybe Piney Peaks will inspire you?"

"Arun, I can't stress enough how unlikely that is. This town . . . isn't me."

"You never know. Even hardboiled city girl Dominique is a big fan of *Sleighbells under Starlight*."

"Her and everyone else," Ves grumbles. "I mean, it's just an old Christmas movie."

"Ah, how could I forget that you run a mile from anything resembling a warm and fuzzy emotion."

Ves grins at his best friend's fond tone. "Speed walk, not run. And probably because you want me to be as happy as you, which is physically impossible. People like Cade are one in a million."

"Meet-cutes are everywhere you look. Save a local business, protect a landmark, fall in love with a wholesome small-town girl. Maybe she's the hot lumberjane daughter of a tree farmer! Kiss under a blanket fort! Break your rule about holiday romance! Do *everything* different. The opportunities are endless."

"You can't find what you aren't looking for," says Ves. "My heart will just have to stay a shriveled, underused prune. I'm not here for love and I'm definitely not desperate enough to watch *Sleighbells*."

Arun groans. "You're *killing* me, Ves. And for god's sake, don't let anyone in town hear you say that! Google tells me they're really proud of it. Cade watches it every winter, and I have to say . . . it's not terrible."

"A ringing endorsement," Ves says wryly. "Anyway, I've hogged you for long enough. I better get a move on. Since I'm stuck here, I might as well be productive and get it cleaned up and ready to sell. Sooner I'm done here, sooner I'm back. And sooner I can find some *real* inspiration."

"Is there a TV?" asks Arun.

Ves blinks. "You realize I'm out of the city, not out of the century?"

"Precisely!" Arun crows. "You have no excuse! Watch *Sleighbells*, you complete philistine."

Ves ignores that. He has zero intention of cocooning himself in the holiday nostalgia that comes so easily to others. "Hold on, you said this was the bad news. What's the good news?"

Silence slinks across their connection. "Erm," says Arun, the word encompassing both sheepishness and guilt. "You arrived in one piece?"

Well, sort of. Ves snorts. Without thinking his eye flicks to the candy cane propped against the wall.

He releases a gusty, defeated sigh. "There's only the bad news, isn't there?"

Merry fucking Christmas to me.

CHAPTER SIX

Ves

An hour later, Ves selects Piney Peaks's highest Yelp-rated restaurant for dinner. The Old Stoat promises traditional American fare that is "heaven on a fork," the finest selection of wines and ales in the Poconos, and a family atmosphere, so he tries not to be put off by the pub's name.

It's just a short jaunt away, so he takes a bracing walk. It's not quite as windy as the city he left behind, but he still hikes his red scarf up to his ears. Less than ten minutes later, as the world tips into twilight, he's welcomed to the beating heart of the town.

Twinkling lights and huge red-velvet bows are strung between black lampposts, lining the street with magic. A quick peek into a side street reveals a winding labyrinth of narrow cobbled lanes leading to bookshops crammed with shelves and glowing with light; store windows draped with tinsel and garlands of ivy; and packed restaurants with outdoor seating, charming red-checked tablecloths, and space heaters leaping with orange flame. Even Ves feels the chill momentarily chased away.

In the town square, everything shimmers silver and gold. Everywhere he looks is lit in snowy brilliance, from the lofty height of icing-sugar eaves to the blanket of snow beneath his feet. Trees sparkle and tiny Christmas-market stalls are squeezed around the steepled church, from where he can hear the sweet strains of choir music. In front of a store called the Chocolate Mouse, a sandwich board announces dates for an upcoming cookie-decorating workshop, a holiday party, and a gingerbread-house competition.

The online pictures didn't do this place justice; the town is completely photogenic and inviting. The kind of place someone could want to stay forever.

Not him, obviously. But someone.

Ves inhales Piney Peaks into his lungs. Even the air is more refreshing, like pine needles and burning wood and walking into a memory that has always hovered just *this* much out of reach.

He's instantly suspicious. Nowhere is this perfect without a catch.

At the Old Stoat, he's seated at a corner booth underneath a loudspeaker playing Christmas oldies and handed a sticky plastic menu. "Haven't seen you in town before," the waitress, Becca, comments brightly, whipping out a stubby pencil and a dazzling smile. "Here for the holidays?"

"Death in the family."

Her pencil freezes over the pad of paper. "I'm so sorry."

In hindsight, he should have just agreed with her. He studies the menu. "What do you recommend?"

"Time is a great heal—" she begins to stammer.

"I meant from the specials," Ves interrupts, a hot flush crawling up his neck.

She rattles through their offerings with the same speed in which she rushes away a moment later. It's almost comforting to know he isn't the only one who finds the small talk painfully awkward.

A raucous cheer breaks out, drowning out the music and drawing Ves's attention. Overlapping voices chatter excitedly and in the hubbub of it all, his heart jolts when he hears a familiar name: *Elisha*.

He doesn't appreciate it; this is the second time today she's given him a shock. Admittedly, in her candy-red sleeveless cropped turtleneck and high-waisted skirt, she makes a better first impression than she did in pajamas. His lips twitch at the memory.

As he watches, a retinue of townspeople continue vigorously shaking her hand like she's some kind of hometown hero and saying things that make her blush redder than the cocktails that keep on coming.

The last thing Ves needs is for her to catch him staring, so he glances away. "Excuse me," he says politely when Becca returns with his maple chai latte and ice water. He nods toward the bar. "What's going on over there?"

"Oh, that's Elisha. I went to high school with her. She's barely been back home for a year, and she's already got Hollywood interested in us again, so everyone's plying her with drinks tonight." Becca grins. "Piney Peaks used to be really famous. Not for skiing or anything, we're not high up enough for that. But because of this old movie that was filmed here in the seventies." Her voice drops to a stage whisper. "And if you're a fan of *Sleighbells*, you'll freak out when I tell you that starting this January, they're filming the sequel at the Christmas House!"

She ends the sentence with a squeal the equivalent of a dozen exclamation points. It pierces the air at the exact moment the song changes and Elisha looks over. Her mouth parts in a silent O of surprise.

Ves's lips thin as he locks eyes with her from across the room. No wonder she was so proprietary when she barged over this morning. Still, he'd spent the day sorting through Maeve's papers, and he hadn't come across any legally binding document that backed up what he's hearing now.

"Is that so," he says coolly. "What an *unbelievable* stroke of luck."

After that, it takes ten minutes for his food to arrive, and another fifteen of avoiding eye contact with Elisha before she finally comes over, armed with two drinks.

"Do you mind if I . . . ?" She juts her chin at the unoccupied side of the booth.

He spears his last piece of maple-glazed ham onto a roasted carrot. "Go for it."

"Thanks." Elisha offers him a tentative smile. "Glad to see I didn't scare you off."

"Ha! Not for lack of trying."

She winces and slides one of the glasses over. "I am so sorry. Again. But I promise that I come in peace! And with an apology cocktail that isn't even half-off for happy hour!"

Ves finishes chewing before saying, "Well, seeing as it's full price, of course I forgive you for almost taking my head off." She looks relieved, so he worries he's letting her off too easy. "Thanks for not bearing any weapons of merry destruction this time," he adds, taking a sip of the red liquid.

He promptly sputters and coughs. "I spoke too soon. What's *in* this?"

"Oh my god, I should have warned you. I just got you what I was having . . ." She shoves his water into his hands. "It's a Spicy Grinch. Like, ginger beer, jalapeños, Tabasco sauce, vodka, cherry limeade?"

He stops coughing long enough to glower and rasp, "Tabasco? That's . . . a normal ingredient."

"I feel awful." And she actually does look quite stricken, so he softens a little. "Sorry about the heat."

"I feel awful, too," says Ves. "It's not every day someone makes an attempt on your life twice."

She buries her face in her hands, groaning. The Tiffany-style lamp hanging above them flashes against her golden rings. "I promised myself I was going to make things up to you. I can't believe I made it *worse*."

He frantically gulps down water to ease the fizzy burning. If this is her trying to do something nice, he would hate to see what she's capable of if she were actually trying to take someone down.

"I hear congratulations are in order," he says, setting down the empty glass.

"What? *Oh*." Her cheeks flush the shade of the drink she's clutching like a lifeline. "Um, yeah. I guess you heard about that?"

"Why didn't you tell me this morning?"

She casts him a disbelieving look. "Before or after I made an ass of myself?"

"Point taken." He tests the Spicy Grinch again, this time prepared for its powerful kick. Vodka isn't his favorite, but the burn from the ginger blended with the maraschino-cherry sweetness is pleasant. Without preamble, he asks, "Is there a signed contract in place?"

She takes a deep breath and looks him in the eye. "Maeve signed all the paperwork, but since the house has changed hands ... I need permission from you as the new owner. It hasn't occurred to anyone else yet, but right now, the future of this movie depends completely on you."

Her honesty surprises him, but not enough for him to be truly sympathetic. He lets his eyes rove freely around the room, at all the happy people made even happier by this one woman, before returning to her face. "So everyone's fêting you for something that doesn't even exist."

"*Yet*," she counters.

"Putting the cart before the horse, then, aren't you?" He knows his eyebrow is doing that sardonic arching thing his ex-girlfriend hated when Elisha scowls.

She flips her hair. "Not if you're nine hundred horsepower."

He's curious despite himself. "Are you?"

"Nah." A beat passes. "I'm probably an even thousand."

Ves hides the hint of his smile in his cocktail, taking another sip. He refuses to be charmed by her. "And modest to boot."

"The truth is, I may have said some things to stick it to my smarmy, now married ex-fiancé. And you know how quickly small-town gossip travels. Or I guess you don't, but—"

"And I don't plan on sticking around long enough to find out, so if you're going to ask me for my permission to film at the Christmas House, the answer is no."

Elisha blinks. "That's it? An unequivocal no?"

"That's it," he confirms. "My life is in the city. I'm not looking to get tied down with other obligations. Selling the house is my only priority. I don't want my limited time here to be any more complicated than it needs to be. Quick in, quick out." He ends with a note of finality, hoping that's the end of it.

Something shifts behind her eyes, like she's recalculating. "I get it. You probably don't want to be away from your family this close to Christmas, if you celebrate." When he doesn't say anything, she tries again. "Or your girlfriend?"

"I don't date over the holidays."

Her nose scrunches. "Why did you say that in the tone of 'I don't wear white after Labor Day'?"

Ves shakes his head. "I'm only here to deal with Maeve's estate and that's it. Famous house like that should have no problem selling."

"You're not . . . tempted to hang on to it? Even a little bit?"

He doesn't know how to answer. It never occurred to him to keep it, and now that he's here, sorting through everything Maeve left behind, he can't unsee it as hers. Every square foot, every keepsake.

So instead, Ves keeps his focus on Elisha's nails. Their design had looked odd to him before, but he now realizes that they're hand-painted with open-mouthed nutcracker faces. He holds back a shudder. A grim mouth, Chiclet teeth, and vacant, wooden eyes . . . It creeps him out that anything festive should look that empty.

"Of course, it goes without saying that the production would pay you for allowing them filming permission," says Elisha, changing tack. "Very generously. Not to mention the value added to the house when it does sell." She leans in conspiratorially. "A *ton* of people place a premium on owning a slice of history."

His eyebrows draw together. "It's not about money."

"Okay. Well, then, if you wouldn't mind, could you tell me what it is about? Because I can't tell you enough how much I need this to go through. Without your signature, this whole deal falls apart. As far as filming is concerned, they think we're still on schedule and they're set to show up in mid-January. Needless to say, I'm so fucked here." She gives him a sweet, slightly embarrassed smile, toying with a gold pendant at the hollow of her throat that looks like a backward 3, but on closer inspection, is actually a cursive capital *E*. "You'd *really* be helping me out."

Now it's his turn to feel awkward. "Please don't waste your breath. My answer is no."

She huffs. "You're not even going to let me *try* to sweet-talk you?"

"What would be the point?"

"Ves," she says. The simple one-syllable sound of his name coming from her mouth shoots electric tingles up his arms. It's the first time she's used it, he realizes. "You wouldn't have to be involved.

They just need the house from the middle of January to the end of February, tops. I'll take care of everything. You can still be 'quick in, quick out.' Give me five minutes to convince you. That's all I'm asking for. *Please.*"

He clears his throat. She's the one at his mercy now, and he's surprised to discover he doesn't like the feeling. "It's not just the hassle. The valuation expert is delayed. It looks like Aunt Maeve hasn't thrown anything out in the last fifty years. It would be impossible to film anything in that mess. On top of that, I have to work *and* I'm here without my laptop—"

"Work?" she interrupts, voice sharp with disbelief. "Your job didn't give you bereavement leave?"

He can't help but be charmed at her outrage on his behalf. Amused, he says, "I'm a writer. It's not a traditional nine-to-five job. And I have to develop a new idea pretty much ASAP." Which he's still a little bitter about, but shit happens. Ves knows that all too well.

Elisha leans in, eyes sparkling with undisguised delight. "You're writing a book while you're here?"

"Not without my laptop, I'm not. So, thank you, but no thank you. I really don't need to be adding another project to my already overflowing plate. So. You can save your spiel."

She looks as though she's biting words back, but there's nothing she can say that will convince him. If there's one thing Ves is a pro at avoiding, it's mess. And nothing is messier than a damsel in distress, especially one who looks like her who's looking at him like *that*.

Warily, he studies her right back. He can tell she's torn between hounding him some more and letting it go gracefully. He knows which he prefers and, begrudgingly, is glad she hasn't resorted to further pleading.

She taps her nails against the side of her glass. Finally, she asks, "What do you write?"

"Middle-grade fantasy. For kids eight to twelve."

"Oh, fun! You'll have to tell me more about that sometime. I love watching fantasy shows, but I don't read a lot of it. Always been more into romance." She grins like she's about to divulge a secret. "And that overlap of romantasy because *hello*, hot guys with hero hair, shiny armor, and magic? Yes, please."

Ves shrugs. "Well, I mean, that's a kind of fantasy, too. Men like that don't exist in the real world."

He regrets his coolness when she visibly retreats, eyes hardening.

Elisha takes a delicate sip of her Spicy Grinch and eyes him over the rim before pronouncing witheringly, "Clearly."

CHAPTER SEVEN

Elisha

Saturday mornings spent with her family at the Chocolate Mouse are special in a way that Elisha doesn't think anywhere else can top. The emporium smells delicious, like the anticipation of the night before Christmas: crackling logs, stewed cinnamon apples, sweet vanilla, a whisper of pine and frankincense.

In these early hours before Piney Peaks stirs awake, the Chocolate Mouse kitchen quietly hums with the hustle-bustle of activity. The Rowes have been there since the crack of dawn, working in perfect synchrony to chocolate-coat mini Swiss rolls and candy orange wheels and painstakingly layer bebinca.

Elisha stifles a yawn, taking her eyes off the pot of gently bubbling caramel sauce for a second. Her head aches from last night, ninety percent thanks to Ves Hollins and ten percent thanks to way too many drinks.

"Elisha!" her mother scolds, snatching the wooden spoon to give it a brisk stir.

The coconut milk–rich Indo-Portuguese layered coconut cake requires a lot of patience; baking each of the sixteen thin layers—

alternatingly, cake and caramel—takes forever. Messing up at any stage not only means waste but having to start all over.

"Sorry, Mom. I'm paying attention, I promise."

"Honey, we're all good here. I appreciate the help, but between Gramps, Dad, and me, we've got this covered." Anita presses her lips to Elisha's temple. "You've been working so hard, I wish you would sleep in once in a while. Go home and lie down, sweetheart. You look like you had a rough night."

"I want to help! Besides, if I go home, I'll probably find a new way to antagonize our neighbor."

Anita absently smiles as she checks the oven. "That doesn't sound like my daughter."

"Your daughter who turns into an unprofessional train wreck of a human being in his presence."

"Now that *definitely* does not sound like you." Tiny crow's-feet crinkle the corners of Anita's eyes. "You behaved rashly, but your heart was in the right place and no harm was done. Do you think you're putting too much pressure on yourself? It's just a house. Aren't you always telling me that half the time when shooting on location doesn't work out, they re-create the interior sets in a studio?"

"Except the nostalgia of Piney Peaks is the whole reason they're filming here, Mom. A set definitely won't cut it." Elisha sighs. "I have a short list of other homes ready to email first thing Monday, but it's a long shot. The whole town *and* Damian, the director, are counting on me coming through with the Christmas House."

Hearts are set on it. And not just because of Elisha's promises to make it happen. The right location can improve a production tenfold. It's as important as good casting and a killer script. Using the Christmas House for the *Sleighbells under Starlight* fiftieth-anniversary sequel practically sells itself. From the opening scene of the first movie—snowflakes dreamily falling against the dark-green shingles—the cozy, charming mood is set. With every watch, that shot captures a feeling so intangible inside Elisha that the English language has no word to convey it: the exquisite yearning of remaking a heart over and over again.

When Elisha had told Maeve about the director's interest in using the house for outdoor shooting, the older woman's eyes had brimmed with emotion. It had still belonged to her father, Doc Hollins, when the first movie was made. She'd been a young woman then, and pretty enough to get plucked out of the extras and bestowed with a couple of lines, more than any of the other locals. When she shared anecdotes about life on set, blue eyes sparkling and bright, Elisha could swear time rewound the years Maeve wore.

"If I hadn't made such a shitty first impression, I would have his permission locked down by now," she says glumly. "But he doesn't have to be such a Christmas Curmudgeon about it!"

Anita's lips twitch into what could either be a smile or a reprimand. "I imagine," she says gently, "that the poor boy has enough to deal with. If you want to make amends, perhaps what he could really use right now is a friend?"

Elisha mulls it over. She did tell Solana that she could win Ves over with neighborliness, and it's *way* too early to give up. Plus, he seems like the kind of guy who gets grumpy without his morning coffee, and Maeve detested the stuff. She doubts there's anything good in the house. "Could I bring him breakfast?" she asks. "And maybe, like, a welcome-slash-apology-slash-please-don't-hate-me package?"

"That's a wonderful gesture. How do you think he takes his coffee?"

"Black like his soul?" Elisha jokes.

Anita fixes her with a capital-L Look. "A breakfast basket is a good idea, but it won't work miracles."

"Point taken. Um, I remember he had a latte last night . . . can we do a gingerbread one?"

"Of course." Anita hums. "While you're at it, maybe drop off Maeve's cats?" At Elisha's guilty flush, Anita adds, "I know they're cute, but we can't hold on to them forever."

"Couldn't we, though?"

"Don't use that wheedling tone on me, young lady," Anita says with a laugh.

"Maybe one surprise visitor this morning is enough. Gotta work my way up to 'By the way, surprise! You're a cat dad!' Ves doesn't, uh, strike me as the kind of guy who's good with surprises."

It's at that exact moment that her father, Jamie Rowe, wanders over. His apron is dusty with flour and there's a powdery streak on his blond stubble that Anita brushes away before kissing his jaw.

"Surprises always go over better if you bring treats. If you feed him this bebinca, he'll fall in love with you just like I did with your mom," Jamie says with a grin, wrapping his arm around Anita's waist.

"Dad!" Elisha yelps. "This isn't a seduction package. I swear, I have no ulterior motives. Just want to make a better third impression than I did a first one. Or, you know, a second one. Trust me, yesterday was comically bad. The bad of biblical proportions. Burning-the-bebinca bad."

His lips quirk. "Then you better make it a generous piece, because it sure has a lot of ground to cover."

She takes his advice because, in all honesty, bebinca is pretty magical, and when it comes to food, Dad is never wrong. And it's always been there for her, through bad boyfriends and broken hearts and everything in between.

Her first taste of the rich, sweet dessert had been in her grandparents' villa in Goa, all her cousins clustered around her. In the same kitchen where Anita learned to make it, overlooking the same sandy stretch of beach lined with tall and green coconut palms swaying in the breeze.

And every year—in those sacred two weeks after New Year's, when the Chocolate Mouse goes on holiday and Piney Peaks is buried under snow—Elisha's family returns to the yellow house with the mother-of-pearl windows and iconic blue-and-white azulejo tiles. She wakes early to swim in the ocean while jewel-colored birds chatter in the ancient trees, returning in time to sip sweet, foamy whipped coffee on the balcão, the extended porch where her grandmother swaps gossip with passersby.

Ten minutes later, everything is in eco-conscious packaging and Elisha is on her way out the door.

"Bye, Grandpa!" she calls, not bothering to button her coat. "Wish me luck!"

Dave stops sweeping away pine needles. He doesn't ask what for, just recites their usual catchphrase, the same one he's given her ever since she was little. "Go with grace and gumption!"

So she does.

CHAPTER EIGHT

Elisha

Elisha doesn't mind the walk from town to Ves's house, even though the wind this morning is brisk enough to make her teeth chatter. But the trek gets her blood pumping and it's easy for her to be optimistic about how the conversation will go.

Surely in the face of a hand-delivered breakfast, he won't be so standoffish?

"Elisha," she says, trying to match his deeper voice. "Good morning. It's lovely to see you."

Hold up. She scowls. *Would* he think it's lovely to see her?

Granted, she hardly knows the prickly man, but it doesn't sound like him. "Elisha," she tries again. "It's great to—no, that's not right, either. It's . . . tolerable to see you again? What accursed lottery from hell did I win to see you again so soon? Oh god, you again?"

It's deeply annoying that she can easily envision him saying any of those responses.

"Okay, however he greets you doesn't matter," she says firmly. "Remember: grace and gumption." She switches to her brighter voice. "Morning, Ves! Thought you might enjoy a hot breakfast."

Back to his baritone. "Would you like to come in?"

"I'd love to!" she chirps.

This is going well already, she thinks as she trudges up the front steps of the Victorian house. She even believes it when she raises the Green Man knocker and raps once, twice.

Just as Elisha begins to fret that it may be too early to drop in, the door swings open. *Oh my.*

A somewhat sleep-rumpled, frazzled-looking Ves stands there wearing gray sweats and a tee so white it battles with the color of his hair. He has faint pillow creases on his cheeks, like he just woke up, and his feet are bare. Seeing his toes, weirdly, makes him feel much more human, and she has to forcibly drag her gaze up his body to meet his eyes. Which are suspiciously narrowed at her.

"Good mor—" she begins to say.

"Yes? What do you want?"

Her mouth drops. *Oof, already off to a bad start.* She squares her shoulders. His impatience isn't going to deter her. Clinging to her mantra, she hesitantly lifts the brown carryout bag. "I brought you breakfast."

"You brought me—" He frowns.

"Breakfast," Elisha supplies. "I thought we could eat together? I don't know how you're fixed for the most important meal of the day, but my family owns the Chocolate Mouse, you can't have missed it, it's that big brick building in the center of town—"

"You're rambling," he says, cutting her off. He rakes his hand through his platinum hair and sighs. "Just . . ." He looks like he's about to regret what he's about to say next. "Come in."

She scrapes her feet on the mat first, and when she crosses the threshold, it's abundantly clear what she's walked into: sheer and undeniable chaos. Maeve's romance novels have been pulled off shelves and heaped into piles, entire drawers have been emptied, and there are about five patches of visible carpet that he must have been using as a pathway from one end of the room to the other. In short, the living room looks ransacked, and the kitchen table isn't much better, buried under papers and some of Doc Hollins's old file boxes.

She gapes. *"What have you been doing?"*

His jaw takes on a defensive set. "Cleaning."

"You call this cleaning? No, no, buddy. Whatever this is, it's the opposite of that."

"Didn't ask for your opinion," he grumbles, yet still chivalrously takes the bag from her.

"No, the first one is for free," she quips, eyeing the candy cane ornament propped against the wall.

"And *yet* it's still a bad deal," he calls over his shoulder as he heads for the kitchen. But the grouchiness has mostly faded from his voice. "Oh my god, *coffee*." Ves says the word with rapture. "Coffee that doesn't smell like dead rat." He shudders. "Coffee that hasn't come from *that* contraption in there."

"You actually used Maeve's ancient coffee maker? She hasn't touched that since her dad died." A flicker of sympathy goes through her at his visible revulsion. "In that case, I forgive your bad mood."

For a second, she thinks he's going to gift her with another smart-alecky remark. But he surprises her.

"Sorry," says Ves with a rueful almost-smile. "I do appreciate this. I'm just not a morning person."

Elisha files that away under the other irrelevant things she knows about him, along with how cute he looks even when he's grumpy and that his lips part *just so*, revealing lovely square teeth that look whitened a normal amount, not to a freaky fluorescence. She doesn't want to notice these things, much less be flustered by them, but it's inescapable when you're a foot away from hotness.

"I've been up since five a.m.," she says. "And please know I say that in a matter-of-fact way and not in a smug I'm-better-than-you way, which I've been told is how it comes across sometimes."

He slides her coffee cup across the kitchen island in a silent invitation to join him. "Who said that?"

"My ex. The guy I mentioned last night." She keeps it short. The less said about Bentley, the better.

Ves's lips quirk. "Right. The one you were showing off to about scoring my house to film your movie."

"I wasn't—" She starts to contest, then sighs. "Okay, fine, yes. I talked a big game and now I'm in a jam. And not of the delicious, goes-great-on-toast variety, but the oh-my-god-I'm-so-fired sort."

The cup stops halfway to Ves's mouth. "Oh, I see. This is a guilt-trip breakfast." He lofts one dark brow in a silent *Busted*.

"Don't give me that knowing look." She crosses her arms. "I categorically deny trying to manipulate you with spiced crumb cake, lemon loaf, blueberry streusel muffins, and the almighty bebinca."

His eyes light up, and for a second, he looks so elated and boyish that Elisha's heart takes an involuntary tumble into her tummy. Has a smile ever been so transformative in the history of *ever*?

"The Old Stoat, the Chocolate Mouse . . . is every local business in this town named after a rodent?" he asks, sounding appalled.

"Technically, a stoat is a weasel," she corrects absently, more than a little distracted about where his smile went and how she can get it back. "The emporium has been in my dad's family for generations. Like, all the way back to the founding of the town. We're sort of an unofficial landmark."

He taps at the box where Elisha's neat, rounded, all-caps handwriting identifies the bebinca. "I've never heard of this."

"Something else we're known for. Open it," she says. "See those delicate layers? The lighter one is cake sweetened with coconut milk and the brown one is caramel. My mom grew up eating this during Christmastime in Goa, but it's pretty popular here year-round."

Ves turns to open a cabinet, returning with two of Maeve's best china plates and matching forks.

The gold-rimmed buttercup-patterned china was a family heirloom passed from mother to daughter; Maeve tucked it away for safekeeping 364 days of the year, except for the anniversary of her mother's passing, when she carefully removed the fine layer of dust. Elisha has never actually seen it in use before. She opens her mouth in faint horror before she realizes it doesn't matter anymore. The house, like everything in it, is Ves's now.

"Thanks," she says instead, as he hands her a plate.

Ves studies the bebinca. "It seems a bit sacrilegious to cut into this after all that effort."

"Mhm." She grins. "Wait until the first bite hits your taste buds, though. Now *that* is an unholy experience."

His lips twitch. "I hope you're not all talk."

"Guess you'll have to find out."

He makes the first cut and brings the fork to his mouth. When his lips close around the morsel, she leans in eagerly. "Well?"

Ves chews slowly, drawing her eye to the line of his jaw before she snaps out of it. He looks at her with those baby blues, which sends a whisper of a shiver down her spine. What's going through his head? And why does she care so much? Agonizing seconds tick by before he says, "Heaven on earth."

The tension in her shoulders relaxes. His answer matters more than she thought it would. "Really?"

"Would I lie to you?" He pauses before adding reproachfully, "You might come at me with a candy cane again."

"You're not letting that go anytime soon, are you?" Elisha laughs with a trace of embarrassment. Despite it being such a feeble weapon, she'd certainly managed to do some damage—both to her dignity and her own knee. "Keep it if it makes you feel safer."

He scoffs. "Like I don't see the other dozen on your driveway."

"You're really not a morning person, are you?"

He takes a sip of his gingerbread latte. "Not in the slightest. Although the restorative powers of this drink are doing wonders."

"Feel free to come by the Chocolate Mouse if you get a craving." She casts a dubious eye over the house. "Although I'm not sure there's enough sugar in the world to power you through cleaning this mess up."

He pops another piece of bebinca. "I think it calls more for rolling up sleeves and getting right down to it than it does for sugar. Just need to give it my all."

Elisha blinks. The visual imagery of him rolling up his sleeves is . . .

She clears her throat and pretends to take another sip of her latte. Unfortunately, she gulps down rather more than she'd intended. She sputters and coughs, waving off his concerned eyes and wordless gesture to bring her water.

"Well, right now it kind of seems like you're only giving it your some," she says, her tone a little off.

"Are you offering to help?"

She gauges his offhanded reply for signs of snark. Finding none, she considers the question.

Who knows Maeve better than her? Who would give as much time and care to Maeve's most priceless treasures? The more she thinks about it, the answer is obvious: she's the best person for the job.

Even though she already has one. Well, for now, anyway. With a demanding boss who already doesn't like her, and is about to like her even less when he finds out the paperwork on *Sleighbells under*

Starlight 2 isn't tied up with a bow like she promised. Which means it's really going to suck when she sees him at work on Monday.

Elisha tugs her lower lip into her mouth, chewing thoughtfully. In the back of her mind, an idea is flickering to life like a spotty string light. What if she offers Ves some clearly much-needed help in exchange for the filming permission?

A slightly different scenario than the one Solana suggested, but the same concept applies: two turtledoves, one stone. Elisha can be nice *and* get what she wants, which is a present for both her and Ves.

But putting the trade-off into words . . . It would be wrong to take advantage of Maeve's great-nephew. It wouldn't be neighborly. And to her surprise, Elisha wants to be nice to this prickly boy who likes her mom's bebinca and, in his way, makes her laugh. There's no grace or gumption in making him give in—not like this.

"I apologize," Ves grinds out. "I wasn't trying to put you on the spot. I don't truly need any help." At her dubious look, he defensively adds, "It always looks worse before it gets better." He shoves his hand through his straight hair, disheveling it rather marvelously. "The house isn't your concern."

At this, she frowns. "What if I want it to be?"

His frown is equally doubtful. "Why? Ah, this is about the permission again, isn't it?"

Elisha stamps her foot. *"No."*

"My charming personality, then?"

She huffs a short laugh. "Your attitude, personality, and ability to clean house are all atrocious. But I'm going to help you, anyway. For Maeve. For how much she meant to this town and to me. Call it your Christmas gift, if you want. No strings attached?"

Ves hums agreement under his breath, making Elisha wonder what other throaty noises he's capable of. And promptly wants to perish, because he's looking at her like he knows where her thoughts have wandered, and nope. Hard nope. Not happening.

She is not going to notice things about him. And even if she does, she is going to sweep them from her mind and into her mental trash bin. *Swoosh*, gone.

Because of all the insufferable things about him, the way he makes her feel isn't one of them.

CHAPTER NINE

Elisha

It's a Monday morning *and* it's snowing.

Ordinarily, both things that Elisha loves. Today, however, the gray clouds have completely blotted out the sun outside her minuscule office at the Chamber of Commerce. Inside is just as bleak: her boss, Greg Pierce, bitched at her to make coffee even though it isn't her job, and the office administrator was ambushed with the news that their holiday office party had to be canceled due to going a measly twenty dollars over budget last year.

It's already a shitty eleven a.m. And it's about to get worse.

The wheel on her ancient computer mouse bumps and creaks as she scrolls through a long email thread going back five months, all the way to the introductory email from JJ, the personal assistant of *the* famous director Damian Rhys.

That sticky summer day, shuttered away in her sweltering office with a fan that didn't work and the thermostat set a solid ten degrees higher than it should have been in July, Elisha had no idea that her life was about to change. Not even the faintest inkling that the ping of a new email would drop such an exhilarating opportunity into her lap. Hair plastered to her scalp, blouse clinging to every nook and dip of skin, she'd checked her inbox with one hand while using the other to fan herself with a pad of paper. And there was JJ's email, laid out in neat rows of text.

All those months ago, when she read that a big-time Hollywood director wanted to use the Christmas House to film the *Sleighbells* sequel, she had to muffle her scream into her fist. Then reread the email twice to make sure she hadn't missed anything. Then type her reply—and then delete it because it had too many exclamation points and a certain stench of desperation.

Now, after a morning spent clacking away at the keys, Elisha reads her latest message one last time, nutcracker nails resting lightly on the mouse, a familiar anxiety pinching her stomach.

To: June, Jessica
From: Rowe, Elisha

Hi JJ,

Thanks for your last email! We are incredibly excited to move forward, too!

You can count on our full support for next steps. We would love to feature an interview with Mr. Rhys in the next chamber newsletter. We also have a robust database of production support services and crew in the area, and are happy to refer you. The sheriff's department is going to get back to us about traffic control for street filming—more on that soon!

I know you'd expressed interest in the house from the original film, but I wanted to make sure you also saw the attached JPEGs from the photo library I've already shared with you. We have so many beautiful locations around town that I would hate for you to miss these! If any of these gorgeous period homes stands out to you, just shout. We have strong relationships with the property owners and can facilitate whatever you need.

Best,

Elisha Rowe (she/her)

Film & Digital Media Liaison
Piney Peaks Chamber of Commerce

She clicks send.

With a *whoosh* and a flash of panic, the email flies to JJ's inbox. Even though it's too late to take it back, she still goes over her words in her mind. Will it read as glaringly transparent as it does in hindsight? Why didn't she just tell the truth that there was a holdout on the house?

Okay, she knows why. It doesn't matter how many gorgeous homes are in their location database—Damian Rhys wants the Christmas House, no ifs, ands, or buts. While the exact plot of the sequel is tightly under wraps, JJ did reveal that a young Damian got his foot in the door of the industry with *Sleighbells*, working his way up from lowly assistant, and he now wanted nothing more than to honor his start by directing the anniversary sequel. Who knew that a Hollywood hotshot could be so sentimental?

Well, frankly, as far as Elisha's concerned, warm fuzzies and *Sleighbells* go hand in hand. The movie plays nonstop on TV every year, iconic as beloved oldies *It's a Wonderful Life* and *A Charlie Brown Christmas*. One of Elisha's favorite memories is celebrating a snow day by being squished between her parents on the couch to watch it for the first time, sneaking her fourth cookie and, at every kissing scene, scrunching her cold toes in the new socks that Grandma Lou knitted.

Even though Elisha is three hours ahead of California and is unlikely to get a reply anytime soon, she watches her inbox, waiting for that familiar ping. Maybe if she stares at it long enough, she can will a response to appear. *Thank you for these alternate suggestions that are just as good as the Christmas House, Elisha! Damian has selected Rosebud Cottage and would like to personally thank you for your initiative!*

"Elisha!" Greg hammers on her open door hard enough that the wall shakes. He casts a disgruntled look at her many signed posters. They're a reminder that Elisha worked on several flagship Netflix streamers while his career stagnated, leaving the man to stew in bitterness, take zero initiative, and accomplish very little of note. Without preamble, he snaps, "That coffee tasted disgusting. When was the last time you cleaned the pot?"

"Hmm, not sure. If you noticed any gunk, though . . ." She smiles sweetly. "Feel free to take that on."

"That's not my job," he says dismissively, but in a tone that's meant to imply that it's hers. He runs his palm over his gelled hair and makes aggressive eye contact. "Where are we on the Damian Rhys project?"

Elisha's smile grows wider and more wooden. *Unraveling like a bad Christmas sweater. Crumbling like a sugar cookie. Fizzling out like cheap string lights. Take your pick.* "Right on track," she says blithely.

She can tell her answer disappoints him by the way his lips twitch halfway to a frown before he smooths his expression. "Ah," says Greg. "Well. Good. Your friend the mayor will be happy."

She keeps a bland smile on her face, refusing to rise to his bait. If she'd been a man, he would have told her to keep up the good work, maybe even added a hearty "champ" at the end or a congratulatory pat on the back. Offered to give her a hand on such a prestigious project. But he doesn't like her. Never has.

Not even when she interned here as a teen that summer in high school, making the coffee and answering the phones and doing all the grunt work he only asked *her* to do, never Riley, the other intern. Who happened to be a guy. A decent guy, incidentally, who's now their trade specialist, but more importantly? His friend's son. Clearly, Greg doesn't have a problem with nepotism as long as it comes from him.

"Seeing as you're not doing anything important right now," he says, "why don't you go check on Mia? She's still sulking about the party being canceled. I told her not to make any plans after she went over budget last year, but did she listen? *No.* And now she acts like I'm the bad guy here? I will never understand women."

Um, maybe because he is *the bad guy?* If it were humanly possible, there would be actual steam coming out of Elisha's ears right now.

Shaking his head, Greg walks out, but not before adding, "And tell whoever's decreasing the thermostat to quit it! A balmy seventy-eight degrees is just perfect for me."

How does he not hear himself when he speaks? Every word out of Greg's mouth is sexist or insulting, and usually both. If he's not insinuating that she doesn't deserve her job, he's picking on their office administrator for trying to brighten up this sad, soulless place where fun goes to die.

Unsurprisingly, when Elisha heads out to the main office, Mia Liu isn't actually sulking. She's on the phone talking someone through a small-business grant application, being the consummate professional she is, and holds up one finger in silent request.

"Let me guess," Mia says, slotting the ancient corded phone

back in the receiver. "Greg interrupted you to come 'check on me,' right? Like I'm a child?"

Elisha rolls her eyes. She glances around before saying, "Make no mistake, he's the only baby around here. You know he still thinks we clean out the coffee maker when he's the only one who uses it? That thing hasn't been cleaned since, like, *last* Christmas."

He's her boss, so she can't flat-out refuse, but she isn't going to do more than the bare minimum for him, either. It would never occur to him to make the coffee himself, and so he's never seen the discoloration that's probably now permanently stained the pot. Revenge has never tasted so disgusting. Presumably.

Mia grins. "And may I just say, I really hope we pull it off for another year. At least."

"*This is my grown-up Christmas liiiiist,*" Elisha whisper-sings. "You're as petty as me and I love it."

Mia pretends to think, stroking her chin. "Nah, I'm pettier."

But not as petty as their boss. Despite his weak excuses about the budget, both she and Mia know that the real reason the party is canceled is that last year, Greg's way-too-young-for-him girlfriend got drunk, puked in the potted fake ficus, and went home with the chamber's executive director.

"I'm gonna log off my computer real quick and grab an early lunch. Want to join me?" asks Elisha.

"Thanks, but my parents are visiting from Toronto, so I'm going to have lunch at home. No one makes beef noodle soup like my mom."

Elisha grins. "Make me jealous, why don't you?"

She heads back to her office—essentially a broom closet small enough to make a cubicle cry—to log out of her computer. With all the confidential data they deal with, it's office policy, but the machines are so obsolete it takes forever to get back in. Mind already on her own comfort food, she almost misses the notification that she has new mail in her inbox.

When she sees the sender's name, her heart sinks. Evidently, personal assistants from California *do* start their workday at eight a.m. on the dot.

From: June, Jessica
To: Rowe, Elisha

Hi Elisha,

Little confused here. As beautiful as your suggestions are, the Christmas House is a non-negotiable. I apologize if it wasn't clear that Damian chose to film on location in Piney Peaks solely for this reason. Let me know what's going on. We do hope there aren't any problems at this stage.

JJ (she/her)

Personal Assistant to Damian Rhys

Nonononono. That last line is so ominous Elisha can practically hear creepy thriller music in the background. She squeezes her eyes shut. That's it, then. So much for plan B. JJ hasn't even bothered with her usual kind regards because what she probably wants to say is *Unkindly, WTF?* And Elisha wouldn't even blame her. Grabbing her plaid shacket from the back of her chair, she dashes out of her office, ignoring Mia's worried eyes and Riley's strangled yelp as she almost collides with him and his steaming Cup Noodles.

Once she's outside in the fresh alpine air, her heart stops racing. There's an inch of snow dusting the ground, not a significant amount by any definition of the word, but every single creature on two or four legs is charmed. A scruffy squirrel clutching a nut perches on the little red sleigh outside the Chamber of Commerce like one of Santa's helpers, beady black eyes beatifically closed as if to soak it all in. Children in puffy jackets shriek and scrape their mittened fingers into the snow, making bitsy snowballs that melt upon contact. A man walking his dog sticks his tongue out to catch a snowflake; his terrier imitates the action, looking adorable in his Pride flag–colored sweater.

It's hard to stay grouchy when her town is *this* cute. Even harder when she can already smell her lunch wafting over from down the street: garlicky red wine–braised short ribs. Her mouth waters, imagining the fall-off-the-bone tenderness and all the delicious browned bits. Already, she can feel her mood lifting, like the first ray of sun breaking through clouds. An hour spent people-watching from a corner table at her favorite little bistro, dipping into the new romance ebook she'd borrowed from the library . . .

Mood lifted, she raises her hand in passing to everyone she meets, chirping *Merry Christmas!* even though it's still three weeks away. Even Bentley looks happy coming out of the fancy gourmet grocery store at the end of the street, a big brown bag in either hand.

Wait, Bentley? Elisha blinks. And then blinks again.

It's snowing, but not hard enough to pretend she didn't see him. And he's definitely spotted her.

Bentley's starting to shift his bags around so he can wave, and even as her heart jackrabbits, everything else slows down. She knew this would happen. The moment he had entered her pub, all smiles and smugness, she knew. That one day, here she would be, running into him like it was normal. *Normal.* Nothing about seeing her ex-fiancé in her town, on her side of the sidewalk, during her favorite holiday, was normal.

So far from it.

Before he can wave, Elisha ducks out of sight, intending to scurry into the building next door and while away a few minutes until he gets in his car and drives away.

And collides with the person coming out of the bank, cutting off her escape.

CHAPTER TEN

Elisha

All Elisha sees is a bright-red wool scarf before they stumble backward, and instinctively, she clutches onto the person, crushing their lapel. Hands settle on her waist, bracing her. She looks up into the bluest of eyes, the color of a pond before first frost.

"Ves!" she gasps, not letting go.

He pries her off. "Still haven't given up on the bodily injury, huh?"

"I—*what?*"

He shakes his head, twisting his hips to gesture to the door. "Never mind. Are you going in?"

"In? Oh! I don't need to— No, this isn't even my bank. Actually, do you think we could maybe walk in the other direction? Quickly, but also, like, casually."

"Only if I can ask why. Inquisitively, but also, like, fearfully," he drawls.

She ignores the sarcasm only because he lets her loop her arm through his and drag him in the opposite direction from the short ribs she was *this* close to having. As far as her ex's presence recalibrating her life goes, choosing a different restaurant is only the start, she's sure.

"I just thought you looked hungry and could use a hot lunch. Cleaning is such exhausting work, after all. My treat to welcome you to town!" she says airily.

"Riiiiight. You expect me to believe this is all for my benefit?" Ves adjusts the sleek black messenger bag on his shoulder. "Beware of small-town girls bearing gifts and all that."

Okay, one, rude. That isn't even the expression. And two, *rude*. Elisha knows she's an attractive woman. No, scratch that. She's a total babe that anyone should be happy to have lunch with, especially when it's free. What is it going to take to un-Grinch this guy for good?

"I'm welcoming you," she says between gritted teeth, tugging him along. He allows it but maneuvers so she's forced to switch to his other arm on the interior side of the sidewalk. "It might be nice to find some common ground before we tackle Maeve's house, right?"

Ves starts to turn as if to glance behind them. Elisha makes an embarrassing squawking sound. "Pay attention! It's icy here!" She clasps him a little tighter.

He laughs, as if bemused. "Calm down. It's *one* inch of snow. It's nothing compared to last week's snowfall in the Windy City."

"Since I'm apparently responsible for your safety, I'm taking no chances. You're precious goods." She makes the mistake of looking up at him, only to catch him looking back. Brows furrowed, mouth slack. It's the first time since she's known him that he hasn't had a smart retort at the ready.

Until this moment, she'd known he was Burberry coat–model handsome—she has eyes, after all—but knowing it and seeing it in zoomed-in, HD, full brightness is another. Her stomach whirls like the hand-carved spinning tops Grandpa Dave used to make for the emporium. It's disconcerting, to say the least.

"What?" Ves is the first to break eye contact. He dislodges his arm from hers only long enough to fuss with his scarf, making adjustments so minor that she can't see the difference, before letting her have it back.

Blood rushes hot to her face. "Nothing," she says quickly.

Ves narrows his eyes. "A more suspicious 'nothing' has never been uttered."

Elisha doesn't know where to look. Behind, to make sure she's successfully avoided Bentley? At Ves, the human equivalent of the North Pole? Chilly, distant, steeped in mystery?

He palms the leather messenger bag. It's a telling gesture, as though he wants to remind himself that it's there. Splayed out that way, his fingers look enticingly long and, unsurprisingly, neatly trimmed and buffed. She's never been with a guy who has better nail beds than her.

She blinks. Not that she's with Ves now.

Okay, yes, she is with him, but not *with him* with him. They're just going to the same place to share a meal and absolutely not swap spit or any other bodily fluids. A mundane, unmemorable Monday. No mortifying crushes being formed, no delicious down-there tingles. Move along, people, nothing to see here.

She keeps it light with "Yeah, you've got me. I was just trying to figure out whether you've robbed that bank."

"And of the two of us, you think *I'm* the most likely suspect?"

"Well, you *are* wearing all black and acting a little sus about your bag," says Elisha. "Your scarf, on the other hand . . ." Her smile is wry. "Not exactly camouflage. You're clearly new to a life of crime."

Without missing a beat, he asks, "Offering to share your trade secrets?"

She good-naturedly rolls her eyes. "Seriously, though. The scarf doesn't seem like your style. Too . . . homespun." Which is exactly why she loves it. It's chunky and soft-looking, and she might be a little jealous because she's freezing her nips off. She bundles her shacket tighter around her.

Ves arches one dark brow. "And what do *you* know about my taste?"

"Hey, I nailed your sweet tooth pretty well."

She suddenly realizes he's made sure to put himself between her and the street. It's unexpected and oddly touching, a boyfriend gesture she forgot how much she missed.

He scoffs. "That's an easy one. Who doesn't love sweets?"

She hums her agreement. "*That* we can agree on."

He makes sure they sidestep an icy patch. "Anyway, it was a gift."

"Christmas gift from a girlfriend? Wait, I'm being nosy, you don't have to answer that."

"Told you I don't date over the holidays," he reminds her.

Two little kids pulling at their harried-looking mother's hands squeeze past Elisha and Ves on the sidewalk. He angles his body into hers for a too-short second where she forgets to breathe, then pulls away with a mumbled apology. Once again, his chest is in her personal bubble. His very hard, solid chest.

His scent surrounds her, something warm and homey, quite unlike the man himself, but just as undefinable. A jigsaw puzzle with all the pieces scrambled up. She smooths her hands over her corduroy skirt—the color of a roasted pumpkin, cold slipping in with each step—and does her best not to tremble.

Elisha shrugs, swallowing past her dry mouth. "Could have been a past-tense girlfriend. As in 'We broke up, but I'll always cherish her by this gift she gave me.'"

"You keep presents from your exes?"

That tinge of horror in his voice makes her blink. "You don't?"

"If you were mine, I wouldn't let you wear anything gifted by another man."

Let her? His? The shiver running down her spine has nothing to do with the weather. Annoyingly, while she's feeling flustered, he shows no sign of realizing how outrageously sexy his words were. Like everything else he says and does, it's offhand and blasé. Already, he seems to have moved on, while Elisha's stomach is as tangled as badly stored Christmas tree lights.

With a glossing-over cough, she says, "You'll have to tell me the story behind this whole cryptic 'I don't date' thing over lunch."

He says nothing, as if unwilling to commit his mouth to anything other than eating.

Not that *she* wants his mouth for any other purpose, either. Obviously.

"We're here," she says in relief. She reaches for the door handle, but somehow, Ves gets there first.

"After you," he says, holding it open for her. It's such a small, mannered gesture, but one that squeezes her heart. It's been a while since she's been on anything resembling a—

No. This is *not* a date.

And then he promptly confirms-slash-ruins it by saying, "I want you in front where I can keep my eyes on you."

CHAPTER ELEVEN

Ves

When Elisha flounces into the restaurant—a nondescript little place with an iron sign that reads FIRESIDE—with a tight jaw, Ves knows she's taken what he said the wrong way. He never meant to imply that he doesn't trust her or that he's still holding a grudge—okay, he is a *little* bit, but it's nothing a little teasing won't get out of his system.

In truth, Elisha isn't the worst person to spend time with. She's easy on the eyes, has good chat and a rapier wit. He wouldn't mind getting to know that sharp tongue better. And since the state of the house is so horrendous, it looks like he'll get the chance. The week he'd allotted to dealing with his surprise inheritance now seems woefully underestimated.

Ves follows her into the narrow entry, his shoulder brushing against the coat rack. There's just one peg left, so he hangs his coat on top of her inadequate shirt-jacket-type thing that he doubts keeps out any of the cold at all. He eyes the clumps of mistletoe tied with red ribbons hanging from the ceiling. The place is what his New York real estate agent would delicately call bijou and other people would call small and pokey. But the modest square footage isn't what hits him first or most.

Fireside doesn't feel like a restaurant; it feels like being invited into someone's home. A fire crackles in the hearth on the back wall, and in front of it are a pair of plaid wingback armchairs occupied by two older gentlemen nursing drinks and playing a game of checkers. Covering the exposed brick walls are framed newspaper clippings and local art. There's even a painting of the Christmas House in the springtime, flowers in full bloom, the way Maeve liked it best.

Customers are seated shoulder-to-shoulder at long refectory tables that remind Ves of what he always imagined sharing a meal with a big family might be like. A gaggle of grandmotherly-looking women clink wineglasses at the far end. It's . . . nice. More than nice. It's welcoming in a way Ves doesn't think he's ever had before.

Elisha must see his dazed expression, because she says with just a touch of shyness, "I guess I'll just have to give you some good memories to replace the horrid first one you have of me."

There's a twinge in his chest. Damn it. "Elisha, I—"

He's cut off when a stunning Black woman in a blazer raises her arm and calls Elisha's name. That's all it takes for the entire restaurant to start elbowing one another, moving down to make space for two more seats. He trails after Elisha, waiting for her to make introductions.

"Ves, this is our mayor, Danica Pereira, and her daughter, Solana."

Elisha scooches in next to the mayor, leaving Ves to slide in opposite her. Their knees brush, but she doesn't jerk away. *Interesting*, Ves thinks. In fact, she lets it linger long enough for both of them to relax. And then they're just . . . touching. Like it's normal. Like they're friends who don't think twice about it.

It should be weird how *not* weird it is.

With difficulty, he drags his eyes away from her face long enough to shake hands with the other two women. They share the same high cheekbones and impish, pointed chins; same warm smiles aimed his way.

"Ves Hollins," he says, ready to be quizzed about why he's in town over the holidays.

Danica smiles, revealing deep laugh lines. Unlike her daughter's cloud of golden-brown curls, her head is shaved, showing off a cluster of star tattoos behind her right ear. "Maeve's great-nephew. You're all grown up now. I remember you when you were about yea high." Her hand hovers three feet in the air.

"I'm surprised you remember me," he says honestly. "I only visited here once when I was seven."

The moment the words are out of his mouth, he wishes he could take them back. What kind of nephew only visits his aunt once? Especially one who inherits her entire goddamn house?

But Danica's face is gentle as she says, "I'm sorry for your loss. We all loved Maeve so much here in Piney Peaks. Christmas won't be the same without her. But at least her spirit will live on in the movie she loved so much. We're all very grateful to you for letting this go ahead."

His eyes flick to Elisha, who has the grace to flush. He's backed into a corner, not able to contradict the mayor without looking like a prize asshole. Discomfort scratches at his skin, itchy as a too-small sweater. He despises losing control, and he suspects that ever since meeting Elisha, he's being slowly but surely stripped of it.

His father is good in these sorts of situations. He likes parties and he likes people. He also likes other people's wives—which was the whole reason for the divorce that brought Ves here in the first place twenty-three years ago. There's no doubt in Ves's mind that

Karl Hollins would have been able to segue the conversation to something cheerier as easily as breathing.

Ves just smiles awkwardly, mumbles a thank-you, and intently studies the menu.

He overhears quite a few things while he reads: One, literally every person at the table loves Elisha, including his neighbor who spied on him from the porch just that morning, miming the invitation for coffee, whose name he learns is Marcy. Two, in addition to being Elisha's champion, the mayor is a *Sleighbells* fan who is keen to revitalize the town's cultural identity and attract more creative industries, boosting economic development.

And three . . . Well, there is no three, because when Danica talks to Elisha about chamber business, Solana turns her attention to him. "We're waiting on the Char Siu Wellington. The chef makes it with pork loin instead of beef and this amazing honey glaze. If you like twists on tradition and Asian flavors, it's terrific. My favorite sides are the garlic green beans and mashed butternut squash."

He's grateful. Food is a safe topic. "That sounds good. I'll go with both those sides," he says.

When the waiter comes over, Elisha orders the same but with gochujang brown-butter brussels sprouts and a glass of red wine. "I've had a *day*," she says with a sigh, offering no further explanation.

Ves takes a sip of his water. "You don't have to come over tonight if you're too tired."

"No, no. I don't need an out." Elisha smiles awkwardly. "I said I would."

"Oh ho ho," chortles a woman with wispy white hair sitting farther down the table. She looks older than Maeve but her ears are still sharp. "You two have been spending quite a lot of time together, haven't you?"

Now Marcy chimes in, voice gossipy with innuendo. "*I* saw Elisha leaving the Christmas House in her pajamas *quite* early on Friday morning. Did you give her a lovely present, dearie?" More giggles and titters.

Ves chokes on his water. Solana has to thump his back until his coughing ceases. "No, that's not—" he rasps, but the table erupts in gleeful cackles and congratulations. His neck is stiff, tight. Eye contact becomes too difficult. With anyone.

Including Elisha, who's eyeing him with concern. He thinks. Right now, watching the condensation drip down the side of his glass is about all he can manage.

Other people might be able to laugh it off, maybe even join in.

But not Ves. He never could.

His pulse races. His skin crawls. Do all these women live on their street? Do they just peer out the windows hoping to catch their neighbors in scandalous acts? Does he need to keep his drapes closed 24/7 in this town? Does he need, like, three layers of blackout curtains for maximum privacy?

He can't believe that literal strangers are discussing his sex life, which is actually nonexistent at the moment, right in front of him. While merrily ripping into bread rolls and sopping up gravy and patting their lipsticked mouths. It's *mortifying* and they show no signs of stopping. Even Danica's attempt at saying *Ladies, please* goes unnoticed.

All Ves wants is this excruciating moment to end, but he doesn't know how. He's blushing and he hates it. Any attempt at denial will only be met with more amusement, more fun poked at his expense.

His mind flashes back to other meals, when his legs didn't touch the floor and he hadn't yet learned how to block out the sound of his parents' verbal grenades sailing over the length of their formal dining table. They hadn't expected him to participate. At least not until one or the other would try to make him pick a side in their argument du jour.

Elisha leans in but can't make it all the way across the table, so he mimics her pose. "You don't have to look so offended," she whispers. "They don't mean anything by it. It's not like I'm your type, anyway."

His brows draw together. How has she arrived at that conclusion? Regardless, it's not the assumption that's galling him, it's the sheer lack of propriety. He's not used to this kind of open prying from his parents, let alone from complete strangers. Adeline and Karl have always been far too wrapped up in themselves to express an interest in his life. They're his parents, but they're not parent*ish*.

But, he supposes, they must be different around other people—his dad with his 2.0 family that is so perfect it's scary, and his mom with the much younger man she's flaunting all over social media apps that Ves didn't even know she knew how to use.

He steadies his irritation with a deep breath. This is why he prefers staying single over the holidays.

Why he doesn't want to do the obligatory meet-the-parents fanfare where he'll be asked questions about his own childhood and upbringing while picking at tasteless boiled chicken and un- or underseasoned sides.

Why he doesn't want to get into personal territory that will inevitably lead back to his parents' divorce and no, they really aren't all that close. Nope, no plans to introduce them.

Ever since that Christmas during his senior year of college that he joined his girlfriend Claire's family in Connecticut, he's had way too many of those conversations. They might start in different ways, some more subtle than others, but they always end the same way: the girl's parents exchanging looks, confirming with each other that he's not exactly son-in-law material. That his lack of familial relationships is a yellow flag, at best. No doubt if he ever made it to a second meeting, they'd upgrade him to red.

But he hadn't known any of this when he met Claire's family. Her parents were younger than his, having gotten married right out of high school, and Claire's older siblings had all followed suit. They were all warm and loving, or so he'd thought. He'd been envious of how tight-knit they were, wanted so badly to be part of the family one day.

Then he'd come down to the kitchen just in time to overhear Claire's married older sisters telling her that her boyfriend was hot, but *he doesn't really seem family oriented, does he? Isn't it weird that he hasn't been home since he was eighteen? That's almost four years!*

People who are estranged from their own families are usually weirdos...

Guys like that don't usually commit. You want to get serious, right?

Oh, don't get us wrong, he's a nice boy, but he doesn't really fit in with us, does he?

Worse had been what followed, the limbo moment of waiting for his girlfriend to protest, to stand up for him. Instead, she'd just sighed. Like her sisters were merely echoing things she already knew. He still remembers the swift pang in his chest, the way his heartbeat pounded in his ears as he tiptoed his way back upstairs to hastily repack, because until that profoundly humiliating moment, he'd thought he *did* fit in.

He's never made that mistake again. He never will.

That January, Ves and Claire rang in the new year with a breakup. A week into the semester, she reunited with her high school boyfriend. By the time they all graduated college a few months later, she was engaged. Ves unfollowed her the second he saw the announcement on Instagram. She didn't owe him a heads-up, but being caught by surprise just brought all his old feelings of inadequacy screaming back.

Ever since that fateful Christmas, he's tried again and again with other partners, but it always ends the same way. With the cold confirmation carved in stone that Ves is never, *ever* going to be the one.

The food arrives, piping hot and smelling delicious, but he doesn't enjoy it as much as he would have five minutes ago. It's another reminder that one conversation is all it takes to send him back to being that unwanted little boy, waiting on a stoop for someone to let him in. By now it's an old wound, one that doesn't feel quite as lethal as it did that morning with Claire's family in Connecticut.

No, now it's more like picking at a scab.

He can get through this. He always does.

He slices through crisp, crackling puff pastry and takes a bite of satisfyingly fatty pork, gloriously flavored in some kind of sticky, sour-sweet marinade that sends him straight to umami heaven. Having something to do helps most of his tension ebb away.

The rest of the meal passes in relative harmony and quiet—for him, at least. The group of elderly women order what looks like the entire dessert menu and move on to comparing notes on their grandchildren, while the three women closest to him talk about Christmas plans. Elisha tries to draw him back in, but he resolutely keeps eating, answering short and to the point during the brief moments she catches him without his mouth full. Eventually, she gives up.

Solana scoops some of her mash on her fork. "Food's good, right?"

Ves finishes chewing before agreeing. "Just like you said. A perfect recommendation."

"Would you take another from me?"

He can feel Elisha's eyes on him. "About the menu? I'm too full for dessert."

"About the housing market," Solana says bluntly. "I'm going to level with you, Ves. Now isn't the greatest time to list a house. And I sell houses, so I know what I'm talking about. Piney Peaks is pretty year-round, but it's at its most picturesque in winter. Now, imagine you stick a FOR SALE sign in your yard. What do you think happens next?"

The answer seems obvious, but it still feels like he's about to fall in a trap. ". . . Someone buys it?"

"Wrong!" Solana widens her eyes. "New buyers take *one look* at our sweet little town and wonder why anyone would want to leave during"—she finger-quotes—"the most wonderful time of the year?"

He supposes that makes sense. "Does that scare them off?"

"Oh yeah. Big-time." She nods vehemently. "You wouldn't believe how many offers fall through. There's kind of a moratorium on selling houses until after the new year. Not that I'd tell you what to do! But if you were my client, I'd advise waiting. Small tourist towns are a *whole* different beast."

"Wow. Um. Yeah, thanks. I had no idea, so that's really good to know. I can't do anything until then, anyway. There's too much to do around the house."

"Oh yeah?" Solana brightens. "No worries, then. But when you're ready . . ." She pulls a business card from her purse and offers it to him between two fingers in one slick move.

He pockets it, something about the logic not quite ringing true. "Of course, I'll be talking to my real estate agent, too, but thanks for the heads-up. It's much appreciated."

"It's entirely my pleasure," she chirps.

"What are you two whispering about?" Elisha asks, looking between them with a furrowed brow.

Solana winks. "Secrets."

"Tell me, really."

"I did, babes. Secrets." Solana smirks at Ves, nudging his arm like they're in on it together.

He would just have told Elisha, but it's amusing to see her pout, so he goes along. They return to their meal, and his plate is the first one clean when the door opens, a tinkling bell cutting through the chatter.

"Ellie, I *thought* I saw you duck in here earlier," comes a voice, friendly but chiding.

CHAPTER TWELVE

Ves

Ves looks up from his plate to see a good-looking guy around his age enter, brushing snow off his hair. It's the same guy Elisha thought she was doing a good job avoiding, the reason she was so obviously hustling him in the opposite direction. He knows she recognizes the voice when she closes her eyes, mouths what looks like *for fuck's sake*, and sets her fork down with an exaggerated finality.

"Hi, Bentley," she says grudgingly.

Ves's lips twitch. Her greeting has all the enthusiasm of *Oh, look, a blistering boil on my bum.*

The man shakes his head when the hostess approaches. "Didn't you see me wave at you earlier?"

"Sorry, must have missed it."

Elisha still hasn't turned around, so only Ves sees her cheeks flare with telltale pink. Her eyes beseech his for . . . what, exactly? He doesn't know what to read into that look. He doesn't know her well, but he knows her enough that she wouldn't be rude on purpose unless there was a good reason.

Both men take each other in. Ves knows his resting dick face—impressively impassive, according to Arun—will betray nothing. Bentley's the first to break the silent standoff with an easy grin. "Hey, man. Good to meet you in the flesh. Kinda thought Ellie made it up."

Flesh is a word that gives Ves the heebie-jeebies. It's repugnant, right up there next to *moist* and *phlegm* and *yolk*. And made *what* up? Him? Not for the first time, he's taken aback at how everyone seems to know him. It's true what they say about news traveling fast in a small town.

"Same," he replies coolly. He knows his hand is clean, but he wipes it on his napkin before shaking, anyway. He half rises to take Bentley's offered hand.

The grip is extra firm, as if trying to size Ves up. Then, flippantly, he proclaims, "Bentley. The ex."

Ves almost sneers. As though that's a title to be proud of.

So this is the guy who just swanned back into town with a wife and an undented ego. Ves flicks questioning eyes to her, but instead of responding with a discreet nod, there's a nervous tension on her face that looks all kinds of wrong. And Bentley is the one who put it there. Her eyebrows have drawn together to form an "11" wrinkle and her lips resemble a flatline.

He doesn't need to know anything else about Elisha's ex to already dislike him. The man oozes a certain smugness, like his running into them here isn't exactly what he wanted in the first place. What's with the pouncing like he's caught them in the act? Does he want her back?

Annoyed, Ves squeezes back harder.

Elisha's eyes find Ves's. He maps her face, the taut jut of her jaw, the urgency in her eyes. In a tight voice, she says, "We should probably be going, I only had an hour for lunch."

Is he imagining the tremor in her voice? And more importantly, why does Ves care?

"Ves is the new owner of the Christmas House," Danica explains to Bentley, but with absolutely none of the warmth she had shown to Ves.

"That makes sense," says Bentley. "Is that how you and Ellie met? How long have you two been . . . ?"

Ves wonders if that's her nickname. She doesn't *look* like an Ellie. It's certainly not how she introduced herself to him, and he hasn't heard anyone else use it, but maybe it's reserved for people she shares history with. Unlike him, who's gone by "Ves" ever since grade school—only Arun calls him by his full name, and even then, only when he's annoyed.

Belatedly, he understands what Bentley's driving at in asking how they met. Isn't that the first question people always ask couples? A slow smile spreads over his face as it clicks: Bentley thinks they're together.

"It feels like we've known each other *forever*," he says, reaching for the tab before she can. She makes a bitten-off sound of protest, but he scribbles a generous tip and slides his credit card in almost defiantly. And then, in a voice imbued with as much adoration as possible, "I'll get your jacket, love."

He's never been a pet name person, but damn if it doesn't feel good to have someone to give one to, even if it's fake.

Elisha's expressive face flickers with shock, eyebrows comically shooting toward her hairline. *Love?* she mouths to Solana, followed by *What are you playing at?* to Ves.

He doesn't give himself a chance to second-guess the surge of protectiveness as he calmly unhooks their jackets from the peg. He hopes Bentley has seen his coat on top of hers.

Ves shrugs into his, then holds hers out in a subtle way that implies he intends to help her put it on. With a bewildered expression, Elisha lets him. Her face is a cocktail of curiosity, disbelief, and . . . gratitude?

"Thanks," she murmurs, not stepping out of his bubble.

"Nice to meet you all," Ves says to the table once his card is back in his wallet. The oldies are all watching with hungry expressions. "I'm sure we'll be running into each other again soon. Nice meeting you, *Ben*." He senses he has allies in the Pereiras when both mother and daughter give him broad grins.

Bentley's jaw tightens. "Don't forget my soirée. I'll text you the details." Irritation flashes over his face as he sees how close Elisha and Ves are standing. "You're both invited, of course. It'll be nice to catch up and get to know each other."

"Like I said, I'm"—she looks at Ves—"*we're* going to be pretty busy. But we'll see. Tell Tori hi."

Ves frowns. She's already had this conversation? Evidently her ex can't take no for an answer. As Elisha starts for the door, he catches her loosely by the wrist. He can count every single one of her thick black lashes as her eyes widen up at him. "Hey," he says softly. "C'mere. You're going to be cold."

And then in front of everyone, he unwinds his scarf, still warm from his body, and loops it around her neck. Their heated gazes lock. "There," he murmurs. "Gorgeous."

CHAPTER THIRTEEN

Ves

When Ves's knuckles brush the curve of her ear, Elisha makes a sound of delight. The ends of her short brown hair tickle his thumb, the innocent gesture giving him a hot nudge in his pants.

"You realize," she whispers as she steps through the door Ves holds open. Snowflakes catch on her hair, on the apples of her cheeks. "That they're definitely going to think we're a thing now?"

Dismissively, he tells her, "I'm not bothered by what they think."

"You know, for someone who's not a big relationship person, you did a pretty decent job of pretending to be my boyfriend back there," she says lightly.

A bit more than *decent*, he thinks. "Purely for your benefit." He clears his throat, wishing he could clear his mind half as easily. Coming to her rescue was a knee-jerk reaction to witnessing her obvious discomfort. It had absolutely nothing whatsoever to do with the spring-loaded coil of jealousy that unfurled when he saw the way Bentley was looking at her.

To his relief, she takes him at face value. "Thanks, by the way, for paying, but I'll get the next one."

He never intended to let her pay for this one, but he likes that she offers. That it goes without saying there *will* be a next one. That for some reason, he's more than okay with her foregone conclusion.

"Also, thank you for what you did back there," adds Elisha. "You didn't have to, and I know you weren't comfortable with, um, all of that." She gives a little laugh. "The *look* on his face when you called him Ben. It's such a great, solid name, but he thinks it's 'plebeian.' Solana can't stand how pretentious he is, so knocking him down a peg? You've got a fan for life now."

He clears his throat. "How about with you?" For a reason he doesn't want to dwell upon, he wants Elisha to find him impressive, too.

"Oh, goes without saying," she says brightly. "If you want to give me the best present ever, just keep using the nickname loudly and frequently in my presence."

"You've got it." They share a grin that feels a bit like solidarity, a bit like something more.

"And obviously you're off the hook about the party. I'll probably have to make an appearance, bring them a poinsettia flower arrangement or whatever, and make an excuse for you."

That gets his attention. "You're still going to attend?"

"Attend." She eyes him with unconcealed merriment. "Ves, I'm currently wearing your scarf after that possessive little display back there where you pretended to be my boyfriend—I *think* you can be a little less formal. And yes. Probably. As much as I want to go back to pretending he doesn't exist, it's just not realistic now that we live in the same town." She groans. *"Oh my god.* I can't believe that's just a sentence that I said."

"Don't go," Ves says impulsively. "He's just trying to needle you with that nice-guy act." Before either of them can dissect why he even cares, as casually as he can manage, Ves adds, "I realize that I don't know you that well, but dear old Ben didn't really seem like your type."

"My ex-slash-long-story? Well, now that I think about it, it's actually quite a short one. Boy proposes to girl, gets a job in her hometown after graduation, then finds every reason under the sun to delay following through. I was so humiliated I took the very first job offer I could get and ran off to Atlanta."

He's torn between saying *Sorry that happened to you* and *What a fucking asshole*, but then she laughs as if she's trying to brush off the fact that she overshared. So he bites back his instinctive protectiveness and anger on her behalf.

Ves wouldn't mind if Elisha wanted to take his arm again, but she doesn't, although their bodies do brush while they tromp back through the snow. The air between them simmers with an undercurrent that he doesn't particularly care to investigate. He blames his smooth move with the scarf as the catalyst.

"So when did you become an expert on *my* taste, Ves? Spend a lot of time thinking about who's my type?" she teases.

He dodges the questions as well as a rather emboldened squirrel who bounds alongside them on the sidewalk. He's a bit unsure whether Elisha's teasing him or if she doesn't think he has any business thinking about her questionable taste in partners. "Of course not," he says with a huff. "He seemed . . ." *Like he still wants you*, his mind whispers. Ves hesitates, then reroutes. "You don't like him."

Not even as a friend, clearly. Ves himself has parted amicably with the women he's casually dated, neither party invested enough to stay friends. But Elisha's ex keeps going out of his way to stay in her life like some kind of haunted, permanent fixture. It's weird, it's suspicious, and Ves doesn't like it. Or him.

She exhales. "Yeah, that would be why we're exes. What, do you stay friends with all of your ex-girlfriends or something?"

He thinks about Connecticut and paying a small fortune for the Amtrak ride back to his campus apartment on Christmas Day and Claire not even trying very hard to talk him out of it. "No," he says. "But then, I haven't had very many. I date casually and that's about it. I don't do serious."

"Oh, that's . . . Sorry, I was going to say sad, but maybe you have the right idea. Getting serious has never really worked out for me. I just hate being single over the holidays. Especially here of all places."

His boots slosh through a puddle with an ugly squelch. Ves grits his teeth. The suede is *so* going to be ruined by the time he's back at Maeve's. "Is that why he assumed you made me up?"

"Oh, um. Well. Don't freak out. I *may* have implied that I had a boyfriend, and he *may* have assumed it was you because of the whole Christmas House thing. Don't give me that look. I know I'm two for two when it comes to lying to my ex, but in my defense, I really wanted him to think I was doing well."

"Because you're still pining over him?" He doesn't want to examine too closely why the idea bugs him.

Elisha scoffs. Judging by that eloquent response, Ves guesses she isn't.

"No, I just didn't want to be the sucky Oreo," she says.

He spots the scarlet winterberry trees lining the path to the Chamber of Commerce building. They're getting closer to her office and Ves doesn't want their conversation to end. "Oreo? You're going to have to explain that one to me."

"You know, when you split an Oreo apart, one half of the cookie gets the majority of the cream?"

He's going against every instinct he has, but what the hell. "Would you be the successful Oreo if you got the filming permission? I wouldn't want to let you—uh, your mayor—down."

Elisha tugs at his elbow and comes to a standstill, so he does the same. He can sense he's surprised her for the second time this afternoon. "You'd do that for me?" she squeaks. "I mean, her? Me?"

He shrugs. "You're helping me with cleaning the house. Seems only fair."

She bites her lip. "I don't want you to feel obligated."

"I don't."

"Are you sure? What changed your mind?"

He looks at her for a centuries-long moment, weighing his words. "Yes, I'm sure." Then, unable to stop himself, he adds, "And you did."

She opens her mouth, but before she can say a word, he says, "I'm doing this town a public service since I'm genuinely afraid what lie you'll come up with next if you don't get your way."

She purses her lips, eyes alight with teasing. "*So* selfless of you," she coos. Then, in the most serious voice he's ever heard her use, she says, "Thank you, Ves."

He huffs a laugh. "Pull out your phone. I'm going to give you my email address so you can send me whatever I need to sign to make this sequel happen."

She does, opening up her mail app to attach the PDF for him to electronically sign and send back. Just as she's about to put her phone back in her purse, Ves stops her.

Her wrist is chilled against his warm fingertips—she had her hands stuffed in her pockets the whole way back because, he suspects, she left her gloves at home—and skims his pulse in a way that causes an entirely different kind of shiver. "Take my number, too," he says after a hard swallow.

"Okay. Why?"

"Because your house is too far away to stretch two aluminum cans and I have a deathly fear of birds and their 360-degree vision, so carrier pigeon is also out."

"... Fine, fine, fair point." She taps in his number as he recites it. "Is this your way of hinting I need to call before coming over?" She grins. "Just so you know, I was probably almost definitely going to ring the bell this time, my darling stickler for the rules."

He catches his eye roll at the last second. "Shameless," he tuts, liking it far more than he should.

"Can't just let myself in. It'll set those gossips' tongues wagging again."

He arches a brow. "More than the scarf did?"

She grins, conceding. "Maybe not. That was a pretty suave move. Guess you're not as predictable as I thought."

He ignores her heckling, but he's a little miffed to be labeled predictable—it's not usually considered a complimentary trait. "What did you save me as?" he asks, craning to get a look at her screen.

She immediately presses it against her chest. "Your name. Ves Hollins. What else?"

One skeptical eyebrow goes up. "Your face is too squirrelly for that to be true."

She waves her free hand. "That's just how I look."

"You and I both know that your face is *far* from rodentlike," he says with a smirk.

She half pouts, half scowls. "Uh, not the most glowing of compliments, but thanks?"

"Even though this town does seem to have a weird preoccupation with them," he adds.

"I *told* you a stoat is a weasel." She ignores his snort, tucking her phone away, and gives him a radiant smile that sucker-punches every other thought out of his head, including the one insistently screaming that this is a bad idea. "You have no idea how much this helps me out, Ves."

"Yeah, well, wait until you see how much of a mess I made while cleaning."

She blinks. "It's worse than before?"

"Oh, the current mess laughs in the face of the before-mess's face. Really thumbs its nose in it."

Elisha throws her head back and laughs. Squeezes his elbow. Looks at him with sparkling eyes that aren't just brown, actually, but the exact shade of golden brandy. "Lucky me."

As they part ways—her back to work and him in search of packing materials, feeling warmer than he's felt all day—he kind of thinks she means it.

"Hey! Ves!" she yells, hand on the chamber's door. "I still have your scarf!" She starts to head back.

They meet at the same place on the sidewalk in front of her office building. The wind picks up, sending her hair flying. When she visibly shivers, he's glad he loaned her the scarf Maeve knitted for him. He holds up a hand when she tries to unwind it from her neck. "Keep it until tonight," he says. "Can't have you coming down with a cold. Why is it whenever I see you, you're persistently underdressed?"

"Tell you what." Her smile is unmitigated challenge. "A secret for a secret. I'll spill the deets if *you* tell me why you don't date over the holidays."

She must *really* want to know. But being vulnerable in exchange? Giving her emotional ammunition? He's nosy, not desperate. "Doesn't sound like that great a trade-off, Elisha. Care to sweeten the deal?"

Elisha thinks about it—or at least pretends to. "Hmm, you know what? I think you'll cave first."

Ves's laugh is an unsubtle *Dream on*. He starts to walk away.

"This close to Christmas, you want to risk going on my naughty list?"

He isn't flirting. Definitely not. He's doing a nice thing for a nice girl because it's almost Christmas and goodwill to all and yes, okay, fine, that thing about her being the losing Oreo has stuck with him.

Arun would be so proud, Ves thinks wryly. Probably make some joke about Ves's soft marshmallow Peep heart. Which is exactly why, when Arun inevitably requests that Ves regale him with a recap of his Piney Peaks adventures so far, he fully intends to lay it out as strictly business.

Truly, he does need the help: clear out the house, get through the holidays, reschedule the valuations.

That's it, nothing more. He's not thawing toward this small town or the people in it. Not at all.

And he's certainly not counting down the hours until Elisha's off work.

He checks his wristwatch and frowns before he can stop himself.

CHAPTER FOURTEEN

Ves

After returning home, Ves spends the next couple of hours frantically attempting to clean the mess he warned Elisha about but doesn't actually want her to see. It's no joke; the mess has undeniably multiplied. It's like it had rampant bunny sex and is now even more *everywhere* than it was when he arrived.

When his surroundings are this uncontrollable, all he wants is the escape he used to find between the pages of a book. He has plenty loaded up on his phone's Kindle app, but even thinking about books reminds him of the new book idea that he's trying and failing to brainstorm.

He pulls out his phone, thumb hovering over Arun's name. Then forces himself not to call, because it's barely three p.m. and Arun's probably got an eagle eye on an auction for a client's book or negotiating the finer points of a contract like the badass, sharky agent he is.

Ves sighs as he taps open the new messages from his parents, the last one from his dad, saying simply Call me.

Karl Hollins picks up on the second ring. "Ves. Finally."

"I texted you when I got to town."

"I suppose you've called your mother already? Or am I the first one you called?"

Ves bites the inside of his cheek. Thirty years old and this bullshit is *still* ongoing; his father tries to trick him into admitting his favorite parent; his mother claims the title for herself and assumes there's no contest. "I texted you both when I landed. And again when I got to Maeve's. Can we, for once, not play this game?"

"You sound stressed. Are you sure you can handle this on your own?"

If it were anyone else's parent asking, Ves might call it concern. From his, he knows better. "It's all good, Dad."

"You haven't hired any bereavement cleanout services, right? It's a small town. Don't trust them to know what's valuable or not. These people probably think a paint-by-numbers is real art." Karl snorts. "I told you my grandfather had a library full of first editions. And all that art. There's a real Gehry sketch in his old bedroom. Aunt Maeve had a safe-deposit box at the bank. Lots of family heirlooms we shouldn't lose track of. We can hold on to the jewelry, make sure it stays in the family. *Someone* should get to wear it. Doubt Maeve ever did. If memory serves, I recall her being quite plain."

Through the barrage of insults, Ves reads between the lines: *Son, since you're not married, give everything precious to me so my new wife can pass them down to your little sister, Hanna. We don't want your mother having them*—she's *not even a real Hollins anymore, even though she kept my fucking last name just to spite me.*

Karl seems to take Ves's silence for agreement because he moves on. "How are you finding that little backwater, anyway?"

As usual, his father's self-centeredness makes his stomach hurt. Ves sits on Maeve's pink floral sofa, which is every bit as stiff and uncomfortable as it looks. "Piney Peaks is hardly that."

Karl laughs. "They don't even have a Starbucks. Bet Maeve still hasn't replaced the coffee maker."

Okay, fair. On both counts. But maybe the Christmas spirit or whatever is finally getting to him, because he's feeling protective of the town when he says, "I like it here."

"You did when you were a kid, too. Couldn't shut up about the place."

"I remember," Ves says softly, even though the memories have grown cloudier with time, like a vigorously shaken snow globe, fading fast as a dream.

"My parents sent me out to Grandfather's every summer. Hated it there. Had to be on my best behavior all the time because he was the town doctor. You, though. Maeve *doted* on you." Karl's voice is coated in what sounds to Ves like a bit of resentment. "One visit and you wouldn't stop talking about some chocolate shop. Even went ice skating and said it was better than Rockefeller Center." Karl snorts. "Maeve this and Maeve that, drove Adeline up the wall. But then, she's always been a jealous woman."

Aaaaand there it is.

"Dad, there's still a lot I need to do."

Even a hundred miles away, Karl's scoff is no less cutting. "How hard can it be? I already took care of the funeral. You have the easy job."

For one wild flash of a second, Ves wants to switch to video and show him just how easy it's *not*. Instead, he takes a deep, steadying breath and exhales through his nose. There's no point in revealing all the paraphernalia he has to sort through, how many keep-trash-maybes he has to make decisions about. Not unless he wants Karl to head down and take over.

Wearily, Ves pinches the bridge of his nose. That's the last thing he wants. His dad wouldn't worry about making the wrong decision and accidentally throwing something precious away. Karl would be ruthlessly efficient, no second-guessing to slow him down.

The same way he handled Maeve's funeral: a hurried, out-of-town affair given that Maeve was away from home when she passed. The fact that she was only in upstate New York for another cousin's funeral didn't faze his father at all. Karl simply planned something convenient: minimal fuss, just him and his father's family at the service. No thought given to those from Piney Peaks who may have wanted to pay their own respects.

With just his indifferent father and kind-but-distant step-mother there, Ves's twelve-year-old sister, Hanna, hadn't hesitated to slip her hand in his, squeezing tight, as though it were the most natural thing in the world. The grateful way he'd held on to her, the way he hadn't since she was a small child and their age gap didn't seem quite so vast.

It strikes Ves that every family event he can remember has been about duty. Making an appearance, lingering just long enough to be noticed, and then leaving as fast as he can.

"I want to do right by Aunt Maeve," he says firmly. "Like she did for me. However long it takes."

"Sort through the valuables, sell the house, stick the remains in an urn vault. It's that simple, Ves."

"In a dark, dusty mausoleum? She would hate that."

"Didn't know you could commune with the dead," says Karl.

Ves ignores the snippiness. "I'm just saying, it sounds miserable. I thought I'd come back in the spring to scatter her ashes some-where pretty. She always loved this place in full bloom."

"How do you know that? She was always pretty reserved with me." His dad's voice is more complaint than curiosity.

"It was just something she mentioned when she visited me a few years ago in the city."

"Right. Well, do whatever you think is best. Just let me know if I need to show up."

Ves hesitates. "I was wondering what you think about me holding a—well, not quite a wake, but just a little farewell drinks thing in her memory. For the town. Sometime before I leave. Since we took care of the funeral in New York and no one got a chance to pay their respects, I just thought . . ." He trails off.

"Jesus. For the town?" Karl sounds incredulous.

"They really loved her." Ves hates feeling defensive. "It's just a small gesture. If you wanted to come." But even as he says it, he knows that his dad's offer is as superficial and meaningless as this phone call.

"I think it's unnecessary. In any case, your stepmother has a lot of charity gala commitments and then we promised your sister another trip to Aspen. You might be looking at a future Olympian skier." A pause. "Might be hard to swing right now. It's a time for family and truth be told, Maeve wasn't too fond of me."

But I'm your family, too is what Ves doesn't say. *Come for me.*

Ves looks at the chaos around him, and it suddenly looks manageable. At least compared to what's going on in his head. "Yeah. I need to get back to it, so . . ."

"Sure, son. Call me if you need anything."

The empty offer almost makes Ves laugh. Karl hangs up first, a reminder that the Hollinses don't really do goodbyes. They spring in and out of Ves's life when it suits them, and it's never about him. Not really. Despite the divorce two decades ago, the family fallout has been stretching out ever since. He's not sure which is worse: the fighting or the game playing. Either way, he loses.

At least with his new arrangement with Elisha, he's going to come out a winner. He didn't love his dad dissing Maeve and Piney Peaks, but that doesn't mean he wants to linger here any longer than necessary. Once the house is in order, he's out of here, and will only need to return for the valuation the first week of the new year.

Elisha promised that filming would start in mid-January and wrap by the end of February, with no need for him to be on the premises. As long as she takes care of everything, there's no reason why he can't help her out, and hopefully the house will sell by early spring.

The thought comforts him as he abandons the living room and retreats to the kitchen, where he's cleared enough space on the table to sit down with a well-loved Moleskine notebook and his favorite Montblanc pen, a college graduation gift from Maeve. Now that the rest of his schedule is worked out, he just needs to figure out what book concept is going to wow Dominique and prove he knows what a happy family looks like.

Even if it's one hundred percent pure fiction.

CHAPTER FIFTEEN

Ves

Three pages of scribbles, crossed-out words, and defeated sighs later, the knock at the door takes him by surprise. Ves glances at his watch: four p.m.

Elisha's enthusiastic, but surely not so much as to take off from work early? Warily, he approaches the door like it's a snake about to strike. One look through the peephole and he jerks back in shock.

Crowded on the front porch, looking inordinately cheerful, is a group of what he can only assume are carolers. Five adults all wearing red, whether that's stockings or coats or huge, hideous poinsettia brooches, and clutching sheets of paper in mittened hands.

Can he pretend he's not at home? Who just drops by without warning and an actual invitation? Another knock, this one more insistent. What on earth could these people possibly want?

Braced for the very real possibility they're about to sing at him, Ves opens the door. He's sure he looks like a man awaiting his doom, but they're all smiles. "Isn't it too early for caroling?" he asks suspiciously.

A man with black hair and a stubbled jawline laughs. It takes a moment for Ves to place him: the bartender from the Old Stoat. His quarter-zip pullover and puffy jacket hide his impressive tattoo sleeve. In fact, the whole arm has been claimed by an impish-looking old woman with a shock of bubblegum-pink hair. "I'm Adam Lawson," says the man. "And this is my grams, Bibi, and her friends Marcy and Dave."

Ves nods, hovering in the open doorway. "Hello."

"Hi there, son. I'm Jamie. Dave's my dad," says a handsome man with blond hair and twinkling blue eyes, pushing forward to stand beside an older gentleman to whom he bears a strong resemblance. "We just wanted to welcome you to the neighborhood. I believe you've met my daughter already."

Ves blinks. "I have?" Then it hits him, seeing traces of her pert nose and full, bow lips in both her father and grandfather. "Elisha," he realizes out loud.

Dave laughs, a hearty guffaw that almost makes Ves jump. "Bingo! Our girl is pretty memorable."

"We're sorry to meet you under these circumstances," says Bibi. "We all loved Maeve so much. Now, I don't know if anyone's told you yet, but next year is the fiftieth anniversary of *Sleighbells under Starlight*."

"As well as what would have been Maeve's eightieth birthday," says Dave.

"Two pretty big milestones," Adam chimes in. Marcy and Jamie nod emphatically.

"And you see, well, even before all this movie business started, we wanted to celebrate our dear Maeve." Bibi's eyes grow misty. "There's no reason we can't still do it in her memory."

It's a sweet, thoughtful gesture, made worse by the conversation he just had with Karl. Guilt stabs at his chest. The people of Piney Peaks going to this much effort really reinforces what a valued member of the community Maeve truly was. Meanwhile, he can't even remember the last conversation they had. He just saw her name while scrolling his recent call log, but if he picks that thread he's a little afraid that he'll discover it wasn't so recent, after all.

Maybe Marcy reads something in his face, because she quickly pounces. "We're dedicating our Winter Festival to her. As her only family in town, of course you'll want to be there."

Ves finds himself nodding along. It's probably only one day. It won't be any hardship to show his face and appreciate everything they've done—it's the least he can do.

"We're putting together a little sleigh ride through the forest," explains Dave. "Following the same route they did in the movie. We also have cookie decorating at the Chocolate Mouse, ice skating, caroling, a wonderful Christmas Market next to the church, fresh cider stalls, the works! We'd love it if you joined us." His voice becomes extra jovial, as though he's about to impart something wonderful. "I know Maeve would have loved to know you were spending the month enjoying the season in Piney Peaks with us."

A record screeches in his brain. A full *month*? His cheeks and neck and ears suddenly flame with heat. Unfortunately for him, the fair complexion he inherited from both his parents wasn't accompanied by their disinterested composure. He's sure his cheeks have gone all splotchy.

"Oh, I—" Ves is about to explain he'll be too busy with the house to throw himself into the spirit of things in a community he's only temporarily part of when he reads the expectant looks on their faces. Didn't he *just* tell Karl he wanted to do right by Maeve? Declining their invitation is the exact opposite of that.

"You're family," Dave says with conviction, catching Ves's hesitation. "You should be a part of it."

Adam gives Ves an encouraging grin.

A gust of wind slams into him like a wall and slithers cold air past his cashmere rollneck sweater. Ghosting down his neck, his spine. He hates being put on the spot, and yet . . . there is no other answer he can give, other than: "Okay."

An hour later, Ves is still reeling from his "Okay" when Elisha lets herself in without knocking, finding him in the kitchen with his notebook open, pen held loosely between his fingers, and eyes glazed over.

Seeing her pink nose and ruffled hair, he startles. When he gave her the filming permission, he intended to leave things in her capable hands. But as long as he's here, they're sort of in it together. A not wholly unpleasant notion, but not the one he signed up for, either.

"I know for a fact I locked that door," Ves says without looking up.

"You did." There's a creak as she sits down next to him. "My parents have a spare key."

"I'll be wanting that back." He holds out his hand, palm up.

She hands it over, along with his scarf, neatly folded. "A little birdie told me that you're going to be enjoying our Winter Festival while you're here. How did you get strong-armed into all this mandatory fun?"

"Maybe I'm not as predictable as you think," he says archly.

Elisha's lips tic up before flattening back down, barely restraining a grin. "Uh-huh."

"Who told you? Your dad?"

"Nope."

"Granddad?"

She seems amused. "Again, no."

"I give up."

"Solana."

His eyebrows shoot up. "She wasn't even there."

"She's dating Adam. We're in, like, eight group chats. And every single one is buzzing about you."

He waits for her to shoot him a grin, to be included in the joke. When she doesn't, he stares, absolutely perturbed. "Wait, that's not hyperbolic?"

"That's the Piney Peaks gossip grapevine for you," she chirps.

"That's disturbing," he counters.

"Ves, it's a small town. Good news travels fast."

Forget what everyone else thinks—does *Elisha* think it's good news? His skin itches under his sweater, which, at its Bergdorf's price tag, it absolutely should not do.

She leans closer to look at his notebook, bringing the heady scent of cocoa butter and mint. "What are you working on?"

Part of him wants to slam his palm over the paper, but she's already tugged it away. In his sharp, slightly slanted handwriting, he's made a list of things he could write about.

She sweeps over the page, landing on the last line. "Why have you written *journey*, crossed it out, *quest*, crossed it out, *adventure*, crossed it out? Aren't these all the same thing?"

He straightens, groaning at the ache in his back. "It's a brain dump. Anything that comes to mind, I write it down. At the end of the exercise, I weed through and hopefully find what I'm looking for."

"Which is what?"

"A kernel of a story that could grow into actually being a book someday. But right now I'd settle for even just a smidge"—he holds his thumb and pointer a centimeter apart—"of inspiration."

"Seek magic and you shall find it." She gives him a radiant smile, like it's supposed to mean something to him. A quote, perhaps?

Something from a book or movie? Shit, *he* didn't write that line, did he?

"Apropos," he quips. "Wish I had some magic right now."

"You don't know where that's from, do you?" Elisha's smile fades. "It's something Maeve always used to say."

He almost smiles. "Funny, 'Be good' was how she always ended her conversations with me."

It was always strange to hear, especially as he grew older. It made him feel childish, as though he were still that seven-year-old who had to be on his best behavior with an unfamiliar stranger. But now he thinks maybe it was her way of telling him she loved him.

Elisha's eyes crinkle when she laughs. Her very earthy, very lovely eyes. His gut unexpectedly tightens. "Were you frequently naughty?" she asks.

He knows she's teasing him, but he doesn't mind. "Incorrigibly."

"You? I can't see it. I bet you were always on Santa's nice list."

Curiously, he tilts his head. "You're so convinced I wasn't a bad boy?"

"I think you were exceptionally, predictably good."

"Exceptional, am I?"

She opens her mouth, then snaps it shut. He doesn't hold back his smirk. She narrows her eyes. "You did hear *predictable* was right next to it, didn't you?"

He supposes he is: he likes a sense of routine and doesn't necessarily enjoy stepping outside his comfort zone. There are worse things to be, but now, perversely, he wants to prove her wrong.

"What's 'Seek magic and you shall find it' from, then?" he asks, neatly setting his writing materials to the corner of the table at perfect right angles. He uses his fingertip to imperceptibly straighten his pen.

"Oh, it's a line from *Sleighbells*. Maeve was just an extra, but everyone loved her so much that they wrote a couple lines just for her. This wasn't one of them, though. She kind of just blurted it out to fill the silence when Nathan—he played the lead—forgot *his* line, and the director liked it so much, they didn't do a retake. She was encouraging him to take a chance and seek magic and love and possibility with his small-town girl instead of trying to get back to a home where he never fit in."

"Is that why she loved the movie so much? Even your mayor knew what a fan Maeve was."

"I wouldn't say fan, exactly. She always had dreams of being a historian, and, if she hadn't spent so much of her life under her dad's thumb . . . well, that's what I think she was trying to do here." She rises, clapping her hands on her thighs. The move draws his attention to her rusty-orange corduroy skirt and thigh-high black socks, and the couple of inches of skin peeking out. "Speaking of . . ." She flashes him a determined grin. "We're here to get this place shipshape, right? Where do you want to start?"

"How about the living room?"

Once there, Elisha takes in the room with a surveyor's eye. "First, you need to find all the important documents. Electricity and water bills, home and life insurance policies, any stock or bond certificates. What else, what else . . . Oh! Bank statements. The deed to this house. Got it?"

Ves is honestly not sure whether she has too much faith in him or she's just chronically optimistic. He stares at all the loose paper. "You're kidding. In *this*?"

"I know it looks daunting, so don't worry if you can't find everything. I'm sure her bank will have some things on file."

"While I'm doing all of that, what are you going to do?" he asks suspiciously. "Kind of feels like I got the hard job."

She flutters her fingers at him. At his blank look, she sighs. "Do you see these nails? Brand-new. I just painted them last night." White snowflakes stand out against dark, inky blue and silver-glitter tips. He hadn't noticed them at lunch, but he likes them better than the grim nutcracker faces and frightening chompers by a long shot.

She does another fancy hand flourish. "I'm not risking these babies with any heavy lifting. I'll go through the rest of these books and see if you missed anything."

"What could I possibly have missed? They're just some old mass-market paperbacks." He senses he's made a grievous misstep when she stares at him like he's sprouted antlers.

"*These*," she enunciates, "are Maeve's most beloved and extremely valuable collection of romance novels. They might not sell at Sotheby's or whatever, but we—and by that I one hundred percent mean *you*—are going to show them the respect they deserve."

He throws his hands up, flashing his palms in surrender. "I wouldn't dream of doing otherwise. Have at it."

She puts her hands on her hips, looking adorably incensed, though he'd never tell her that. "Are you humoring me?"

He shakes his head. "Never about books." And that's the honest truth. He's not an elitist snob; plenty of his author colleagues are incredibly successful at penning diverse, inclusive romance. They're *New York Times* bestsellers and award winners and some of the best writers he knows.

She looks surprised, like he's robbed her of the fight she was gearing up for. "Oh . . . Well, that's okay, then. Sorry. Didn't mean to jump down your throat. I don't like when people look down on what brings others joy. It's just so unnecessary."

"I do understand that." His mind slingshots him back to the night he told his parents he had gotten a book deal. His father's voice rings in his ear: *Not exactly the next Great American Novel, is it? Well, you're just twenty-four. You have time. Your sister Hanna can read it and let me know what she thinks.*

Ves waits until Elisha meets his eyes. "Trust me, as someone who writes fantasy for kids, I get it."

Her eyes are soft. Understanding, even. It makes him feel dreadfully exposed. His heart hurtles into his throat when her lips part as if to speak. Part of him wants to kick himself for saying that, laying himself so bare before her.

The other, more insistent part, wants to know what will happen next. What this unpredictable, kindhearted, unimaginably protective woman will say. But then, at the last second, she seems to change her mind. As the thoughtful expression drops from her face, he's disappointed.

And then he's disappointed in himself. She's a means to an end. A way for him to get through the holiday with someone resembling a friend and absolutely nothing more. His timeline in town may have changed, but nothing else about his situation has.

He knows he's not *that* guy—the guy who gets the girl, the happy ending. Those are other guys, ones who don't come with his emotional baggage and fucked family history. He should be more wary of her sympathy and her smiles—of getting too close to her, period.

So then why is it so easy to forget?

CHAPTER SIXTEEN

Elisha

"Wow, you've really scourged the kitchen," Elisha says in surprise. Over the last few days, between the hour or two she spends helping Ves after work and his own efforts during the day, they've already made a huge dent. Now, the cabinet doors are splayed wide open to air out and there's still a hint of lemon all-purpose cleaner hovering in the air. Maeve kept the place as clean as she could, but the gunk built up quick in a working kitchen. "Oooh, nice, you got rid of the musty smell."

Ves wrinkles his nose. "That's not all. I also degreased the range hood and inside the oven." As if he can't help it, he does a full-body shudder.

Blech. Elisha knows how filthy those get. With sympathy and just a sprinkle of amusement, she says, "Please tell me you had rubber gloves on." His glower is all the answer she needs. She hides her laugh behind a fake cough that even *she* doesn't buy. "Um, thanks for being a true gent and not involving me?"

His scowl doesn't drop. "You're not getting off that easy. You're doing the next gross task. De-squirrel the rain gutters or evict the family of rats nesting in the crawl space."

"You've got it," she says brightly. Not, she thinks, that it will ever be an issue. The only thing in Maeve's gutters is clumpy brown leaves and the old Victorian doesn't even *have* a crawl space.

He looks suspicious at how easily she agreed. Her gaze snags on the kitchen table, and she quickly blurts out, "You got your laptop! And a . . . whatever that thing is."

"Arun sent them." Ves grins and pats his MacBook Pro, then the thermos-looking object.

Okay, she likes him surly and broody, but her heart jolts with a happy little *ping!* when she sees his explosive handsomeness. One little grin did that?

Oh lord, she really does have to make him smile more often.

Oblivious to her giddy thoughts, he continues, "It's a travel coffee press. I know it's a little extra but I can't survive without it, and trust me, Arun has already teased the hell out of me."

Elisha throws up her palms. "Far be it from me to criticize a man and his coffee habits."

She wants to be as delighted for him as he clearly is, but there's a little thought in the back of her brain that now that he has his favorite Starbucks grounds and his fancy-schmancy press, he won't take her up on the standing offer to swing by the house and have breakfast with her family.

She blinks back the warm and fuzzy daydream she's had of him since they sparked at their first meeting: In it, he comes over in a dress shirt at seven thirty in the morning, hair still wet from his shower, trying not to show how much he's enjoying the fuss Anita is sure to make over him. He'll sip from a Ben Lomond High School Film Society mug she had printed in high school and still has twenty more of sitting in a box in her parents' garage. Maybe ask her the story behind it, and she'll tell him that after all the trouble she went through to convince the administration and get a teacher sponsor, only the kids who wanted easy extracurriculars to pad their college apps showed up.

After frustrating months of being constantly outvoted on their weekly movies, she eventually left her own club. Undoubtedly, because he's Ves, he'll tease her about not being over it (true) and probably figure out that spring day in tenth grade when she stomped all the way home in the rain to comfort-watch *Sleighbells* with Maeve is why she's like a dog with a bone about this whole movie filming in Piney Peaks (also true).

It would be so nice if a man understood and supported her instead of mocking or undermining her. Is Ves that guy? When she first met him, looking down his nose at her (literally), she wouldn't have said so. But now? Is it him who's changed or just her feelings toward him?

"What's that smile for?"

She comes back to him with a start, swallowing furiously when she sees that his glacial eyes are trained on her. She replays his question, suddenly unsure about everything: the uncertainty in his tone as if he isn't sure he's allowed to ask, whether the seesawing in her stomach is because of indulging in her little daydream or his scrutiny. "Um, just noticing how much progress we've made? I can actually see the kitchen table and most of the living room carpet."

Ves takes in the kitchen, brow furrowed, and she wonders if he sees the same mental before-and-after she does. In all the common living spaces, they've sorted through the salvageable appliances and furniture for donation, bagged old magazines and newspapers for recycling, and de-doilied all the surfaces. Of which, to his disgust, there were many. Elisha even tackled Maeve's bedroom yesterday, setting the less worn items aside for a local thrift store where she remembers they took Grandma Lou's wardrobe.

"Yeah, it's a good start," he says at last. "Better with you here."

She's pleased with the acknowledgment. "Oh, I meant to tell you! When I was in her bedroom, I found her musical jewelry box. I was obsessed with it when I was younger, there was a spinning ballerina and it played *Silent Night*. But, um, unfortunately I was so little that I lost the key. So, if you come across an antique-looking one . . ." She trails off, seeing his expression. "I know, I know, it's a bit like a needle in a haystack, and if it could be found, Maeve would have likely discovered it years ago, but . . ."

He regards her steadily. "She mentioned it in the will. I'll keep an eye out."

She flushes. "It's just, I think she had some jewelry in there? Probably costume stuff, but it's still really pretty. If you wanted it for someone in February."

Ves looks bemused. "Oddly specific. That's two months from now."

"After Valentine's Day, you'll have plenty of time to find that post-holiday girlfriend, Mr. Ves I-Don't-Date-over-the-Holidays Hollins." Would a wink be too playful? He seems uncomfortable with teasing, but he also gives as good as he gets, so she chances it.

He snorts. "Subtle. And I categorically deny the implication I don't date over the holidays because I'm a cheapskate who wants to skip the expense of a present and a nice evening out." Before she can dwell too long on what a *nice* evening in the city with Ves Hollins might entail, he counters with "Since you insist on being nosy again, are *you* going to tell me the story behind your lack of appropriate outerwear?"

Hey, her black fleece-lined leggings and oatmeal-colored sweater are covering every inch of her. It's chic *and* cozy, a hard combo during the chilly months, when everyone prioritizes function over fashion. Her only concession to the weather is her winter boots, with chunky soles to grip the ice and waterproofed to keep snow out. After too many slips and teeters on the way to work, she has *definitely* learned her lesson.

"I'll have you know that this is perfectly adequate both for the workplace and for walking home *and* for spending time with you." She plucks at the turtleneck collar puddled around her neck for emphasis, swallowing when Ves's eyes do an unblinking meander down her body, leaving tingles in their wake .

"Is that what we're doing here?" he asks, voice wrapping like velvet around each syllable.

Despite the loose, boxy fit of the sweater, he seems riveted. She swears the temperature rockets up ten degrees. The urge to thaw that implacable frost in his eyes has never been stronger, and so she tilts her neck a bit, rests her other hand on her cocked hip, and lets the moment linger.

The first time she saw him, he'd been a little disdainful. At the pub, amused by her doggedness, but adamant that his permission was off the table. At breakfast, weirdly lost and vulnerable and so damn relieved to see that cup of coffee. And every time since then he's been, well, maybe not a *perfect* gentleman, but she can excuse the occasional bout of crankiness. Might even enjoy it a little.

She's seen so many different facets of this man, but this is the one she decides she likes best.

The one that makes her skin prickle and goosebump with the concentration of his stare. All hungry heat and clenching jaw, as if he likes what he sees but is also just a little tiny bit mad about it. The collar of his dove-gray dress shirt is unbuttoned enough that she can see the hollow of his throat. If she follows that neat line of buttons down, past the leather belt and his narrow hips and those slim-fit trousers pressed to within an inch of their fiber-loving life . . .

With difficulty, she drags her eyes back to his face. His irritation has melted, leaving behind a remnant of a knowing smirk. Okay, so they've both been caught checking each other out. Now what?

Ves runs a hand across his face and exhales. "What are you doing to me?"

Her heart trips, tumbles into her stomach. How far does she want to take this?

While she's panicking, the doorbell rings. Ves visibly jolts, looking more discombobulated than she's ever seen him. She counts the seconds that tick by with each of his harsh, staccato inhales. They both hover, making no move to leave the kitchen, even when the bell peals out again. The noisy, jarring reminder shatters their suspended what-if moment that neither of them was brave enough to reach out and grab.

"You should get that," he says hoarsely, pinching the bridge of his nose.

Her lips unstick long enough for her to say, "It's *your* house. Ergo, ipso facto, you are who they're here to see." Wait. Why is she talking in Latin? She doesn't even know Latin!

With one last stare, Ves leaves the room. It's like his presence was the black hole sucking in all the oxygen, because the moment he's gone, she can breathe again. What. Just. Happened.

One minute she was just sassing him a little, which has kind of become their thing. The next, it's like she transformed into some kind of seductive siren, luring him to make a move.

And even though it terrifies her, she wants him to. She thinks she's wanted him to for a few days now, if she's being honest. God, what a mess.

"Elisha, your grandfather is here," Ves's disembodied voice calls.

Here? Now? Surely not . . . She barely manages to school her expression in time.

"I know how hard you two have been working, so Anita sent me over with dinner," explains Grandpa Dave as he follows Ves into the kitchen, bundled up nice and warm in his puffy coat. He beams at Elisha as he sets down two large, familiar CorningWare containers on the table, enough to feed the three of them and then some. "We have a butternut-squash-and-spinach lasagna and apple crumble for dessert. If you stick this in the oven to warm at three hundred for fifteen, honey, I'll be back with some vanilla ice cream. Or do you want rum raisin? Can't go wrong with butter pecan, either. Say, son, what do you think?"

Ves blinks. Whether it's at the amount of new information or the ease with which it's delivered, absorbing him into the fold like he's another grandkid. Or maybe it's the fact that he has to offer an opinion.

The emotional 180 is a bit much, even for Elisha. "Grandpa, you didn't have to—"

He cuts her off. "Nonsense. Ves needs to eat, doesn't he? And Marcy told me he threw out all the pots and pans, so how was he going to cook?" He raises a bushy answer-me-*that*-young-lady eyebrow.

"Trash day was this morning," says Ves.

Grandpa grunts. "Yup."

"How does Marcy know what I threw out?"

Grandpa shrugs, nonplussed. "I imagine she lifted the lid and looked."

"In my trash," Ves says slowly, offended and appalled at the same time.

"Well, yes." Grandpa Dave looks at Elisha. "How about vanilla. Can't go wrong with a classic."

"She nosed through my trash just because? Does she want something? A memento to remember Maeve by or—" Ves flaps his hands in an aggravated manner.

"Oh, Marcy keeps an eye on everyone," Elisha says with nonchalance.

"Two, usually," says Grandpa Dave.

Ves's mouth hangs open. Elisha waves a hand. "We're all used to it—"

"Imagine getting used to it," he mutters. "Which house is hers, anyway?"

"The one with the herd of lighted reindeer in her front yard," says Elisha.

"And the second-story telescope," adds Grandpa, sotto voce.

"Doesn't exactly help clarify," grouses Ves. "When you consider every house in this neighborhood has gone completely overboard with their decorations."

Hmph. Overboard or just *enough* board? She coughs. "Except one."

He shoots her an irritable glance. Oh goody. This, at least, she knows how to deal with.

"You'll get used to the, um, prying," says Grandpa. His blue eyes twinkle. "Folks here are very friendly, and everyone knows everyone, so naturally a newcomer invites a little curiosity. Now, ice cream." He wags his finger. "Speak now or forever hold your peace. I don't want to get back from the store and you kids tell me that vanilla is the most boring flavor."

"I'm sorry, sir," says Ves. He rests his forearms on the back of the nearest chair. "That's very kind of you, but this is all a little . . ."

Grandpa Dave seems to understand that this is about more than just indecision over the ice cream. He reaches out to pat Ves on the back. "Not to worry. I'll get vanilla and butter pecan. Never did like cold raisins in my dessert."

He bustles out, calling over his shoulder, "Three hundred degrees, Elisha! Back in a jiff."

A moment later, the front door shuts, leaving Elisha and Ves alone.

CHAPTER SEVENTEEN

Elisha

W ell," says Ves. "At least one of you rang the bell." A smile inches over his face, begrudging and barely there, but there nonetheless. "He reminds me of movie grandparents. All kind and jolly. I like him."

The warmth Elisha felt only moments ago now travels up to her heart, going in circles a few times like a cat curling up in a basket. And then settles in, tail tucked in tight, all cozy and snuggled up for the foreseeable future. It means something that he likes her family, their bebinca, their town. Her.

"I'm glad," she says simply. "Sorry he was kinda giving orders in your kitchen, but um, I told you before, right? Maeve was family. That makes you . . ." She can't look at him while she says this. "That makes you family, too." Even though the way she feels about him definitely isn't familial. Or even neighborly for that matter.

And then she grabs the vegetarian lasagna and hurries to the oven before Ves can see her blush. She ignores the tickle on the back of her neck, which is either her messy bun coming undone or the prickly sensation of his stare. Either. Both.

After a moment of stalling, she turns around, expecting him to be doing something else, or at least pretending to, like she is. But no. He's waiting there. Waiting for her. She fidgets, not sure what to do or say. Whether he expects her to say anything at all.

She likes him, and even though his response to her earlier was nonverbal, her gut tells her that he likes her, too. But again, she isn't sure what to do with that. Because as tempting as the vision of Ves spending time with her family is, she can't ignore how uncomfortable he seems with anyone getting close enough to know him.

What is he so scared of? That someone might actually like him? Or that someone won't?

Her daydream doesn't feel so solid anymore. It's less and less of a possibility with every passing second, floating away like a wisp of dandelion fluff scattering in the wind. Maybe that's a good thing, because if it weren't for that bolt of yearning earlier, she would never have flirted with him.

Oof, all this is making her head hurt. He's like one of those nesting gift boxes, all wrapped up in pretty paper and sparkling string, one leading to another to another to another until *finally* the prize is reached. Something tells her that he could be worth the effort, but is it even doable in the time she has?

Ves clears his throat. "They were nonstick."

Her relief that he broke the silence first is mingled with confusion. "Um, what?"

"The things I threw out. The coating was burned in patches, like the nonstick wore off years ago."

"Oh. You don't have to justify anything to me, Ves. You can do what you want. If it wasn't worth keeping, then . . ." She shrugs. "That's that."

"Right. Exactly." He interlocks his fingers together, then releases them. He appears as if he's working up to something important.

"Elisha, I know I'm not the easiest person to deal with. And we butt heads."

Understatement. Her lips curl into a smile. "A lot."

He nods. "A lot. But you've been a good friend to me. And I haven't said it enough, or at all, so . . . thank you. For your kindness and your help. It isn't a small thing to me."

When she thinks about what she wants to be to him, *friends* isn't the first thing that springs to mind.

"That's what we do around here. We welcome." She waits a beat, then cheekily adds, "Well, and also go through your trash, apparently."

He gets her back without missing a beat. "Just for that, I'm going to ask your grandfather what aversion you have toward winter outer garments."

Her mouth drops. "You wouldn't! That's cheating."

"Not if we didn't set any rules."

"Fine." She crosses her arms. "Let's set them right now."

"I'm back!" The front door slams.

Ves smirks. "Sounds like he's back early."

It's not even the big secret that he seems to think, but Elisha hisses at him like it is. "Don't you dare play dirty, Ves Hollins."

Dryly, he says, "I'm quaking in my L.L.Bean house slippers."

"You know, we get their catalogs in the mail every year around Christmastime and I always wondered who they actually work on." She pauses dramatically. "And then I met you."

"'Met' me? 'Met' is not a synonym for a little light trespassing to start your morning off right."

"You are never going to let that go, are you?"

Ves opens his mouth but snaps it shut just as Grandpa Dave ambles back in.

"I remembered your mom had vanilla in the freezer, so I saved myself the trip to the store," explains Grandpa Dave, holding out the tub of ice cream. "Sorry about just letting myself in, son."

Ves laughs and puts it away. "It must run in the family."

Grandpa laughs too, a big boom that peters out into a gentle chuckle. "Not every couple has such a memorable first meeting. At least you got a good story out of it."

Oh no, she has *got* to clear this up. "Grandpa, we're not a—"

"No, no, I know you're not. But if it ever happens, you've got this tale handy," he says cheerfully. "Ves, has Elisha taken you to see the Enchanted Forest luminarias?"

"Again, not a couple," Elisha says hurriedly. "And I'm *sure* he isn't interested in our little small-town traditions. Right, Ves? He has better stuff to do. I mean, he hasn't even seen *Sleighbells*."

"They filmed one of the most romantic scenes in the forest just outside of town," explains Grandpa. "For the movie's fiftieth and her eightieth birthday, I was hoping to surprise Maeve this Christmas with the original sleigh. Elisha found it on one of those auction sites. It's a bit run-down right now, but nothing that can't be fixed." He falters. "I . . . guess there's always next year."

"I'll find the time to help you," says Elisha. "As soon as I get everything scheduled for the cast and camera crew's arrival in mid-January, I'm all yours, okay, Grandpa?"

Ves's brow furrows. "I thought all you were waiting on was my permission to film the outside the house? What else do you need to do?"

"Well, this production is a huge deal. The director, Damian Rhys, is super particular and everything has to be just so. My job is making sure he stays happy, and since my boss is a dick who'd rather see me crash and burn, I'm basically on my own." She waves a hand and exhales deeply. "Which is fine. It's all fine. It's just a lot of work to rebuild our database contacts and put ourselves on the map again, but that's *literally* why I'm here. To start from the ground up. I promised the mayor I knew what I was doing, so I need this to go smoothly."

"Danica probably doesn't realize how much you've been handling on your own," says Ves, frowning.

"He's right. We're all excited about the sequel, but we don't want you running yourself ragged," says Grandpa. His lined face creases with worry. "Forget about helping me with my little project. You have more than enough on your plate."

"I can do it all," she insists. It's what she's always believed and she's not going to let anyone—not Damian, Greg, or Bentley— distract her from operating at one hundred percent efficiency. "And I will. With grace and gumption, right, Gramps?"

"No one's saying you can't, honey. But there's a reason you had a whole department under you in Atlanta," Grandpa says gently. "You should ask Danica to assign you an intern to share the load."

The oven timer dings and Elisha whirls toward it in relief, grabbing the oven mitt. "If the two of you are done tag-teaming me, can we eat? I'll just swap this out for the crumble."

"Elisha." Grandpa's tone is stern. He doesn't whip it out often, but when he does, people listen.

"I can help you with the sleigh," says Ves. "I can't say I know my way around a toolbox or anything, but if you show me what to do, I'm a quick learner."

She almost drops the crumble, reaching the rack just in time. "Really?"

"Really?" repeats Grandpa Dave, equally surprised.

"Yes," Ves says simply, setting three plates on the table and three forks neatly to the left of each. He meets Elisha's eyes and says, half challenge, half promise: "Seems like the neighborly thing to do."

CHAPTER EIGHTEEN

Elisha

As Elisha quickly figures out, agreeing to help clean out a cavernous two-story Victorian house and actually knuckling down to do it are two very different things. By the end of the first week, her shoulders, back, and tailbone ache, her manicure is hopelessly chipped, and her fingertips are rough from handling hundreds of yellowing paperbacks. She hasn't struck gold yet, but she knows she's going to hit pay dirt soon. Won't it feel amazing to victoriously hold up some rare romance books and gloat in Ves's face?

She's bone-tired, but nothing is going to stop her from making trivia night at the Old Stoat. After a quick bite at home, she changes into black fishnet stockings and a midnight-blue velvet midi dress. The fabric clings to her curves, showing off toned calves and just enough cleavage to get sent free drinks at the pub tonight, win or lose. Trivia night is a twice-monthly standing tradition in Piney Peaks, complete with friendly-but-not-really axes to grind against the reigning champs, which hasn't been Elisha's team, Came to Sleigh, in a good long while.

As she sweeps matching metallic eye shadow over her lids, dusts champagne highlighter across her cheekbones and the tip of her nose, and pops on a candy-red lip gloss, she contemplates going home with someone at the end of the night. It's pretty much the only thing that will work out those little kinks in her back that she always seems to wake up with these days. Pro: sex. Con: everything else.

She's pretty sure her parents can put together what happens the nights she doesn't come home, simply firing off a *Don't wait up!* text so they won't worry, but she truly does not want everyone in town to know her business.

"Thank god it's Friday," she proclaims the second she steps into the Old Stoat.

A cheer immediately goes up as the other patrons echo the sentiment. Seconds later, chairs scuffle against the wooden floor as more people spill in behind her. On the far side of the room, the trivia master is getting his lectern and mic set up, while Becca, who always works trivia nights, clears tables and lays out answer sheets. She looks up when Elisha enters, grinning. "You look hot!"

Several people turn to look, including a few guys from high school who still think they have a shot and two who tried to corner her under the mistletoe last year. Ha. Hell would have to freeze over—*twice.*

Elisha studiously avoids eye contact with anyone who's checking her out. "Thanks! You too! I love those dangly snowflake earrings."

"Lisha, hey!" Solana twirls on her barstool and waves her over. Adam's working the bar tonight, like he does every Friday, and he has a Spicy Grinch waiting for her on the counter.

"Adam, you are a prince among men," Elisha says, taking a sip with one hand while wrenching off her black peacoat with the other. She sets her micro purse on the bar and hops on an empty seat. "You have no idea how much I needed this. My entire week snowballed from one thing to another. I am fucking *desperate* for two whole days off from Greg's snipes and digs. Two days without JJ micromanaging me because she clearly thinks I'm some small-town hick who can't handle this project."

"Oh, no, why do I sense this is another three-Grinch-problem kind of night," groans Solana.

"Ha! No. Trust me, I've learned my lesson."

Adam laughs. "You were good for business last week, Elisha, but let's not make a habit of it, yeah?"

She good-naturedly rolls her eyes. "I'd pinky-swear with you, but I can't bend my finger."

"If you have frostbite, it's your own fault," Solana scolds, but she briskly rubs Elisha's hands, anyway.

"It's not that cold out. I'm just stiff from spending eight hours behind a desk and another two helping Ves. On one hand, my inbox is finally at zero and all the permits are squared away. On the other, the more time I spend with him, the more obvious it is that—"

"You want to lick his candy cane?" Solana bats her eyes.

"Lana!" Elisha whisper-screeches. Adam, used to them, simply rolls his eyes with a fond smile at his girlfriend. "My god, woman. Not everything is about sex."

"True, but the boy is fine and he's practically made of holiday fling material, hint hint."

Elisha fixes her with a look. She may no longer consider Ves to be Piney Peaks's very own resident Christmas Curmudgeon, but jumping his bones is *not* the move. Sure, he's single and attractive, but those are bare-minimum qualifications. And yes, he has a biting streak of humor that emerges whenever he's feeling a bit prickly or when they're just having fun, but again, he's not the guy for her. Just because he's sticking around for a bit longer than a week doesn't mean he's looking for love or roots.

"I'm just saying," says Solana, "you wouldn't have these little aches and pains if you spent more time thinking about getting *him* stiff." She hums meaningfully. "Or maybe you would, but in a sexier way."

"And that's my cue to go wash some glasses or something," says Adam, taking two steps to the left.

Elisha yelps and reaches out to grab him by his black tee. "No! Stay! You're my ally."

He lets himself be dragged back.

"Adam, you're a man," she says.

"Well spotted," he says dryly, crossing his arms and showing off his impressive tattoo sleeve.

"So, what do you make of him?"

"Honestly, I don't get why he's gotten under your skin so much." Elisha sputters. "Wait, let me finish. Okay, unlike the two of us"— Adam gestures between him and Solana—"you haven't known everything about him since kindergarten—so what? Here's what we do know: It took some convincing, but he gave you the filming permission. He's sticking around for the Winter Festival even though we, uh, pretty much ambushed him." He looks a little sheepish. "You said he offered to help Dave out when he didn't have to. And he's taking good care of Maeve's place, by all accounts. Seems like he's a good guy."

"'By all accounts'?" Solana grins and cups his cheek. "Babe, you've been gossiping."

"Eavesdropping," Adam corrects, leaning into her touch to kiss her wrist in a suave move that makes Elisha's heart squish. "Right now, everyone who comes to my bar is obsessed with three things: Christmas, the movie, and Ves Hollins. Not necessarily in that order."

Solana giggles and pulls Adam in for a proper kiss, a lingering one like neither can get enough. Elisha's torn between looking away to give them privacy and staring long enough that maybe, just maybe, some of their love can rub off on her a little. She wants what they have so much that it actually *hurts*.

It's not even just the sex with a regular partner that she misses, or always having a surefire date so she doesn't look hopelessly single at yet another get-together. It's sweet moments like this, the quiet intimacy of a look, a word, a gesture to understand another person and knowing exactly what they need.

They break apart when down the bar, someone emits an admiring whistle. Adam tosses a rag at the guy, who picks it up and laughs, ordering a round of beers for his trivia table.

"Wait, I know a fourth thing," says Solana, eyes sparkling as she sips her spiced rum punch. "The Chocolate Mouse holiday party. All the ladies in my office under forty are hoping Ves is going to be there this weekend."

Coals glow hot in Elisha's chest. "He doesn't even live here!" she exclaims.

"Doesn't stop anybody from hoping. Anyway, your grandpa definitely invited him," Solana says casually, as though she hasn't just dropped a huge and messy piece of information in Elisha's lap.

Elisha keeps her cool. If by *cool* she means spinning on the stool so fast she nearly topples off and Solana has to steady her shoulders right in the nick of time. *"What?!"*

Returning from the other end of the bar, Adam nods. "It's true, I helped them drag out the sleigh this morning from Dave's storage unit. Your gramps is pretty good at putting people on the spot. He invited him and Ves accepted."

This stumps Elisha, who until this second didn't think Ves had actually meant to devote so much time to helping her grandfather. And now that she knows otherwise, she's left with an uneasy feeling.

"And your grandpa has been leaving flyers for the party all over town," adds Solana, using her chin to point to the cotton-candy-pink sheet of paper tacked up on the bulletin board next to the pub's front door.

"Look, I'm only saying this because I'm forced to be here," says Adam. "But, Elisha, you talk about this guy all the time. There's something sparking between you, and it's not animosity. Why not give it a try? What do you have to lose? Have yourself a fun, casual Christmas romance." He frowns, casting a critical eye around the pub. "Beats your other options around here, honestly."

Solana seems utterly smitten by the idea. "And oh my god, you should have seen it. It was so cute how he had Elisha's back with Bentley." Her smile is utterly wicked. "Oops, I mean *Ben*. It was very hot how jealous Ves got."

"Boyfriend standing *right* here," Adam points out with an amused chuckle.

"Since when did you two take up meddling as your new couple activity?" Elisha demands. "'Holiday fling material'? 'Fun, casual Christmas romance'? You're both singing from the same hymn-book."

"Guilty," says Solana, entirely unrepentant. "But it's because we love you, my darling!"

"And you deserve to be happy," Adam says quietly. "We love having you back home, and we know you chose this to be close to your family and the business . . . but you're lonely. No, don't deny it. We're your best friends. You really think we can't tell?"

Elisha's heart takes a swan dive into her stomach. "Guys, sure, he looks gallant galloping around on a white steed, and yes, he's saved me twice. But he's so closed off and he's going to leave soon, so I shouldn't even want to, and *ugh*!" She brings her palms down on the table with a huff, and wordlessly communicates with Adam for another Grinch. "He's still kind of a mystery, isn't he?"

"I can tell you a few things," he offers, springing into mixing action. "One, he likes Nutella hot chocolate with a good book. Two, he prefers a corner booth, but he hasn't got it tonight. Three, he's here at trivia night and Riley is about to kick him out of your usual table."

"There's no way Ves is—" Elisha turns to survey the room. "Never mind. I'll catch you guys after?" She digs in her purse for her lip gloss. After a quick swipe of Fenty courage, she bounds off the stool with her drink in hand, beelining for the two men.

CHAPTER NINETEEN

Elisha

Elisha can tell that Ves has clearly been camped out at the table for a while: a clean plate with a few bread crumbs and a dab of leftover coarse-ground mustard, and a half-eaten pistachio-and-cranberry brownie on the plate in front of him, along with a beat-up paperback with an expensive-looking pen sticking out midway through, as though it's been used as an impromptu bookmark.

He takes a calm sip of his hot drink and regards her thoughtfully. "Let me guess. This is where the cool kids sit, and newcomers aren't allowed."

At the other end of the table with just a seat separating them, Riley Studebaker swigs his beer, looking massively peeved. "That's not what I said. I *said* that if you're going to sit here, you're on the team."

"Thanks, but no thanks." Ves uses his knife and fork to primly cut a small piece of brownie. "I'm here to sit and read and eat my dinner in peace." He pops it in his mouth and chews.

"Didn't Becca tell you that every other Friday is trivia night?" Elisha asks, setting her hands on her hips. Her voice isn't as cool as she hoped, not when fizzy full-body tingles tease that she's not exactly unhappy to see him there. In fact, anticipation pulls at her stomach, shortens her breath.

Ves's eyes flick to the answer sheet on the table, then back to her face. Well, his gaze does snag on her chest first, just for a second, before he snaps it up. Only a hint of pink on his cheeks gives him away.

She's irrationally proud that she's seemingly stunned him speechless in her sexy dress, but before she can savor the victory, Riley opens his mouth to argue some more.

"Oh, this is ridiculous." Elisha marches to the empty seat between them and sits. "I'm sure Riley has explained this is Came to Sleigh's table, but since everywhere else is full, it looks like we'll have to share. Anyone got a problem with that?" When Riley gives a terse nod and Ves returns to his book, she sighs. "Great. It's settled, then."

Her shoulders brush both men's, but only Ves's makes her pulse flutter and breath catch. He smells unfairly good, more than anyone has a right to. Like sliced green apples, tart and juicy. A little bit like dinner, pan-fried bread and sausage and spicy mustard. And just a tad like Maeve's house: faded lilacs and old paper, and a tingle of eucalyptus cough drops. Somehow—don't ask her how—she isn't put off. It's sexy. Isn't that a thing when you like someone? Everything they do becomes attractive?

Carefully, in a way she hopes is casual, she lets her calves rest against his under the table. It's only in the way that his finger stumbles on its way to turning page 246 that she knows he feels it. And when she leaves her leg there for the next ten minutes while they wait for the rest of the team to arrive, she swears he just keeps rereading the same page. She's not even sure his eyes move. Or blink.

Mia gets there with a minute to spare and everyone else cuts it close, blown in on a gust of wind and the trivia master's one-minute countdown. He taps the mic, muttering "Testing, testing" like he does every Friday. A squeal of feedback splinters across the room and he throws his hands in the air. "Sorry, folks!"

"Solana isn't joining you?" Ves's murmur is so low she almost doesn't catch it.

Elisha leans closer, until his breath ghosts across her temples. "Nah, she never plays. Her boyfriend, Adam, works Friday nights, so Solana hangs around the bar to keep him company. They keep their own score unofficially and crow their asses off if they could have beaten the winning team. Which, to be fair, isn't often because they're too busy flirting with each other to catch most of the questions."

She can see his lips curl in an almost-smile. "Such ruthless competitors," he drawls.

"Ves, we don't have nightclubs in Piney Peaks. This"—she gestures around the room—"is what most of us single hotties are doing on Friday night. So you better believe we're all playing to win. Dork Academia almost always takes first, and—sorry, never mind. I know you don't care about this small-town stuff."

He opens his mouth to say something, but a blur of a person slides into the seat opposite Elisha, his knee knocking hard against hers.

Reproachfully, Richard Breckenridge, last year's Mistletoe Miscreant #1, says, "Elisha, I thought you said the team was full." He glowers none too subtly at Ves.

Damn it. Richard's had a thing for her since high school and has the nose of a bloodhound when it comes to finding mistletoe so he can suggest they go for a kiss. Either that or he carries the stuff around in his pocket in case of an opportune moment—she really wouldn't put it past him.

Mia catches her eye and makes a face that her boyfriend, Isaiah Osuji, the purchasing manager at Fireside, the restaurant his Chinese-Nigerian parents own, mimics. They think Richard's weird, too.

"Ves is new in town and just observing," Elisha says firmly. "We're still waiting on Kat and Adhira, but with Mia, Isaiah, Riley, and me, we have a full team of six and that's the max, sorry."

Richard counts each member off on his fingers as if to make sure she isn't trying to pull one over on him. "Huh. Yeah, there's six of you. I should take it up with the trivia master, make it an even seven."

Ves makes a choked laughing sort of noise.

"Mm-hmm. Good idea, bud. 'Even seven.' That's definitely a thing. You go do that," says Riley. He catches Elisha's eye and smirks. Everyone knows that one does *not* mess with the trivia master, except for Richard, apparently, who squares his shoulders and determinedly heads off like he's going to battle.

"That looks like it's going over well," whispers Isaiah, exchanging a high five with Riley when the trivia master angrily blasts Richard at full volume, amplified even more thanks to the mic.

"What's the word for when you're totally tickled by something shitty happening to someone?" Mia whispers, trying not to laugh.

"Schadenfreude," Ves says without looking up from his book. Elisha glances over; interestingly, he's still on page 246.

As trivia night gets under way, Ves silently consumes the rest of his brownie, orders a second hot chocolate, and turns a few more pages. His leg stays flush against hers, filling Elisha with a giddy thrill and an urge to jiggle her leg in delight. But she doesn't in case he gets alarmed enough to shift away.

God, is she so hard up for touch that a mere leg is exciting her? Well, in her defense, it is a really warm, sturdy leg. The kind poets write about, rivaling even Michelangelo's *David*. She glances down at his slacks and wishes she were brave enough to put her hand on his thigh. Not even that high up or anything.

Lord, she has it bad. She fists her hands in her lap instead and tries to stop sneaking peeks at him.

But it doesn't mean that she's not excruciatingly aware of everything he's doing while the team bickers and whispers and frantically scribbles down answers. His thigh tenses when Elisha has the right answer about contestants of a popular dating reality show but Mia's equally adamant that her own answer's correct. And it relaxes when the rest of the table agrees to go with Elisha's suggestion.

Almost like he has something invested. Which is . . . interesting.

Because reality TV isn't the kind of entertainment she thinks Ves would watch, so how would he know if she was right, anyway? Which means . . . maybe he just *wanted* her to be right? For her sake?

She doesn't have long to question it, because the next question barrels out and it all moves quick, quick, quick. Kat Kwon, whose parents own the stables where Grandpa Dave boards his horse, nails which racehorse won the Triple Crown in 1973 ("Secretariat, obviously! How have you people been friends with me this long and you *still* don't know that?!"). Isaiah knows sports and food (and obscure geography-related knowledge, since he knew that Switzerland eats the most chocolate and Coca-Cola was the first soda consumed in outer space) and Mia is ace at celebrity drama and notable figures ("The first name of Secretary of State Alexander Hamilton's wife was Eliza, honestly, do you people not watch musicals?!").

There's not a person in this room who can outdo Elisha on television and movie knowledge, and Riley knows a little about a lot of things, especially when it comes to world history, current events, and languages, which is why he's so successful as their chamber's trade specialist *and* their team captain.

Unfortunately, Adhira Ambani, Riley's best friend and town cardiologist, and their sixth team member, has to run when her babysitter calls, but not before furtively whispering that the heart has four chambers, which pushes Team Came to Sleigh into second place. Holding first, Team Dork Academia—comprising two high school teachers, an optometrist, and a veterinarian—shoots daggers from the other side of the room.

"Hey, man, you're off the bench," Riley informs Ves. "We're putting you in play."

Ves shakes his head. "No, thank you."

"Not a request. If it's not you, Richard is going to shove his way in and that's completely unacceptable. I need Elisha fully focused on winning. The books-and-literature category is coming up next and we're counting on her. So you're in. You don't have to do anything. Just lean in when we discuss the questions and pretend to take part so we look full up."

It's a perfect solution, Elisha has to admit. Keeps Richard at arm's length *and* includes Ves. Win-win.

"Come on, Ves. I know you've been following along with the game," says Elisha. She nudges his arm with hers, enjoying the solid feel of muscle through his light gray sweater. "Don't think I didn't notice—you're not as stealthy as you think. You clench and unclench your jaw when it's a hard question, like you're stumped, too, but don't want to show it. You let out a breath you've been holding when we take a random guess and it turns out to be right." She lets her eyes beseech him. "Please play."

His eyes narrow at her. It seems to take him forever to reach a decision. "Fine," he says brusquely.

She perks up, unable to hold back her grin. "Really?" When he answers with a small nod, she has the ridiculous urge to throw her arms around him, which she doesn't act on, but she does indulge in a quick squeeze of his knee.

The unexpected touch makes his lips part and his eyes soften, as if he's surprised it takes so little to bring her joy, or maybe because now he knows he's the reason for her smile.

In the very next question, Elisha is both vindicated and relieved that he said yes. "Name the author of the 1986 novel featuring a castle that can fly that inspired the Miyazaki animated fantasy film," says the trivia master. "The clue is in the question, folks!"

She racks her brain, scrounging around for an answer. She knows this, she *knows* this. The other tables look similarly baffled, except for Dork Academia, who have already written their answer and are sitting there with self-assured grins. Elisha leans in, whispering so the other teams can't overhear, "It's *Howl's Moving Castle*, but I don't remember the—"

"Diana Wynne Jones," says Ves, confidence in every word.

Riley runs his hand through his golden curls. "Are you sure?"

"He's right," Elisha says quickly. She meets and holds Ves's impassive blue eyes. "I remember now."

"If it's acceptable to everyone, I'll write it down," Ves says.

The pencil, a short, stubby thing, like the ones golf players use, is nearest to Elisha. In fact, it's rolled up right next to the curve of her palm. She hooks her pinky around it at the exact moment Ves reaches out. His fingertips, deliciously warm and light against her skin, jolt electricity straight between her legs.

With a sharp inhale, she clamps her thighs together. The sound doesn't go unnoticed by Ves, who draws his brows together but doesn't move his hand away. Neither does she.

There's a ravenous, giddy desperation humming through her

entire body. Their eyes lock, brown on blue, the undercurrent of the *something* started a few days ago simmering between them like a kettle about to shriek. Of this much she's sure: she wants him.

Now, here, while the abandoned pencil rolls off the table and clatters to the floor, and his strong arms wrap around her to sweep her on top of the table. Okay, probably not *right here,* right now, but soon. She'll combust if she doesn't chase the spark between them.

"We have two seconds left!" Mia leans in to hiss, glossy black hair falling into her face. "Move it!"

Ves snatches the pencil and jots down the answer. His writing isn't the hurried scrawl Elisha thinks it would be; it's all precise, neat lines, even though the pencil point is rounded and blunt from use.

"And the answer is . . ." The trivia master pauses for effect, scanning the tables to make sure all the pencils are down. "Diana Wynne Jones!"

"Damn it!" one of the high school teachers yells. The rest of the team slumps over and groans.

"Oh my god, does that mean we're tied with Dork Academia?" Mia throws her arms around Isaiah's neck for a hug. "Hell yes!"

All the other competing tables are bummed out but flash stealthy thumbs-up their way and a brave someone shouts out, "Nice one!" Even the trivia master gives them a big wink.

"Not bad, newbie," says Riley, sticking his hand over the table. "Thanks for stepping in."

"Yeah, no problem." Ves shakes his hand, but his eyes are on Elisha the whole time.

It's almost as if he wants her to know he didn't do it for Riley. It's something she's noticed about him, the way his words are deliberate and purposeful, even when he's laughing or bantering.

And that's when Elisha realizes that there's no getting around it—she is full on crushing on her emotionally unavailable new neighbor. And whatever else he might feel about her, he's interested. She's spent enough time fending off Mistletoe Miscreant Men at the bar to recognize it.

The rest of the evening goes by in a blur, and when it's over, Came to Sleigh comes in first place. Ves is the reluctant recipient of back claps and vigorous handshakes from practically everyone in the pub. He shifts his weight from foot to foot, not quite returning the handful of hugs he gets, but not recoiling, either. He even awkwardly pats Mia's shoulder when she launches herself at him with a hug, ears bright pink as he looks helplessly at a giggling Elisha.

"How is it that despite your best intentions, everyone seems to love you wherever you go?" she asks when she finally gets Ves to herself.

"Trust me, it only happens in Piney Peaks," he says gruffly.

"Nah, you're just lovable," she says breezily.

With a diffident shrug, he says, "You're the only one who thinks so."

"Come on, I see Solana's saving us seats at the bar."

He scoffs, falling into step beside her. "So, what do we win for first place?"

"Our team drinks for free tonight." She grins. "So, uh, can I buy you a drink? No Grinches, I promise."

His laugh comes out strangled. "Would you believe me if I said I wouldn't mind getting used to them?"

CHAPTER TWENTY

Ves

Of all the junk Ves has unearthed in Maeve's house, wrapping paper isn't one of them. Great.

"I need help," Ves says the second Arun picks up the phone.

His best friend doesn't skip a beat. "Book, house, or mental?"

"D, none of the above. I bought a box of nice chocolates earlier today to say thanks for dinner, but I can't just hand them over as is, can I? It needs wrapping paper or a nice gift bag, right? I want to make a good impression. But should it be Christmas related or just . . . regular pretty?"

"Regular pretty?" There's a muffled conversation as Arun presumably relays the question to his husband. "Wait, did you have dinner with the girl next door?" Forgetting to lower his voice, Arun imparts to Cade, "*Every* straight guy I know has a thing about girls next door."

Cade also forgets to whisper in response. "Not just straight guys. I hooked up with *all* the boys next door when I was a teenager."

"And that's why we aren't going to your parents' house for Christmas."

"Yeah, that's not why. *You* insisted on spending our first Christmas together as a couple."

Ves coughs to remind them of his presence. "For the record, Elisha isn't next door, she's across the street. And the thank-you isn't for her, it's for her mother. She's the one who made dinner."

"O-kay," says Arun. "So, which one are you dating?" he teases.

It takes every facial muscle Ves has to not grind his back molars. "I hate you."

"You love me." Arun shushes Cade, who tries to interject again. "Okay, so, first of all, was this a romantic dinner? And, more importantly! Why am I only finding out about this now?"

Ves sighs and explains. "I told you Elisha is helping with the house. Her mom made us a nice lasagna and some dessert the other night. Her grandfather brought it over and he was literally right here, man. Didn't exactly set the mood."

Before either of his friends can ask if he *wanted* it to be romantic, he hastily asks, "So how do I wrap these chocolates? And what do I do about the food containers? I washed them, obviously, but it feels awkward to just knock on their door and be like, 'Thanks, here's your stuff back and this box of chocolates to show my gratitude.'"

Even Ves knows that's ungracious, but he has no idea how to play this. He has to assume Arun knows stuff like this, because he and Cade just moved into a town house near him in the East Village where their neighbors actually bring welcome cookies and just-because-it's-Friday bottles of wine like they're in a sitcom. Ves has lived in the city his whole life and has never encountered people that eager to be friends.

"So this was a *homemade* meal," Arun says slowly. "From

scratch? Not, like, lasagna sheets with a bag of frozen peas and a jar of Ragú?"

Ves is appalled. "What lasagnas from hell have you been eating?" He hears Cade snicker in the background.

"He who mocks can fend for himself," Arun snaps. "And he who laughs doesn't get sex tonight."

Both Ves and Cade shut up quick.

"Chocolates are nice, but impersonal," says Arun. "We just got some lovely peppermint bark from the sweetest little Midwestern girl two doors down. I'm making some polar bear–shaped sugar cookies in return. They're so cute, I'm coating them in buttercream icing and desiccated coconut—"

Ves crookedly smiles. Arun could ramble about baking forever if he and Cade let him.

"—Anyway, my point is, it's always a classy move to return containers with something homemade inside."

"Okay, so where would I get that?"

Arun breathes noisily. "From your home."

Horrible realization bubbles in Ves's gut. "So when you say homemade, you mean . . . actually made in my home . . . with my actual hands." He stares at the limbs in question, trying to work out the mechanics.

"That would be the definition, yes."

In the strained silence that follows, Ves is positive the soft gulping sound is Cade or Arun unsuccessfully trying not to laugh. Possibly both of them. *Probably* both of them.

"I'm hanging up now," says Ves.

"Wait—"

Ves slips his phone into his pocket. He can fry up bacon, poach an egg, maybe even do a mushroom-cheese omelet if he's feeling fancy, but none of his cooking, let alone his baking, is at a level that he can offer it as a return gift. Why must people like Arun go to all this polar-bear-cookie effort? If everyone could just do nothing, then they wouldn't have to bother with these social niceties.

Except . . . that's how a Grinch thinks, isn't it?

He leaves the containers for later and decides to bring the chocolate box in the gourmet grocery's prettily decorated bag and marches for the door with it hooked around his pinky. As he heads down his front path in his favorite Chelsea boots and meets the sidewalk, he can't help but wonder which window of the house opposite is Elisha's. If she's already at the Chocolate Mouse party. What she's wearing. Whether she's thinking about him.

Ves groans, running a hand over his face. Adjusting his thick red scarf over his buttoned, immaculately lint-rolled coat, he trudges on toward Main Street. Flurries dance around his head, big ones the size of quarters. Every step tempts him to catch one on his tongue like he's seen some of the kids do.

He's thirty years old and is no stranger to snow, so there's no *need* to be this wistful, but when has he ever noticed it like this before?

Everyone's breath steams in the brisk mid-December air. People make eye contact as they pass Ves: smiling old men doffing flat newsboy caps, women in outrageous stiletto-heeled boots clutching their dates' arms as they head into brightly lit restaurants. He sidesteps the sandwich board outside the Chocolate Mouse to let a middle-aged couple pass, returning their smiles in a way that still feels a little forced.

The party is well under way by the time he arrives. No one hears the bell tinkle or sees him enter, which gives him a moment to take it all in. The fragrance hits him first, as though he's dived headfirst into a giant bowl of spiced punch. If he has to be sentimental, he would say that it smells the way Christmas-scented candles only *wish* they could. Where the vaulted ceiling, open to both the first floor and the ivy-draped balconied second, gleams silver and gold. Fairy lights twine with translucent paper snowflakes, glittering against silver acorns and gold-dusted pine cones.

Ves breathes in sugar cookie, spruce, and mulled wine. There must also be a wood-burning fire somewhere, because the back of his throat tickles with the hint of smoke, and something else, too. Spicy and citrusy. As he makes his way past the entrance and the opportune mistletoe suspended from oak beams, peppering the aisles full of tall shelves stacked with nutcrackers and ballerina figurines, he discovers the source: bundles of cinnamon sticks and clove-studded oranges strung across the mantel.

Every single lamp is on, casting halos of light against the party-goers, who are milling around sipping from cut-glass goblets and nibbling at finger foods. There's plenty of space for the large crowd, as though the floor plan has been rearranged to look less like a store and more like an experience. Choral Christmas music plays from vintage-looking radios that have an iPhone plugged into the dock. There are lush wreaths and artificial trees everywhere, decked out in ornaments and tinsel, white cotton fluff banked in clumps to resemble snow.

Nothing about this is garish at all. In fact, it's kind of perfect. Enchanting, even.

His attention breaks when two blond women start to approach him, whispering in each other's ears and giggling. A redhead in the corner abruptly ignores the man speaking to her in favor of ogling Ves.

"Ves, you made it!" booms Dave's voice. He makes his way through the crowd, bypassing the blonds so fast that by the time he reaches Ves, he's a little ruddy-cheeked. Although that could also be from the generous pour in his tumbler. He pumps Ves's hand exuberantly with both hands.

This time, Ves's smile comes naturally. It's impossible not to be fond of Elisha's grandfather, who has always greeted him with warmth and welcome. "I thought you said it was just a little party?" He arches a brow at the room. It's like the whole town is here, with more people bustling in by the second.

Dave smiles and scratches at his gray scruff. "The more the merrier, right?"

Ves can't say he agrees. It sounds like a nightmare for catering.

"Elisha's somewhere over there," says Dave, pointing to a far-flung corner beyond a mini forest of lit trees. He gives a fond laugh. "Probably evading her Mistletoe Miscreants . . ."

"Thanks." With a parting nod, he heads in her direction.

Elisha faces away from him, blocking his view of the man she's speaking with. She is, unsurprisingly, wearing a pointy green hat with a huge red pom-pom. But even though that's what draws his attention first, it's her slinky black bodycon dress that makes his mouth go dry.

He rubs at his jaw when he sees its open back. His fingers flex, yearning to splay across her skin. Even with that ridiculously un-sexy hat, she's still the most gorgeous woman he's ever seen. The realization slams into him, leaving his skin prickling icy-hot, like a persistent windburn.

Before he knows what he's doing, he's striding toward her, determination in every step.

CHAPTER TWENTY-ONE

Ves

Once Ves is close enough, he overhears "For the *last time*, Richard. Take your mistletoe elsewhere before you make me do something decidedly un-elflike."

Protectiveness and jealousy rear in his chest. "Everything good here?" Ves asks Elisha, but it's Richard who answers.

"Yes, *we* are fine." He squints, not bothering to hide his irritation. "Hey, you're the guy from trivia!"

"Ves Hollins."

"Richard Breckenridge." He doesn't extend his hand to shake, maybe because he's holding a bunch of mistletoe in each fist. "You're the reason I couldn't get parking."

"Pardon me?"

"All the women here." Richard scowls. "They're all here for *you*. You're fresh blood."

Ves turns to Elisha, a panicked thought suddenly occurring. "I'm not the guest of honor, am I?"

She places one hand on her hip and the other on her chin.

"Inadvertently. Honestly, I can't believe you actually showed up." But she seems happy about it.

"Of course I did. Your grandpa invited me. Though he did say it was just 'a little party.'"

Richard laughs meanly. "Get ready to get 'caught' under the mistletoe, my poor, deluded dude."

"Hey." Elisha's eyes flash. Without another word, she reaches out to grab his mistletoe. "Stop ripping apart our decorations. I do *not* want to see you with them again. You work your way *up* to a kiss, get consent, and preferably you don't just lunge at people who have known and rejected you since high school!"

With a wounded look, the man slinks off.

"It needed to be done," Elisha says decisively, eyes narrowing after him.

"You won't hear an argument from me," says Ves. If he's being honest, he didn't like seeing Richard that close to her. Wondering whether he'd placed his hand on Elisha's bare skin, skimmed the curve of her spine. It makes something primal in his chest crackle and spit like a roaring fire without a grate to contain it.

"No argument? That's a first." But she's smiling. At least for a moment, the delightful curve of her lips seems to share a secret. "God, this is why I hate being single over the holidays. Every guy who you turned down in the past pops up out of the woodwork thinking you're now desperate enough to say yes. There are Richards everywhere." She sighs. "I'm sorry Grandpa tricked you into coming."

Ves can only assume Dave was doing a little meddling of his own. "Why didn't *you* ask me?"

She wrinkles her pert little nose rather adorably. "To a Christmas party? I just assumed it wouldn't be your thing. A full house of people all interested in you? Unavoidable mistletoe? Boatloads of small talk with inquisitive townspeople? I wouldn't want you to feel uncomfortable."

Okay, granted, it's not the way he'd most like to spend his evening, but if it means she's there, too . . .

His chest simmers like a pot of bubbling wassail. She *gets* him. She cares if he's uneasy about certain situations. She intuits things about him without needing to be told. Has he ever had a woman care like her?

Ves takes a beat too long to respond, because the next thing he knows, she presses, "Since you're staying, are you volunteering to be my anti-Richard? My mistletoe repellent?"

Each word is repugnant in its own way. "You really know how to flatter a man," he drawls.

Her cheeks turn pink. She fidgets with her glass and looks down at her Dr. Martens lace-ups, mumbling a barely coherent "You know what I mean."

It's cute how she gets nervous around him. And gratifying, considering how he feels right now. The room is excruciatingly hot or maybe it's just his proximity to her that makes him want to rip off his scarf and jacket. Not even hang them up properly. Just throw them to the floor before he takes her hand and leads her past the trees and into a corner where nobody will find them for hours.

"Oh, you need a drink," says Elisha. Her hand lands on his for a quick touch that isn't even close to enough. "I'll go grab us some. I'll be right back." She darts through the crowd before he can stop her.

"Excuse me." Someone lightly taps at his shoulder. "You're Maeve's nephew, right?"

He turns to see the redhead from before. She tosses her big, bouncy curls in a flirtatious manner, smiling with glossy red lips.

"Her great-nephew." He tilts his head. "I'm sorry, you look so familiar, but I can't quite place you."

She laughs. "I'm Charity. You probably recognize me from trivia night. Dork Academia? The name was my idea. I teach English at the high school. I used to teach middle school, and your books were always a favorite in my class. The next one's coming out soon, right?"

"Mm-hmm," he says with the same rigid smile that only emerges when he's uncomfortable—like now, when this inevitable question about what's next comes up. "It's nice to meet a fan," he offers when the silence lingers.

Charity laughs again, but this time she couples it with a hand on his forearm. Applies a little pressure so he knows it's not just a casual touch. "The kids are your fans. Never said I was." When Ves's smile falls, stung, hers goes from sharp to sultry as her fingers walk up his sleeve. "But I can always be . . . persuaded."

A hand unceremoniously shoves a drink between him and Charity. The first thing he sees are nude, polished nails with a Santa hat across the tip. There's only one person they could belong to. Relief surges through him with embarrassing speed. The next thing in his vision is a diamond tennis bracelet on a slim wrist. And finally, the beautiful—and clearly irked—woman it belongs to.

"Your drink, Ves," Elisha grinds out, perhaps unintentionally loud, because the very next thing she does is scowl like it's all his fault. Her surprising jealousy coaxes a small smile to his lips.

He takes the opportunity to detach from Charity. "Thanks, Elisha." Their fingertips graze as he accepts the goblet. The tiniest frisson of electricity zaps him, and he feels the shiver reverberate up his whole arm. Elisha looks somewhat mollified.

"It was nice to meet you, Charity," he says politely, but with finality. "Have a nice night." And with that, he holds out his hand to Elisha, palm up.

She takes it, looking pleased. "Enjoy the party!" The second they're out of earshot, she says, "You're lucky Riley's too busy flirting to see you fraternizing with the enemy."

"Enemy?" God, she's adorable.

"Member of the opposing team. Whatever." Elisha guzzles the punch. "Jeez, it's hot in here."

Ves takes a tentative sip of his own drink. There's a definite burn under all the sweetness. Crisp cider, tart cranberry juice, and enough rum to please a pirate—or a whole crew of them. "And the punch is strong."

Her smile is impish. "It usually is when Grandpa makes it."

That tracks. "Uh, this is for you." He peels the handles off his wrist and holds the bag out to her pinched between two fingers. "Your mom, actually. To say thank you for dinner the other night. I don't know what she looks like, so I thought I'd just . . ."

"Like me, but more tan and way too chic to be caught in an elf hat." Elisha takes the bag and peeks inside. "The annual holiday party has always been more Grandpa's thing, so Mom and Dad are having a much-needed date night at home. Good choice on the chocolate, though! These are her favorites."

Relief pools in his belly. And suddenly, as their gazes lock, it's not relief anymore, but hot lava and insistent desire to kiss the small talk right out of Elisha Rowe, put both their mouths to far better use. He wets the seam of his lips, heartbeat quickening.

"What?" She touches her face, as though worried about her makeup. "Do I have something . . . ?"

Ves is robbed of breath. Her eyes are multidimensional with the fairy lights playing across her irises, bouncing off the highlight artfully placed on her cheekbones, the dip of her Cupid's bow. His eyes are drawn to her lips, where they linger long enough that Elisha notices.

She swallows. "Ves? You're staring at my mouth. Not that I have a problem with that, but, um, why?"

"You're beautiful," he says honestly. He can't remember the last time he's said that to a woman. If ever. Or if he has, if he's meant it the way he does right now, with the force of his whole heart.

There's a light smattering of freckles across her nose, a couple on her cheeks, left over from summer, possibly. His heart aches that he won't be here long enough to see her in strappy summer dresses that cover even less of her than her winter ones do now. Missing out on seeing her run around in flip-flops, wondering if she's equally vigilant about her toenail art. He can imagine her painting white-and-yellow daisies and perfect pink tulips.

He visualizes those nails tugging at his hair, bringing him closer for a kiss. Maybe skating down his back to make him shiver. Wrapped around his cock as she looks up at him, thick black lashes fluttering over her cheeks as her mouth closes around him.

If he were smart, he wouldn't feel so victorious that Elisha was jealous over a woman he didn't even fancy. He wouldn't have wanted to shove that damn mistletoe in Richard's throat and watch it scratch all the way down.

And when she looks at him like she is right now, he wouldn't want to reach behind her, cup her neck, squeeze it lightly as he brings his mouth down to hers. Press her into a corner somewhere to steal that kiss and then a thousand more, just to be safe. Nibbles down her neck, across her collarbone.

Fingers tiptoeing across her warm back, tracing that cursive *E* on her fine golden chain that he can't stop thinking about. Slipping his fingers underneath, feeling its warmth from her skin. She's wearing it now, the gold letter glittering at the hollow of her throat. He wants to kiss it and then keep going down, down, down.

He swallows roughly. "Is there someplace quiet we can go?"

CHAPTER TWENTY-TWO

Elisha

Elisha's heart trips over itself as she leads Ves to the storeroom, far enough away from the party that the chatter is only a dull hum in her ear. Does he actually just want a private place to have a chat? Or is he speaking in code?

When she had her own apartment in Atlanta, *coming up for coffee* usually meant sex first, then coffee the morning after, presuming he spent the night. If she was at a bar or club, *getting out of here* meant getting *into* her panties. But in the middle of the Chocolate Mouse, does the code mean something different?

She flips the switch and the lights take forever to crackle on. One by one, the panels above them come to life. Boxes full of extra decorations are stashed here, worn trees with crooked or missing branches, and various other odds and ends from the store floor that need fixing.

By the time Elisha turns around to ask Ves if this is fine, hinges squeak and she quickly discovers *someplace quiet we can go* is code for reaching behind him to lock the door without looking. His eyes are on her, only her. Elisha's breath hitches.

Without the distracting shimmer of the store decorations and all the dressed-up people, Ves sharpens into focus. Eyes the shade of the softest denim, ringed by black eyelashes. Pure blazing want bleeds across his face, from the unblinking intensity of his stare to the way he wets his lower lip.

The way he's looking at her makes her feel like she's taken a deep guzzle of hot tea that's settled low in her belly.

"I've been wanting to kiss you all night," he confesses, eyes boring into her like he can see her leaping heart, hear her humming bones.

"You just got here."

"I know."

Without another word, she snakes her arms around his trim waist, pressing herself into the solid heat of him. His eyes reverently shut, then pop open when she gets on her tiptoes to press her lips against his.

The angle is all off at first, their mouths meeting too hard, too hungry, too desperate. But then he tilts her chin and it's *good*. So fucking good that if this dress would allow it, she would jump on him in a second, wrapping her legs around his waist.

As it is, his thigh slides between her own, and the friction is so delicious that all the unresolved, tangled tension threatens to unspool her into a writhing mess.

His mouth molds against hers until she melts against him, his hands greedily moving up and down her bare back, blunt nails tickling her spine, knuckles grinding pleasurably against her tailbone. She moans, a reedy, whining thing that makes him smile against her lips.

"Someone likes that," he whispers.

Oh, she *absolutely* does. "Mm-hmm," she says, nipping at his bottom lip when he stops. She makes a sound of protest, shoving at his shoulders, then clenching her fingers around the fabric of his jacket to bring him closer. There's way too much space between their bodies for what's about to happen, what her core is crying out for.

When he resumes that divine strumming of her spine, she feels his erection brush against her belly. The double whammy makes her more frantic, more eager for the solid press of his body against hers.

It's been too long since someone's touched her like this, and the kiss is *good*. His lips are soft but firm and coaxing, stoking the need in her gut that's already roused from flicker to flame. The tingles start behind her ears at first, then pinball in berserk zips, zings, and zaps to every other part of her.

She's ridiculously turned on. Part of her wants this to be rough and passionate, the way a quickie can be when she's desperate for another person and greedy for release. But as lust-hazy as she is right now, it isn't lost on her that they're in her family's place of business. She inhales, resting her hands on his shoulders, the move putting a few inches of distance between their heaving chests.

His mouth presses soft kisses up her neck, his nose tracing her lobe. His voice is low and urgent as he mumbles beneath her ear, "Is this okay?"

It takes a moment for the question to compute and two more before her dry throat unsticks. "Yes," she whispers. "It's more than okay."

His smile reminds her of that moment before plugging in the Christmas tree, the startling magic of seeing every little rainbow bulb come to life all the way to the starlit top. He starts to go in for another kiss, his blue eyes fixed on her lips, but she brings a finger up to land on his Cupid's bow.

"You should do this more often," she says.

The corners of his mouth creep up. "What? Kiss you?"

She rolls her eyes. "No. Smile." She brings her hands up to frame his face, letting her thumbs crook and stretch his smile a bit further. "You're sexy like this."

"I look like the *Joker* like this," he says flatly, but his eyes are soft.

She shuts him up with another kiss, tangling her fingers in the hair at his nape to bring him closer. He obliges, hands splayed across her back, then moving down to squeeze her ass in handfuls. He smells like green apple body wash, but his jawline prickles with stubble that isn't yet quite visible. Thrilled with her discovery, and more than a little curious how the friction would feel against her inner thighs, she caresses his cheeks.

"What are you doing now?" asks Ves.

"Admiring you," she says frankly, this time kissing him with tongue. His swipes against hers in an exploratory taste, and his groan reverberates in her mouth.

"You taste like Christmas came early, Elisha," he whispers, hot breath making her lips tingle and stomach fizz. Hearing the roughness of his voice, she can't stop herself from grinding on his upper thigh, wedged between her own.

"You haven't made me come yet," she quips, rewarded with his flared nostrils and sudden, ragged intake of breath. She shakes her head. "That's my spearmint mouthwash you're tasting. But peppermint is the far superior Christmas flavor."

"Don't know about that. Another taste and I might be singing spearmint's praises." He says it in the same cool, unaffected way he says everything, but she knows his tells now. He's teasing her, because that's their thing, but he's also letting her know that he wants another kiss. More than one if that look in his eyes is anything to go by.

She initiates another, and this time, when his hands graze her hips, she lifts one leg to wrap around his waist, hiking her tight dress out of the way. Without a word, he scoops her up behind her thighs, bracing her against the wall. He catches her gasp in his mouth as her breasts nestle into his chest, his straining erection positioned so, so close to where they both want it to be.

Too many clothes separate them. She whimpers, wanting even more of her skin accessible to his mouth. Ves is making her feel so good, nibbling and sucking at her collarbone until every single one of her muscles clenches around him. There's no way she's stopping this now. Propriety be damned.

She's about to tell him she's on birth control when, dimly, she hears a *BANG BANG BANG!* "I think someone's trying to get in," she says, wriggling down his body.

Ves takes a moment longer to come to, blinking several times before he takes a step back and drags his hand over his face. "This isn't the way I imagined this going. I wanted to tell you . . . well, just that I'd be lying if I said I never wondered what this would be like."

"You weren't the only one."

The knob jiggles, making them both jump. Another *BANG!*

"What the fuck," she says, mouth dropping. "Just a second! I think the door is sticking!"

What? Ves mouths.

"It happens in winter," Elisha says defensively, trying to unlock the door as quietly as possible. "The wood contracting or whatever. The point is, it's a plausible excuse. I'd rather *not* explain why the door is locked. Oh! Hey, take off your coat."

She practically pulls it off him while keeping the door shut with her foot. By the time she swings the door open, fake smile superglued in place, she's confident she can get through this with minimum embarrassment. That is, until she sees who's on the other side.

"Ellie!" Bentley exclaims in surprise. "What're you doing in here? I was just looking for a place to hang our coats. The other room is full." He peers into the room, all geniality dropping as soon as he spots Ves. With a dark expression, he says, "Oh, it's *you*."

Elisha hopes her voice is cool, calm, and collected. "We were actually just setting this up as an overflow room." She gestures to the coat she's holding. "I can take yours and Tori's, too, if you—"

"No, you know what, I think Victoria's probably ready to leave." Bentley backs up. "We should get home while she's still ovulating."

Oh wow, just throwing that right out there, huh? Elisha isn't sure whether wishing them good luck is appropriate considering he's her ex and she's certain Tori deserves better than him.

"Okay," she says simply, not sure why Bentley looks momentarily disappointed. He recovers just as quickly, beating his retreat into the sea of people to seek out his wife.

"He was trying to make you jealous," Ves observes.

"Trying and failing," she counters with a scoff. "That ship has well and truly sailed. Actually, no, it's sunk to the bottom of the ocean in the harbor, no survivors, no hope of salvage."

Ves grins, grabbing her hip to bring her closer. "You're a vengeful woman when you want to be."

"Mm-hmm," she hums. His eyes drift down to her throat and he swallows. She flashes a saber-toothed smile at him, shimmying to close the last inch between them. "It's my best quality."

"Well, maybe not the best."

Intrigued, she tilts her head. "Oh?"

Elisha sucks in a breath when his hand slides up her arm, rounds her shoulder, then gently circles her throat for just a moment before cupping her jaw. His palm is firm and warm and delicious. She almost moans from the sexiness of it, the sudden shock of wanting him to squeeze, but not ready to ask him to.

There's a fine tremble in her legs that wouldn't let her move even if she wanted to, as his intense blue eyes pin her in place. He presses close, lips moving against the corner of her mouth. She feels rather than sees his mouth curl in a smile.

"But it is one of them," Ves whispers.

Her breath catches.

She's about to ask him whether he wants to finish what they started when the lustful expression wipes off his face and he smoothly takes a step back.

"Lisha, finally! I've been looking for you!" Solana elbows her way through the crowd, nearly upending the two chocolate martinis she's carrying. Behind her follows Adam with two glasses of his own. "Candy Cane Olympics are about to start! You and Ves should join us at the starting line."

"Thanks, babes." Elisha accepts her glass, inhaling Baileys Irish Cream and chocolate liqueur.

Adam hands a martini to Ves. "It's a weird Olympic torch relay thing. Only when they pass the 'torch,' or in this case, candy cane, the next person has to add their own onto however many are already hooked. Then they have to walk to the next person without dropping it or touching any of the other candy canes."

"Everyone's pretty tipsy, which makes it funny to watch, but somehow Grandpa Dave always wins," Solana confides, grinning.

"That must be why the drinks are so strong," says Ves. "Smart man."

Adam laughs. "C'mon, let's go watch *Ben* make an ass of himself. It's just for fun, but man, he's so competitive."

Elisha raises an eyebrow. "He's still here?"

Solana lowers her voice so the boys can't hear. "Yeah, with a face like a fucking storm cloud. I feel awful for Tori, she's wearing the prettiest dress but he's barely paying attention to her. Did you see how unhappy she looks?"

"Uh, no, I've been—" Elisha fumbles, not sure she can trust her best friend to keep a straight face if she admits what she and Ves were just up to. "Busy helping Grandpa."

Solana sighs. "Lisha, my darling, once again I remind you that I know all your tells."

Elisha forces every muscle in her face to relax. "I'm not hiding anything."

Solana lets a beat go by—just long enough for Elisha to think she bought it—before casually asking, voice dropping an octave lower, "So you and Ves, huh? Is his little lord a-leaping? His piper piping? His cock a-crowing?"

"Lana!" Elisha's cheeks burn and she can only hope that whatever Adam is saying to Ves is distracting him from this conversation. "Please don't refer to my sex life in 'Twelve Days of Christmas' euphemisms."

"Do you have another carol you prefer?"

"The one called 'I love you but shut up'? Do you know that one?"

Solana smiles gleefully. "Can't say I'm familiar, no."

"*Lana.*"

"Fine, fine! Adam and I will get out of your hair." With a long-suffering sigh, Solana throws back her drink and drags her boyfriend off to watch the inevitable chaos of the Candy Cane Olympics.

"Things aren't going to be weird now, right?" asks Elisha when she and Ves are finally alone. With the game about to start, the crowd has thinned a bit.

"You mean since I overheard your best friend discuss my erection?" he asks dryly.

"She wasn't talking about your erection, exactly—Wait, you still have a hard-on?" She lets her eyes drop to subtly gauge his . . . state. He wasn't kidding. She can't stop herself from smiling. "*Oh.*"

He levels an exasperated look at her, but his voice is fond, and just slightly rough as he says, "You look pleased with yourself."

"Looks like I have reason to be." She smirks, hot pride cascading through her like shooting stars, every tingle aiming for the frustrated nerves between her legs. She takes a sip of her chocolate martini, licks her bottom lip. "Maybe we should do something about that."

It's gratifying when his eyes flick beyond her, darkening with desire. A thrill races down her spine when he meets her gaze again, expression torn. It's unlike her to suggest any sexcapades in places she could get caught, but for one wanton moment, she wants him enough to throw all caution to the wind.

"I *will* fuck you," Ves promises. "But first, do you think it's too late to sign up for that candy cane game? I'd like to see the look on Ben's face when I beat him."

"You mean it?"

Ves shoots her a devastating grin. "Which part?"

CHAPTER TWENTY-THREE

Ves

He never thought he'd say this, but Ves is actually kind of getting used to being in Piney Peaks. Not forever, obviously. But it's a quaint little town, a vacation from the norms and routines that usually guide his days.

For example, when was the last time he just ambled anywhere in the city? It's always point A to point B in the most efficient way possible. He takes the subway everywhere with his AirPods in, the latest podcast prattling away in his ears, studiously avoiding eye contact.

But here, he can't so much as walk out his front door without someone waving at him, saying something jovial and silly, like *Nice weather we're having, huh?* when the temperature is in the single digits and Ves has zero inclination to shiver through an outdoor chat. He can't even head down Main Street without someone recognizing him as Maeve's nephew and offering their sympathies.

If he thought his new fame as Came to Sleigh's trivia secret weapon was too much before, it has nothing on the attention he receives after being crowned the Candy Cane Olympics champ.

And even that pales in comparison to the wildfire gossip that spread after Marcy and Bibi caught the blushes and open affection between him and Elisha last night at the holiday party.

So he avoids Main Street entirely and meanders down the winding lanes that caught his eye his first night here. The bookshop is his first stop, an indie painted a Shire green with SPELLBOUND SPINES handpainted in glorious gold Gothic lettering. Across the storefront windows is a mural of books of varying heights, a renowned fantasy title on each spine. The front door is between *A Wizard of Earthsea* and *Alanna: The First Adventure*. With a smile, Ves steps inside to meet his people.

Fantasy has always been there for him. Even long after he discovered that, try as he might, there was no magical portal at the back of a wardrobe to take him away. Even when his parents fought, even if he was sent to his room for no reason other than to get out of the way, his books were always there. And when he felt most alone growing up, he knew it was between the pages where he could always find a family.

Ves peruses the latest middle-grade fantasy, finding his own titles among the *H*s on the shelf, before moving on to the adult section, walking out with the latest Jemisin, Bardugo, and Schwab.

In a vintage candy store lined with enormous glass jars full to the brim, he buys Christmas ribbon candy, soft and chewy caramel, and several scoops of gummies. It's the same place he bought the chocolates for Elisha's mother, and the owner, an apple-cheeked elderly lady with pince-nez and several sweet stories about Maeve, is thrilled with his return and insists on giving him free samples of pistachio-and-rose Turkish delight.

His stomach grumbles as he passes a blue-painted toy shop. Small children and their parents are pressed close to the picture window, their breath fogging up the glass as they watch an electric train chug resolutely around the tracks, disappear beneath a snow-covered tunnel, and emerge on the other side with an exuberant *choo-choo!* The locomotive is black, with a red nameplate that glints gold on the turns, reading PINEY PEAKS EXPRESS, while the boxcars that make up the body and the caboose are the same bright, candy-apple red.

The set is detailed and expensive with a whole Christmas village and tiny figurines. More of an adult indulgence, really, but it doesn't stop the kids' wide-eyed wonder or the way they pull at their parents' hands to go inside. He can't remember if he ever tugged on his parents to get his way. Ves watches the children's enraptured faces, their parents' fond and not at all impatient expressions, and his heart lurches.

"Oooh, doing your Christmas shopping early?"

"Window shopping," he replies without turning. He would know that voice anywhere. Now that he knows what her soft gasps and breathless sounds of pleasure sound like, there's no way his mind can expunge them. "How do you sound so perky after the number of drinks I saw you consume last night?"

Elisha laughs and comes to stand next to him, crunching her way across the fresh snowfall looking very sweet in pink booties, blue jeans, and a pink-checked blazer. She has a Nikon camera hanging from a strap around her neck. "Mom asked me the same thing when she came downstairs and saw that I was already up." She flashes him a cheeky grin. "Guess it's my superpower?"

"Maybe."

Doubtful. Because when he sees her, it's like the overcast gray of the world rolls back to reveal a literal ray of human sunshine. *That's* her superpower.

Her dark hair just brushes her lapels, falling over the apples of her cheeks as she peers into the window. The bright lights dart across her face, speckling it golden. Without thinking, he reaches out to tuck her hair behind her ear. She stiffens slightly, then relaxes, giving him wide eyes and a faintly confused smile.

With his leather gloves on, it's a clumsier tuck than he thought. It takes him a couple of attempts to successfully get all her hair, and bafflingly she keeps still, letting him finish. Except for one moment when she actually leans into his touch, infuriatingly close, and gives him those storeroom eyes, all but pleading for him to be tender in other ways, too.

His heart trips over itself. Several times, like a Slinky tumbling down a staircase. And when he lets his gloved fingertips linger over her cheekbones, she bites her lip. By the time he's done, her mouth is as pink as her cheeks.

If only he didn't have his gloves on.

The yearning is a swift, lethal punch. He wishes he'd taken them off first, because now he can't stop wondering if there would have been a tiny spark if he had only touched her with his bare hand. A day ago, his head would have written it off as static electricity, but today, he knows that his heart wouldn't be able to deny his feelings for her.

He tries to ignore how something as simple and innocent as her wide-eyed stare makes his cheeks tingle. It's nice to know he's not the only one affected. The tension is palpable, but in a good way, like either of them could go in for a kiss right that second.

"Let me guess, you like the train and the little model village," she says.

He drops his hand down to his side. Is her voice oddly hoarse? Maybe she's coming down with a cold. It wouldn't surprise him with today's weather forecast. See, even now, her blazer is unbuttoned. No hat, no mittens. He bites back what he wants to say. Why is she so reckless? Why does he care?

"I'm that predictable, am I?" he asks instead of what he really wants to know.

She hums under her breath. "Yes, but you surprise me from time to time."

His heart stirs. He's about to promise that he'll do it more often from now on, but he stops himself just in time.

That's not something he can promise, is it? Not in good faith, anyway. He knows himself and even though he's gone a little out of his comfort zone while he's been here, he's still the same old Ves, with the same flaws that were dealbreakers for Claire and so many other girlfriends over the years.

He may have fit in at trivia and at the Chocolate Mouse, but this isn't his world. He needs to remember that.

Elisha points at a snuggly-looking brown teddy bear with a red cardigan. "I have one just like that."

With relief and gratitude for her change of subject, he falls into their familiar banter. "Pride of place in the center of your bed?" he teases.

She snickers. "Don't you worry about what's on my bed."

"Impossible. My curiosity is piqued," he drawls. He gestures at the camera. "What's that for?"

"Oh, Piney Peaks always looks so pretty after it snows, so I thought I'd take some pictures for our database. Productions won't come if they don't know what we have to offer." She holds the camera and pretends to snap a picture. "Click! Spotted in the wild: a New Yorker acclimatizing to the magic of a small town and unwillingly enchanted by local toy shop."

His neck gets hot. "Quit it. You're encouraging the ogling."

"Hmm." She brings one hand to her forehead, shading her eyes and scanning their surroundings. "Nope. Don't see any ogling going on here. You're not as interesting as you think."

Ves tuts. "There you go, lying again. You think I'm fascinating."

She throws her head back and laughs but doesn't deny it. At the hollow of her throat, her tiny cursive *E* sparkles. "You beat Bentley and helped us win trivia *once*, and now you're so full of it. By the way, you do realize Riley wasn't kidding, right? If you aren't with us next trivia night, he *will* show up at your house."

A vision of the blond team captain trying to drag Ves out the door floods his mind. Maybe the whole team will crowd his doorstep, Elisha cackling in the background as he's swept to the pub. He mentally swipes away the image. "But your team is full."

"Well, as it turns out, Adhira would rather spend her Friday nights with her husband, Sam, and their daughter, so . . . looks like we have an opening. I mean, it's up to you. It's just twice a month, and obviously, we'll be on the lookout for someone to join us in the new year, but until then, we could spend some—I mean, *you* could have some fun. Get out of the house before you get old and creaky."

A commitment of just a couple more game nights? He can do that, can't he?

Her eyes take on an evil glint. "Unless it would cut into your reading time," she says sweetly.

Thank god she doesn't know he'd been more focused on her than the words in front of him that night. Ves clears his throat, relieved, and mentally congratulates himself for having the wherewithal to play it so cool. "I'll think about it," he says.

"Awesome," she says brightly. Then, "You know, I wasn't expecting you to join in the fun at the party last night. Not that I'm complaining—watching you win was pretty hot."

"Pretty hot?" he echoes.

"Scorching."

His mouth forms around the word, barely stopping himself in time.

As though she hasn't just sent all the blood rushing straight to his cock, she asks, "Can you wait here just a second? I need to run in really quick." She squeezes his arm like it'll anchor him in place and slips inside the toy shop. She doesn't seem to realize he'd do whatever she wanted right then, just because she was the one to ask.

Through the glass he sees her pick up the bear she'd been admiring, take it to the register, and hand over a credit card. It's only a couple of minutes before she's back, toting the bear in a sparkly red gift bag stuffed with silver snowflake tissue and gently swinging it while they start to walk.

"Thanks for waiting. Want to grab lunch? I did promise to treat you one day."

He *is* pretty hungry. "Yeah, okay," he agrees. "Did you buy a companion for your bear?"

"Oh, no. It's for the Chocolate Mouse's toy drive. We have this big Giving Tree and on Christmas Eve my parents throw another party for the whole town and any of the kids can take a toy. There's usually a lot of swaps, and a *ton* of wrapping paper strewn everywhere later," she says with a tiny wince, "but that's part of the fun. Everyone deserves a present."

Ves typically writes a check to the children's hospital and area food banks back home, but it feels so impersonal compared to what they do here. When he's back in the city, he resolves to donate his time, too. Maybe become a Big Brother or offer a scholarship to someone who wants to study English in college.

"That's really nice, Elisha. I'd love to contribute." Belatedly, he realizes it's come out as a statement and not a question, and he rapidly worries he overstepped. "I mean, if that's okay," he tacks on.

"Of course it's okay! It's more than okay!" Her eyebrow is doing something weird, like she's puzzling out why he thinks it wouldn't be? "Just something to keep in mind, most of the kids are under twelve, but honestly, anything is appreciated. And don't wrap it beforehand! We do it at the store. Oh, here's my car."

She stops at a red Chevrolet, an old model that's clearly been well maintained, squished between two fancier cars on the slushy street. "Want to just drop your stuff in the trunk before we head to lunch? I can drive you home after."

Home. The word makes him feel a little funny. "Sure."

CHAPTER TWENTY-FOUR

Ves

Elisha takes him to a cute little hole-in-the-wall bistro, the kind that wouldn't stay secret for long in the city. Concrete floors, iron barstool seating, and huge Edison bulbs dangling from the exposed rafters. The server, wearing both a rainbow and a trans flag pin, leads them past a wall plastered with flyers advertising local bands and karaoke nights, seating them right at the window.

"So, running into you was a happy coincidence, but I did have an ulterior motive in asking you to lunch," says Elisha. She waits a beat until he nods at her to continue.

"Well, okay," she says with a shaky exhale. "I . . . I like you, Ves. And part of me still isn't sure why, because we're nothing alike and you aren't my usual type, but I do. I hate tidying up and yet, when I'm helping you, it doesn't feel like work. Or it does, but not in the way that makes me want to avoid or hate every second of it. And I have to think it's because I'm spending that time with you. So— and hear me out here, okay?—I was thinking that . . . maybe I wouldn't mind spending even more time with you."

Now she's looking at him with those big brown eyes, silently willing him to say something. To have an opinion. Seeing that anticipation on her face makes his throat dry and his mind go as blank as a new Word doc. The pressure builds and builds until something in her eyes dims a bit.

No, absolutely not. He *cannot* have that. Not because of him. Anyway, disappointing the sunshiniest girl in Piney Peaks would probably get him run out of town with pitchforks and flaming torches.

"How is that different from what we're doing now?" asks Ves. He can't look at her face, so he focuses on removing his gloves, plucking one finger loose at a time before sliding the whole thing off.

"Look, people are already speculating about us. They have been since you stepped in oh-so-gallantly with Bentley, and I know the way we were at the party last night didn't exactly shut down the rumors. Speaking of . . . say hi to Marcy."

Elisha waves at the parka-clad figure stopped on the sidewalk to peer through the bistro window at them. To Ves's horror, Marcy seems to take that as an invitation to join them, because she starts toward the door before frowning and shaking her head. She taps her watch as if to say *Can't, sorry, there's somewhere I need to be*, and continues on her way.

At the aghast look on his face, Elisha's lips twitch like she's trying not to smile.

"So you just want to pretend to date?" Ves asks, wondering if he should be intrigued or offended.

"God, no. It's not about what anyone thinks of us. It just occurred to me last night that you and I are going to act on our attraction for each other sooner or later, and before that happens, maybe we should have the conversation about where this is going. So what I mean is: let's *actually* date, but with a deadline."

He's catching on. "So it ends on our terms without either of us getting upset."

"Exactly. To be perfectly candid, I know you're leaving town in a few weeks, and we aren't looking for the same things in the long term, so I'm not expecting our relationship to, like, turn into anything?" She ducks her head, looks at the paper menu like she's actually reading the specials and doesn't already know her order by heart. There's a little tap-tap-tap below the table, like her boot is working overtime. "We're already spending so much time together, and since we clearly have chemistry, it wouldn't be such a leap to have a little holiday romance, or even just holiday sex, if you're game. Just casual, no strings attached."

Ves's throat has gone from Saharan dry to feeling as if someone's shredded his vocal cords into Christmas confetti. He's never been propositioned like this before, all pragmatic and transparent. And definitely not in public, in broad daylight—well, broad cloudiness. *Shit*. Where's the server with the water?

When they show up with ice cold glasses of water, Ves croaks out, "Scotch, please. Make it a double."

"The second least expensive one," says Elisha. "Sorry, but you'd be better off buying a bottle from the store. Don't you *know* how much hard liquor costs at restaurants?"

He laughs weakly, gulping down water that does absolutely nothing for his stampeding heartbeat. "Yeah, I have some idea. Look, it's not that I'm not, uh, flattered, but I'm not so sure this is a good—"

That seems to amuse her. "I'm not proposing marriage, Ves. I just don't want to be alone over the holidays and I'm guessing that you don't love it, either."

No, I don't, he thinks. And then immediately checks himself— where has that thought come from?

The server returns with his drink and asks if they're ready to order.

"I'll have the roasted chestnut soup with sourdough bread, not the whole wheat. And the grilled salmon with fig glaze," Elisha rattles off.

"Same," says Ves, relieved he doesn't have to make a new decision while he's still working through the old one. He takes a bracing sip of his scotch before he braves eye contact with Elisha. "Can I think about it?"

She tilts her head and regards him in a way that makes him suspect he's just behaved in a way she finds entirely predictable. "Sure," she agrees. "Just not too long. We don't have forever."

Luckily Elisha has the gift of gab and steers the conversation to small talk, which Ves usually detests but is now thankful for. The soup arrives, sweet and nutty, and the fish is delicate and flaky, grilled to perfection. He bites back the impulse to tell her that her lunch choice is excellent, because it may lead them both down the road of wondering what *else* she's right about.

If he isn't careful, he's actually going to agree to date her just to get rid of this restless, agitated vortex of energy. Which he's not going to do, obviously. And to drive it home, he stabs harder at his fish.

This should be an easy yes, so why is he hesitating? He dates girls, treats them well, enjoys their company—and that's it. He doesn't date exclusively and he's always up front about that. The second someone doesn't take him seriously about keeping it casual and their toothbrush magically appears next to his on the bathroom sink, he knows it's time to bail out.

He doesn't wonder what they're doing when they're not with him, doesn't see something cool or funny or gross and immediately want to share it with them. It sounds bad, but once they're out of his vicinity, he doesn't think about them much at all. Getting emotionally involved has never worked out for him.

So what Elisha's offering is, well, perfect. There's no real reason to hesitate, and yet he can't shake the feeling it's his heart making the choice for him rather than his head.

They're midway through their post-lunch coffee when Ves feels Elisha's foot slide against his. "You hadn't been to the Chocolate Mouse before yesterday, had you?" she asks, not moving her leg. She isn't *doing* anything, just silently reminding him that she's there, waiting for his decision.

His pulse trips. "No, I . . ."

The truth is, he'd been avoiding it. He can't put his finger on why, though. It's not like he hasn't thought about it every time he's on Main Street.

The emporium is enchanting and welcoming, buttery-golden light spilling through the windowpanes and the wafting scent of cinnamon and sugar. No one is immune to its charm; even locals who must pass the store regularly pause in front of the gold-and-red spiral columns on either side of the front door, hesitating only seconds before ducking in. And now having been inside, he can understand the impulse. It's the kind of place you never want to leave, and if you do, you want to return as soon as possible.

Elisha's waiting for a response. How long has he been lost in thought? He clears his throat. "I just hadn't gotten around to it, I guess."

Maybe out of some long-buried self-preservation instinct? If he had to put it into words, he'd liken it to eyeing the biggest, most exciting-looking box under the tree, but already knowing that what was underneath all the ribbon and sparkle was never meant for him.

She wraps her hands around her cup like she's seeking heat, even though it can't possibly be warm anymore. "Another thing you needed time to *think* about, I guess."

It's the knowing way she says it that gets under Ves's skin. As though she has him all figured out, cobbling together an idea of him based on, what, exactly? His responses to shit that has always been out of his control? But he doesn't want her to know she's hit a nerve, so he finishes his coffee in one gulp. Lukewarm, just as he thought.

"Some of us do think twice before leaping into situations," he says icily.

Her laugh sputters out, stunned and maybe a little hurt. "Right. Yeah, okay."

Three little words. Three little words—the equivalent of one of those jagged ice spikes dangling from a roof. Three perfect stabs straight into his heart. Why the fuck was he just so mean to her?

"Sorry," he mutters, trying to look at her so she knows he means it. Instead, she's staring steadfastly out the window, a purse to her lips he's never seen before. Another stab. *He* put that expression there. "I don't like people making assumptions about me."

"I get that," she says softly. She turns her head about thirty degrees as though she's still deciding whether he's forgiven or not. "I guess that, um, even though I expected you wouldn't say yes right away, I still . . . well, I wanted you to. Didn't realize how much until just now. After we kissed, I thought . . ." She looks embarrassed. When he's about to apologize again, she faces him head-on like she did before. "But you've got one thing wrong, Ves."

He's so relieved at being forgiven that he doesn't even care. "What's that?"

She does a fluttery motion with her hands that seems intended to convey something. "You think that I'm rushing into things, don't you? Like when we first met and I got the wrong end of the stick—erm, wrong end of the candy cane. And our kiss was pretty impulsive, too, I'll grant you, but I know what, and who, I want. The truth is, I was attracted to you the first moment I saw you."

"You mean when I had my back to you and *you* had a weapon raised?"

She stomps on his foot, enough to show her annoyance but not enough to hurt. "Maybe not the very first moment. But the first time I saw your face, yes."

Then, deviously, as though she can't let the compliment stand without evening it out, she adds, "That was before I got to know your personality, obviously."

And then she gives him the most spectacular smile.

He groans and whisks the napkin off his lap. "Just get the damn bill."

CHAPTER TWENTY-FIVE

Ves

Ten minutes later, Elisha's frozen fingers work the key inside the padlock on a gate while Ves looks on, a half frown of concern on his face. It sets in deeper as she leads him up the dirt road to a barn that's peeling strips of white paint on the outside but will be warm and cozy with hay inside.

"Thanks for agreeing to a quick stop before we head home," she says over her shoulder. "Damian's assistant wanted some pics of the stables. Won't take longer than a few minutes."

"Working on a weekend? You really love your job." He huddles behind her while she opens the barn door, wondering if she feels the warm puff of his breath on her neck. He fights the impulse to drop a kiss on her nape, skim his lips all the way up to her ear, suck on the flutter of her pulse. "Are you sure we're allowed to be here?" he asks instead, fisting his hands against his thighs to keep from reaching for her.

She half turns, close enough that her lips could kiss the slant of his jaw. "My friend Kat Kwon's family owns the stables and I have a standing okay to visit whenever. You met her at trivia night; she manages the stables while her parents spend the winter in Florida. We used to sneak in all the time when we were younger."

"Breaking and entering even at such a tender age?" he murmurs.

She doesn't move away, even though the door is open. "We weren't all such Boy Scouts."

Ves can't help but tease. "Problems with authority and character-building team activities?"

Her answering grin is pure menace. "What can I say, extracurriculars cut into my TV time."

"Why did I have a feeling you'd say that?" Ves mutters, complaining to the dreary gray sky above.

There's an unexpected note in her voice that tugs at him when she leans in to whisper in a breathy caress against his cheek, "Don't think you have me totally figured out."

But he'd like to.

Before Ves can reply with a zinger of his own, Elisha takes him by surprise. Her soft, cool lips graze the corner of his mouth, just enough to be a barely-there kiss. That side of his face tickles, nostrils flaring as he takes in her sensual scent—sweet mint, woodsy chestnut, and cozy vanilla. He leans into it, goosebumps peppering over his suddenly flushed skin. His pants tighten as his stomach swirls with dizzying pleasure, and Ves has to close his eyes and set his jaw to keep from embarrassing himself with a groan.

"The day you become predictable, Elisha Rowe, would be a very sad day, indeed." He barely recognizes his own voice, all low and hoarse and wolfish like that.

"Stick with me and I can teach you a thing or two."

Stick with her. The fog in his mind clears: her flirting is taking a battle-ax to his defenses, devastating his walls in the best-worst of ways, and it scares him how little he rues their demolition.

"You teach *me* about impulse control?" he drawls, offering her an unimpressed arch of his eyebrows and a slightly disapproving hum under his breath.

Her smile is impish. "Or about not controlling it."

Ves definitely knows which one he prefers, especially when she looks at him like that. It takes every muscle in his face not to smile at her unrepentant cheek. Unfortunately, it's about the only physical response he can control, because fuck, he hardens further. Either he underestimated her charm offensive or it's been longer than he cares to think about since he's been with a woman.

"Just saying, think about it," Elisha chirps.

Believe me, I am, Ves thinks. *With you right in front of me, how can I do anything but?*

He notices that she waits just long enough for the offer to sink in before entering the barn. The sway of her hips is going to *kill* him. He clears his throat and decides to shift the subject to neutral ground.

"The Kwons leave their barn unlocked?" asks Ves, following her inside where it's every bit as warm as he knew it would be. The scent of leather and horse musk hangs heavy in the air.

"It's a safety hazard to lock the stall and barn doors. If there's a fire or another emergency, the folks arriving to help won't be able to get inside in time. Didn't you see all the security lighting outside? Plus the property is padlocked and all the horses are microchipped."

He's glad to hear of the precautions in place, but he still feels a little uneasy being in a place he isn't sure he belongs. "So tell me, what did teenage Elisha get up to when she snuck in?" asks Ves.

"There's a lot of trails around here, so the stables would be chaotically busy during the day with people getting tack on or taking lessons or mucking out stalls. But the evenings were all ours. Kat knew how much I loved horses and kittens, and, well, you need a few cats around to take care of the vermin." She pauses, eyeing him. "Do *not* make a rat joke, I swear to god."

"I wouldn't dream of it," he says swiftly, even though one had been on the tip of his tongue.

"My parents didn't want to add another responsibility to their plate, so I never had a cat growing up. But the litters in here were so sweet and they always got adopted out super quickly, so Kat let me play with them. I was always jealous that she got to keep a couple for the barn," she says with a laugh. "How about you? Any pets growing up?"

"My parents didn't want to shuffle a pet back and forth along with a kid. So I'm not really a cat person, or a dog person, or an anything person, really. And yes, my exes have all pointed out how weird that makes me, so you don't need to repeat it," he says with finality.

With a guilty flush she says, "Wasn't going to." Then, softer, "Guess Kat could always take two more . . ."

"What was that?"

"Oh, nothing." In a particularly squirrelly way, Elisha hastens to a nearby stall. "This pretty lady here is Noelle," she coos, scratching the black mare behind her inky forelock. Noelle whuffs, nosing against Elisha's arm in search of treats. "I'll bring you apple slices tomorrow," she promises.

To Ves, she explains, "He doesn't get to ride as much these days, but Grandpa boards her here for free in exchange for Kat's family using her in lessons. She's gentle with the older kids and adult beginner riders."

Ves rubs Noelle's nose, rewarded with a pleased whicker. "She's huge."

"Mm-hmm. She's a Clydesdale. Kinda what they're known for. She's eighteen hands, which is about the same height as me." Elisha removes the cap from the camera lens, pockets it. "Ever ridden one?"

"Not a Clydesdale, but yeah, my parents used to send me to horse camp every summer when I came home from boarding school. I actually attended one of the best equestrian programs."

He sees the camera freeze halfway to her eye. "I thought you grew up and went to school in New York City?"

Why does she sound so tentative? "I did," he confirms.

"So you went to boarding school in the city? The same place where your parents lived?"

There's no mistaking how aghast she sounds, her pitch rising and then falling as she fails to modulate her voice. But Ves doesn't know how to answer her implicit *Why?*

Maybe once upon a time he wished his family could be different, but he's long realized that it's easier to accept people and things as they are than to feel sorry for himself over what they're not. If he hadn't adjusted his expectations, he would have sunk into bitterness instead of merely embracing resignation. And what good would all that hurt and anger have done, anyway?

Wishes are like dandelion fluff: pretty but useless.

They hadn't done him any good when he'd been turned away at the New York Public Library after exuberantly racing past the lion statues on the steps, eager for his very first library card, but too young to get one without a parent signature. He'd begged Adeline to take him for weeks, but she could never find the time. He'd hoped to make her proud by getting it all by himself, but instead, hopes dashed, he'd returned home. Dejected and bracing himself for the scolding when his parents realized he'd snuck out with his MetroCard without permission. They hadn't even noticed.

And wishes didn't magically make Karl interested in taking him to the American Museum of Natural History. No, he'd had to wait for a school field trip. And forget about riding Le Carrousel in Bryant Park—he'd been too old when he finally did see it, coaxed onto the horse only because Arun's younger siblings had begged him to join. And even then, it had been Arun's parents who had waved to him. Not his.

No, wishes were for children who hadn't yet learned that it was better to have *goals*.

Goals like not needing anybody who didn't need him.

"Ves?" Elisha prompts, startling him back to attention.

After a long moment, he says, "Different boroughs. After the divorce, it was more practical for me to attend one school for stability." He thinks the explanation is more than sufficient, but she's still waiting, holding her camera like it could bite her. Not snapping pictures, even though that's what they came here for.

It's as though she's waiting for him to say something else. Something more. It's what she always wants from him, he realizes. Just that little bit more than he's ready or willing to give.

It should terrify him. It should irritate him. It *should* be a hell of a lot of things, but not the one thing that it is: exciting.

This woman is practically a stranger. So why should he want to rise to the challenge and actually meet her expectations? No, not meet. Exceed. He's never been so infatuated, so intrigued with someone he barely knows. But *is* she really a stranger?

She's impulsive and she's generous and she's got the biggest heart of anyone he knows. She loves to eat, relishing bold flavors, and she likes her cocktails sweet and boozy. She's never dressed for the weather but always makes him feel warm all over. She gets defensive about romance books, and she loves being right. She cares about a movie Ves has never seen and a great-aunt he's ashamed to say that he barely knew. And, most surprising of all, she cares about *him*. When he's given her no reason to.

What surprises him is how much he wants her to keep doing it.

He shouldn't need this woman.

And yet he does.

Ves's decision is made in an instant. In a millionth of an instant.

"Okay," he finds himself saying. "Let's do it. You and me, no strings attached."

He knows he's made the right choice when Elisha's smile drop-kicks his heart straight into his throat.

CHAPTER TWENTY-SIX

Elisha

After work the next day, Elisha practices what she's going to say before she rings Ves's doorbell. Now that they're "together," it can't be as simple as "Hi." Maybe she should go for a kiss on the lips? Just a peck. Or maybe more? Definitely no tongue. Not on the doorstep, anyway. Better yet, she'll keep it casual.

But that's a bit hard to do when she's wrangling way too many anxious thoughts and a basket full of cats.

As she's alternating between "Hi" and "Hello" in her head, she tilts her gaze up and squints at the fir needles and classic red bow greeting her at the front door. A wreath.

She's quite sure that it's not one of Maeve's, and it certainly wasn't there when she left for work in the morning. The design is simple. If it were her, she would have gone for a fancier ribbon, maybe a velvet one with gold trim, juniper berries, and frosted pine cones. But she can see how Ves would pick this one; it's traditional and not overly adorned, much like the man himself. A smile grows on her face.

"Hello," she starts again. No, too formal. Breezy would be better, but after she's been unable to get him out of her head all Monday, it's not looking remotely in the realm of possibility. "Hey," she tries. Yes, that's an improvement!

"Are you having a conversation with yourself?"

She spins—well, as much as she can when her arms are full—and comes face to face with Ves. "Hi. Hey. Um." Her eyes hastily avoid the amused curve of his mouth and drop to the reusable bags he's carrying. He's gone to the gourmet grocery, unsurprisingly. He probably has fancy cheeses and alcohol with a vintage older than 2018 in there.

"Sorry," he says, shuffling past her to unlock the door. "I hope you weren't waiting long."

"No, not long." She hovers behind him, shifting the weight of the basket from arm to arm, not sure what to do when he steps aside and lofts a brow at her. She stares back in confusion. "What?"

Ves swings the arm holding two bags toward the open door. Then uses his foot to kick it open a little wider. Her cheeks burn and it has nothing to do with the way the wind has suddenly picked up.

"Oh," she says, embarrassed that he was waiting for her to go in first, and she hadn't even realized. She scrambles across the threshold, toeing off her shoes at the door while he locks the door behind them. "New wreath? It's very you."

"Just doing my bit for the neighborhood," he replies diffidently, but he looks pleased she noticed.

"Well, I feel more cheerful already," she says brightly.

"Yeah, yeah," he says with a melting smile. "It's all for you."

Thor's distinctive purr rumbles out of the basket. Elisha darts guilty eyes to Ves.

"What have you got there?" he asks. He puts cold cuts, cheese, and greens in the fridge, boxed soups and croissants in the cabinet, and leaves everything else bagged on the counter.

"Thor and Thorin." With a sheepish smile, she tips the basket a little sideways. Ves blanches as Thor, a ginger shorthair tabby, stretches out his paws and yawns. Thorin, a Ragdoll mix with thick black fur, is even less inquisitive about his new surroundings and doesn't bother to open his eyes. "They were Maeve's, but, um, I know you're not a cat person. And I didn't want to assume you'd want them. They're neutered and house-trained, but pets are a lot of responsibility, especially if—no offense—you're not used to it."

"None taken. Where have they been this whole time?"

"My house. I didn't want them to be taken to a shelter and none of Maeve's friends could take both, and the boys shouldn't be separated. Plus, with all the reorganizing, they would have just added to the chaos. But now that the downstairs is almost done, I figured they wouldn't be underfoot. If you wouldn't be comfortable, though, that's absolutely not a problem."

She lightly laughs, reaching in to scratch behind Thor's ear. He purrs and arches into her touch. "I'll admit, at first my parents weren't too keen when I took charge of them, but Dad was the first one to cave, and it didn't take much longer to win Mom over."

"I'm in your debt." Ves comes closer to peer at the basket. His face is totally impassive, which makes Elisha worry a little, since the adolescent cats, barely a year old, are especially cute.

"Not at all," she says. "Maeve loved the little guys, so I was happy to take care of them."

To her surprise, Ves reaches for Thorin without hesitation, pulling him against his chest. Always happy to be held, Thorin settles into the crook of his arm, baby style. Elisha stifles an *Awwwww*, schooling her expression when he looks at her. "Are you sure no one else wanted them?" he asks.

"Afraid not. But that's not a guilt trip! Like I said, we're happy to hold on to them. It's your choice."

Watching him with them makes her insides all gooey, the way Solana gets when she sees Adam with his baby nieces and nephews. It isn't like Elisha doesn't know that Ves can be tender, but as he rubs his hand comfortingly up and down the Ragdoll mix's thick black fur, her heart grows at least ten sizes. She takes a mental snapshot to relive later, maybe when he's being extra grumpy and she needs to recall that he was once this goddamn soft. It makes her want to smoosh kisses all over his face.

Ves bites his lip and the gesture is so uncertain that she practically hears the hiss of her super-inflated heart puncturing. "I don't . . ." he starts to say, then stops.

She fills in the blanks, imagining what's running through his mind. *I don't want them. I don't know if I'm allowed to give cats milk and I actually think a black cat is unlucky and obviously all this makes me completely unsuited to the responsibility. I don't think I'm cut out to be a cat dad. I don't think pets suit my lifestyle. I don't think this is a good idea.*

Idly, he scratches Thorin's neck, brow so furrowed in concentration that she doesn't think he realizes the cat's happy squirming is getting hairs all over his expensive-looking cardigan. She waits it out.

"I don't know how to do this," Ves says finally. "I've never had a pet." She tries not to be disappointed, about to tell him it's okay, she's happy to take them back, will convince her parents *somehow*, when he adds, "But I can learn. Will you help me?"

It's the exact opposite of everything she expected him to say. But then she remembers boarding school and horse camp and spending summers with neither parent. And she sees him tickle under Thorin's chin with such a gentle look on his face, and she thinks she gets it.

"Of course I will," she says. If her voice is a little tight, a little too close to tears, he either doesn't notice or doesn't press her on it.

"Elisha?"

"Yes?"

With a hint of amusement, he asks, "Thor and Thorin?"

"What can I say, Maeve was a huge Marvel and *Hobbit* fan. Her favorite party trick was coming up with six degrees of separation between me and all the Hemsworth brothers."

He stops cuddling Thorin. "You're kidding."

"Nope, she didn't kid around when hot guys were concerned." She gives him a wry smile. "What surprises you the most?"

"All of it. She visited me in New York a few times since I graduated college, but to me she will always be the kind, little old graying lady who smelled like cookies and played explorers all over the house with me. Not this . . . horny grandma who named her cats after hot fictional men."

"Well, you were her great-nephew. She probably loved you like a grandmother. She doted on me, too, but, well, even with the huge age difference, I think at the heart of it, we were friends."

Ves chuckles, dodging Thorin's swishing tail as the greedy boy begs for more affection. "God, there's so much about her that I don't know. The weird shit is kind of the best part, too."

"She was making up for a lot of lost time," says Elisha. "I never thought of her as old, you know? I don't think anyone else did, either. That's why it came as such a surprise when she died." Quietly, she adds, "And it sucked even more that she was so far from home when it happened."

A pensive look falls over his face. "Was she happy?" he asks quietly, like he's afraid of the answer.

Elisha rolls the question around in her mind before answering. "You know, I think she learned to be. I don't think it was easy and she had guilt sometimes. She originally stayed behind in Piney Peaks to care for her father, so there was probably some resentment.

But she really believed in remembering roots, where she came from. And balanced that with the dream of spreading her wings and taking flight. That one just came to her a lot later in life than most people. She never said so, but I think that's why the *Sleighbells* sequel mattered so much to her. It was a reminder of the best time of her life, her lost love, her ... well, her regrets, too. I think she wanted a chance to re-create the magic."

Ves looks pained. "Do you think that's possible? To wish for something different than what you have?"

"Why not? It's your life. Who else will chart your future if not you?"

"You say it like it's that easy."

"Of course it's not easy. But it's still worth doing. All the best things are. And don't forget, everything in life happens because someone first wished it so."

CHAPTER TWENTY-SEVEN

Elisha

Following their conversation about Maeve, Ves has withdrawn into himself. It's clear that his great-aunt weighs heavy on his mind, and for a moment she feels horrible that she's dumped the care of two energetic cats on him. But then she wonders if maybe that's the best thing for him.

While the cats reinvestigate the house and Ves inventories all the papers lying around and ticks boxes off his to-do list, she continues sorting through Maeve's old paperbacks.

If she closes her eyes and focuses hard enough, Elisha can just about hear Maeve fussing over her, smell her stovetop hot cocoa and popcorn. Before Grandma Lou passed, the two women and Elisha enjoyed weekly after-school Hallmark movie nights. Maeve would have the heavy-bottomed saucepan and a value bag of kernels waiting on the counter while Elisha and Lou clinked their way across the street. By the time the popcorn stopped exploding, Lou had the chocolate liqueur and vodka back in her handbag and two White Russians chilling in Doc Hollins's old-fashioned glasses.

"You were right," says Ves, breaking into her nostalgia.

"Huh?" Elisha blinks away the memory. She hastily sets aside the floppy, dog-eared romance novel she's been holding for the last several minutes. "I mean, *obviously*. But you'll have to be more clear regarding what I'm right about."

"The important documents," explains Ves. "Between what was lying around the house and the stuff the bank gave me, I have it all. Dad wasn't sure, but I checked and found out that the house is paid off and Maeve's covered all the utilities for the next few months. It's perfect timing."

She absently flips through a yellowing paperback. "For what?"

"To list the house in March as soon they're done filming. Don't worry, Solana told me all about the importance of when to sell in the Piney Peaks housing market."

Her brow furrows. Probably boring real estate stuff. "Um, okay."

It is a little weird to hear him so casually mention selling up and leaving town, but she always knew they wouldn't last. It's better this way, anyway. Unlike with Bentley, where the breakup stretched out like taffy, knowing their end date brings certainty. And with certainty comes less chance of getting hurt.

"Adding to the Elisha-is-always-right canon," she says, smirking, "you'll be happy to know I have found not one, not two, but three treasures that you, Mr. What Could I Possibly Have Missed?, absolutely, unquestionably missed. Eat crow, Ves Hollins. Wait, no." She smiles evilly. "Eat fruitcake."

He drops the manila accordion file that presumably holds all the paperwork she set him to find. "You're kidding," he says, joining her in her fortress of books on the living room floor.

To her surprise, he crosses his legs under him pretzel-style, his knobby knee bumping hers. He brings with him the scent of crisp, juicy green apples. She inhales greedily, trying not to imagine a hard green Jolly Rancher gliding across her tongue. "Here, look.

Two out-of-print Nora Roberts and Madonna's *Sex*. You know, I didn't even know Maeve had these?"

"Between all the medical texts and fiction, I'm sure there's a thousand books here. How would you?"

"Oh, this used to be like my own personal library growing up. Mom and Dad were busy working, and back then Grandpa Dave still had his wood workshop at the Chocolate Mouse. Grandma Lou had early-onset arthritis and couldn't help with the baking anymore, so she took care of me after school. We spent a lot of time here." Elisha's grin is fond. "She could sure handle the cocktails, though."

Ves looks startled before he catches himself. "I know Maeve was close friends with you and your grandma, but I didn't realize that you practically grew up in this house. Do you think we ever met?"

"Ah, you mean were we ever childhood sweethearts?" Elisha gives him a teasing grin.

"Shut up," he grumbles. His arm wraps around her waist, tucking her into his side.

She scoots closer. "You said you were seven last time you were here, right?" When his face falls, she realizes it was the *only* time. Quickly, she moves on. "I would have been four. Maybe we had a playdate or something? I'll have to ask my gramps. Grandma Lou might have mentioned it."

There's something a little lost and wistful in Ves's expression that suddenly makes her wish she hadn't said anything. He's studying the neat piles of books she's meticulously arranged around them, absent-mindedly playing with the tortoiseshell button on his gray cardigan. She watches him nervously, afraid that he's going to tear it off and it'll fly somewhere into the mess, unable to be found, and even if they do find it, she has no idea how to sew a button back on. Would he? Yes, probably.

Probably he keeps all his spare buttons in the tiny plastic baggies exactly for this sort of occasion. She thinks about all the hotel bathroom sewing kits she's saved up over the years that she hasn't used once. She can thread a needle, but that's about it. *Probably* he is a real adult who knows how to sew buttons and even iron shirts and read full-size newspapers instead of just Internet headlines.

"So you can sell these online if you want. They're pretty rare and valuable," says Elisha. Her voice comes out aggressively loud and she wishes she wasn't vigorously brandishing said books under his nose. "Or I know a couple of used bookstores in town that pay good money for collectibles like these."

"Maybe you should hold on to them. Maeve would probably approve."

"No, I—" There's a tight knot in her chest. "It's yours. Your inheritance."

For a moment they just stare at each other, until she places all three books in his lap. Her hand lands much higher up his thigh than she'd anticipated. He jolts, his knee knocking hers again. He makes a frazzled sound that sounds like a mashup of *oomph*, *fuck*, and *sorry* all at once.

His hands curl around the books' edges, both thumbs running over the pristine covers. "I hate being responsible for this," he says finally. "It shouldn't be me."

"Yeah, I can imagine this is kind of a lot for people our age. Are you sure you don't want to ask your parents to come help? I mean"— she suddenly realizes how it sounds—"not that I mind helping, obviously. It's just . . . they might be a better support for you?"

She gets that they're not close, but if your son has a whole house thrust upon him, how can neither parent care enough to show up and make sure he's okay?

"Parents. Help. Support. Pick the one that does not belong," Ves says dryly.

"Fuck. I'm sorry." She leans her head against his shoulder, her hand finding his. Her thumb works slow, soothing circles against his knuckles. When he grunts, the taste of his breath—minty toothpaste and chocolatey coffee—ghosts over her mouth. "Can I ask . . . why Maeve's family wasn't close with her, either? She was the loveliest person. It just doesn't seem, well, fair."

"Doc Hollins was my dad's grandfather. Everyone always knew that she was the old man's favorite. Kept her at his beck and call, according to my father. Daughter, receptionist, general dogsbody." Ves's lips form a scowl. "Her life was on hold until he died, so in my mind, she earned every penny. But by then, it was hardly a secret she would inherit everything. And the family hated her for it, though god knows none of them needed the money. Still, her older brother, my own grandfather, used to send my dad, Karl, here year after year to worm his way into the will."

The look of disgust on his face reveals all she needs to know about what he thinks of his family. "That's awful. And that's why he isn't here? He's pissed the inheritance skipped a generation?"

"Not pissed at me. But entitled? Very much so. Dad's never been good at . . . being there. He's better with my sister, Hanna. But then, I guess he's had all these years to learn." Ves visibly hesitates, scraping his front teeth over his bottom lip. "Karl cheated on my mom, Adeline. A lot. They sent me to stay here with Maeve during their divorce because their lawyers thought I shouldn't be pulled into the fighting. It was upsetting at the time, and say what you want about divorce lawyers, but at least theirs had my best interest at heart."

Her heart shrivels. No, crushes. Like the crispy shell of a meringue demolished in a clenched fist. He spoke more fondly of literal strangers than his own parents. No wonder Maeve left it all to him; she must have wanted him to know that he would always have a home here.

"Are you close with your sister?" she asks, now that she has an opening to be nosy. "I bet every only child says this, but I've always wanted a sibling."

"We text. Sometimes whole conversations in GIFs." Ves laughs under his breath. "I go to all the stuff she invites me to and I take her out to Chinatown every couple of months for this fish-shaped waffle soft serve with red bean paste in the tail that she loves. Hanna calls herself my official beta reader. But it's hard," he admits. "I was already an adult when she was born. I'm old enough to be her dad. It makes it hard to be a brother, sometimes. But we're not nothing."

"She sounds sweet," says Elisha. "I know I don't get a vote, but I'm glad this house is yours and not anybody else's. Maeve knew seven-year-old you would have to go back home, but she also knew you would always want to come back."

If there's a way a smile can be both hopeful and sad at the same time, Ves wears it on his face now. "Can you tell me something she shared with you?" he asks. "About me, I mean."

"Um, well, I remember this one Christmas . . . It was freshman year of college, and my first visit back home. It was the first one after Grandma Lou died, so I visited Maeve as soon as I got here. I was expecting her to be sad. And she was, of course, but you know the first thing she did? She told me all about her Thanksgiving trip to New York City. She saw her great-niece for the first time but what she was most excited by was her great-nephew taking her to see a Broadway show and eating at a restaurant with a Michelin star. She could see the Brooklyn Bridge from his fancy-schmancy loft."

Ves laughs. "It's far less impressive if you knew the caveat that that was actually my mom's apartment, her settlement in the divorce, and she let me live there all through college. She also told me to show Maeve a good time and charge everything to my dad's credit card. But before you think I was too spoiled, I'll have you know I worked part-time at McNally Jackson for my sake bomb and sushi money."

The tense moment is broken. Elisha can't hold back her giggles. "Oh my god, you were a *hipster*."

"Hey." His knee bumps her, this time on purpose. "You take that back."

"Never," she vows. Another bump, also on purpose. Now they're just grinning at each other like fools and she's once again struck so fucking hard: Ves should smile like this more often. Not that smirky thing he does when he's being all aloof, or the neutral school-picture-day smile when he's uncomfortable.

Ves holds her gaze. "If it makes you feel any better, when I graduated the next year, I moved in with Arun. We both needed a roommate and I wanted to stick it to my parents that I didn't need their money anymore." He grins. "We had a prime view of the dumpsters and unless we closed the windows, the place reeked of greasy takeout. Sadly, in summer we *had* to leave the windows open because the air conditioner was always broken and our shady landlord only got off his ass for female renters."

"Wait, Maeve told me about this trip, too!" Elisha nearly bounces in place. "She said you gave her your room and slept on the couch. I remember thinking how sweet that was."

It's like some magical moment is suspended over them, sequestering them from the rest of the world, far away from shitty ex-fiancés and greedy families and cluttered houses. It's just him and her, staring at each other in a way that isn't weird in the slightest. He's all cheekbones and beautifully square jawline, barely-there stubble a few shades lighter than his dark brows. His blue eyes don't look quite as glacial and his lips aren't in their usual grim line.

Their hands are still connected and letting go is the last thing she wants to do. She swallows, heat scorching up her neck and prickling over her collarbone. In fact, now that she's up close and personal, she's stunned to discover that his wide upper lip has a perfect candy pout. *Well, then.*

Trying to hold on to the moment, she says, "Why didn't you ever come back to Piney Peaks?"

His eyes shutter, and that's when she knows. That this answer is the irreversible flick of the first domino that will send all the others tumbling down. "You ask a lot of questions."

She senses that she's overstepped. "Too personal?"

He hesitates.

". . . or too painful?" Elisha guesses.

"In this case, they're the same thing," says Ves.

Her voice is small as she murmurs an "I'm sorry" that she feels all the way down to her signature alpine-white toenails. She's been blabbering on about the sweet childhood memories she hugs close to her heart, thinking she's giving him a little piece of Maeve, when all she's doing is alienating him further.

Ves cocks his head to the side. "For what it's worth, I do wish I'd come back. When I was a kid, she was the only one who ever really cared about me. My parents didn't exactly love that, so they never sent me here again. It's ridiculous they cared enough to be jealous over her relationship with me, but not enough to actually do any-thing to fix theirs. And yeah, I was too little to have any choice about where I went, but as an adult? There's no excuse. I guess I just . . . I wanted her to be my family so badly. Wanted to live with her instead of my mom and dad. And that's embarrassing, to want what you know is so impossible. So I pretended that Christmas here in Piney Peaks never happened. So you see, Elisha, you're not the one who should be sorry."

Her heart wrenches. "I am, though. Not about being nosy. Well, not *just* about that, anyway. I meant . . . I don't think I ever told you how sorry I was. That you lost Maeve, too. Yes, she meant a lot to us here. But she was your family. Your *actual* family. And I've been sharing all the memories that you never got to have."

He shrugs, seems to be trying his best to sound indifferent. "Secondhand stories are just as good."

But Elisha knows him better now. Maybe not a lot, but enough. "No, they're really not," she says. She stands, steps over a wall of her fortress, and offers him her hand. "Want to change that?"

He lets her haul him up. "What did you have in mind?"

"Magic." At his unimpressed look, she sighs. "We're going to seek some. Go grab your coat."

"Magic," he repeats. "But it's almost dinnertime."

"Don't worry, I'm buying."

He scowls with that stern, absolutely not kissable mouth she's absolutely not ogling, absolutely not at all. "Elisha, that's not what I—"

"I am offering you an *adventure* and you're thinking about dinner? Ves, you're a human, not a hobbit."

He looks visibly startled.

She enjoys this victory. "Yeah, that's right. I know Bilbo Baggins."

At his deep inhale, she decides that he's relenting like a stick of butter sitting near a sunny windowsill. He must feel otherwise, because he vehemently shakes his head. "Don't give me that look."

"Ves." Impulsively, she squeezes his hand. The one she hasn't let go of yet. "Because of you, I was able to get back to the *Sleighbells* director and say everything was fine. The movie is under way and the town is thrilled. Even better, I got to not look like the sad singleton I am in front of my ex-fiancé, who's rubbing his happiness in my face every chance he gets. Do you get how much you've helped

me? Most people just have to deal with seeing their ex on social media. But Bentley is my *literal* ghost-of-boyfriends-past haunting me here on my own streets. That's fucked up. And you being here makes it . . . better. So let me give you this. I promise you'll like it."

When his face remains frustratingly blank, Elisha tries again. "Or, even if you don't like it, you'll probably be polite enough to pretend you do so I don't feel bad, and that's fine, too."

There's the tiniest crack in his stoic façade. His eyes soften and for a second, perhaps just one, they drop to her mouth. In a voice edged with doubt, he asks, "My accompanying you means that much?"

"It's not about me. It's what it'll mean to you. And like I said, you're free to hate it." She gives him the bright and merry smile she's perfected down to an art form. It's the one she uses during difficult work situations to infuse optimism and enthusiasm back into the room. "But," she adds, looking up at him from under dark lashes and aiming every last ounce of her conviction his way, "I *really* hope you don't."

CHAPTER TWENTY-EIGHT

Elisha

The movie theater is empty and eerily quiet when Elisha and Ves arrive, thanks to five screenings showing at the same time. She buys Milk Duds, Junior Mints, and Swedish Fish in the lobby, then motions for Ves to follow her into the *Sleighbells* memorabilia room off the main hallway. They pad over the worn purple carpet into a space painted Hollywood red and filled with glass cases, dreamy black-and-white photographs, and mannequins wearing shearling coats and cloche hats over bell bottoms and bell sleeves.

Jamming a fish gummy in her mouth, Elisha points to a behind-the-scenes picture of the cast sitting on the hood of an old-school Mercedes roadster. In the film, it was cherry red and glossy. Her snowflake-painted nail taps at the glass in front of a beautiful blond woman's face. "Doesn't she kind of look like Claudia Schiffer?"

Ves leans in, bending slightly to squint at the face. His lean fingers play with the ends of his scarf, dangling below his waist. "Who?"

"Supermodel. Gorgeous. She did a cameo in *Love Actually*." When he shows no sign of recognition, she gasps in mock outrage.

"Don't tell me you haven't seen that movie, either! Sacrilege! Hugh Grant is in it!"

He looks unimpressed. "Don't tell me that's another holiday favorite of yours."

"Of course not." A beat. "It's my second favorite. Followed by *The Holiday* because Jude Law."

"Because Jude Law what?"

She blinks. "That was the end of my sentence. Does it *need* any other qualifier?"

He blinks back, like he's never met anyone like her before, which is silly, of course, but she can't stop thinking it. Finally, Ves nods at the photograph. "You could have mocked me for my lack of movie and celebrity knowledge at home instead of making me walk all the way into town."

"Don't be grumpy. How do you not recognize that platinum blond hair and smile?" In a sad little voice, she teasingly asks, "It's Maeve. Don't you know your Maeve?"

Ves snorts, a sound that's so at odds with his unruffled appearance that she has to laugh. He stuffs his brown leather gloves into the breast pocket of his gray cashmere wool topcoat. "Don't tell me you misuse Chamber of Commerce time by looking up *Lord of the Rings* quotes before coming over."

"For your information, funny man, they happen to be my number one favorite movies."

She can't decipher the emotions that sprint across his face because he returns his attention to the photograph. There, in tiny black type, is the caption. Cast names left to right, and there, squeezed between the leads, Nathan Landry and Heather Frederick, is Maeve Hollins. Bouncy blond hair and a big toothy smile. Unlike the other women shrieking sex appeal in mini dresses and towering pumps, Maeve's wearing wide-leg aquamarine corduroy pants, a white dress shirt, and a mustard sweater vest. From the gossip Elisha's heard her whole life, Doc Hollins was flattered by the use of his house in a real Hollywood movie, but he didn't want his daughter getting any ideas about running away to L.A.

Maeve's not wearing any real adornments either—unlike Heather's iconic pearl necklace with the ruby-heart pendant, dazzling even in such miniature—unless you count the daisy tucked behind Maeve's ear and Nathan's arm around her waist. She looks like a woman in love and, just like every other time Elisha's seen this picture, something sharp and pointy pierces her heart.

"Maeve had one just like this in her jewelry box," says Elisha, pointing at Heather's necklace. She smiles at the memory, faded at the edges, but still strong. "She let me play dress-up with it when I was little. The box was gorgeous, too. Antique. And there was an engraving on the bottom. 'To M, From D.'"

"D for Dad, maybe." He glances between the photo and Elisha. "It would still look great on you, now."

She bites her lip. "You never happened to find the key, did you? I hate that it could be lost forever."

"I'm not giving up the search," he promises, brushing his hand over hers. It's warm and familiar, and a little scary how much she's already grown to crave his touch. Her breath hitches. She'd almost forgotten how an honest-to-goodness crush should feel. Just like this: exciting and nervous and sparkly, like she's glowing from the inside out.

"I can't believe this is how Maeve looked in the seventies," says Ves. "She's . . . so young. And her dad just let her rot in that house all those years, taking care of him? Not letting her have her own life? What the fuck."

She knows what he means in those three little words. It's disconcerting, seeing Maeve at age thirty, just a couple of years older than Elisha now. Her whole life ahead of her. What the fuck, indeed.

Sometimes she imagines the picture coming to life, Maeve blowing a cheeky kiss and a wink before slipping behind the wheel of the roadster. Maybe one of the cute gophers or sound technicians gets in front with her, maybe even the leading man himself. And Maeve puts the car in gear and goes anywhere. Goes *everywhere*.

"Doc Hollins was scared to be alone, so he guilted her into staying," says Elisha. "But she didn't hold a grudge. She was very much the sort of person to let things go and look ahead, you know?"

He makes a disgruntled sound. "What did she have to look forward to in Piney Peaks?"

"One, *rude*. Although I know what you mean, so I'm going to let that one slide." She hip-checks him. "But two, you see all this stuff in this room? It's stuff she collected from the set or chased down on eBay over the years. In another life, I'm convinced she would have been a historian. It was always her passion and I think a lot of things would have been different if she had the chance."

She chances a peek at Ves. He still wears outrage and dismay on his face. "In the last year since I've been back, I was helping her. I even got in touch with Nathan Landry to ask if he still had the stocking with his character's name on it. Here, look."

She leads him to the faux fireplace at the opposite end of the room. "Grandpa Dave carved this from some old reclaimed barnwood." She's proud when Ves runs his fingertips over the mitered edges and the immaculate crown molding of the mantel surround, clearly admiring the craftsmanship.

"We have everyone's," says Elisha, pointing to each of the cast's red stockings in turn. "It all came together this summer. Mr. Landry wanted to deliver it in person, but his health wasn't up to it."

Personally, she always thought that something had gone on between him and Maeve, a feeling that was confirmed when her elderly friend had seemed particularly bummed out when he had to cancel the trip to Piney Peaks.

"This is why you wanted the filming permission so badly. Why the sequel is so important," Ves realizes out loud. "It wasn't just about your job. It was always about Maeve." He looks at her with an awed sort of fascination. "Do all small-town girls have big hearts like yours?" His words are teasing, but there's also something genuine there.

"Speaking for the Small-Town Girl Society of which I am, of course, both president and founding member, yes. We are a deeply underappreciated demographic, especially by big-city boys."

He scoffs. "The last word I'd use to describe you is underappreciated, Elisha. You're . . . probably the most loved person I know. Universally so. Would I go so far as to say you're the beating heart of Piney Peaks?" He waits until she's looking at him, heart thump-thump-thumping in her chest like it's about to pop out like a cartoon character's. "Yes," he says softly. "Yes, I would."

"Ves . . ."

"For what it's worth, nothing about tonight has been a disappointment," he says. "Our first meeting notwithstanding, nothing about *us* has been, either. I don't think you could do anything to turn me off you even if you tried."

She doesn't know what to say. What to *do* with that. He's kinda just trusted her to hold his heart for as long as he's here. It's weird and it's nice and it's the last thing she ever expected and suddenly the only thing she wants.

"Oh my god, I'm going to have to upgrade you," she says faintly. "I can't believe you were an elf and three grimy old socks."

"*What?*"

She throws her hands around helplessly. "The emojis I used instead of your name in my phone. That first day I decided that you have to work your way up to 'Ves Hollins.'"

"I just told you that I like you *and you*—" He pinches the bridge of his nose. "Only in Piney Peaks."

"You were just very cute so I'm going to pretend I didn't hear the tone of that sentence."

"I'm happy to repeat it louder."

"That's it. You're now the baby angel emoji." She taps her chin. "Maybe even three of them."

"Hell, Elisha, I'll take a dozen Santas over that."

As she flounces away, she hears him mumble, "Gonna make a law one day about the evils of your smart mouth during the holiday season, Elisha Rowe."

She grins all the way out of the movie theater. "Mm-hmm. Good luck, *baby.*"

CHAPTER TWENTY-NINE

Elisha

In bed later that night, Elisha lies on her side, cheek pressed into her silk pillowcase. She inhales the lavender oil she daubs to aid a good night's sleep and watches Ves's shadow move behind the curtain of his second-story bedroom across the street. He's just an unexciting blurred shape. She's watched him a few times before, not on purpose or anything. She likes to leave her curtains open to sleep in the moonlight streaking across her bed, and in the morning, dawn wakes her better than any alarm could.

Tonight, her nighttime routine is just as methodical as all the others, but then something changes.

Decrepit old butterflies start to flap their ragged, time-worn wings. Slowly, at first, like they don't remember their strength, then more fiercely, until all the dust and cobwebs are shaken off. And then they take flight, fluttering away while she's in her pug-patterned lilac pajamas and Ves is too far away to do anything about it.

She inhales sharply. Her earlier fullness from the cauliflower steak and potato-leek soup at the vegetarian restaurant she took Ves to is replaced by something insistent and hungry.

Her right hand drifts to the waistband of her flannel bottoms, fingers slipping underneath. Cool fingers on warm skin. She bites her lip and lets her hand move lower. She wishes Ves had kissed her after he'd walked her home. She thought that had been his intention when he'd accompanied her across the street, all the way to her front door, which was disarmingly sweet and entirely unexpected. He could have just parted ways when they reached the cul-de-sac, he to his house and she to hers.

So the fact that he didn't means something. Then again, the lack of kiss *also* means something. She sighs and pulls her hand free, unsatisfied with this line of thinking and everything else, too. Maybe the revelations of the evening had just been too heavy.

Across the street, his bedroom light turns off. But a second later, her room glows.

She snatches the phone under her pillow. One new text message.

Ves: You still up?

Elisha hesitates over the keys only long enough not to talk herself out it.

Elisha: Yes.

Ves: Thanks for dinner tonight. I had fun.

Elisha: Me too. Sorry they seated us right in the center of the restaurant. Swear I didn't plan it! 🙈

Ves: Not sorry that Ben got a good view of us, I'll bet. He was fuming.

That makes her smile.

> Elisha: To be fair, that could be because he
> was seated near the restrooms, though . . .

Bentley had already been in the restaurant, sitting with some of
the guys Elisha had graduated with, mostly ones she'd turned down
at the Old Stoat or one of the many holiday parties over the years.
Whatever. They'd fake-smiled their way through it when Elisha
and Ves had to pass them on the way in and out.

A new message from Ves bubbles up.

> Ves: Wouldn't it be funny if all your
> exes were teaming up to make a new trivia
> team?

> Elisha: HAHAHA NO WHY WOULD YOU
> SAY THAT 😬 🙄 😖 They'd probably call it
> Elisha's Exes and think it was clever.

> Ves: You weren't kidding about spurning all
> of them?

> Elisha: What can I say, everyone wants me
> 💁

An ellipsis bubble pops up. Disappears. Then it's back again. In
the time it takes her to reread her last message, analyzing it for any
clues as to why he's waffling with his reply, he stops typing.

She wishes she had gone with a different emoji in her last message, one that isn't so cocky. The laugh-crying emoji, maybe. That

one shows she's clearly joking around. She squirms, trying to get comfortable. Wait, what if he's fallen asleep?

For a second, she's miffed. But then she imagines him nodding off, phone falling to his chest when his hand goes limp, *Elisha* the last thing on his mind. That's not so bad.

Her fingers fly over the keys.

> Elisha: Guess you fell asleep! You have the
> right idea, I have work tomorrow ugh.
> Anyway, good night! xx

She's about to turn the screen dark and go to sleep when he starts typing again.

> Ves: Then I'm honored you chose
> me to date.

She blinks her fuzzy eyes at the screen. That's it. No banter. Just a solid statement of fact.

He probably assumes she's not looking at her phone anymore, because he follows it up with another message immediately.

> Ves: Good night.

No *x*'s or emojis. She's learned that's not his style.

Once, she might have thought he was uptight, reserved, far too cool for her liking. But now she knows better. He's honest to a fault, and always means what he says.

> Elisha: My parents have been hounding me
> to invite you over for dinner.

She frowns, then deletes and retypes the whole thing.

> Elisha: Oh, with everything going on, I
> almost forgot! My parents wanted me to
> invite you to come over for dinner
> tomorrow. I'd love it if you came. DON'T
> FREAK OUT, OKAY? It's literally just a fam
> dinner. Low stakes, great food.

He answers at once.

> Ves: Thank your parents for me and tell them
> I accept the kind invitation. Sleep tight,
> Elisha.

And a second later—

> Ves: xxx

CHAPTER THIRTY

Ves

Ves is positive that the only thing more uncomfortable than dinner with his own family is dinner with someone else's.

A long-held belief that he has revised just once over the years at the many family functions he's spent with Arun and his large extended Indian family. But no matter how loved he's made to feel, or how many delicious and syrupy gulab jamun they always pile his bowl with because they know he's adored the deep-fried Indian dessert since childhood, he's not *actually* family, is he?

Arun's mother may kiss his cheek and call him *son*, but it's Cade who has formally joined the Iyers, not him. The next time he sees them, he knows it will be different. He knew it the night of Arun and Cade's sangeet, when, with a bittersweet pang, he wondered if he would ever again fit into someone's family. The feeling of being the odd one out persisted through the singing and the dancing, and later that night, when he removed the ice-blue and silver kurta and churidar, it seemed to reinforce that he couldn't keep this family any more than he could keep his own.

Even though Ves knows that nothing good can come of getting attached to Elisha's family, he still wants to make a good impression. So he buys an expensive bottle of wine from the liquor store as a hostess gift and braces himself for a night of dancing around awkward questions about his own relations. Now here he is with their daughter, on their stoop, too chickenshit to ring the bell.

"Why are you being so fidgety?" Elisha asks, reaching up to unbutton the top of his dove-gray dress shirt.

"Whenever I've met a girlfriend's parents, it's . . ." He's hesitant to meet her eyes. "Never gone well."

"Then it's just as well that I'm not a girlfriend," she says firmly. "It's just dinner, and you've already met two-thirds of my family. Now stop worrying. You'll get premature frown lines."

Personally, he thinks it's a bit too late for him; he's already sprouted a few white hairs since meeting her, but when he pointed it out, she'd retorted that his hair was platinum, so how could he tell, anyway? Sounds like girlfriend logic to him—she's always right, he's happy to let her think so.

"I wish you'd showered and gotten changed," he says, eyeing her outfit. "I feel overdressed."

She's in the same black leggings and oversize sweatshirt she wore to help him move furniture around after work. It says HOT CHOCO- LATE AND CHRISTMAS MOVIES in faded lettering, a graphic of a VHS and an anthropomorphized mug filled to the brim with marshmallows holding hands. It's . . . creepy. Or cute. He can't decide.

She pooh-poohs him. "It's winter, I barely sweat. Anyway, I *told* you it's a casual family dinner. I don't know why you ironed your trousers and tucked in your shirt. Now ring the bell."

"Why me?"

"I'm not ringing the bell of my own house, Ves."

"But you'll argue with me outside it?"

Her smile is pure devilry. "I'll argue with you anywhere."

Yeah, he'll bet she would. But he rings the bell to cut the squabble short, pleasantly surprised when her eyebrows shoot up as though she didn't expect him to give in. He will never tell her to her face, but he enjoys surprising her. Showing her that she doesn't have him all figured out. That beneath the buttoned-up, inflexibly practical persona is a man taking baby steps at being unpredictable.

The door swings open, bringing with it the mouthwatering aroma of home cooking. Anita wears a black vegan-leather skirt and a fuzzy gray sweater shot through with enough silver thread that she sparkles at every angle like a ball of tinsel. "Hi, kids! Welcome, Ves. Please come in."

"Thanks for the invitation, Mrs. Rowe." He politely steps across the threshold, offering her the bottle and the bouquet of red amaryllis blooms and white peonies he picked up at the florist's on Main Street.

"Please, call me Anita," she says with a laugh, shutting the door behind them. As Ves passes her, he's stunned when she does a quick kiss-kiss to the sides of his cheeks. It doesn't bother him, he just doesn't expect it, so he gapes like a fish until the shock settles.

Should he return the gesture? No, he's taken too long, the moment has passed. And he definitely can't shake her hand now. It's too late and too formal and—

Oh, Anita's already pulling her daughter into the house. Elisha doesn't seem to notice anything amiss, either. The boulder of pressure on his chest eases. Maybe his first impression isn't as shitty as he thinks.

"Thank you, the flowers are beautiful, Ves. We're thrilled to finally have you over! As you can imagine, this is the Chocolate Mouse's busiest season, so we've barely had a moment to ourselves this December." Anita's brown eyes dance with her daughter's mischievousness. "We would have come over as soon as we knew you were in town, but much to everyone's surprise, our daughter beat us to it."

"Including mine," Ves says wryly. "Emphasis on *beat*."

Elisha scoffs and gestures to her knee. "Hey, the only one injured that day was me."

"Poor baby," says Anita, giving Ves an apologetic smile that speaks of endless love for her reckless daughter. Her dangly silver earrings glimmer when she turns to call for her husband, "Jamie, honey, Ves is here!"

After Ves and Elisha toe off their shoes, Anita leads the way to the kitchen. He pauses to look at their family photos lining the walls. For a second, it bothers him that clearly nothing is in chronological order. In the next, he's already too distracted to care.

Elisha bright-eyed and red-lipped in her high school graduation cap and gown, looking cozy in a group pic with a handsome dark-haired boy he doesn't recognize, arm wrapped around Elisha's shoulders like it belongs there. Must be an old boyfriend. Other faces, ones he knows, round out the group: Solana Pereira, Adam Lawson, Riley Studebaker, Adhira Ambani, Becca Rosen, Isaiah Osuji, and Kat Kwon.

Ves squints at the boy, aging him up in his mind and wondering if he's still in town—and if so, with any luck he's got a spouse and is absolutely haggard after three kids, all under five. And then promptly wants to roll his own eyes at the ridiculous, petty sensation of being jealous over a teenage ex.

But he's stared at it too long, and now feels like it has to be addressed. "You two were cute," he says, turning around to smirk.

"So cute that he couldn't wait to get out of what he considered a 'dead-end small town' the second we graduated. Now keep it moving," whispers Elisha. He's about to protest when her hand lands on his ass and pushes him along with enough vigor that he actually *does* keep walking.

Toddler pictures of Elisha at the Chocolate Mouse, so engrossed in wrapping herself in copious amounts of tinsel that she looks like the most adorable sparkly mummy he's ever seen. Why are people so embarrassed about baby pictures? He doesn't get it. He'd love if he had any of his own.

"Ves."

"What? I'm literally in motion."

"Too." She jabs her finger in the small of his back. "Slowly!"

"Who rushes on a scenic route?" Granted, he does. Or at least, he used to. But now he's finding that when the view is her, there's no end to the detours he'd take to learn everything about her.

"He who wants to live to eat dinner," Elisha deadpans.

But Ves has an unfettered opportunity to drink in all these little time capsules of her life, and he's not just going to walk on by without appreciating them. Other than the yearly school picture, his own childhood was never displayed proudly throughout his house when he was growing up.

Now it's the Rowes on holiday somewhere tropical, a teenage Elisha in a yellow string bikini that matches the color of the house behind her. She holds a green coconut with both hands, teeth clamped around the straw sticking out of it. Her parents hang in the background, dotted along the shoreline.

It's only been seconds, but he can feel her impatience mounting. Why? She's cute as . . . His mind flails. Well, cute as a button, he supposes, a phrase he's never used in his life and can't imagine where he heard.

"I absolutely need your middle name for situations like this," she groans from behind him.

"Andrew," he says absently, still unaccountably hungry for these peeks into her life.

He skips several frames, only to land on a gap-toothed Elisha holding a red lollipop in one hand and the paw of a soft cuddly toy in the other. His eyes widen, recognizing it as the bear from the workshop.

He twists at the hip to point it out to her, grinning like they were playing the world's easiest game of Where's Waldo?, if Waldo were a brown bear hidden in plain sight. She rolls her eyes, unimpressed with his not-so-subtle sleuthing. Poke, poke. He sighs and lets her shepherd him into the kitchen.

While Anita runs the tap to fill a vase, Elisha's dad pulls a roast chicken from the oven. Their kitchen counter is covered in dishes that look like Le Creuset, which he only recognizes because of Cade, but he's far more interested in what's inside them. It's enough to feed the whole street, he's sure.

"Hello," says Ves, letting his hand drop when he sees Jamie's oven-mittened hands, patterned with red roosters. He settles for a polite smile instead. "Everything smells delicious."

Jamie grins back. "I should hope so, I've been at it for hours."

Anita lightly swats her husband's shoulder with the dish towel she just used to dry her hands. "Don't listen to him, Ves. He loves cooking."

"I'm hopeless in the kitchen," Ves offers, because all three of them are looking at him with expectation, and he doesn't want to let them down. "There's so much choice in New York and I pick up a lot of prepared meals at Union Market or Whole Foods, so . . ."

Suddenly, he wonders if he shouldn't have mentioned that. What if they think he's a spoiled rich kid who's too lazy to learn to cook? That he throws money away? That he lives on two-minute noodles?

Four years ago, at the last holiday he'd ever spent with a girlfriend's family, his ex Nora's dad had apparently been a bit miffed that Ves hadn't offered to help him fry the Christmas turkey. It wasn't rudeness, though; Ves simply had no idea what a raw bird, a metal trash can, and five gallons of peanut oil were doing on the driveway, or that Nora's past boyfriends had usually used fry time as a way to bond with her dad. End result: Ves had not impressed the patriarch.

"Then you should start joining us for dinner," Jamie says easily, tossing the rooster mitts on the counter. "We're not usually this fancy, but we always make enough for extras. Comes in handy after a long day. Sometimes even with something you love, like me and cooking, it's the last thing you want to do."

Ves smiles uncomfortably. He knows he's definitely not going to show up at mealtime just to eat like a moocher, but the offer is a kind one. "Can I help with anything?"

"Oh, that's so sweet." Anita hands him five shiny knives and forks. "I've already set the plates, but if you want to just place the silverware—Oh, Elisha, can you check the dessert? Grandpa will be here in a minute and then we'll be ready to eat."

As Ves distributes the cutlery, Elisha heads to the fridge, peeking inside.

"How are you finding Piney Peaks so far?" asks Jamie, bringing over one of the covered dishes.

It isn't the backwater Ves's dad described it as, that's for sure. But it's also not a place Ves can imagine staying for longer than a few weeks. It's a quaint little town, especially all dressed up for the holidays, but a guy like him—content with his city life—doesn't fit in here.

"It's . . . different," he says, opting for the diplomatic answer.

"It grows on you," Anita chimes in. "Honestly, when I met Jamie in college—why yes, that *is* his ancient NYU sweatshirt I told him to change out of—I never thought I'd leave the city, but here we are!"

"Ancient?" Jamie indignantly points down at the faded purple sweatshirt. "It's my favorite!"

Elisha catches Ves's eye and good-naturedly rolls her eyes as if to say *Yeah, they're always like this*.

He eyes her own sweatshirt and hopes his expression conveys *Like father, like daughter*.

She gets it at once, huffing at him.

While Anita and Jamie continue to squabble as they bring all the dishes to the table, Elisha grabs a chilled bottle of wine from the fridge and pours out five glasses on the countertop.

"See? Told you it was casual," says Elisha, slipping to his side.

"I'll believe you next time," he promises, taking the drink she offers.

Mirth flickers on her expressive face. "Even if I tell you it's an Ugly Christmas Sweater party and you *have* to wear one to get in the door?"

He's amused at the thought. "Your dress code is that discriminating, is it?"

"Well," Elisha says in an exaggerated, gossipy voice, "my guest list is the crème de la crème of Piney Peaks society."

"In that case, how could I resist donning a Rudolph sweater?"

Her eyes glimmer. "Even if his nose lights up with a red bulb?"

With the utmost seriousness, he responds, "Well, if it doesn't, is it even *worthy* of being an Ugly Sweater?"

The soft clatter of a lid being removed reminds him they're not alone. He looks up to see fond expressions on both Jamie's and Anita's faces, quickly masked as though they didn't want to be caught. Anita grabs the other two wineglasses.

When the doorbell rings, Jamie excuses himself. "That'll be Dad," he says, clapping Ves's shoulder on his way out. "Grab a pew, son."

"Sit next to Elisha," says Anita, shooing both of them toward the only two plates side by side. Elisha claims her spot, drawing her legs under her to sit cross-legged.

Ves waits until Jamie returns with Dave, thinking he'll finally get a chance to shake someone's hand. He readies himself to thrust it out, even though he saw the man yesterday to work on the runners for the sleigh. Dave glances at the outstretched hand, then, to Ves's astonishment, pulls him into a hug.

Ves breathes in the scent of wood shavings, Werther's caramel candy, and the faintest trace of cigarette smoke. None of these things have any special significance to him, so why does his chest ache?

It's the strangest thing. The last time he felt like this was . . .

Hmm. A long time ago. When Maeve gave him that handknitted red scarf. That, too, was without warning. Snuck up on him out of nowhere, a foreign rush of emotion that he's never had the words to describe. It's like a hand around his heart, digging in its sharp nails at irregular intervals, whenever Ves thinks the sting has passed.

Anita sniffs. "Dave, have you been hanging around at the Cheery Chinchilla?"

Ves is released. "Absolutely not," says Dave staunchly, but then he ruins it by winking at Elisha.

"Oh, Dad," Jamie groans. To Ves, he explains, "It's this little hole-in-the-wall hangout spot. It's probably not even up to code and it's the farthest thing from *cheery*, believe me. The floor is perpetually sticky, the walls stink of stale smoke, and the average age of the occupants is, what, eighty?"

"Probably less now," says Dave. "Had a few funerals this summer that lowered it."

"Because all you old coots go there to drink and smoke. Dad, your heart, you're not as young as—"

"James, who's the dad and who's the son here?"

Jamie sets his jaw. In that moment, he looks exactly as determined as his daughter. Ves remembers that same unyielding expression on Elisha's face when she came over at the Old Stoat to sweet-talk him his first night in town. Good to see she comes by it honestly.

Half out of genuine curiosity and half to gently remind the family of his presence so they'd stop bickering in front of a guest, Ves asks, "Did you say Cheery Chinchilla?"

Elisha sputters into her glass of wine, resolutely not looking at him.

Misunderstanding, Anita shakes her head. "It's tucked away on one of the side streets, but it's definitely not one of Piney Peaks's must-see destinations."

Ves keeps his eyes on Elisha. "But a chinchilla is a . . . what, exactly?"

"It's a close cousin to the armadillo," she shoots back, managing to keep a straight face.

He works his mouth from side to side. "Hmm, I don't think that's it."

"It's, like, basically an aardvark."

"Nope, not buying it."

"Ves, just *say* you don't know your basic mammals and let's move on."

"Is this flirting?" asks Dave, head swiveling between the two like he's watching a tennis match.

"The weirdest kind I've ever seen," Jamie says with a laugh.

Anita looks like she doesn't know whether to be amused or exasperated. "Elisha, stop teasing the poor boy. Ves, a chinchilla is a rodent. A cross between a mouse and squirrel. Now, can we eat?"

CHAPTER THIRTY-ONE

Ves

Moooooom." Elisha groans, cheeks blooming a splotchy pink. "How could you sell me out like that?"

Anita blinks. "What? It *is* a rodent."

Ves grins victoriously. Elisha, on the other hand, is supremely mature and sticks out her tongue.

But she doesn't have long to pout, because Jamie starts plating up the food. Everything smells amazing, traditional holiday fare mingling with the familiar fragrance of masala.

"Ves, do you eat shellfish?" asks Jamie.

"I do."

The first serving on Ves's plate is prawn pulao, basmati rice flavored with onion, ginger, garlic, green chilies and plenty of whole spices, cinnamon and cardamom the most prominent. The tangy, peppery dish is unfamiliar to him, but he loves the plump shrimp on top, the slightly shriveled peas and cilantro studded throughout, and the lime juice drizzled liberally on top. The first scent is so divine he could have happily eaten a whole plate of it, but as each additional dish is uncovered, he starts to wonder how he can possibly make room for it all.

"I think you had the right idea wearing stretchy pants," he mutters to Elisha.

She stabs at a shrimp, holding her fork aloft in victory. "I'm *always* right."

Next, Ves slurps his first tisrya, clams in a savory green chili and coconut paste. It's followed up with a slice of chicken, which is rubbed with spices and herbs and doused in melted rosemary lemon butter. Coating his roasted potatoes in the drippings is sweet, sweet heaven. The sides aren't skimpy, either: fried okra, perfectly golden, crunches in his mouth, a sharp contrast to the tender succulence of the grilled paneer-and-red-pepper skewers. Sweet-corn fritters and garlicky broccolini are served on the side, simple but equally delicious as the main dishes.

He asks about each new dish before he eats, turning the new and unfamiliar words over in his head until he's pronouncing them correctly. When the sweet-and-sour fish vindaloo is served in small bowls with steamed white rice, he inhales greedily. The aroma is unlike anything he's had before. The red curry is thin compared to the chunks of firm cod, the broth strong with the pleasingly sour tang of feni, a Goan brandy that makes Ves think of tart, crisp pineapples and scorching summer vacations.

The flavors here are different from the takeout in the city or the comforting vegetarian food Arun's mom makes. He's never eaten food like this before and his taste buds zing with excitement.

"Nope, you won't find these dishes in most American restaurants," Anita agrees when he tells her, smiling when he mentions that he loves the chicken biryani he's eaten in the city. "It's all naan and tandoori chicken on most restaurant menus, isn't it? But Goan cuisine is different since Goa is on India's western coast, so it's famous mainly for seafood dishes."

He's glad she said that, because he wasn't able to place it, and he's dreadfully afraid he's asked a few too many questions. "Oh," he settles for saying. He's still reeling from the knowledge that Anita and Jamie cooked all of this for him. Yes, when his parents were still together, they had multicourse meals, but those were always prepared by the chef. And when he was deemed old enough to join them at the table, he would eat fast enough to be excused so he could escape back to his room and his books.

But something must show on his face, some sign of his curiosity and ignorance, because Elisha takes pity on him. "Portugal colonized and ruled Goa for four hundred fifty years until independence in 1961," she says around a bite of prawn pulao. "There's a lot of Portuguese influence on our food, which is why the flavor is different from what you may be used to."

"You may have seen some of our family photos on the way in," says Anita. "My parents' ancestral home is in Pernem, which is in north Goa. It has a tiny population even compared to Piney Peaks! My mother missed home, but I grew up in New York City, so I've always been a bit of a city girl at heart. We went back to Pernem to visit family regularly, and after my father retired last year, he and my mother decided to live there permanently."

"The beach life," Dave says with a wistful sigh. "Can't wait for January."

"What's in January?" asks Ves.

"Our annual trip to Goa. We always take a two-week holiday after New Year's Eve," says Jamie. "Looks like we'll both be leaving town around the same time, huh?"

Ves wishes he could take his question back. At the worst possible moment, his tongue decides to go on vacation, too, so his mouth takes turns opening and closing.

"Or maybe you've changed your mind about leaving?" asks Anita. She's looking at Ves, but she gives herself away when her eyes flick to Elisha for just a second, as though she's trying to gauge how much her daughter wants him to stay.

Okay, it's obvious that they know there's *something* going on between him and Elisha, but how much? That they almost went for it in the Chocolate Mouse's stockroom? Oh god, what if there were security cameras and the whole family saw him sliding his hand up her thigh in grainy black-and-white? His tongue makes an unfortunate return, this time feeling too thick and fuzzy for his mouth, and he swallows desperately.

"Mom, he has a life back in New York. He can't just up and relocate." Elisha refills his glass of water and gestures for him to take a sip, while Dave looks on with mirth.

Actually, as an author who could work from basically anywhere with a decent Wi-Fi signal and back support, Ves *could* just up and relocate. But obviously that's beside the point. Not even worth pointing out. Especially not since she's shut it down so quickly.

"Of course he does," Anita says brightly. "We'd just love to get to know you better, Ves."

"New blood is always good," Dave says around a mouthful of rice and vindaloo.

Jamie laughs. "Way to sound like a cult, Dad."

Sorry, Elisha mouths behind the rim of her wineglass.

Dave makes a grumbly sound of disagreement deep in his chest. "A cult wouldn't want Ves. He's got lots of folks who'd miss him. Where would I be without my apprentice woodworker?"

"Probably further along than where you are," says Elisha. Without warning she grabs Ves's hands. "Soft. Uncalloused. Have you even *held* a piece of wood?"

He's still recovering from the sudden snatching of his extremities to put together the reason why Jamie and Dave are rollicking with laughter, and even Anita's turning away to unsuccessfully hide her giggle.

Elisha groans and unceremoniously drops his hand. "You people are all awful."

As the family continues eating and chatting, Ves tries to get back to normal, only to realize . . . nothing about this is normal for him. It's been surreal ever since he crossed the threshold. Hugs and jokes and laughter. Conversation that doesn't leave him out. Same as Arun's family, he's never once been made to feel like a guest, but rather part of the family right away. They're both families that want him there.

And he *wants* it to be, with a profound yearning that he hasn't felt since . . . well, since he was seven, and all he wanted was—No. He couldn't have it then and it's still not his now.

The shrill ring of a phone cuts through the conversation. Elisha squints at the number flashing across the screen. "Seriously? It's after work hours!" She sighs. "Oh, nope, actually, I guess it's still the workday for Jessica June."

"Who?" asks Jamie.

Anita clucks her tongue. "It's Damian Rhys's assistant."

Everyone falls silent so Elisha can answer it at the table, which is another oddity to Ves. Even now, his father always answers phone calls in a furtive way, leaving to go to another room. It's probably a leftover habit from the days Karl used to sneak around behind Adeline's back.

Long after his mother discovered the affairs, Karl continued playing at discretion, but even as a child, Ves knew what it meant when his father left the table and his mother waited for him to come back, picking at her plate long after her food went cold. On those nights, Ves wouldn't rush away to his room and the solace of his books. He always stayed, even if she didn't seem to notice or care that he was there.

Suddenly, in the cozy warmth of the Rowes' home, he feels itchy and uncomfortable in his own skin. Everything here is so different, and he isn't sure he likes it.

"Hello?" Elisha squirms in her seat. "Oh, hi, JJ. How are—Yeah, it's almost eight here, but it's no problem. Oh, really? Yeah, no, that's—Yeah, yeah, I can always ask. Of course. I'm not sure how possible it will be, but—Mm-hmm. Well, I'll definitely do my best."

A beat. Her gaze cuts to Ves's. "Yes, he's a relative." Another pause, where Elisha's eyebrows pinch. "Not a problem at all, I know you're working round the clock, it's all go-go-go." A few more niceties and she hangs up, setting her phone on the table with a sigh.

"Everything okay, sweetie?" asks Jamie.

Ves fists his hand in his lap, inconveniently plagued by the urge to reach out and smooth his fingers over her brow until she relaxes her face. Every muscle is taut, her nostrils are flared, and there's a distinctly unhappy set to her mouth.

"Uh, just a surprise?" Elisha angles her body to face Ves. "So JJ wanted to give me a heads-up that Damian is interested in coming down here early with a skeleton film crew to get some pre-production footage. Check the lighting for when they start to film next month. Promotional stills. Stuff like that."

He shrugs. "I suppose that's fine?"

She takes a deep breath. "Well, here's the thing," she says hesitantly. "He wants to do some of it *inside* the house. ASAP. Like, this weekend. Apparently, he got his start as an assistant on the original movie and actually knew Maeve, so he wants to get in there. But, obviously, I know that's not what we agreed to, so . . ."

Even if Ves couldn't feel all four pairs of eyes staring at him, his answer would be the same. "You really have to ask?" he asks.

Her eyes widen. "No, I know! I knew you'd hate the idea! I just had to make it seem like I was actually going to run it by you, but I'll let them down easy."

It feels like he's wearing an itchy sweater while sweating profusely, so every horrible wool fiber is plastered tightly to his skin. He clears his throat, which is also wadded with skeins of detestable scratchy yarn. Joy. "I meant," he says, voice rough, "that I'm in this now, Elisha. I'm with you. All the way to the end."

Her eyebrows are still drawn together, like she hasn't grasped what he's trying to say.

"As long as they're gone before the valuation people get here, they can have whatever they need," he clarifies, waiting for it to click. When it does, her brows shoot almost to her hairline and the sound she makes is similar to the one that had escaped her throat when he'd sucked the crook of her shoulder just right during their first kiss. Damn if he doesn't feel rewarded by surprising her yet again.

"You're not kidding?" She scans her family's faces as if they have more information than she does. "Seriously, Ves? People underfoot? Being kicked out of your own house?"

"I can check into a hotel for a few nights," he says. "No big deal. Hotels around here are pet friendly, right? Thor, Thorin, and I will be just fine."

Momentarily, it surprises him how readily he's accepted the cats into his life, but then it doesn't: they're his responsibility, but more than that, they're *his*.

"Yeah, but uh, forget about any chain hotels," Elisha replies. "We don't have any of the big ones, and I don't think you'll want to stay at any of the motels, but I can call up the B&Bs and see if there's—"

"Sorry, hon," says Dave, looking sheepish. "That idea's out. There definitely won't be any room at the inn, I'm afraid. At *any* of the inns. There's that cozy Christmas mystery writing retreat going on right now, remember? And I was just chatting with Marcy on the way here; she always has the lowdown on everything. Places are already booked up." He brightens. "Well, except . . . I do know of *one* . . ."

"Whatever it is, we'll take it!" Elisha's brown eyes entreat Ves to murmur his own agreement.

Dave grins, flustering Ves with a bold wink. "Chez Rowe!"

Ves thinks staying with Dave won't be too bad—they've been spending time together, anyway, and he's grown to really enjoy the man's company—but apparently he's come to the wrong conclusion, because Anita declares, "Dave is right. We won't even hear of you going to a hotel when you can stay in our guest room, Ves. You're basically family. More potatoes?"

CHAPTER THIRTY-TWO

Ves

"Last night, you meant that I'd be staying with you at your place, right?" Ves asks, watching Dave get to work on repairing the thoroughly rotted runners for the sleigh. They're in the workshop behind the Chocolate Mouse, where Ves has spent the last few days learning how to split wood along the grain, the properties of hardwoods with excellent bendability, and how to unpick splinters from his hand without his eyes watering—much.

Dave laughs and slaps his thigh. "I live in a one-bedroom apartment. You can take the couch if you want, but I guarantee you'll find Anita's guest room more comfortable."

"I'm sure I can find somewhere else," says Ves. "It won't come to that."

That's the end of the chitchat for the next couple of hours.

Since day one, Dave has been patient and explains everything, sometimes twice, to make sure Ves gets it, but the rest of their time is devoted to doing their respective tasks. The man works hours on end on his many projects—custom cribs, reclaimed barn door headboards, rocking chairs—for people around town. Dave spends most of that time in silence, or humming Presley, Sinatra, or, surprisingly, Mumford & Sons. Ves envies that focus, especially since he still hasn't made any progress on his next book idea.

By the time they finish making the curved ski runners, it's almost noon. Ves usually asks Dave to lunch, but the old man never takes him up on it, citing the meals Anita sends him home with. And now, having been the recipient of the same generosity, Ves knows he'd much rather devour the leftovers in his fridge Anita insisted on packing for him. There's enough for him to be set for both lunch and dinner.

His phone rings when he's halfway down Main Street, Arun's name popping up on the screen. "Why did you send me a picture of sleeping cats at three a.m. last night?" his best friend asks without preamble.

"You always offer to send *me* pet pics."

"Which you say you delete without looking at, which is physically impossible, by the way."

Ves huffs. "Fine, I look. They just don't have the same effect on me as they do on you."

"Oh, pfft! If you're done lying to yourself, just admit they make you all squishy, too," Arun says with a good-natured snort. "But seriously, what's up? Why cats. In the middle of the night. Answers, please."

"I couldn't sleep last night and thought they looked cute curled up together. They refused to pose earlier. Every single photo came out blurry or with tails blocking the lens. Jeez, I thought you'd like it. My mistake."

"Don't pout. I need more information, Veselin Andrew Hollins."

Ves winces. Other than his parents, Arun is the only person he still associates with who knows his full first name. He hates it. It reminds him of the first year at boarding school when the other boys called him Vaseline, even in front of the teachers.

It's been *Ves* ever since. Not Veselin, the boy who cried at night. Not Veselin, whose textbook pages were gloopy with petroleum jelly on his second day. Not Veselin, who had thought if he went to the child psychologist without making a fuss, maybe his parents would get back together and then he wouldn't have to go back to that school for a second semester.

Ves is a man who none of those things could happen to. Ves is someone who is in control, and that's how he likes it. How he plans to keep it. Changing what works will only invite crushed hopes, and it's not a taste he cares to familiarize himself with again.

Arun gasps at Ves's silence. "Plot twist! Did you, the most city person to ever city, decide to settle down and get closer to your homespun roots, falling for the girl next door, saving a local business, ideally one owned by her mom and pop, and then, cherry on top, save some kittens from a tree?"

"Roots?" Ves's lips quirk. Karl's family emigrated from Germany, and Adeline has never quite been able to give a straight answer about her background; her side of the family had a habit of estranging themselves at the earliest opportunity, so he's never known that half of the family tree. Just another way they're fucked up. "Arun, small tourist towns are not my roots. And *I keep telling you*, there's no falling happening. Her parents' business is probably the most profitable one in this whole town. Have you been watching Hallmark again?"

"... No?" Arun's voice lilts at the end. It's his tell.

"I blame Cade for this."

"It's just so ..." Arun sighs. "Real."

Ves stands to the side to let a group of brisk joggers overtake him. "It's a film set."

"Oh, if only places like that existed in real life." Arun's voice rises dramatically. "Oh wait, they do! Welcome to Piney Peaks! God, I wish I was there right now."

"Okay, that proves nothing. Piney Peaks is the exception, not the rule. And, if you think about it, isn't the whole town basically a set? They're so committed to dining out on *Sleighbells*'s success for as long as possible that they're really playing up the whole cutesy charm."

Arun grumbles. "Getting back to your cat acquisition . . ."

"They were Maeve's. I inherited them."

"And you just found out?"

"Elisha didn't want to stress me out with them right away."

Arun laughs. "She knows you well."

"But, I don't know, now that they're here . . . I think I would have been fine with it? They haven't clawed the furniture or pointedly pissed on the carpets. Thor and Thorin have been pretty chill so far."

"Excuse me, *who* and *who*?" Arun sounds incredulous.

"*I* didn't name them," Ves says defensively, not wanting to get into Maeve's celebrity crushes. "Actually, it's good you called. You saw Dominique's email about the arrival of my author copies?"

"Yup, I'm cc'ed on everything."

"Do you think you can get her to send me some books early? And if you go to my apartment, grab some of the first two and mail them to me here?"

"Yeah, don't see why not. Are you doing a school visit or something? Aren't schools already out for winter break?"

"The Chocolate Mouse runs a toy drive and I thought it would be nice to offer some of my books."

"Damn, you're a regular Christmas elf *and* a cat dad," teases

Arun. "I'll toss in some of my other clients' books, too, if that's okay? I have some of the sweetest picture books."

"That would be great," says Ves. "You're the best."

"This can't possibly be the first time you've come to this conclusion."

"Lifetime or in recent memory?"

Arun laughs. "You shithead."

"You called me Veselin, asshat. I haven't heard that in years."

"Mea culpa. I will never again insult you or your fur babies."

Ves cringes. It sounds like the kind of thing that goes in social media captions. "Never say *that* again, either. I'm imagining Gizmo from *Gremlins* now and I. Blame. You."

"Fine, fine, whatever you want. Keep me updated on the pet sitch, though? I'm still trying to convince Cade that we should get a corgi, so I'll be living vicariously through you for now."

"Done," Ves says with a grin.

"Anyway, the other reason I called," says Arun. "I know it's kind of late notice, but I had this idea for our first married Christmas together that we'd throw a super-sophisticated, aspirational dinner party. And, of course, it's not Christmas without our best friend! Next week. Do *not* try to get out of it, none of this third-wheel nonsense. You're coming and that's final. That way you can save me some shipping and collect the books yourself."

"You're holding my donations hostage?"

"I'm a good agent and even better friend," Arun says smugly. "Let's call it incentivizing my client."

Ves doesn't even need to think about it. "I'm there," he promises, and he hears the breath of relief all the way from Arun's home office.

"And definitely bring Elisha," says Arun. It's less of an ask and more of an edict. "You know," he continues, a smirk in his voice, "the girl you aren't falling for."

"We're not that kind of couple," Ves says distractedly.

He pauses in front of an antique shop window, gaze snagging on a vintage trinket jar. Amber glass with a metal top, polished to a brilliant gleam, and sporting a pretty finial.

But what captures him the most are the dozens of rusty old keys stuffed inside. The shop is closed for lunch, which isn't a problem, because there's something he needs to get first.

"Not the kind of couple who eat? Who socialize?"

"She has to work. This movie is really important to her. Production starts here in mid-January."

"I respect the work ethic, but don't count her out. This girl is something special. She's got you cooing over cats and bitching less and less about being away from the city. It's practically a Christmas miracle."

Ves inhales pine and snow and what smells like fresh bread baking in a nearby restaurant. His next exhale is pure patience. "It's nothing of the kind. I do not *coo* and I do not *bitch*."

Arun laughs. "Wrong and *so* wrong. Come on, man. You never date over the holidays, but now you're abandoning your golden rule for this one girl? I don't remember the last person you dated who lasted more than three months! How long is that feasible or are you waiting to exhaust every woman between eighteen and eighty?"

"Leave it, Arun."

"No, I won't. I know you'd probably prefer that I butt out," Arun says frankly. "But what kind of friend would I be if I let you miss out on having the kind of love you've wanted your whole life?"

"The kind with boundaries?"

"Ves." A frustrated exhale.

"Look, I hear you, but this is what you're not getting: the whole reason this even works is because Elisha and I are both in complete agreement that this is over when I leave. We're not making plans for the future, which is inevitably how this always goes wrong, and I'm sorry, but a double date with my married best friends definitely qualifies as a plan."

"But that's the best part," Arun says quietly. Every trace of his flippancy is wiped away, replaced by careful and considered words that reach straight through Ves's chest and target his heart. "Having someone to make those plans with. Whether that's running away for the weekend or just sitting down to go over the grocery list. Knowing that what you want and what they want are the same. Meeting that person who makes you forget that you ever even had a type."

Ves scowls. Arun is using his soothing agent voice now, like Ves is one of his clients who needs hand-holding to get through a hard truth. It's irritating and, more importantly, unnecessary.

"I get that you're keeping it casual," says Arun, "but how long are you going to be happy with that?"

"Not all of us want to get married by thirty," Ves reminds him.

Arun laughs. "*Please.* I'm not my mother, I'm not trying to marry people off. I just don't want you to be lonely. And the last couple of years, I know we haven't had as much time for each other—no, that's not fair. I know it's on me. More clients, more work, Cade, the wedding, it's all one giant black hole."

Well . . . yes. All true. But it's not like Ves has ever begrudged Arun his happiness.

"I'm not *lonely*," he says, like it's a bad word. He doesn't know the words are a lie until he catches sight of his reflection in the shop window, his words replaying on a loop in his mind. And he just knows. "And, uh, maybe don't call your loving husband the equivalent of a time suck?"

"Fuck. Yeah. You know what I meant, though." Arun curses under his breath. "Shoot, I gotta go. Cade and I are meeting some friends at Punjabi Grocery and Deli for samosa chaat."

"All right, have fun. Tell Cade I said hi."

"Only if *you* don't forget to tell Elisha she's invited! I'll text you the details. Send me more cat pics!"

Ves struggles with what to say, finally settling on "I will." If his tone is a bit off, Arun is too rushed to notice, and Ves is grateful for it.

After hanging up, he glances one more time at the keys crammed into the jar before walking on, eager for the warmth of his house, his reheated leftovers, and to check that the cats haven't chewed his laptop cord. But as he makes his way down Main Street, he's no longer thinking about any of it.

He imagines a music box and a *maybe, just maybe* long shot paying off. He imagines New York City and Elisha in it. He imagines a Christmas with a girl he likes and the friends he loves, and he smiles.

CHAPTER THIRTY-THREE

Ves

Ves returns to the antique shop later, having knocked more things off his to-do list around the house, and waits at the register for the owner. The old man is currently helping a customer take down several ornamental picture frames from the wall in what's clearly a huge purchase. Ves sighs, drumming his fingers against the counter.

While he waits, he reads the latest text from Elisha. She's been coming over every day after work, but still, it's hard not to be disappointed that she's busy tonight.

Elisha: Spending the evening with Solana and Adam, join us at the Christmas Market later for wassail and shopping if you want! It's open until 10 p.m. and we'll be there until close! Might need to borrow your 🧤 if I get cold 😀

He snorts and taps at the screen with his thumbs.

Ves: Hilarious.

Elisha: Pfft. You know I look good in red.

Ves: You look good in everything.

Fuck! Why did he send that?

Elisha: Including your sheets? 😉

His heart trips over itself and he stiffens in more ways than one.

Ves: Are you flirting with me?

Elisha: Clearly I need to be less subtle about it . . .

"Can I help you, young man?"

Caught by surprise, Ves nearly drops his phone. The owner slowly ambles over, eyeing the trinket jar and music box on the counter in front of Ves. He points and says, "Don't think that's one of ours, but the glass is ten dollars. I can dump the junk out for you."

"I'm actually more interested in the keys," says Ves.

"The keys?" The man's wiry white eyebrows bunch together. "They're just odds and ends. Worthless. Don't fit into anything, that's why they ended up here."

But if even one of them fits, it'll be worth it. "I brought my own music box," says Ves. "The original key was lost a long time ago, but I was hoping to check and see whether any of these would work. I'm happy to buy the lot. And the jar."

The old man keeps staring. "You're Maeve's boy, aren't you?"

"Erm. Her great-nephew, yes."

"I'm Jimmy. Remember you from when you were a kid. Quietest little boy I ever saw, but you sure did love your chocolate." The man laughs, smacking his own barrel chest with his hand. "No family of Maeve's is going to pay me to try a few keys. Here, take this stool. Sit down, you won't break it. That's fine Pennsylvania Dutch crafts-manship, that is. You go on and try those keys, see if they sing for you."

Ves attempts to protest, but the man tugs at him until he finally relents and takes the offered seat. "Thank you," he says, a little em-barrassed but nonetheless grateful.

Jimmy grunts. "What's so important about getting in there, anyway?"

Ves tests the first key, which looks a bit too small, but looks can be deceiving so he's intent on trying it anyway. "Maeve left this to someone. I don't want to give something without a way to open it."

"Seems like a lot of trouble," says Jimmy, looking dubiously at the three keys Ves has already discarded. "I've got some more lying all over the shop. Want me to grab them for you?"

"If it wouldn't be any trouble."

Jimmy hoots. "Of course it's trouble, but I'm keen to see how this goes now."

It takes three hours and Jimmy keeping the antique shop open ten minutes past its seven p.m. closing, but somewhere after a few hundred keys, they hear it. The tiny click of sweet, sweet success.

Jimmy gasps even louder than Ves, fully invested in their quest. Ves's hands reek of metal, his fingers are stiffer than they are after pulling an all-nighter to meet a writing deadline, and he hasn't been able to feel his ass for the last hour.

But it's worth it when the lid opens to reveal the box's secrets: a small, chipped ballerina, velvet-lined compartments filled with brooches and costume jewelry, and a yellow Post-it on the mirror that reads *For Elisha Rowe* in faded ballpoint. Jimmy gasps again when he recognizes the name.

"Thank you, sir," says Ves, standing to shake the man's hand. "I couldn't have done this without your help." His shoulders ache and his behind is still numb, but they fade to nil compared to the joy blooming in his chest. Likely, the value of the contents is purely sentimental rather than monetary, but he suspects that unlike his father, Elisha won't mind. He'd rather Maeve's jewelry go to her than anyone else.

"You sweet on the Rowe girl?" asks Jimmy, a hint of awe in his voice.

How does he answer that? "We're seeing each other," says Ves. "She's helping me with the house."

"Yup, Marcy and Dave told me about that. Still selling up?"

"That's the plan," Ves says absently, studying the box. It's deeper than it looks, hiding at least one more compartment level than he guessed. He works his thumb into a corner to pull it up.

"Holy shit," says Jimmy, getting the first look. With reverence, he says, "That's from *Sleighbells*."

Everything comes to a standstill. Heather Frederick's pearls are nestled snugly into the velvet bottom.

Why—*how?*—does Maeve have this?

CHAPTER THIRTY-FOUR

Elisha

"You shouldn't have given me your scarf," Elisha chides after work the next day upon hearing what feels like Ves's hundredth sniffle. "I wasn't even that cold." They're on Maeve's old-fashioned floral sofa, which Ves has covered in gray wool throws in an attempt to make it cozier and less, well, hideous. Thor and Thorin scamper between table legs, enjoying all the extra space that leaves them plenty of room to play.

"Wanted people to see you in it," he mumbles from behind a Kleenex.

Those darn hibernating butterflies make a reappearance. Clearing her throat brusquely, she moves on. "It was fun having someone to wander around with me at the Christmas Market last night. I usually hang with Solana and Adam, but it sucks being the third wheel. Especially when it's all couples and families browsing and it's just a reminder that . . ." She shakes her head, scooching closer to him. "Anyway. I just wish you hadn't gotten a cold because of me."

Another sniffle. "If it makes you feel any better, it wasn't because of the chill."

"No?" She lays her head on his arm, lets her fingers dance up and down his forearm. He's a little resistant at first, like he isn't sure what she's doing or how to respond, but when she keeps doing it, he relaxes into her touch.

"It's all the dust," he says. His arm wraps around her, lightly at first, and then, when she burrows closer, he squeezes her to his side.

She laughs. "What dust? We've cleaned this place spotless."

It's true, all the junk is gone. The small-town gossip grapevine worked for good: some of the aged décor has gone to thrift shops or friends, thanks to Marcy spreading the word that Ves wanted to make sure that all of Maeve's friends had a little sentimental something to remember her by.

Most of the movie paraphernalia that was still in the house will grace the theater museum, enough for another couple of exhibits, much to the Preservation Society's delight. The paperwork has all been organized or shredded, as needed. The well-loved romance novels have been donated to the Piney Peaks Friends of the Public Library book sale, and the three rare books are in the window of the local used bookshop, the proceeds given to the church's soup kitchen. There's nothing left to do except wait for the film crew and valuation experts. Her heart pinches, but it's not like she didn't know this would happen.

He shakes his head. "Not dust from here. I was at one of the antique shops on Main Street before meeting you last night. Damn, I would have preferred to not be a congested mess when I gave this to you," Ves says ruefully. "But take a look at the jewelry box."

"What?" Elisha follows the direction of his gaze. The box is placed on the nearest end table, the wood gleaming under the light of the lamp. On top of it is a brass key, such a tiny, nondescript thing that at first she mistakes it for being part of the lid. Her eyes light up. "Oh my gosh! Where did you find it?" She scrambles to reach it, bringing both back with her. "Wait, this . . ." Her brow furrows. "This isn't how I remember it. I know it's been forever, but I'm pretty sure it was silver."

But it fits in the lock nonetheless.

Elisha runs her fingers gently over the treasures inside. "I remember Maeve wearing all of these," she says. She pries the top layer off, almost dropping it in shock when she sees what's below. "Oh my god, Ves! Did you—" She catches the soft look on his face. "Did you know this necklace was there? How did you find the key?" Bewildered, she waits for answers.

"I'm as surprised as you. I tried every single key the antique shop had. When one actually worked and revealed the pearl necklace at the bottom . . ." He trails off. "Didn't Maeve tell you it was the *Sleighbells* necklace and that she left it to you?"

She blinks. "The real necklace?"

"In her will, she said she left the jewelry box and all its contents to the one person she knew would appreciate them: you. I didn't want to say anything until we could get it open without destruction," he admits. "I thought you wouldn't want to smash the box."

Her eyes grow misty. "You thought right. Thank you, Ves." She takes a moment to collect herself, taking a ragged inhale as her fingers reverently run over the smooth, glossy pearls. "Maeve never said a word." She holds the necklace in trembling fingers, vision blurry with tears. "Everyone just assumed Heather Frederick had kept it, but she never wore it in public again and she was always so cagey about things she took from the set."

Holding a part of her favorite movie—of her town's history—in her hands is amazing enough, but what means more to her is the effort Ves went to for this to even be possible.

Carefully, she replaces the necklace and lifts her eyes to his. "You did all this for me?"

He nods. "And as far as the key being different, you're right. Look at the grooves and notches. There, do you see? It's a generic shape. I bet a lot of accessories would open with this kind of key. Probably how Maeve jimmied it to add the Post-it."

Elisha's mouth drops. "You mean there's a chance I could have just used one of my old diary keys all this time and it would have worked?"

His lips tic upward. "You kept a diary?"

"Uhhhhh," she hedges. "It was a way to track movies I watched."

"And that needed a lock?" He grins. "Exactly what kind of X-rated movies were you watching, Elisha?"

Hearing the way his voice goes deep and teasing, every cognizant thought in her brain turns to static. She imagines the warm press of his body, the way her back will arch off the mattress, how her snowman nails will rake his back. He must catch some micro expression of lust on her face, because he leans in.

She mirrors his move, breath hitching.

"I'm sick," he reminds her. Still in that same goddamn sexy register.

"I know." Reluctantly, she pulls back and gives him a sheepish smile. "Sorry."

"Don't be." His voice is rough. "I'll be better tomorrow and then I'll want that kiss."

She grins at his confidence. "How about I give you something else that won't involve our mouths meeting?"

His eyebrows raise.

"Not like *that*. I meant I'll tell you a secret." Somehow, he manages to look both disappointed and intrigued, and she can't help but laugh. "You wanted to know why I don't bundle up like a marshmallow, right?" At his eager nod, she continues, "The answer is going to be so anticlimactic, but here it goes."

He links their hands, drags their joined fingers to his lap. "I don't care. I want to know everything about you, Elisha."

"When I was little, I used to get sick all the time in winter. Ear infections and colds like clockwork. Even with all the flu shots and everything. So my mom would make me wear thermal layers and puffy jackets and earmuffs *everywhere*, even those trapper hats with furry earflaps. Think of the puffiest jacket imaginable, then multiply it by three. And don't get me started on those gloves with so much padding that I could barely move. My parents wouldn't even *hear* of fingerless gloves."

He makes a sympathetic face.

"It felt like wearing those school-spirit foam fingers. I eventually grew out of it and stopped falling routinely unwell when I was like, nineteen? But it's hard to forget how uncomfortable it was and the way I could never dress cute like the other girls. It's why I hate being stifled with heavy coats now." She grins. "Your scarf is the exception, though. It doesn't constrain me. It makes me feel . . ."

Safe. Protected. Yours.

Elisha strangles the impulse to say any of that. She clears her throat. "Warm."

"I'll always loan you my scarf if you need it," says Ves. He smiles crookedly, although she's unsure whether it's due to her explanation or the DayQuil. "Even if you don't need it. You look cute in my clothes."

Okay, those butterflies are in full freaking flight now. She resolves to ransack his drawers later, borrow his softest shirts and maybe sneak a pair of his boxers to wear to bed. That impulse could be the DayQuil talking, too.

"I'm sorry my secret isn't very exciting," Elisha murmurs, bringing his wrist up to her lips to press a soft kiss against his pulse. "Pretty anticlimactic, huh?"

Ves's inhale rattles, and she flatters herself that it has more to do with her touch than his sickness.

When he speaks, his voice is rough. "For the record, nothing you could ever tell me about yourself could be anticlimactic. I will take any random crap info about you. You can tell me that your favorite color is pink and your favorite food is Italian and your favorite hobbit is Samwise, and I promise you that I will be fucking fascinated because it's you."

She snuggles closer, needing to feel the warm, solid feel of him. If he weren't sick, she would be climbing him like a pine tree. "Oh yeah?"

"Yeah." His voice is soft, wistful, like he really wishes he could kiss her right now after all. His palm skates up her jawline, caresses her cheek, all to finally tuck her hair behind her ear.

"Lavender. Thai. Pippin."

"What?"

"Favorite color, food, hobbit."

He laughs under his breath. "That last one doesn't surprise me one bit."

She turns her face just enough to drop another kiss on his wrist. "Tell me yours now."

He looks bemused. "My what?"

"Why you don't date over the holidays."

The happiness in his eyes promptly extinguishes. He looks in the other direction. "Oh, that."

"Hey." She cups his chin, draws him sweetly to her. "You don't have to."

Suddenly, she wishes she could take her question back. Does she really need to know? It doesn't matter in the end, does it? After all, the one thing he doesn't do, he's doing it now with her. She's the exception, not the rule.

"The holidays have never exactly been . . . easy for me," he says finally. "It started because of my parents. Mom wanted to do all the family Christmas traditions we'd always done, and Dad, well, he just didn't want to be part of the family anymore. It was different when I came here. And I don't just mean Christmas was better that year. Maeve made *everything* better. I wanted to stay here forever."

He bites his lip. "When I went back home, I found out my parents had decided to send me to boarding school. I didn't want to go, but they were suddenly fighting less so I thought if I did as they wanted, we'd be a family again."

His eyes shutter, and Elisha hates so much that it's because of her nosiness. Silently, she squeezes his hand. It can mean whatever he wants it to mean: the strength to continue the story or the space to say nothing.

Eventually he says, "But that's not what happened. And by the time I realized it, they were already living separate lives. Even though we lived in the same city, I saw Arun's parents more than mine. They welcomed me into their family. He was in my year at school, so I spent most holidays with them, even the ones I didn't celebrate. I even asked my mom if I could go live with Maeve, but she got pissed at me, and by then, I was practically one of the Iyers, so I stopped asking."

Elisha's heart squeezes. If Ves's mother had said yes, Elisha would have grown up with him. Played street hockey with the other kids in the cul-de-sac, snuck out of the house as moody teenagers. God, she would probably have had the biggest crush on him. The thought makes her insides squirm.

"This sounds incredibly weird," says Ves. "But I don't think I've ever had a traditional Christmas with both my parents since I was six, and I can barely remember it. And inevitably, when you're dating someone, they want to know about your parents. Sometimes it's even first-date material, just to make sure you're both on the same page about family values."

Here he pauses, pain flitting across his face, a reminder of a re-opened wound. "But if you're really, really unlucky," he says softly, "someone will invite you home for Christmas and their family will grill the shit out of you. Then, they can't or won't wrap their head around your dysfunctional upbringing, because they don't want to accept that this is just how some families are. This is how both my parents *choose* to be, and nothing will ever change them.

"But the women I've dated always think there's *hope*. That maybe *they* can bring my family back together. They think if they meet my parents, we can clear it all up in one conversation, like my feelings and memories were just one big misunderstanding. But this is real life." His laugh is bitter. "You don't always get a happy ending, not even at Christmas."

The way they've been raised is so different. Elisha doesn't know what to say, except that, yeah, he's right. The Hollinses might be capable of change, but for that, Karl and Adeline have to actually want it. And maybe Ves is right that this is the way they'll always be. It's sad, sure, but it's naïve of anyone to think that they can meddle and magically fix things just because *they* selfishly want to try.

"Sorry you asked?" Ves asks.

"A little," she admits. "Mostly I just . . . is it okay to say that I hate your parents? Or strongly dislike, if that's too harsh a word."

"I don't particularly like them, either, so." He shrugs. "Go for it."

She waits for him to follow it up with something like *I don't like them, but I love them*, but he doesn't. "So, what would you be doing right now if you weren't here?" she asks. He still hasn't let go of her hand in his lap, so she wraps her other arm around his shoulder and into his hair, teasing the fine strands at his nape, enjoying the feel of his soft blond hair against the pads of her fingers.

"Right now? This time of year, I'd be . . . hmm." His voice goes a little sleepy, and she likes to think it's from her tenderly stroking his neck instead of nostalgia for his city routine. "I'd have a full belly from Katz's Delicatessen. Walking it off. Probably stopping at my favorite street vendor for hot chocolate. Maybe a museum or a bookshop. See a show later. I watch *The Nutcracker* every year."

The things he's mentioning sound nice, and she's not one to knock anyone's traditions, but . . .

"Do you put up a tree?" she asks.

"We have one in the lobby of my building."

She's bemused. "But that's not the same as your own tree."

"I don't think a lot of New Yorkers go around cutting down ten-foot-tall evergreens. Especially not ones who don't have an elevator."

"Okay, as admittedly charming as it looks in movies, I don't like using real trees." Ves instantly gives her a disbelieving look. "Hear me out! I know it may seem counterintuitive because they're plastic, but they can be reused year after year. Sustainable! And real trees drop sap and needles, so mess. And people are so picky about height and bald patches that so many trees just get chopped down into mulch after Christmas Day." She makes a face. "Think about all the small woodland creatures who make their home in those trees."

"You're a regular Snow White, aren't you?"

"No. I don't like birds. They're creepy. Same goes for squirrels."

He laughs out loud.

"Would you maybe want to put up a tree here? And decorations? I'm sure Damian won't mind a bit more cheer; in fact, he'll probably *want* to get a feel for the place while he's here. I think there's a box around here somewhere with all Maeve's holiday stuff." She definitely remembers sweeping out all the autumn stuff from the hutch in the kitchen.

"Uh, you do remember we're cleaning the mess out, not putting it back in, right?"

"Yes!" She pulls her hand free from his to lightly swat his thigh. "Decorations are not *mess*."

He reclaims her hand. "Politely disagree."

"Okay, forget all the bric-a-brac and the Santa cushions and the little LED Christmas houses. What about just a tree? We can keep it simple. Lights, ornaments, tinsel, nothing over the top. Like your wreath! Super tasteful! Come on, don't tell me you're not a little excited? We can do it however you want!"

"Our traditions . . . weren't like that. My mom hired someone to decorate. Christmas was always a 'look, don't touch' holiday in our house. I've never decorated for the holidays before."

Her energy goes down a notch. She gets the feeling he never put out cookies and milk on Christmas Eve, either. Karl and Adeline don't sound like the kind of people who would humor their son that way. "I'll be your first," she says with a wink, trying to get the levity back. "I promise I'll be gentle."

"I'll only have to take it down again before I leave. Or maybe Damian will want to decorate the inside to match the original movie. It's pointless effort."

"I'll help put it up and take it down!" A wily thought pops into her mind. "Plus, it'll look great in pictures when you put the house up for sale! Really charming and inviting. One of the other houses down the street had multiple offers last year because of how cozy it looked. The couple wanted to move in right away because they could see themselves raising a family here. *And* we—you—get to enjoy it in the meantime."

A slow frown spreads over his face. "Multiple offers during Christmas? But Solana said—" He breaks off, furrows deepening.

She blinks at him. Is that so surprising? It's a desirable area to live, after all, and proximity to the Christmas House has only increased house values.

Before he can say another word, she plows on. "I'll make us a pot of Maeve's hot chocolate and whip up a big batch of popcorn. Salty and buttery, mmmmm. Oh, and I bet *Sleighbells* is on TV!" In fact, she knows it is. "We can make you your own traditions."

He looks into her eyes. "You said *we*. So they're *our* traditions."

"Well—" She hesitates, then agrees. "You're right. Our traditions."

She tries not to think about the fact that they're not really traditions if he won't be here next December.

Why did he have to go and say that? Making her want things. She was just trying to cheer him up, show him that what he wants is within reach. Don't have traditions? Make them. Every beginning has to start somewhere, right?

With an expression that suggests he's found a lump of coal in his stocking, Ves sighs. "Fine."

It's halfhearted agreement with absolutely zero enthusiasm, but it's a win and she'll take it. Impulsively, Elisha kisses him on the cheek. He turns pink immediately, and in the spontaneity of the moment, she forgot he was sick. But what she doesn't forget is how soft his eyes look as she clambers off the sofa. "Are you well enough to help me carry the boxes down from the attic?"

"Probably not." He gets up anyway, giving her a melting smile. "Lead the way."

CHAPTER THIRTY-FIVE

Elisha

It's times like these that Elisha really regrets giving back her key to the Christmas House. She's been knocking on Ves's door for the last five minutes and she knows he's home. Where is he? He knows she always comes over after work, and this Friday is no exception. This time, instead of her knuckles, she uses her fists.

The door swings open, revealing a disheveled Ves. "Sorry, I was just in the middle of something."

Elisha runs her eyes up and down his body. "Oh?"

He gives her a look and steps aside to let her in. His rumpled appearance is a good one: damp blond hair combed back, ends just starting to curl; a white cotton tee and cozy gray sweatpants with the faintest dusting of . . . is that dust? No, it can't be. They've swept, swabbed, and vacuumed the house within an inch of its life. He swats at the white marks on his upper thighs and knees, but it only rubs them in further.

She doesn't even get a moment to bask in the charm of yesterday's decorating spree—Christmas tree all lit up and the thick green garland draped over the fireplace mantel, trimmed with rustic pine cones, red ball ornaments, and gold berries—before she smells it. "Um, Ves, what's burning?"

"Nothing," he says quickly.

She gives him a doubtful harrumph and sets straight for the kitchen. Resting on the counter is an aluminum-lined tray with a dozen charred discs that maybe, in another life, could have been called cookies. "Please don't tell me you're entering the Winter Festival cookie exchange with these."

"Hell no, just trying something new. It's not as bad as it tastes," he says with an embarrassed laugh.

She picks one up and contemplates eating it. "You mean it's not as bad as it looks?"

Ves points to a cookie that's been nibbled at the edges. "Uh. No, it's definitely as bad as it looks. But just know that it tastes even worse."

She promptly drops it. "If you wanted to sate your sweet tooth, you should have dropped by the Chocolate Mouse." She tries not to think about another appetite that hasn't quite been sated.

He might be doing the same, because he's staring at his ruined cookies with a look of abject fascination. "Yeah, I know. I just wanted to try my hand at it."

"Shame," says Elisha, picking one up and letting it *thunk* down with a wince. "These hallongrotta could have been really good if they're anything like the ones Maeve used to make."

"Hallongrotta?"

The confusion in his voice surprises her. "Yeah, these cookies. They're Swedish butter cookies with a raspberry jam center, right?"

"I've always just thought of them as thumbprint cookies. I remembered she made them with me when I was here. I pressed my thumb in each one and she filled it with the jam. Do you think they were a family recipe or something? My mom didn't know what I was talking about when I tried to describe it to her. So I just assumed she didn't know because Maeve was Dad's aunt, not hers."

"Maybe? I think she learned this from her grandmother? She said she was Bulgarian and Swedish on her mother's side and German on her father's." Elisha laughs. "Maeve was always trying out new recipes to get in touch with her roots. We loved her schnitzel but drew the line at blood sausage."

He looks like he's repressing a shudder. "Thankfully my memories aren't as gruesome. I'll go with cookies any day."

"Oh, she made these for us, too! They were always a hit at the Christmas cookie exchange." Suddenly, it occurs to her. "Wait, are you sure you didn't get conned into joining this year? I mean, I know Marcy can be wily, but surely even she wouldn't think these were fit for public consumption."

Patches of red flare in his pale cheeks and she immediately feels shitty. He clears his throat. "No, I just wanted to bake. Truly."

She grins. "Getting in the Christmas spirit, are we?"

He snorts. "No. Believe me, I'd much rather buy than make. I'm not great with my hands."

"Um, beg to differ." She shoots him a wink before her gaze snags on something. "Oh, what's that? Making friends other than me already, huh?" His face turns tomato red, but he doesn't get there in time to stop her.

She snatches a card off the table. It's a fairly generic cream greeting card with a gold tree on it. She pops it open, thoroughly intending to roast him if it's from one of the old ladies on their street who she suspects fancy him just a little bit.

Instead, she reads this: *Dear Elisha, Anita, Jamie, & Dave, thank you for inviting me to dinner and making me feel so welcome in Piney Peaks.*

It's short and sweet. No flowery words or painterly phrases, for all that he's a writer. He's sparing with his words and always to the point, which is more impressive to her than all the lyrical prose in the world, because she knows he always means what he says.

She looks between the card in her hands and her mother's ceramic dish. The last time she saw it, Anita was piling leftovers into it for Ves to take home. The dish is clean now. "Wait, the cookies are for us?"

"Were," he corrects. "I wouldn't risk anyone's teeth with these. They're going straight into the trash."

"Do it after," she says, voice rough.

"After what?"

She drops the card on the counter and surges forward to kiss him. Even though her heart is all gooey, there's nothing soft about her kiss. It's a hungry gnashing of teeth and lips as they find their rhythm. Her hands delve deep into his hair, alternating between the scrunches that make him grunt and the tugs that make his hips buck against hers.

She breaks the kiss only long enough to hoist herself onto the counter. Ves makes a soft sound of concern, using the oven mitt to push the still-hot tray as far away from her as possible. "My hero," she whispers, circling her legs around his waist and pulling him flush against the counter.

He smooths her hair, not going in for her mouth right away, which baffles her. Instead, he cradles the back of her neck and smooths the flyaways around the crown of her head. What a strange preoccupation he has, making sure he can see her face at all times. She smiles despite the stab of impatience in her gut telling her to hurry the fuck up. There it is again, that needy whine slipping out of her throat before her teeth have the good sense to bite it back.

How does she want him so much? This isn't like her. She isn't the girl who jumps on counters and propositions men over lunch and tries to hit them with lawn ornaments, and yet . . . here she is, wet and panting in Ves Hollins's kitchen, guilty of all those things.

At least she hasn't made the biggest, most fatal mistake of them all, yet. Falling for a boy who already has one foot on his way out of town.

He must read some of the apprehension in her face, because his hand stills in her hair, looping around her back. He's not really touching her anymore, but she's still hyperaware of him. The pounding of his heart against her own, the heat of his skin so incandescent that it makes the blood in her veins froth. The longing in his eyes slides to something infinitely more serious. "Do you want me?"

"No, I'm kissing you out of sympathy," she says playfully. "Those cookies were really awful."

"Elisha."

She loves the way he says her name. Gritted between his teeth. He's exasperated, but now she wants to hear him say it like that while his cock is sheathed within her, like he's trying to restrain himself. As if he's delirious with pleasure at the feel of her muscles contracting around him.

Oh yes, she wants to hear what sounds he'll make then, whether her name will be whispered with benediction or growled as a curse. Maybe both. She hopes it's both. Of course she wants him. It's the easy answer, the one that will let her fuck him without wondering about tomorrows.

"I want you," she says, consenting clearly. "I want this."

"Good. I do, too." And then he whisks her off the counter.

"Ves!" she yelps, clamping her legs tighter around his waist. "What are you doing?"

He keeps walking. "Kitchen sex is unhygienic."

Her mouth drops open. "Because what we were doing was going to be so neat and tidy?"

He nips at her ear. "Bedroom."

She doesn't want to wait. She unwinds her legs and plants them firmly on the ground. "Here."

Ves looks around. "In the living room?"

"Why not?" There's a rug in front of the fireplace. It's got a nice, thick pile, and she knows it's soft, so it won't irritate her knees or back. "Grab a condom, will you?"

She shimmies out of her black leggings, hopping on one foot when the legs snag on her socks. In her peripheral vision, he looks utterly transfixed. Slack-jawed. Goosebumps prickle over her skin, following the path of his gaze. Elisha grins, plucking off her wool socks. Judging by the unabashed want on his face, Ves has been longing for her at least as long as she has for him.

Finally, she rips everything off except her bra and panties. They're plain white, nothing fancy, but his eyes still devour her like they're silk. Elisha gets on her knees and bends forward, her favorite position, and looks back at him over her shoulder with a quirked, expectant eyebrow. "Well? It's fucking cold, Ves. You coming or not?"

Before she finishes the sentence, he's already in motion. He pulls his tee over his head, revealing toned, lean muscles and mouthwatering hip bones with the faintest dusting of golden hair.

With a ragged inhale, she turns away. But not to give him privacy. Instead, she luxuriates in the soft sounds of clothing being removed, hurriedly folded, and then the swish of him as he approaches her from behind. The condom makes a soft crinkle as he tosses it on the rug next to her.

Ves seems to instinctively know what she wants, hands large and warm and roving as they stroke the soft skin of her stomach, the dip of her waist, the generous swell of her hips. She holds her breath as his fingertips, slightly rough, skim the waistband of her panties. He doesn't go further, and she lets him know exactly how she feels about *that* by leaning against his chest, soundlessly asking for more of his touch.

He laughs at her impatience and plants kisses in the crook of her neck. Elisha closes her eyes, lets her head tip back to give him better access. He sweeps aside her hair to drop a flurry of ticklish little pecks. Even though she's not touching him—yet—his body subtly shivers at her back.

"Ves," she says, but it comes out like a plea.

He doesn't make her wait. With one arm slung under her breasts, pulling her to him, the other is free to snake past her rounded hips and push aside her underwear. She gasps when his fingers find her center, parting her enough to find her slick with desire.

With a hoarse groan, she rocks her hips, wanting the soaked panties off so he can move freely. But Ves seems completely unbothered by the fabric's frustrating texture against her pulsing nerves. Instead, he seems content to work one finger inside her, then another, rotating his wrist to draw a strangled cry from her as his thumb hits her clit. At the sound, his hardness swells against her ass.

He keeps an irregular rhythm of tight circles and coaxing thrusts and teasing strokes until she's grinding against his hand, panting and tossing her head. Her upper chest is a blotchy red and her thighs tremble as she tries to chase her pleasure, but he seems to know exactly when to switch it up, pulling her back from the edge just in time to start the cycle all over again. The delicious torture goes on for indeterminate minutes until finally, *finally*, he seems to think she's hit her breaking point.

"Come for me," he whispers, breath fanning against her cheek.

Body poised to snap, she does, gasping as her eyes squeeze shut.

Her orgasm hits her hard and fierce, and she rides it out on his fingers, sure that her underwear must be soaked. When it's over, she sags against him with a tired laugh.

He pulls his fingers from her to gently caress her upper arm with the side of his palm. "You okay, Elisha? Do you want to keep this position?" he asks.

"Yes and yes," she says, barely able to recognize that husky, hoarse voice as her own. "But after that, missionary. I want to see you."

"Those are my favorite, too." He kisses her neck again, mouth dragging wetly to her shoulder. Before her brain can catch up with reality, he's unclasping her bra, then slipping his hands between their bodies to start removing his own clothing.

She flings her bra away, followed by her underwear.

"I should have lit the fire," says Ves. "I don't want you to be cold."

Elisha loves how considerate he is of her comfort. "I won't be," she tells him. "You'll keep me plenty warm."

He hums agreement under his breath, then places his palm at the small of her back in silent request. She obliges, dropping to the rug. Using her forearms to prop herself up, she only has to wait for a moment, listening to the condom wrapper tearing open, before his hands find her waist. His thumbs, a little rough after the woodwork, rub soothing circles on her hot skin before they disappear as he takes himself in hand and lines himself up with her entrance. She wiggles her hips, opening her legs wider.

His first thrust is long and deep, and they both moan from the sheer pleasure of it. "Elisha," he groans, like he's barely holding it together.

She twists her head around to look at him, suddenly regretting that she could miss seeing his expression during their first time. His hair hangs in his face and his chest is glistening as it rapidly rises and falls, and when their eyes lock, she can tell that he's close.

Ves's thrusts are steady and firm at first, but after she clenches around him, he starts to piston in and out harder. His fingers dig into her hips, gripping her thighs so he can move deeper inside her. His release ramps up quickly, but before he comes apart, his hand works between their bodies again, so close to where they're joined, and pinches at her clit. With a raspy cry, she follows him over the edge.

He doesn't pull out right away, choosing to scatter kisses over her spine. Lower, lower, lower. Her breath catches, but he stops. His breathing is uneven when he finally collapses next to her. By this point, her arms have gone wobbly like Jell-O and there's no pretending that she has the strength left to move. So she slumps on the rug, rolling onto her back while she waits for her pulse to calm.

They lay together for a moment, listening to the faraway howls of wind outside and the faint trilling of Thor and Thorin somewhere in the house.

"You good?" she whispers.

Ves opens an arm to her and she wastes no time in cuddling into his side. He gives her a tired but satisfied grin. "I'm with you," he says simply. He kisses her forehead. "How could I not be?"

CHAPTER THIRTY-SIX

Ves

I n the end, Grandpa Dave was right about every inn in town being full right before the holidays, so when the weekend rolls around, Ves ends up across the street in the Rowes' guest bedroom, after all, Thor and Thorin in tow.

"Thanks again for putting me up," he says as Anita unnecessarily fluffs his pillow and double-checks that he has an extra quilt folded at the foot of the bed along with his towels.

"It's no trouble at all." Anita is gracious, even though he can tell his gratitude embarrasses her. "Now please stop. Once was more than enough!" She squeezes his shoulder before turning to leave.

"Thanks." He winces as it comes out automatically. "Sorry."

She gives him a soft, achingly maternal smile. "I'll let you get ready."

He and Elisha have been invited out to dinner tonight with Damian Rhys, who, somehow, managed to book two rooms for himself and his camera crew. He can only assume Damian's staying somewhere on the outskirts of town or maybe just flashed his money around to find accommodation. Downstairs, the soft mumbles of conversation trickle up to Ves, along with the mouthwatering aroma of Jamie's cooking.

He sets his laptop aside, document of book pitches abandoned, before changing into a thick cable-knit navy sweater, tugging out the white collar of the shirt underneath. As he pads across the carpet to open the door, he's relieved to find it doesn't creak like Maeve's, so he's able to slip out in total silence.

Elisha's room is opposite his and her door is wide open, offering him a tantalizing peek at her inner sanctum. Without stepping all the way in, he pokes his head through.

Her walls are dove gray, bed linen a pristine white and perfectly made. Her quilt is a pale shade of rose, matching the curtains, which are thrown wide open to let every bit of sunlight in. Even now, the last of the daylight spotlights her bed completely. He smiles, imagining her sprawled out like a cat.

"Wanted proof about the whereabouts of my teddy?"

He turns when he hears her teasing voice. "Maybe."

"I *told* you not to worry about what's on my bed," she retorts, taking a step closer until they're both standing on opposite sides of the doorway. Her fingers play with the pearls around her neck.

"How was your trip?" he asks, even though what he really wants to do is grab her and kiss her senseless. "I still can't believe your work ethic in agreeing to do this on a weekend."

"It was super cool that I got to take a little field trip a couple towns over and speak to their tourism office. They heard about what I'm trying to do here and they wanted to chat about how we could work together. Greg was Greg. He wasn't thrilled about local assets being 'let loose' for community outreach, but Danica was the one who arranged it." She rolls her eyes. "No one asked *him* to come, though. He naysayed the entire time and complained about giving up part of his Saturday."

"Fuck him. Once everyone sees Piney Peaks star in *Sleighbells* again, you'll be overrun with interest," says Ves.

She lights up. "You're that confident in this town?"

"I'm that confident in *you*," he corrects. He enjoys the way she ducks her head, hiding her pink cheeks from him but completely unaware of the way the color spreads to her upper chest. He wants to draw his tongue across her collarbone, see how far down the flush will go. See her wearing those pearls and nothing else.

She cocks her head. "You know, you ask me about my day more than any of my exes ever did."

"To be fair, you haven't had that many, have you?"

She laughs. "I don't want you to be fair. I want you to take the compliment."

"Consider it taken."

Their eyes meet. "I, um, just wanted to say something," says Elisha. "I know it's just for a night or two until Damian leaves, but I don't want to . . . do sexy shenanigans . . . in my parents' house."

"I want to stay respectful, too," says Ves, relieved they're both on the same page. This is one less thing to fret about. The last thing he wants to do is repay Anita and Jamie's kindness by having sex with their daughter while they sleep just a few doors down. "Wait, did you just say 'sexy shenanigans'?"

She scowls. "I expect some *disrespectful* things to happen the second he leaves, however. Like, the *very* second."

God, she's perfect. Sweet as buttercream but tough as his shitty cookies when she wants to be. "Agreed," he says.

"But." She tilts her face up to his. "Kissing is allowed."

He bends until their noses brush. "Noted." And then his lips descend on hers. He gives her kisses like flurries, soft and unhurried, wrapping an arm around her waist to glide his thumb under her shirt. She moans into his mouth, giving his tongue a quick, hard suck that makes his hips buck.

"Is inviting you to New York for a dinner party Arun is throwing also allowed?" he asks when they finally part for air.

"Ask me and you'll find out."

"Would you like to come to a party with me on December nineteenth, Elisha?"

She grins. "I would. My ex-boss from Atlanta is in the city and emailed me to meet up, anyway."

"Wanted to make me work for it first, though," he says wryly.

"Ves, if I wanted to make you work for it, I would have wrung way more concessions out of you first."

"Minx."

"You secretly enjoy it," Elisha says, undulating her hips against his.

"Only because I would happily give you whatever concessions you wanted. Even"—he leans closer—"sexy shenanigans."

She bites her lip. "Like what?"

"Like parting your soft thighs, crawling between them, and making you orgasm over and over until you couldn't take it anymore. Like what you taste like when you come undone. Just a flick of my tongue to make you tremble and quake all over again. Folds slick and dripping as I lap at you. Your sweetness glistening all over my face. What a pretty mess you'd make."

Elisha visibly swallows, brown eyes almost black with desire. He hears her breath hitch as she says, "I can't believe you said that to me right when I have to get ready for dinner with Damian."

Ves grins. "It'll give you something to look forward to."

CHAPTER THIRTY-SEVEN

Ves

R ight on time!" cries Damian when the pair arrive at Fireside at eight on the dot. He's got a Pierce Brosnan look going on, all tan and gray and svelte. He gets up to shake both their hands, and if he notices their lips are both a little swollen, he has the grace to ignore what they were doing mere minutes before their dinner reservation. His eyes catch on Elisha's neck for a moment before quickly sliding away.

Ves's chest tightens. It wasn't a lustful look or anything, but he wonders whether Damian thinks Elisha is available. Maybe he does this with all his movies, used to his star power getting him what he wants, even when he's three times a woman's age.

"It's surprisingly empty," says Elisha, glancing around almost as if she expects other customers to pop out from under the table.

"My doing, I'm afraid," says Damian. "I wanted to make sure we were alone tonight."

"Oh, I see." Elisha smiles at Ves. "Damian Rhys, this is—"

"Ves Hollins," the older man cuts in smoothly. "I read it on the location release agreement."

"It's good to meet you, Damian," says Ves, placing his hand very deliberately on the small of Elisha's back. "Let me take your jacket, love."

She lets him take it. With so many free pegs tonight, there's no reason for them to share one, so with some reluctance, Ves uses two.

A waitress comes out with a bottle of chilled champagne and a basket of bread rolls. If she finds the cleared-out restaurant strange and the presence of a Hollywood director surreal, she doesn't show it.

"So, Ves, you have the same last name as Maeve Hollins?" Damian asks the moment they're alone again. "I admit, part of asking you both to dinner is because I was . . . curious . . . about your relation to her."

"I'm her great-nephew."

Damian's voice sharpens. "Karl's son?"

Ves's lips part. "Y-yes. How did you—"

Damian interrupts with an abrupt "Is she here? Does she live with you?"

"Who, Maeve?" Ves is having trouble keeping up. How does Damian know who he is and not that the woman he's asking about is dead?

"I swung by the Christmas House earlier but no one answered." Damian rakes his hand through his hair, appearing to be in some agitation. His eyes flick to Elisha. "I'd like to see her before I leave."

She places her hand on Ves's thigh. It instantly reassures him. "Damian," she says, "I'm so sorry if I'm misunderstanding, but exactly how well did you know Maeve?"

At once, Ves can see the qualities that make her a good film liaison. Cool head in a crisis. Concise questions that get right to the heart of things. Professional demeanor that puts people at their ease.

"Well, yes." Damian picks at the collar of his white dress shirt like he'd rather rip it off, be anywhere other than here, having this conversation. Ves can relate. "Since we did the original movie together all those years ago, I thought it would be nice to bring this full circle. Christmastime, the house, the town . . ." He frowns. "She's not still mad at me, is she?"

"You knew her from *Sleighbells*?" Ves blurts out.

"I was one of the producer's assistants," Damian says tersely. "And the only one who knew how much she did for the movie."

Elisha leans in, the V-neck of her red dress dipping dangerously into cleavage. This time, Damian doesn't even seem to notice. "What do you mean?" she asks, catching Ves's eye long enough to exchange a *WTF?* look.

Damian makes an impatient sound, affection and frustration battling in his voice. "Maeve became close with all of the cast and crew, but especially with Heather and as time went on . . . Nathan, too, who was a known flirt. There was a lot of gossip on set at the time, everyone assuming Maeve and Nathan were an item. But it wasn't true. They encouraged the gossip and played their close friendship up only to hide the real story—the fact that both the leads were having an affair, Heather gifted the necklace to Maeve in thanks."

Elisha gasps. "Wait, Nathan and Heather?"

"Back then, Heather was still married. Maeve believed in true love but she also knew that in those days, a scandal that huge would have ruined everyone's reputation and maybe even torpedoed the movie. The studio ran a tight ship and no one wanted Hollywood's golden girl accused of adultery, even if nobody liked that lout of a husband of hers. So my Maeve stepped in to help. She cared more about Heather's career than the bad publicity. Of course, the multiple affairs and drinking eventually did that anyway." Damian shakes his head. "What a waste."

Ves's throat constricts, taken aback at this unknown chapter of his great-aunt's life. So Maeve's supposed love affair wasn't with Nathan, after all. He glances at Elisha to see how she's taking it. Fascination, devastation, and fresh seams of grief rip over her face. "How do you know any of this?" he asks.

"Because she was *my* sweetheart. She was a few years older than me, but it didn't matter to us," Damian says simply. His gaze fastens on Elisha's necklace, eyes growing misty. "Now will one of you please tell me how I can reach her?"

Their champagne sits untouched as Elisha breaks the news.

Damian stoically looks away, showing them his profile and the one solitary tear that he allows to escape. He doesn't sob. Just makes this awful noise. It's guttural and raw, an involuntary reaction to gut-wrenching news, even when delivered as gently as it can be.

"She left the house to you." Damian states it as a fact, looking at Ves for the first time in minutes. His eyes are bleak, and the face that Ves thought handsome just a few minutes ago now looks ravaged. "I just assumed she was still—And then when I saw the signature on the paperwork, I wondered why it wasn't her name. Whether she might have married, had a son . . . When I saw your name, I assumed you might have been that son."

Damian's laugh is forced and harsh as he tears his gaze away from Ves to crumple the cloth napkin in his fist. "So I decided to come down here for the pre-production shots myself, see Maeve. But now . . . Well, we're here, anyway, and my team can wrap this quickly. We should be out of your hair in a couple of days, Ves. I'm sorry to have inconvenienced you."

"That's fine," Ves replies, trying not to drum his foot on the floor. "Whatever you need."

Damian's smile doesn't reach his eyes.

"Do you want to give dinner a rain check?" asks Elisha. "I can't imagine how much of a shock this is after driving down here expecting to see her."

"Teaches me to call first, huh?"

Ves forces his lips to form the facsimile of a smile.

Damian opens his menu, all business again with a stoic set to his face. "We're here, may as well eat. There's just one thing. Ves, do you plan to keep the house?"

"Well, I hadn't intended to," says Ves. "I live in New York."

"But the two of you are together?"

Ves glances at Elisha, feeling horribly put on the spot.

"Only until he leaves," she says finally.

"Sounds like me and Maeve. She couldn't leave, I didn't want to stay." Damian loses himself in thought for a moment before coming back to himself. "The prerogative of youth, I suppose." He gives Ves a speculative look. "So, it would appear you're in need of a buyer. I'd like to make you an offer. Some of the best moments in my life were in that house, with Maeve, and I don't think I could bear for new owners to move in and make changes. Not so soon."

And then in the next breath Damian quotes a price so extraordinarily high, well over market value, that Ves is sure his eyes bug out. Elisha's certainly do.

"I don't know what to say," says Ves.

"Say you'll sell."

CHAPTER THIRTY-EIGHT

Ves

On Monday morning when Damian leaves, pre-production photography all wrapped, Ves goes back home. It's strange, but until the moment he shook Damian's hand and promised to sell it to him, the Christmas House didn't feel like home.

As he crosses the threshold now, it does. The sense of belonging sinks into his bones as soon as he's through the door and his overnight bag thumps to the hardwood floor. So does the hard pit in his stomach that makes him think he's made a dreadful mistake in selling what's become *his* to someone else.

"Hey, don't dawdle!" Elisha scuttles through the door behind him. "Did you forget you promised to come to the Chocolate Mouse today for the cookie decorating workshop? This is one of my favorite Winter Festival activities!"

"I think we've established that I'm a hazard in the kitchen," he says dryly.

"Oh, I don't know about that." She winks. "We achieved some pretty good results last time."

He laughs and puts an arm around her. "I guess that's true. Do we have time for some more of those 'good results' before the workshop? The one I don't remember signing up for?"

She has the grace to look sheepish. "Grandpa Dave strikes again. You know he considers you family when he starts volunteering you to do things at the emporium."

Like I'm another of the man's grandkids, Ves thinks, pleasantly surprised at the fondness that sweeps through him. Maybe a few weeks ago the meddling would have bugged him. No, no maybe about it. The intrusion of a perfect stranger, however well intentioned, would have grated like sandpaper. But now, it just makes him feel a sense of belonging to this place, these people.

As it turns out, when Ves and Elisha arrive at the Chocolate Mouse, their presence seems surplus. It's a full house, with cookie-making stations set up across the shop floor. All the decorations from the holiday party are still up—snowy clumps, shiny ornaments gleaming reflections back at them, tinsel and string lights strewn everywhere—lending to the impression that they're contestants on a fancy holiday baking show.

Momentarily mesmerized, Ves tunes back just in time to catch the end of Elisha's conversation with her grandfather. "Nonsense," Dave insists, "I've saved you a spot and you're here now. Come on, get those coats off and stand at your station."

"But Grandpa, you said you only needed us to make up numbers if there weren't enough sign-ups and there are, just take a look around, oh my god even *Bentley's* here—"

"You can't let Ves down! Look at him, he's so excited."

He is? Ves blinks when Dave gestures at him with a pastry bag filled with a hideous green icing.

Elisha sighs. "Fine, but we're not going to have fun." She casts an irritated look over at her ex-fiancé. "Especially since the only station left is right next to his."

"The early bird gets the cookie," says Dave.

"Not how the saying goes, but *fine*." Elisha grabs Ves's arm and leads him to their station. Pre-made shortbread cookies in the shape of boxy sweaters are already laid out, along with several icing bags and edible decorations to make buttons and patterns.

"Hi, Elisha," says a woman who must be Bentley's wife. She's pretty, with a genuine smile and excitement in her face as she picks up a dish of snowflake sprinkles. "These are so cute. You're so lucky to have this place year-round. My parents put all the decorations up the day after Thanksgiving and take them down right after New Year's. If it were up to me, I'd at least have the lights up every day of the year."

"Thankfully for our electricity bill, it's not up to Victoria," says Bentley. He's the only one to laugh.

When his wife flushes with embarrassment, Elisha says, "I know exactly what you mean, Tori. This is my favorite place in the entire world, except maybe for my grandparents' beach home in Goa. Whenever you need a dose of Christmas injected straight in your veins, stop by. Mom runs an awesome candle-making class in January, and we do a Cowboy Christmas during summer, which is always a great excuse to dig out the boots and fringe." She grins. "It's so extra, but I love it. I can give you the details, if you want?"

Tori's enthusiasm, for some reason, makes Bentley bristle. Ves studies the other man under the guise of familiarizing himself with everything on their station. Why did they even move to this town if *Ben* isn't keen to throw himself into local activities? The way Bentley's eyes dart to Elisha with an odd frown of disappointment confirms Ves's suspicion that he's still trying to get some kind of reaction out of her. Jealousy, maybe. Does he want her to be a bitch to Tori or something? The opposite is happening here.

Elisha and Tori chat about upcoming events until Dave takes

center stage to walk them through the best tips and flavor combinations for their cookie decoration.

"And don't forget!" he says with the biggest of grins. "As a couple, you must make at least one Ugly Christmas Sweater cookie to enter the contest! This is one of our most popular Winter Festival activities, and the prize is a doozy! Winners get their choice of their very own solid chocolate mouse! Brain fillings range from sweet to salty to plain disgusting." He winks.

"He's talking about the bubble gum flavor," Elisha whispers in Ves's ear. "I actually designed it to look like a veiny brain, but it has the consistency of a Tootsie Roll. The kids love it, but uh, it didn't go over super well with the grown-ups."

"Ellie's always been a kid at heart. Christmas year-round at the emporium, this obsession with *Sleighbells* . . ." Bentley chuckles like he finds it ridiculous, shaking his head at the pastry bag Tori offers him. He even goes so far as to cross his arms like he doesn't want to be here and is definitely not planning on participating. "It's cute how she never sees things how they really are, but how she wants them to be."

"You mean like when I was too naïve to realize you were never going to move here?"

The words fly out of Elisha so fast that Ves doubts she meant to do it.

"What?" Tori looks between her husband and his ex. Finally, she turns to Elisha. "He's never going to give me a straight answer, so I hope you will. I know you two dated, but he planned to move here for you?"

"That's debatable, actually," Elisha says at the same moment Bentley snaps, "I did mean it at the time!"

Elisha's glare softens when she looks at Tori. "I'm sorry, I didn't mean for it to come out like that. I really don't want to rehash the past, but it's hard when it's walking and talking right in front of me." She waves a disgusted hand in Bentley's direction. "We had plans to live here together after we graduated, but he got a better job offer, so he took it and didn't tell me until I was already back in town."

"Ellie, this is exactly what I meant when I said you live in a fantasy world," Bentley says, condescension dripping from every word. "Did you really think this place would be enough for me?"

Tori's mouth drops in obvious outrage. "Excuse me? I grew up around this area."

"I didn't mean it like—" Bentley massages his forehead.

"So why did we move back here?" Tori demands. "If it's so *beneath* you."

At this, a few people around them glance over.

Ves thinks this is the moment. When he'll finally discover whether Bentley just wanted to rub his new life in Elisha's face or whether he wants her back. Either option is as distasteful as the man himself.

"It doesn't matter to me whatever the reason is," Elisha says quickly, as though the same idea has occurred to her and she doesn't want anything admitted in front of Tori. "The fact is, I've moved on and while I generally like to stay on good terms with my exes, I'm willing to make an exception for you, Bentley. You treated me like shit and if that wasn't enough, not only did you never apologize for it, but you showed up back here and keep acting like you and I are friends. Let me be very clear: we aren't."

With an open-mouthed choking sound, Bentley starts to say, "Ellie—"

"I hate when you call me that. It's *Elisha*. We've had this argument a dozen times."

"Sure, sorry." He doesn't look like it.

Ves tenses his jaw, aching to call the asshole out, but knows it's the last thing Elisha wants to happen while Dave is running the workshop. Instead, he calmly selects a piping bag and creates a hot-pink outline around the cookie to corral all the icing. He floods it with lime green that reminds him of Shrek and then picks out matching sprinkles to create a border on the bottom.

"Look, I think I just need to say this. I hoped it wouldn't be necessary, but clearly it is." Elisha takes a deep, bracing breath. "It's not Piney Peaks that's beneath you. It's *you* who is unworthy of our town and everyone in it."

Pride fireworks in Ves's chest at her firm, no-nonsense delivery.

Bentley gives them all hard stares. "Victoria, we're leaving." When she doesn't move, his expression turns ugly. "Victoria?"

A bottle of sprinkles slams down hard. *"It's Tori!"*

Bentley storms out without another word, nearly crashing into another cookie station on the way.

Tori releases an uneven, choked exhale.

"Are you okay?" asks Elisha.

"I honestly don't know."

"Here," says Grandpa Dave in a gentle voice, heading over to join Tori, who looks at him with visible gratitude. "Why don't you try these?" He holds out a packet of popping candy. "Let's do some stripes on your Ugly Christmas Sweater cookie. Grab some of that icing, sweetheart. Do you like yellow and purple?"

Ves isn't sure how much he's overheard, but is once again struck by the older man's ability to get right to the heart of every hard situation. With Tori under Dave's wing, he gives all his attention back to Elisha. "I'm proud of you," he says, kissing her forehead. "I know it would have been much easier to ignore him."

"I'm glad I gave him a piece of my mind," she admits, relaxing into him. "I probably shouldn't have forced the issue right now, but

I can't quite bring myself to regret it. I hope the scales have fallen from Tori's eyes way faster than they fell from mine. And that she realizes she deserves better."

With one last look at Tori, who's in good hands with Dave, Elisha aims a high-wattage smile at Ves. "Now, are you going to wow me with some truly horrible sweater designs or am I going to win this on my own?"

"Hey, I've been carrying us so far. It's your turn," Ves says, snaking one arm around her waist while the other taps his chin. "Now, how ugly can we make this?"

He's one hundred percent positive he doesn't want to put this much food coloring into his body, but if she keeps looking at him like he's Christmas come early, he just might be convinced. As Elisha pros and cons the technical difficulties of using licorice bits to make reindeer antlers and a cinnamon Red Hot as its nose versus using icing, a feeling of contentment steals over Ves.

He didn't want to come, could certainly think of far more pleasurable activities to spend their time doing. But as he watches her brush her hair out of her face, getting a smear of icing on her cheekbone that he wishes he could lick off, he realizes there's nowhere else that he would rather be.

CHAPTER THIRTY-NINE

Elisha

In her dream, someone's calling her *love*. Someone with a laugh like silver bells, like waiting for winter all summer long, to finally wake up to the first frost spiderwebbing across the window and knowing that at last it was here, welcoming you home.

"Elisha, it's time to wake up. We're almost here, love."

Love. There it is again. It feels nice, as nice as the warm arm securely around her. One eye blearily opens as she recalibrates, taking stock of where they are. It isn't the glamorous view of midtown Manhattan's skyline she loves or the exciting whizz of every geographically impossible tourist attraction jam-packed into the travel montage of a movie. Instead, she's greeted with the gray-and-brown concrete walls of a bus terminal and a sore neck.

She stretches the stiffness out of her legs and cracks her neck before grabbing her suitcase, a tan carry-on size that was perfect for taking the bus on the two-hour journey from Piney Peaks to Manhattan's Port Authority Bus Terminal. Ves handles the subway with ease, like he knows it like the back of his hand. Which, she supposes, he probably does. After disembarking from the train, they walk three blocks until arriving at Ves's East 2nd Street apartment. By the time they get there, she's thankful her mom insisted she wear the heavy peacoat.

She lets him remove it after they make the three-flight walk up. "I know we just got here," she says around a yawn. "And what I'm about to say makes me a terrible tourist, but please let me just crawl into your bed and stay there until Arun's party?"

As much as she's looking forward to tonight, they have a packed schedule full of sightseeing and a catch-up lunch with her old boss, Veronica.

Ves huffs a laugh, buries his face in her neck. "Now why would I have any problem with that? I hear that terrible tourists make *excellent* girlfriends."

Is he sniffing her? He does that a lot. Nuzzles his nose against her skin and inhales like he can't get enough. No man has ever craved her the way that Ves does. She arches her back, teases him with her ass right up against his growing hardness. "Hmm, nope. I don't think I've heard that."

"Well, you do come from a really tiny town . . ."

"Fuck you," she says with a sigh, wriggling to give him better access.

"Where do you think I'm going with this?" he mumbles into that shivery spot where her neck meets her shoulder. The sensation springs her from eighty percent awake to a full one hundred percent, especially when his breath and body heat starts to warm her up.

"I've been away from home for so long," Ves continues, wrapping both arms around her waist, squeezing her flush against him. "I miss my bed. My sheets. And I have this image of you rolling around on them wearing that black lingerie I like, or maybe nothing at all, wrinkling my perfectly ironed sheets into sheer fucking devastation."

"Thank god you're hot, otherwise the fact you iron your sheets would be a real turn-off."

His lips brush the back of her neck. "Smart mouth."

Without breaking his embrace, she twists to face him. "Put it to better use, then," she says breathlessly.

Ves doesn't wait a second longer. His mouth crashes down on hers, hungry and seeking. His large hands frame her face, tilting her chin to better meet the angle of his kiss. Every lean, muscled inch of him presses into her, one thigh nudging hers apart so her denim-clad pelvis rubs tantalizingly against his leg.

She always thinks he's sexy, but when he takes control like this, she grows wet for him.

He kisses her the way she loves, hands weaving into her hair, then slipping free to trail down her back and cup each of her buttocks. Kneading like the bread she's positive he's never made in his life.

She winds her arms about his neck, gasping when her breasts make delicious friction against his chest. He growls in reply, deepening the kiss. His tongue coaxes hers to give way to him, stroking just right. With a low moan, she digs her fingers into his shoulders. Each one begs for more, more, more. The vibration rocks through her, heat pooling low in her abdomen.

Kissing her the entire time, he walks her backward, presumably toward his bedroom. At this point, her eyes are fluttering shut in desire every two seconds, but she still tries to get a good look at the living room. It's sun-flooded, with tall bookshelves lining white walls and neutral rugs against parquet floors. A collection of nice black-and-white abstract prints above a gray sofa.

A few more steps and the back of her knees hit the bed. His

mouth applies the perfect pressure, firm and insistent, but still tender. When he tugs at her bottom lip with his teeth, she goes boneless in his arms. If Ves weren't holding her up, she would have collapsed in a heap on the bed, all tightly coiled desire and trembling legs.

She likes kisses like this, without too much tongue. Just flurries of pecks, darting tongues, a little biting, and his hands exploring everywhere.

"Undress me?" she whispers against his mouth, core clenching with want.

She doesn't have to ask him twice. His hands work the large tortoiseshell buttons on her chunky cardigan while hers move to his trousers. A few tugs and they're off. He makes a bitten-off sound when she kicks them aside.

"You didn't *really* want me to stop to fold those neatly, did you?" she asks sweetly, sinking to her knees and peeling off her camisole to reveal her black La Perla bra.

He smolders down at her, clearly liking what he sees. In addition to being her most expensive lingerie, it's also the skimpiest. It has just enough lace to cup her breasts and cover the nipples, but it's sheer everywhere else. "Trust me, love, I have swiftly reprioritized," he says with a rough laugh. His hands curl into her hair for just a second, and it feels like a kiss.

"Mm-hmm, I thought so." She yanks down his briefs.

He's hard and erect, and she fully plans on sucking him like a Popsicle. But first . . . She gives him a few hard pulls that have him groaning, then wraps her right hand around him, bringing the head of his cock to her mouth. His hips twitch at the first puff of her breath across his sensitive skin, but she doesn't take him in her mouth right away.

First, she blows cool air across his length, which brings forth a full-body shudder and a tiny pinch of his brows. Next, she traces the outline of her lips with his head achingly slow, and then swirls her tongue over his tip, drawing a broken moan from him. He tastes salty and musky, uniquely Ves, and he's trembling in her grip like it's taking all his effort not to thrust.

She brushes her palm underneath him from base to tip, then makes a circle with her thumb and middle finger. They don't quite meet. God, she wants him inside her right now. While she's marveling at his thickness, he reaches out to grip her chin. Dazed, she looks up.

Those beautiful baby blues lock onto her lips. "Fuck, Elisha," he says. "Don't play with me."

Without further ado, she hums and takes a few inches, then a few more.

His gasp is strangled, but he holds himself still. She works up and down his length, taking him deeper until he hits the back of her throat. She hollows her cheeks and sucks until his hand tangles in her hair.

She flicks her eyes up at him.

"I don't want to finish in your mouth," he says. "Not this time, anyway."

Elisha pulls away, a trail of saliva clinging from the tip of his cock and her mouth. He barely gives her time to swipe it away before he kisses her, tongue delving deep in luxurious exploratory swipes. Ves trails soft, open-mouthed kisses down her neck, the side of her breast, her ribs, and is sucking a mark into the dip of her waist when she suddenly realizes where he's heading.

"Return the favor next time," she says, grabbing his hair to stop his descent. "I need you inside me."

"As my lady commands."

He teases one finger inside her, laughing when she whines and twists her hips to take him deeper. "You're so wet for me," he marvels, and before she needs to beg him for release, he lines himself up and plunges home in one sure thrust.

Stars explode behind her eyelids as he gives her a second to adjust, then begins moving, every stroke measured and slow against her walls, making sure to hit every single nerve. Her hands roam his back and buttocks, squeezing in encouragement when he hits at just the right angle to make her cry out.

"Look at me," Ves says between gritted teeth, tendons in his arms straining to keep his weight off her.

She does, until everything tightens and his thrusts become erratic. Moments before they both crest, he buries his face in her sweaty neck, kissing the flushed skin.

"Ves, I'm all gross," she says with a giggle.

He lifts his head to look at her. "You? Never."

His words are so solemn, his eyes so serious, that she laughs again.

With a growl, he pins her arms to the headboard and in one swift stroke, Elisha isn't laughing anymore.

She's moaning his name instead.

CHAPTER FORTY

Elisha

"You're late," Arun says instead of hello when Elisha and Ves turn up at 7:05 p.m. "But you're here and it's almost Christmas and you brought my favorite wine, so you're forgiven." He hugs Ves with both arms, then turns to Elisha. "Are you a hugger?"

She laughs and throws her arms around him. "What do you think?"

"I *think* you're the best thing that's ever happened to my best friend." Arun's hug is extra tight, like he's committing something he can't put into words behind the gesture. "Come in, Cade's dying to meet you."

The Iyers' apartment is as wonderfully eclectic as the couple themselves. Elisha can easily pinpoint each man's influence on the modern-slash-shabby-chic aesthetic: soft black walls, leather sectional, and monochrome photography blended with plenty of floral soft furnishings and worn furniture, replete with nicks and scratches. Arun wears a sharp navy suit and his hair is styled in a suave undercut, all clean lines and lots of volume. A bit like he's auditioning for the next Bond. Cade, on the other hand, wears a

KISS THE COOK apron and Birkenstocks, and looks like he listens to James Blunt.

"So glad you could both make it," Cade enthuses. He has a light French accent and shoulder-length curls that he brushes back with an impatient sound. He apologetically gestures to his spattered apron. "Sorry, thanks to this mess, I won't hug you. *Someone* insisted on throwing a dinner party and then had a panic attack at the idea of cooking for eight people."

Arun winces and takes the bottle of wine from Ves. "It's true. I may have woken up at two in the morning to panic-google 'How to take the stress out of cooking.'"

Cade gives him a lopsided smile and prompts, "And the answer is?"

Arun sighs. "Get your ridiculously hot, super-thoughtful husband to do it for you."

"I must have missed the part in your vows when you promised to do everything Arun delegates," Ves drawls, giving Cade a wink and slinging his arm around his best friend's shoulders.

"Oh no, they were in there," says Arun. "So obvious they didn't even need to be spoken. Went unsaid. But they were definitely there."

"I don't think marriage vows written in invisible ink are enforceable," says Ves.

"Fuck off," says Arun, putting him in a headlock to mess with his hair.

Elisha watches with her mouth open. Who *is* this Ves?

Boyish, carefree, not even bothering to smooth himself after a bit of roughhouse? In Piney Peaks, she's sure, if someone had grabbed him like that, he would have immediately fixed his hair and then gotten all stony jawed and monosyllabic until the sulk wore off. Actually, no, back home no one would have thought he was even approachable enough to, well, approach.

"Can I pour you a glass of wine?" Cade asks. He nods toward the two men, who are already poring over one of the thickest books Elisha's ever seen. "It's one of the most anticipated fantasy novels for next year and Arun scored an early copy for Ves. Trust me, they'll be occupied for the next ten minutes with that."

"Actually, feel free to put me to work. I'm more than happy to help." And, selfishly, she wants to know more about Ves, and she's not sure Arun will spill all the messy details about his best friend.

Cade grins like she's already won him over. He hands her a fork and a big mixing bowl. "Awesome, can you smash these garlicky potatoes?"

"Oh my god, are you a chef?" she asks in amazement. On the counter, he already has bacon-wrapped haloumi drizzled with herb pesto and speared with toothpicks, and champagne chilling in a bucket of ice. Between the cauliflower gratin broiling in the oven, beer-braised pork resting on a chopping board, and cheddar rolls keeping warm in the bread basket, the kitchen smells orgasmic.

"Ves, I love her!" Cade shouts. When Arun and Ves come out of their book-infused stupor, he waves his hand at them to go back to what they were doing. "No, I wish. I work in finance. Specifically financial crime risk assessment. I worked as an analyst in France for many years until my firm moved me to New York." He gives her a nod of approval when he sees her work with the potatoes. Thankfully, he gave her an easy job. "What about you? Arun said you're a film liaison? What is that like?"

"Yeah, I help coordinate location work, but more importantly, at least to me, I do a lot of the groundwork to show film and TV stakeholders how our town can work for them. There's a ton of

places all over the U.S.—the world, really—that could be revital-
ized. So many movies get tax incentives to film in Canada and Aus-
tralia these days that people don't always think to look closer to
home."

"You're doing a good thing for your town, Elisha." Quietly, he
adds, "You've been good for Ves, too. He looks more than just
content—he looks happy."

Finally, an opening for her to dig a bit more. But just as she's
about to ask him to share some stories about Ves, there's a commo-
tion at the front door. Suddenly, more people are pouring into the
house. It then hits Elisha: this is a real, *actual* adult dinner party.

She looks around the apartment. Everything here is just so
damn nice. White taper candlesticks in brass holders gently billow
with flame. The Instagrammable square plates and the garland
draped from one end of the dining table to the other add a bit of
rustic charm to the otherwise modern place settings.

Arun and Cade aren't more than a few years older than her, and
their lives are already so damn *together*. They have a mortgage and
a marriage and maybe even a five-year plan? No, they probably have
a twenty-five-year plan, that's how adult they are. They aren't back
home living with their parents and making no-strings-attached
deals with guys. She wonders if Cade would still think she was so
good for Ves if he knew the truth.

"Hey, you good?" Ves is suddenly at her side, peering at her from
under those lush dark brows with concern.

She forces herself to smile. "Yeah, why?"

"No reason," he says slowly. His eyes zigzag all over her face. "You
just looked pensive for a moment and I . . ." He runs his hand over
her ear like a lock of her wavy hair has come loose from the pearl
barrette. But she knows it hasn't, which means he just wants to touch
her. "I was worried," he concludes. "I don't want you to feel left out."

"I don't! Oh my god, Arun and Cade are so nice. The best." She reaches for his hand and takes it in both of hers. He immediately slides his fingers in between hers, interlocking them. It's cute and it makes her want to kiss him, but before she can get on her tiptoes and tilt her chin up, a petite blond-haired woman pops up at Ves's side, wearing an anime shirt and a striped beanie in the pink-blue-white trans flag colors.

"Hey, you must be Elisha!" She sticks out her hand. "I'm Hero Crane."

Elisha frees her hand from Ves's grip with an apologetic smile. "Hi, it's nice to meet you."

"Hero and I did the same English degree at NYU," explains Ves. He reclaims Elisha's hand as soon as possible. "She gave me some of the best critiques I've ever received. We stayed in touch after undergrad and I ended up referring her to Arun."

"And now he represents both of us!" Hero beams. "Hey, maybe you can convince this guy to finally co-author a graphic novel with me?" She nudges Ves with her elbow. He doesn't budge an inch but lets her poke at him with the kind of indulgent smile he only gives to people he likes.

"Our professor had an ax to grind about graphic novels, so this has become Hero's white whale," says Ves, making a face. "Hero's idea is great, and she definitely doesn't need me to write it. Plus I'm only stick-figure qualified at drawing, so . . ."

"I'll do all the art and at this point you know it as well as I do," Hero argues. "And it's right up your alley. Magic? Adventures? Zero parental supervision?"

"Hero!" cries Arun. "You must try one of these pesto bites. They're divine." When she's distracted, Arun knowingly mouths at Ves: *You should do it.*

"You're reluctant?" Elisha asks, watching Ves play with her

hands, twisting the stacked silver rings on her index finger. She can't figure out whether he's truly distracted or simply stalling for time.

"It's just . . . it's a commitment." He doesn't look up. "Arun loves the idea as well, but starting to write a book with a friend feels like a good way to not have that friend anymore. It's not worth losing someone over."

"Doesn't seem like she feels the same way."

When he sighs, she's afraid she's overstepped.

"Putting myself out there never ends well, Elisha," he says quietly. "Arun is terminally hopeful on my behalf, but people like you and him don't understand. *Can't* understand."

"Can't understand what?"

"People who are so loved by everyone can't understand what it's like for people who aren't."

She hates the way he says it, as if he's resigned that this is how it's always been and will always be. She wants nothing more than to prove to him just how untrue it is. Flabbergasted, she lets him lead her to the dining table, where she's squeezed between him and Arun.

The guests don't waste any time digging in, even though Cade jokingly bemoans that the food that took him hours to cook will be devoured in under one. He catches Elisha's eye and winks.

But she can't smile back. Because after one bite, she knows one thing that is irrevocably, incontrovertibly true, even if she isn't ready to say it. She's done the silliest thing she could do with Ves Hollins, Christmas Curmudgeon, Toast of Trivia, and Small-Town Girl Rescuer: fallen in love with him.

CHAPTER FORTY-ONE

Elisha

How long have you been up?" Ves's voice is sleep-roughened and the sound of it goes straight between Elisha's legs. How does someone so pretty have a voice like sexy gravel? He angles his body to better hold her, chest rising and falling in an enormous yawn.

Shivering against him, she presses herself even closer, until her lips skate across his jaw and up behind his ear. She can smell herself on his skin, sugar cookie crossed with his green apple body wash.

She's very much a morning person, and it's usually a struggle to stay in bed after she's woken up, but for him, she tries. Surprisingly, he's a cuddler. Even in sleep he wraps himself around her tight, and it's no different now. His bed is cozy, the blankets warm with their shared heat, but she imagines it will be a different story during summer's sweltering humidity.

Except . . . they won't be sleeping in the same bed by the time summer comes. The valuation experts are scheduled to come the first week of January, Damian will close on the house and head back to Piney Peaks to film only a week after that, and Ves will be . . .

Here, in these gray silk sheets, maybe spooning some other girl to sleep at night. At least for a few weeks, and then it'll be someone else. Because he doesn't do serious.

She's still okay with that, isn't she? No, she can't think about the future right now. She'll just enjoy the moment, where they're both in the same place at the same time, and, if she can rouse him fully awake, maybe they'll join as one before she overthinks this.

"Not too long," she says, rolling her thumb over the curve of his ear. She can tell he likes it when he makes a purring sort of noise deep in the back of his throat. "You're cute when you sleep."

One eye blearily opens. "Yeah?"

"Yeah," she whispers, tracing her tongue over his lobe. He cranks the other eye open now, but she still doesn't have his full attention. "When I first met you, I thought you had an unfriendly jawline. Now I just want to kiss it all the time. What's up with that?"

He laughs and snuggles deeper into his pillow. "Sometimes I can't believe you're real, Elisha Rowe. Every single time I say your name like that, first and last, I'm reminding myself that you aren't some snow angel fueled purely by coffee and good cheer, sent to un-Grinch me."

She giggles and nips at his bare shoulder. He growls and hugs her tighter. "You're only, like, two-fifths Grinch," she says, studying him intently. "Pre-me, though? You were a solid one-quarter."

"It's too early to be discussing your bad math." His hand weaves between them, touching her exactly where she needs to be touched.

She grinds against his questing fingers, seeking more, but he keeps his caress intentionally light. Grazing her outer lips with a finger that feels like a feather, then flicking her clit with some pre-ternatural ability at knowing exactly when she's grown impatient.

He works one finger inside her, giving her leisurely strokes until she whines for a second. "I'd much rather you focus on *this* two-fifths," he says, kissing the corner of her mouth at the exact moment that two of his five fingers scissor inside her.

Does he really think that she's thinking about anything but that right now? Maybe some people go limp as a dead fish for a five-minute fumble, but Elisha believes in being proactive in all areas of life. To that end, there's still something she wants to talk about, and in about a second, he's going to make her forget her own name.

She clamps her legs shut, keeping his wrist in a stranglehold. "I liked meeting your friends last night," she says, squeezing her thighs in warning when he tries to pump in and out.

He seems to realize this is important to her, because he goes still, even though his eyes remain wary. "Glad to hear it. Arun was afraid he'd never get to meet you."

"Does he usually meet the people you date?"

"No. Not because I don't want him to. There's just no point when it's not going to go anywhere." He wiggles his fingers inside her and she's so wet that she can actually *hear* it. When he grins with a look of what she can only describe as exceedingly lustful pride, she hides her face in his shoulder.

"Hate you," she mumbles against his warm biceps.

"Lies," he announces. "You love me."

Before she's humiliated further, before he reads the truth of his flippant comment on her face, before she blurts it out when she comes, she hurtles out of bed. "Oh my god, I have that meeting with my boss! My old boss! Erm, I mean, former boss. Okay, I have to—Where's my underwear—Is that my, no, wait, that's yours—Actually do you mind if I just—" She whisks the sheet off to drape around herself as she lunges for the bathroom.

"Elisha!" he bellows, scrambling for the comforter discarded at the foot of the bed.

"Sorry, sorry!" she calls back through the door.

"I thought it was a lunch meeting! It's only seven a.m.!"

"Traffic!" she screeches back, twisting the shower's hot water tap.

When there's only silence, she's relieved. Ves has probably drifted back to sleep, comfily cocooned and dreaming about whatever he dreams about, which is probably not what *she* dreams about, and anyway, it was her idea to keep this casual, so why is she staring at herself in the mirror, pathetically watching two fat tears roll down her cheeks?

There's a soft tap at the door. "Elisha, I find you exasperating at the best of times, but by some kind of magic, you manage to charm me despite my best intentions. And right now, you're not charming me."

She gulps back a sob, clutching the sheet tighter.

"You're scaring me," he finishes softly.

What? She opens the door to find him standing there in his briefs. He's holding himself close, like he's cold from dashing after her without taking the time to even pull on a sweater, and pillow creases are still etched on his face. Immediately, she feels bad for making him worry. "It wasn't locked."

"Considering you ran in here, I didn't even try to open it. In case you wanted space from me."

How can she tell him she doesn't want more space, but less? As in, miles less space between them. Preferably the most she can handle is across the street. None of this bus and multiple subways business.

"I'm sorry I scared you."

He tangles his hand into her messy, unbrushed hair, fingers massaging her scalp. It's comforting and she can't help but lean into his touch. His palm cups her cheek, stays there. "Talk to me, my love." His voice is hard, insistent, granite. But his eyes are gentle, and she *wants* to tell him, but a keen sense of self-preservation and an even healthier dose of fear that he won't feel the same makes her hold back.

"I don't want to talk anymore," she says hoarsely. "I just want you."

"Elisha," he begins to say, but she cuts him off, surging up for a kiss. They both have morning breath but she doesn't care, letting the sheets puddle on the tile floor. Realizing that she doesn't want him to feel anxious about it, she bends and scoops up the sheet, haphazardly folding it.

"Leave it," he says, rubbing the back of his neck like he's embarrassed. "I just want you."

"Shower with me?" she asks, stepping behind the glass sliding door. She's trying to distract herself as much as him. "Rough and fast," she says when he steps out of his underwear.

Perfect, she thinks two minutes later as he bends her at the waist to brace her palms against the tile. *Perfect*, she thinks when he digs his fingers into her hips as he positions himself behind. *Perfect*, she thinks as his thrusts pick up speed, driving them both to the hard finish she craves, eradicating every single thought from her mind that she wants a whole lot more from him than just sex.

The thought becomes harder to deny afterward, when he takes such good care of her. Ves drags a sudsy washcloth across her trembling body, grazing tender nipples and quivering thighs, diving between them and hitting that bundle of nerves that makes her curl into his palm with a keening cry.

When he lathers her hair with his shampoo, piles it high on top of her head and massages her scalp, combing out the tangles. When he tenderly wraps a towel around her and gives her those soft, heated eyes, like she's everything he could ever want. When she lets the towel fall, water droplets still clinging to glistening skin, and lets him show her that rough and fast can be fun, but sweet and gentle can sate them both, too.

CHAPTER FORTY-TWO

Elisha

I'm so glad you could take this meeting, Elisha," says Veronica Fox, throwing back her martini at lunch later that day. At sixty-five years old, Veronica's unlined face and black cherry lipstick are exactly as flawless as Elisha remembers. "It's terrific that we were both in New York City at the same time."

Someone else might chalk their aligned schedules up to a stroke of luck or a sign from the universe. But Elisha's former boss from Atlanta doesn't believe in either of those things—only in hard work.

"I don't know if you're still in touch with anyone from our old office," says Veronica, running a hand through her sleek silver layers. "But you may have heard that I left to go out on my own."

This is Veronica to a T. When other people might be looking forward to retirement, she's taking her lifetime of experience to start her own company. Just another one of the reasons why Elisha admires the woman so much. "No, I hadn't, actually. But wow, that's so exciting!" Elisha sips at her cranberry gin fizz before asking, "Are you based here now?"

"Secured the premises last week. Just a few blocks away." Veronica flashes her a smile full of perfect whitened teeth. "And you know me, I poached all the best before I left. With one notable exception, of course." The curve of her lips is all fox now. "So, how's that little hometown treating you?" she coos.

Oh, it is so obvious where this is going. Not the quick little catch-up chat Veronica's email intimated, after all. Friends don't take *meetings* with friends. This is a job offer.

Or at the very least, an interest check. This place certainly has the vibes for it. The kind of spot where someone takes out a client or does a deal. Elisha casts an eye around the room; the dimly lit wood-paneled Lower East Side restaurant is filled with young professionals in thousand-dollar suits poring over the well-curated wine list.

Elisha wants to impress her boss, prove that resigning from the Georgia Film Office was the right move for her. That she isn't in the career standstill Veronica clearly seems to think she is. "You may have heard about the *Sleighbells* sequel?" Elisha's vindicated by the surprise registering on the older woman's face. "It was a slow start, but we're gaining some real momentum now."

Her momentary victory goes downhill quick.

"Ah. You mean that's the only interest you have so far," Veronica says dismissively.

Elisha crumples the cloth napkin in her lap. Goodbye festive tree fold, hello ball of crushed fabric. She frowns. "That's not what I—"

"Don't bullshit me, dear. I know what 'gaining momentum' means. You have jack squat except one movie and the hope that it will lead to more opportunities, am I right? I know I call you the fairy godmother of film, but even a magic wand can't turn Pokey Peaks into something it's not."

"It's *Piney* Peaks, and I'm not trying to change it into anything. Our local history is exactly why we deserve to be a filming destination again. I'm just taking us back to our roots."

"Our, we, us." Veronica sighs. "Can you really tell me that you see a future there?"

"Of course I—" Elisha sets her jaw, staring Veronica down. "I love my job and my town. With the right investment, Piney Peaks could be exactly the kind of success story that gets other towns to follow in our footsteps. And even if it's not *yet* the trailblazer that I believe it can be, the mayor went out on a limb to make me a position in the Chamber of Commerce. I made promises that I have to see through, and even if it doesn't work out, I have to try."

"That's very . . . sentimental, Elisha." Veronica's nose crinkles like she'd rather use another word. The rest of her face doesn't, a testament to her excellent Botox. "And I understand and admire your tenacity, to an extent. But to inject that kind of investment into their economy, well, to be perfectly frank, I just don't see it happening. Don't think me heartless, my dear. I'm only thinking of you!"

Elisha looks at her askance.

Veronica, indefatigable as always, says, "You've *somehow* got Damian Rhys, but this discount-Hallmark production is a one-off between his big-budget movies, I guarantee you. Don't throw away a very promising career to molder away in a place that would never allow you to grow."

When Elisha says nothing, Veronica reaches out to pat her hand. "I'm sorry to give you a dose of realism, dear. But if nothing else, it would appear that my offer comes at an opportune time for you."

Elisha hears her out without interruption. It's definitely flattering to be thought of, but it's tough to choke down the mushroom ravioli that, ordinarily, she'd find delicious.

Veronica is smart, passionate, and driven, all characteristics that will serve her as well here as they did in Georgia. Traits that Elisha acknowledges they have in common, unwillingly impressed by the spiel. Neither of them likes to quit, which is why Veronica will keep at her until the dessert menu arrives.

The coffee-and-amaretto panna cotta comes highly recommended by their waiter, a flirtatious young man who gives most of his attention to Veronica as though he knows where his tip is coming from. She sighs after him, stabbing her dessert spoon into the wibbly-wobbly cooked cream. "God, he would be an excellent lead in a rom-com. I should ask him if he's interested in being an extra in something," she muses. "You never know, he could be Netflix's next darling. And I could be the one to discover him!"

Elisha's amused despite herself, licking some of the chocolate syrup off the back of her spoon. Typical Veronica. She might be a shark, but she also goes after things pretty wholeheartedly for someone who claims she doesn't even have one. "You do remember you're not a casting agent, right?"

Veronica swats the air as if to ward away Elisha's words. "I'm a little bit of everything."

"Well, thank you for the offer, Veronica. I'm honored you still want me after you cleaned out half the office. And I'm not saying it's a definitive no, but for now, I'm happy where I am."

"You could be happier," says Veronica. "Especially when I tell you that I don't want you as just another one of my liaisons, Elisha. You whipped that office into shape. If you come on board, it will be as my partner. Well, not fifty-fifty, of course. Junior partner. Very junior. Seventy-thirty? Perhaps just twenty. We can negotiate later! Now, where's that waiter, you simply *must* try one of these Negronis to celebrate."

298 · LILLIE VALE

"Veronica, I haven't said yes!" Elisha's eyes widen. "We don't have anything to celebrate!"

"You mean you—" Veronica's hand limply drops into her lap. "You aren't just playing hard to get?"

"Have you ever known me to play games?"

Veronica sniffs. "Who knows what habits you've picked up in Pokey Peaks."

"Veronica."

"Fine, fine. Piney Peaks. What if I said a seventy-thirty split was back on the table?"

"It's not about the—"

"Twist my arm, why don't you!" cries Veronica, smiling with all her teeth. "Fifty-fifty partnership."

That was fast. Almost like it was what Veronica wanted all along. Elisha waits for her to take it back, to walk it back down, maybe offer ninety-ten in her usual blasé way.

Veronica waits, too, steadily meeting Elisha's gaze over the rim of the Negroni she guzzles down, signaling for another as though negotiating is thirsty business and every second she spends in Elisha's company dehydrates her further.

Elisha needs to confirm that this is for real. "You meant it about an equal partnership?"

"If I have to." Veronica's sigh is dramatic. "Now that you know all my cards, can we celebrate?"

CHAPTER FORTY-THREE

Ves

Ves is sure that something has Elisha spooked. She's been acting oddly all day, and even though she's physically right next to him, part of him feels like she never came back from lunch. He wants to smooth the pinch between her brows that reminds him of the quotations button on his keyboard, wants to anchor her to him when her eyes start to glaze over like she's technically looking at the Fifth Avenue window displays but not really seeing them.

He's not having fun, either. Which is annoying, yes, but bafflingly, he's more upset for her sake. Because this is the exact kind of magical extravaganza she lives for: crystal snowflakes suspended from vaulted ceilings, frolicking woodland creatures, gumdrops and lollipops that look good enough to eat, heaps of that cottony fake snow, life-size animatronics, thousands of LED lights . . .

It's one thing to catch her delighted gasps in his mouth when they're in bed together, read the exhilaration racing in her eyes as she hurtles to the finish line seconds before him. Bringing her pleasure with the warm press of his body, the heat of his mouth and the thrust of his hips. But this is different.

He just wants to give her this simple, innocent enjoyment. And if his heart pounds like a whole herd of stampeding reindeer in anticipation of the enchantment on her face? Well, he'll cherish that all through this cold winter and hold on to it in those quiet moments in the months to come when he finds himself imagining what color she's painting her nails, where she is and who she's with, whether she's meeting strangers and turning them into friends with the same effortless ease with which she won over Ves.

"Is everything okay?" he asks delicately.

Elisha jerks back to him, lips twisting in an abashed smile. "Sorry, just work. I know, I know, I'm the worst! But I'm all yours now, promise."

His own lips tic up. "So what you're saying is your every thought is of me?"

"*Eh*," she says with the biggest grin he's ever seen. She threads her arm through his, pulling him closer. Whenever she does this, her feet tend to slant and he has to straighten their trajectory. He doesn't mind; it's just another way he finds himself adjusting to her. She squeezes his biceps. "You'd like that, wouldn't you?"

To be someone she thinks about with a frequent, horrendous regularity?

Yes, his brain whispers with no hesitation at all. He wants to be that person for someone with an intensity that should scare him, but it doesn't. Which is itself scary. Because it makes him think that the reason he isn't running in the opposite direction is *her*.

But he matches her levity when he says, "Maybe only every other thought. I'm not greedy."

He is, though. He rakes his eyes over her face as she laughs, giddy and sweet, memorizing the sparkle of her brown eyes, the curve of her lips, the reddened tip of the pert nose he has the sudden urge to drop a kiss atop. When he acts upon the impulse, she giggles and gives his arm another squeeze, snuggling even closer, half hiding her face. She looks up at him at the exact moment he makes the glorious mistake of glancing down again.

His entire world tilts. The pleasure centers of his brain detonate like a Vegas slot machine and he forgets his own name, or, apparently, how to walk, judging by his sudden stumble.

"What the fuck, Ves," Elisha says through a giggle, and it sounds like sunbeams bursting through clouds. He comes to with a disorienting abruptness. "Are you okay?" she asks. "I know I was the distracted one a few minutes ago, but did you have a drink while I wasn't looking? Or maybe ten?"

He wishes. God, a finger's worth of Glenfiddich would be good. "Icy patch."

She looks down at the almost completely dry sidewalk. "Hmm. You sure you're good? We can head back to your place if you want."

Ves clears his throat. A momentary lapse, that's it. He needs to get this back on track before he gives himself away with the force of his yearning. He likes her. *Likes*. Not lo— That other word. "Trying to weasel out of doing all the things on my list, Elisha Rowe?"

She makes an offended sort of grumble. "No way! We still have to ice-skate in Central Park, see the Rockefeller Center Christmas tree, and—"

"None of those things are on my list," he interrupts. "They're for tourists."

"I *am* a tourist."

"I did everything you wanted us to do in Piney Peaks," he points out. "Without complaint."

"Ha! You're kidding me, right? You definitely complained. Okay, whatever you have planned for me, can we fold a few of my things into yours?" She pulls her arm from his, patting down her pockets before coming up with a folded sheet of notepaper from the

Chocolate Mouse, candy cane borders with a whiskered mouse in the corner wearing a cute Santa hat and bow tie.

He scans the locations, which are plentiful and, more importantly, a logistical nightmare to get to before they go home tomorrow evening on the last bus out to Piney Peaks. He hands it back to her pinched between two fingers. "These are where tourists go for photo ops."

She snatches it. "Exactly. And all my favorite movies have been filmed there."

Ves groans right there on the street, getting a startled look from passersby. "You're making me a fangirl right alongside you," he accuses.

"Darn, you figured out my nefarious evildoer scheme." She stands on tiptoe to press a kiss on his cheek. Or it would have been, if he hadn't turned his mouth at the right time so her lips landed at the corner of his mouth. He knows without checking that there will be a sticky mess of her glossy pout left behind.

"Ves!" she chides, rubbing at it with cold fingers that are once again not wearing mittens. She looks like she's biting back a smile. "You're a mess. What am I going to do with you?"

His traitorous mind answers for him: *Love me.*

His mouth, thankfully, is more circumspect. "Tell you what," he says. "Give me that list again."

"Are you going to make fun of me?"

Ves sighs. "Probably. But I'm also going to get you everything on your Christmas wish list."

She skids to a stop so fast that for a second, he thinks she's hit the nonexistent ice, too.

"Everything?" she asks coyly.

He never overpromises or underdelivers. "Everything," he confirms.

CHAPTER FORTY-FOUR

Ves

With a groan that rumbles down his throat and slingshots all the way to his toes, Ves reaches his peak. He finishes seconds after Elisha, his body flush against her sweaty, naked skin, pressing her into the mattress. She's glowing a gorgeous shade of pink all over, and the sleepy, content smile playing on her lips as she looks at him under lowered eyelashes almost gives him an erection again. With regret, he slides out and discards the condom but snuggles back in bed immediately, resting his head on her shoulder.

"I'm not cold anymore," she whispers, pressing a kiss to his temple.

"Good. Any objections to me making you shiver for a different reason?" He lightly draws circles and swirls over her skin, rewarded by her giggles and trembles when he does figure eights across her nipple until it stiffens again. He rolls it under the pad of his thumb, pleased when she hisses and stretches like a cat, angling her body into his.

When she's this happy, it's easy to forgive her for spending the rest of their evening doing utterly pedestrian things like visiting famous spots from *Breakfast at Tiffany's*, *Serendipity*, and *Enchanted*. A single smile from her and he's a goner. He will happily play tour guide if it means earning as many of those smiles as he can.

They're scheduled to hit the rest of Elisha's list tomorrow morning, mostly beloved sites of movies Ves has never seen but has been pertly informed he *will* as soon as they get home. Date night or threat, he doesn't much care as long as he's spending it with her.

God, he could spend forever touching her. Making her writhe under his fingers, his cock, his tongue. He's about to put all three to good use when his phone goes off, its shrill, inconvenient ring shattering their post-sex bliss.

Elisha's bare stomach rises and falls rapidly as he pulls away. "Better get that," she says with a pout.

He presses a quick kiss to her shoulder in apology before reaching for the phone on the nightstand. The number on the screen looks familiar, but it's not in his contacts. "Hello?"

"Hi, is this Ves Hollins?"

He fights to keep his voice even when he feels her toes stroking his calves. "Yes, who is this?"

"Oh, hey, this is Shane from American Asset Appraisals. When we last spoke, I know you were eager to get back home and, again, I can't apologize enough for the holdup on our side. I wanted to let you know that we were able to clear our schedules earlier than expected. We can get the whole crew out to do this valuation in double-quick time so we can be out of your hair tomorrow itself. I realize it's short notice, but are you available in the morning? We prefer for the homeowner to be on the premises."

"Tomorrow morning?" It's a lot sooner than Ves had expected. He glances at Elisha, who gives him a satisfied smile and a tantalizing lip bite, her hair splayed across his sheets.

"Sorry again," Shane says. "We can stick to the first week of

January if that's more convenient. Happy to do whatever makes you happy!"

Happy? Happy is here, with Elisha inches away from him, warm and willing, burrowed in his sheets, giving him those eyes that let him know she wants him again. He hesitates, not sure how to respond. Nothing about this timing is convenient, but isn't this what he wanted? A quick visit in and out of Piney Peaks?

It's been years since he's made a Christmas list, but even if he'd made one this year, falling for a small-town girl with the biggest of hearts wouldn't have been on it. Maybe this is for the best, a gift in disguise. An out before he gets too attached.

"I appreciate it, Shane," says Ves, closing his eyes against the sight of her rolling onto her stomach and burying her face in the pillow. Against the spine he pressed kisses down just half an hour ago, the curve of her sweet cheeks that the sheet doesn't quite cover. "Ten o'clock is just fine. I'll see you then."

"Making plans for us tomorrow?" Elisha asks as he hangs up.

His heart twinges that they have to cut the trip short. That he'll change their tickets so they can catch the earliest bus tomorrow morning to make the two-hour journey home. "I'll tell you after," he says, trying to ignore the disquiet in his heart as he takes her into his arms again. "First, I want to do this."

And then he kisses her, like it's not just a want, but a need. Like it's his last night on this earth, because, in a way, it feels like it is.

CHAPTER FORTY-FIVE

Ves

Thanks again! Have a good night!" Ves waves the valuation experts goodbye from the doorway, a conflicting cocktail of emotion brewing in his chest. With two whole teams doggedly working through the day, he now has the final appraisal of all the books, art, and jewelry left in the house. He doesn't quite know what to do with the information, let alone with himself. Does he bring some of it back to New York? Should he send everything to an auction house?

God, he actually doesn't care about any of this right now. All he wants is to get back to Elisha. She'd taken it in stride when he'd broken the news to her last night and had even laid her head on his shoulder on the ride back to Piney Peaks early this morning, scrolling through all their pictures. But her energy was all off, the sparkle dimmed from her brown eyes and a gloomy pout on her lips as she'd headed to work straight from the Piney Peaks bus station.

"So this is it, huh?"

He glances up to see Elisha standing on the sidewalk in front of his house. He scans her face quickly; her smile is back, or at least a facsimile of it.

His laugh comes out in a white puff. She's changed out of her work clothes, wearing sweats and the same bunny slippers and pom-pom beanie she had on the day they first met. It's cold outside, and she looks ridiculous, but in a way that makes him want to drag her into his house and straight up to bed. He wraps his fingers harder around his still-hot mug of coffee as if physically restraining himself from doing so.

"It doesn't have to be," he offers.

She works her mouth from side to side. "I think it does," she says quietly, as though she doesn't want to say the words. "Long-distance relationships don't work for me. I know you're nothing like Bentley, but if it has to end, I'd rather it be quick, you know? Not dragged out. That just makes it worse."

He exhales. "Yeah." There's no argument he can make to refute her. She's one hundred percent correct, even though walking away from her feels all kinds of wrong. He can't even bring himself to go back inside the house. Honestly, he doesn't know if it would make it easier or harder if she were to ask him to stay. He doesn't know if he *wants* her to put that on him. He doesn't even know what he'd say if she did.

"Think you've changed your mind about dating over the holidays?" she asks.

"No," he replies, mouth curving into a smile. "That was just for you, Elisha Rowe."

She rolls her eyes, but he swears she looks pleased. "Lucky me."

He gives her one last look. Damian isn't in a rush to take possession of the house, but Ves doesn't want to overstay his welcome, making things harder both for him *and* for Elisha. Dragging things out the way she obviously dreads.

So he raises his mug in the air, tips it in her direction, and gives her a nod. They had a great December together, but on Christmas

Day, it all comes to an end. Not just the Winter Festival he promised to stay for, but the whole Piney Peaks bubble, where everything he ever wanted seemed within reach.

"Hey!"

He turns back to her.

"I *am* lucky, you know," she says. "I'm really glad I met you, Ves Hollins."

His chest twists like someone's wringing out a wet rag. Her words have a note of finality, like this is a goodbye. And he wishes it weren't.

All these weeks he'd cursed the valuation specialists for not being here on time, forcing him to wait it out. Giving him the time to fall for the town, for her. The memories he's made here won't melt away like morning frost. They've stacked one on top of the other, a steadfast tundra in his mind.

And now? Now he wishes he'd never picked up that phone call last night. Then maybe he'd be cocooned in bed with her, happy and sated, not out here shivering and bereft of her warmth. Christmas is almost upon them, but he feels like he's already clutching a lump of coal.

"I feel like I've known you forever," he says, but even so, it's not nearly enough.

He wants *more* and he wants it with her.

But how would that discussion even go? After everything she's done to make her career work out in Piney Peaks, he can't see her giving it all up to move to the city. After losing Maeve and her grandma Lou, of course she wants every possible day she can get with Grandpa Dave. She wants to learn the ropes of managing the Chocolate Mouse so she's ready to take over one day—hopefully far in the future—when her parents retire.

Everything she loves in her life is here. He'd be the biggest jerk to even ask her for more.

Elisha's smile is bittersweet. "I'm not ready for it to be over."

Their shared sentiments won't change anything. This was a nice holiday, but he knows he doesn't belong here, no matter how easy it was to pretend he did. And her stance on long-distance relationships won't change. So they're at an impasse. Maybe it's just better to part on good terms.

The brisk air steals his oxygen, or maybe it's just looking at her beautiful face and knowing that it's all coming to an end.

"Me neither," he admits. *We said no strings*, he reminds himself. *No strings*.

"But are you still going to stay?" She falters. "For Christmas, I mean. The end of the Winter Festival. You said Damian told you to take your time, so you could—I mean, if you wanted."

She's giving him an opening. It's the exact opposite of no strings, and he latches onto it with the grip of a desperate man.

"I'll be home—I mean, *here* for Christmas," he promises.

CHAPTER FORTY-SIX

Ves

Adam proposes to Solana in the Old Stoat after Friday-night trivia, five minutes into his shift, two feet away from Ves and Elisha. The happy screeches pound in Ves's ears, even though he puts on a good face.

"Congratulations," he says, shaking Adam's hand and returning Solana's hug.

His blood buzzes pleasantly when he sips his wassail, and then it positively electrifies when Elisha bridges the gap between them with her hand, lacing their fingers loosely together. He likes her friends, so he's happy to be part of their moment, but it's with a bittersweet twinge that he acknowledges a new beginning on the eve of his own new beginning's end.

"I want a spring wedding!" Solana exclaims giddily. She thumps her empty glass of wine on the counter, voice loud and merry. "Ves, it's so beautiful when everything is in bloom. Beautiful like Elisha! Don't sell your beautiful house, either! You'll need it when you come back!"

He lofts a brow. He wonders if he can get drunk Solana to admit that she was steering him in the wrong direction regarding the housing market. He'd figured out her meddling a while ago.

"Oh, bless." Elisha kisses her friend's cheek. "You don't even have a date fixed yet, you drunk mess."

"Well, we will! And Ves should be there! As your plus-one, obviously!"

His heart doubles in size. It's humbling that his presence isn't just wanted, it's expected. As though, *of course* he's going to be there on the day of the wedding day, what absolute *nonsense* to think otherwise!

Solana gets caught up in another round of celebratory drinks and thankfully the subject is dropped, but her exuberant proclamations have sobered him right up.

All Ves can think about is what color Elisha will paint her nails in spring. In summer. Seeing the flowers Maeve loved so much. Putting her to rest somewhere really beautiful.

Another year of trivia Fridays and wiping the floor with Dork Academia. Asking Elisha to move in with him, making the Christmas House truly theirs. Getting up early on the weekends to pitch in at the Chocolate Mouse and learning how to make bebinca, if they'll let him in on the family recipe. Double dates in New York with Arun and Cade. Asking Grandpa Dave what their next woodworking project will be.

God, he wants this life so fucking much.

Ves doesn't want the Piney Peaks bubble to be popped by reality—he wants this life to *be* his reality. He wants this life in a snow globe to put up on a shelf, beautiful and tangible and his.

"Forget coming as Elisha's plus-one," says Adam, leaning in to speak into Ves's ear. "We want you in the wedding party."

Before Ves can do more than gape at him, Adam claps him on the back and heads off. As he and Solana flit among the crowd accepting congratulations and well wishes, it occurs to Ves just how quickly they accepted him as one of their own. At no point has either of them judged him or made him feel less than. No one in Piney Peaks ever has.

Maybe it's not that he's unlovable or that there's anything wrong with his relationships. Maybe it's that the tight-knit families of the Claires and Noras of the world are just shitty people who don't understand that not everyone is like them.

Not everyone is fortunate enough to be loved unconditionally and unreservedly by the people who brought you into this world. But that's a reflection of them, not you.

It hits him like a sucker punch: if he leaves, he'll never get a chance to see if he and Elisha even have a chance in hell.

"Sorry about her," Elisha says now, casting a fond look at her friend. "She knows we were keeping this casual, but she doesn't know that it's over for good when you leave."

His stomach gives a sour lurch.

She sucks her teeth. "Shit. I didn't mean 'for good.' I meant—"

"I know what you meant." He hopes his voice doesn't sound as hollow as he feels. "It's getting a little much in here. Can we step outside for some fresh air?"

She hops off her stool and goes with him to the door. He holds it open for her before following her into the night. Lumpy snowflakes are gently tumbling down to join the untouched snow brushing streets, cars, and rooftops. It's like someone's dusted icing sugar all over the town.

"Beautiful," Elisha breathes, tipping her head back. "Looks like it's going to be a white Christmas."

"Beautiful," he agrees, looking at her instead.

She must hear the catch in his voice, because she burrows into his arms. He holds her close, sheltering her from even the slightest gust of wind, knowing that if he could, he'd do it for the rest of his life.

"You're cute when you're all cuddly," she says, words muffled into his chest. Her hands wrap around his back, squeezing tight. "I don't want to let go of you."

He tucks his head on top of hers. "I was going to say the same thing."

"I said it first."

He starts to snort at her adorable, triumphant tone, but then disguises it as a laugh. "Fine, you win."

Piney Peaks is so quiet. Literally, not a creature is stirring. Main Street twinkles with lights, but everyone is inside houses or restaurants. Spirals of smoke puff out of chimneys, trailing up to the stars before fading away entirely. The Christmas Market surrounding the church has wrapped up for the season, and as the church bell chimes ten times before plunging the town back into silence, Ves shivers.

In New York, it's impossible to escape the sheer amount of life that hums on every street corner. He's never stood outside in the open air and felt like one of only two people in the universe. It brings a clarity like he's never felt before, along with a rush of determination to get this off his chest before his courage dwindles. "This is going to be the happiest and saddest Christmas of my life, Elisha."

She pulls back to look at him. "Ves . . ."

Swiftly, he shakes his head. "No, let me say it. I know we said we wouldn't do strings, but every inch of me is so goddamn knotted up in you that I can't just go home and bury everything that's happened in a box. I can't. No, not can't. I *won't*. At this point, it's a physical impossibility to walk away from this. From us. I want to keep seeing you. We can make this work."

There, he's said it. He's handed her his heart and now he has to trust she won't break it.

Elisha's inhale is ragged. "Ves, I . . . I like you a lot. But I've done the long-distance thing before. And I know you aren't Bentley, and maybe things will be different for us, but I don't want to be naïve little Elisha again. I can't feel like that again. All those years ago, when I waited and waited for Bentley to join me like he promised, all I could do was cling to the belief that he wanted a life here with me as much as I did. That he was choosing *me*. And with every missed day, with every excuse, I still wanted to believe in him so much. I put the kind of stock in us that kids put in Santa Claus."

Her self-deprecating laugh skewers Ves's heart as she continues, "I kind of hate myself for saying this, because I believe in the underdog beating the odds, but I can't put myself through that kind of disappointment again. You know I came back home for my family, and it's still just as important to me as ever. I can do weekends with you in the city, but eventually that won't be enough for either of us. New York is your home. Piney Peaks is mine. Do you see that ever changing? Can you honestly say you'd be happy with having a girlfriend you only see a couple of days a week?"

The honest answer is no, he wants her every day, but they can still try, can't they? "We can text. FaceTime. And I can come visit you here. We have options."

Ves tries to sound confident, but fuck, he's already coming around to her way of thinking. Technology connects people, but it's also a reminder of the distance between them.

He wants to wake up every day with her legs tangled in his, her hand splayed possessively over his chest, her morning frizz tickling him as she buries her face in his neck. He wants to hear all about her day while cooking dinner together before cuddling up on the couch with Thor and Thorin and hot chocolate with way too many marshmallows to watch a film. He wants to end the night making love and falling asleep in each other's arms.

Anything else would fall woefully short of what he yearns for.

"I love that you want to try," she says, sounding impossibly kind. As she always is. "And we can still be friends, obviously, but this has been my best Christmas in years, and it would break my heart if all these lovely memories were tarnished by a messy breakup. You mean too much to me." Her eyes plead with him, made luminous in the reflection of the streetlamps. "Let's just enjoy the next few days? I don't want to ruin what we have. That's why I think it's best if we end things when you leave. Fantasies never live up to reality."

But if you let fear stop you, then what we have will only ever be memories is what he wants to say.

"You're probably right" is what he says instead, tabling his thoughts before they can leak out of him.

"We'll always have Christmas," Elisha says quietly.

Somehow, that makes Ves feel worse.

Because, in his heart, he is still a boy who believes in fantasies and getting the girl and happily ever after.

CHAPTER FORTY-SEVEN

Ves

Thorin wakes Ves up on Christmas morning with a swish of his tail. Ves sputters around a mouthful of fluffy black cat hair, shooting upright in bed to glower at him. Thorin primly licks a paw and jumps from the bed, landing nimbly on the floor next to Elisha's clothes from last night.

"Merry Christmas," she murmurs, throwing an arm around his waist and pulling him back down.

"Merry Christmas," he says, dropping a kiss on her temple.

She smiles, sighing contentedly.

Ves stares down at her in bewildered astonishment. How can she look so at peace when his insides feel as shaken as a snow globe?

How does he just get up and deal with the fact that there's a last time for everything? A last kiss. A last sleepy morning snuggled together in bed. A last time he's going to be the person he is right now, with her, in this quiet moment before they go to her house to celebrate the day.

How is he supposed to be okay with any of this?

Elisha blearily cracks one eye open. "I can hear you thinking."

He makes a noncommittal sound as he strokes her forearms, grazing his fingertips up and down. He knows how much she enjoys the languid touches, the way it takes him a long time to tire. She especially likes when he does it to her spine, shivering when he reaches her tailbone.

If they had time, he'd show her how much *he* likes that whimpering sound she makes when he lulls her pleasurably boneless, then picks up the pace until they're both frenzied with want.

But they're all out of time.

They shower together, taking turns under the hot water, slipping the loofah around each other's bodies until they're both slick and sudsy. No quickie this time, just a sensual re-anchoring to the present moment as they stare into each other's eyes and exchange sloppy kisses.

When they head across the street armed with presents, he almost feels like he's ready for it.

Jamie opens the door and takes Ves's jacket. "Merry Christmas, you two!"

"Don't you both look lovely," says Anita, beaming. "New sweater?"

"Thank you, yes. I got it at this little shop on Main Street." Ves glances down at his color-block sweater with pride. He usually sticks to solid, neutral colors, but he went a little wild with this one: beige, white, navy, and gray. Before meeting Elisha, he would have called it an ugly Christmas sweater.

"This is his idea of colorful," says Elisha, looking up at him fondly.

Jamie eyes his daughter's outfit. "At least someone dressed up for Christmas Day. You, young lady, are wearing the same thing as yesterday."

Her face turns red. "I'll go change!" she yelps.

Anita shakes her head, smiling. "Come on, Ves. Dave's already here."

In the kitchen, they find him scrambling eggs and turning perfectly golden-brown sausage in the pan. "Just in time!" he exclaims, twinkling at Ves.

This time, when the hug comes, Ves embraces it. Dave's arms are strong and sturdy, the whisper of sweet peppermint tingling Ves's nostrils as his chin meets the older man's shoulder. He never knew his grandparents, but he imagines a hug from them would have felt like this.

Dave pulls away with a resigned smile. "When do you head back to New York?"

Anita's waiting for his answer, too, as she pulls cinnamon rolls from the oven, baby-blue snowman mitts padding her hands. The scent of rich browned butter and caramelized brown sugar is intoxicating.

"Tomorrow," says Ves, unable to muster a smile in return.

"Did everything that you wanted?" Dave asks lightly as he carefully rotates the sausage.

"Yeah, explored the shops in town. Visited the Christmas Market. Did all the touristy things. I'm glad I stayed for the Winter Festival, got to meet you all."

But they both know what Dave was really asking.

Elisha slips back into the room just as everything is being pulled out of the oven. She's changed into a buffalo-check miniskirt, knee-high black socks, and a tucked-in black turtleneck. "Oh my god, Dad, Gramps, all this smells amazing!" She grabs a plate of maple-bacon scones and joins them at the table, sitting next to Ves.

"You look beautiful," he says.

She grins. "So do you." She cups his cheek, running the soft pad of her thumb over his cheekbone. "Christmas is a good look on you. You seem happy."

He catches her hand, laces their fingers together. "It's not Christmas that makes me happy," he replies in a voice too low for anyone else to hear.

"Don't stand on ceremony," Anita says with a laugh, pouring out cups of steaming coffee. "Help yourselves, everyone!"

They all open presents as they eat, which is new to Ves. When he was growing up, presents were opened only after a formal breakfast, and with Arun's family's, first thing upon waking up. As a kid and teenager, he'd spent many winter breaks at their house, and Arun's younger siblings would drag everyone out of bed without even a chance to brush their hair or teeth to gather around the tree.

Dave shovels a scone in his mouth and benevolently waves a hand. "Ves, Elisha, go on."

Even in this, they're total opposites. Elisha rips into the wrapping paper with abandon, while Ves carefully slides his finger under the tape to wiggle it loose.

"Writers' Tears Irish whiskey?" Ves holds it up by the neck, grinning. "I can guess who this is from."

Dave guffaws. "Will it help you write? Probably not. Will it make the writing more pleasurable? Almost undoubtedly."

"It's perfect. Thank you."

"My turn," announces Anita, handing a lumpy present to her husband, who tears into it.

Jamie holds up a brand-new NYU sweatshirt. "You shouldn't have!"

"I'm going to throw out your old ratty one."

"You *really* shouldn't have," he says with a long-suffering sigh that seems more playful than put out.

Jamie promptly dons both his new sweatshirt and a gorgeous plush robe before diving into the manual for his top-of-the-line air fryer.

Dave is delighted with the new tools and beverage refrigerator for his workshop, a beard grooming kit, and, from Ves, an engraved flask.

Anita tears up at the diamond solitaire necklace and matching bracelet, wine subscription, and, from Ves, a couples spa certificate.

Elisha gets gold huggie earrings and a black moto jacket from her parents, a Sephora gift card from her grandpa, upcoming concert tickets from Solana and Adam, and a red money-envelope adorned with gold foil embellishments from her grandparents in Goa.

Between bites of a perfectly roasted squash-and-bacon hash, Ves opens his gifts: he gets a cozy cream cardigan with beautiful tortoiseshell buttons from Anita and Jamie, along with an assortment of their homemade candy from the Chocolate Mouse and a few small, fluffy cat toys. Elisha surprises him with Solana's present, a set of pencils with funny sayings on them and a faux leather journal. Waiting for him in the city are new AirPods from Arun and a temperature-controlled mug from Cade—Arun is truly hopeless at keeping secrets that aren't work-related.

When his phone rings, he's enjoying himself so much with the Rowes that he almost doesn't hear it. "I have to take this. It's my sister," he explains. Everyone falls considerately silent as he answers.

"Merry Christmas, Ves!" she shrieks down the line. He hears both his father and stepmother repeat the greeting in the background, more perfunctory than cheery.

He's bemused at his sister's exuberance. "Merry Christmas, Hans. Did you have fun skiing?"

"Yeah! Did you get good presents?" she wants to know.

"The best," he confirms.

"Nuh-uh. Not the *best*. You haven't opened mine yet. I'll give it to you the next time I see you, that way I know you'll come."

He half frowns. "You know if you want to see me, you just have to ask, right?"

Uncertainty trickles down the line. "I guess, but Dad always says I shouldn't bother you because you're busy and you're an adult, so . . ."

"You never bother me, Hanna," he says firmly. "Ignore Dad. I'm always here for you."

She drops her voice, a little scandalized, impressed, and apologetic all at once. "I forgot to tell you that you're on speaker. He heard you say that."

He laughs under his breath. "Don't worry about it."

"Dad wants to talk to you. I'll text you after."

A second later, Karl says, "Please do not tell your sister to ignore me, Ves. That undermines me as a parent."

"Yeah, sorry, I shouldn't have said that. But what am I supposed to say when she tells me— You know what, never mind. Just . . . stop making her feel like she's a nuisance."

"Fine," comes Karl's clipped reply. "I'm always the bad guy."

Ves really doesn't have the energy for this conversation. And especially not with the Rowes right there, all of them eating uncomfortably, not making a peep. Even though they can only hear one side of the conversation, he knows they've picked up on his change of tone. "I'm having breakfast with the Rowes. Why don't I call you back later?"

"You take calls in front of other people?"

"I'm not you, Dad." What he really means is *I have nothing to hide.*

"No need to call me back. I just wanted to wish you a Merry

Christmas." The call ends, which Ves was expecting, knowing how curt Karl can be, but it still stings.

"I didn't know you had a sister, Ves," Anita says lightly when Ves puts the phone down. "It's nice that you're so close."

"We weren't always," he admits. "We have to work at it. She's much younger than I am."

"You have a big family?" asks Dave.

Ves glances at Elisha, then away. "No, but maybe someday."

Dave grins. "Then younger siblings are good practice."

Jamie coughs. "Dad, you do realize your children—my older siblings—tormented me all through childhood, right?"

Dave stabs a sausage. "You were the baby. That's different."

"Well, I guess hiding in the kitchen with Mom taught me everything I know about baking," says Jamie.

"Grandma Lou would have liked you, Ves," Elisha says decisively. "Right, Grandpa?"

Dave gives a sage nod. "Oh, undoubtedly."

Tears prick at Ves's eyes. "This fruit salad is amazing," he says, digging through the festive medley. A mint syrup is drizzled over cut strawberries, honeydew melon, red and green grapes, and kiwis, everything sprinkled with jeweled pomegranate seeds. "Anita, Jamie . . . I'm going to miss your cooking as much as I'll miss all of you."

"No talking about sad things today," Anita says brusquely.

Jamie reaches out to clap Ves on the shoulder. "We'll miss you too, son."

The lump in Ves's throat grows impossibly bigger. If anyone finds it odd that he hides his expression by studiously staring at the fruit he's eating, they're too polite to say so.

"You haven't opened mine yet!" Elisha cries, sliding a rectangular package to him.

It's wrapped in glossy red plaid paper, scattered with sprigs of holly. He gives it a light shake. There's a good weight to it. "A book?"

"Close." She glances at her family, unable to restrain her full-blown grin. Whatever secret they share is seconds away from coming out, and all of them look on with anticipation. Still, no one hustles him as he neatly removes the wrapping.

It's a photo album. He opens it, coming face to face with dozens of pages filled with pictures of himself. In the earliest, he's a baby swamped in a lacy white frock, professionally posed even though he can barely hold up his own head. In later ones, he's a well-dressed toddler sitting in his mother's lap, his father standing stiffly behind them. He doesn't remember ever seeing these at home.

But what truly knocks the air out of Ves's lungs is the overexposed photo of a seven-year-old him in what is clearly the Chocolate Mouse, face screwed up because of the younger girl next to him grinning into the camera, dangling a milk-chocolate mouse by the tail in front of him. *Elisha.* A rascal even then.

And after that are a few more pages of him as a child at the Christmas House; excitedly holding the reins of a stationary sleigh; reading some enormous medical tome with a look of intense concentration . . .

Finally, he raises wet eyes to the Rowes. "How did you get all these?"

"I went through all the old albums," says Elisha. "Maeve and Grandma Lou took a lot of pictures when I was growing up. I figured that Maeve would have some of you, too, over the years."

Ves turns to the last page. There's him and Maeve. She's just given him the red scarf and he remembers pulling out his phone for a quick snap. She'd waved him off, pulling out an old disposable camera, insisting a real picture was better. She was right. If he'd taken a picture with his phone that day, it would be uploaded and forgotten in cloud storage. He probably wouldn't have looked at it again.

He closes the book with reverence. "Thank you," he says hoarsely.

When they get ready to go back to his house a couple of hours later, Grandpa Dave takes them aside for a second. "Are you planning to meet up in the city for New Year's Eve?" he asks. "I have to head up that way to pick up some reclaimed barnwood. We could coordinate."

"Oh, Grandpa." Elisha glances at Ves before answering. "He always spends New Year's with his best friend's family. We're actually not going to do the whole long-distance thing. It's too complicated."

For the thousandth time that day, Ves is second-guessing her decision and his earlier agreement. But he doesn't want to disagree with her publicly, so he shuffles silently into his shoes.

Dave shakes his head. "There's nothing complicated about love, Elisha. It's you kids who are *making* it complicated. Everything is possible with a little gumption."

CHAPTER FORTY-EIGHT

Elisha

The day after Christmas, Ves leaves at an ungodly hour of the morning. The whole street turns out to wave him goodbye, even Marcy in her terry bathrobe and hair curlers piled high on top of her head. Elisha joins them, but she and Ves already said their private goodbyes last night, between feverish kisses and gentle thrusts.

It's harder than she thought to see his luggage disappear into the trunk of his Uber, Thor and Thorin in the back seat, plaintively mewling. Long after everyone else goes back inside, she stays on the porch, staring down the road even though his Uber has already disappeared.

And for the first time, she feels cold.

"Pancakes or Belgian waffles?" her dad asks when she groggily makes her way back into the kitchen, blinking back tears. Her eyes sting from the wind, from not enough sleep, from possibly making the biggest mistake of her life.

"Pancakes, please." She clambers up on a barstool and groans, holding her head in her hands.

"How are you, sweetie?" Jamie asks, looking sympathetic. "I hope the cats don't give him too much grief on the journey . . . they're not used to the carriers. You can call and check up on all three of them. Should only be a couple of hours as long as his Uber doesn't get stuck in holiday traffic."

"No, we decided not to—" She stops herself. She doesn't want to talk about Ves right now, not when it's still so raw. It's the last thing she wants to put into words. But in her haste to change the subject, she instead blurts out the very thing she had been trying all week to keep from her parents. "Do you remember Veronica Fox? My old boss in the Georgia Film Office?"

She immediately wants to take it back. The pan sizzles with the first pat of cold butter Jamie tosses in, quickly melting enough that he can coat every inch. "Sure," he says.

Elisha takes a deep breath. She started this, she might as well see it through.

"I met up with her while I was in New York." Elisha watches as the batter hits the pan, immediately sizzling. "She offered me a job. And I . . . have to decide if that's something I want."

"You'd have to live in the city?" Jamie flips the pancake. It's a little thicker and browner than usual, the way first pancakes often are. "But that's great, right, honey? You'd be closer to Ves."

Which is exactly why she can't let that be a factor in her decision. She can't base her career decisions around a guy who she's only casual with. What if she accepts Veronica's offer, thinking he'll be stoked to have her closer, only to find out down the line that he's not into it?

She doesn't think he'd be like that, but she's been wrong before. And she doesn't want to uproot herself, even if it's just a couple of hours away, for something that could be nothing. Especially since she came back to her hometown for a reason, and that reason hasn't changed. She wants to be near her family. And Veronica can offer her a lot, even a fifty-fifty partnership, but the job will take her away from something irreplaceable: home.

"I think that's partly why I'm hesitating," Elisha admits. "I don't want to be tempted because of him."

"But it *is* a temptation?" Jamie clarifies, getting to work on the second pancake.

"I'd be lying if I said it wasn't. But it's not just him. I adore Piney Peaks. I think I'm doing something good here. There are already a ton of film and TV opportunities in New York. I can't help but think that I'm kind of unnecessary there. Anyone can do what Veronica wants me to do. But unearthing gems like our town all over Pennsylvania? That's . . . that's like magic, Dad. And there are plenty of towns that *want* to do what I'm trying to do here. With Danica's support, who knows where this could go?"

Jamie smiles. "Elisha, you know what it sounds like to me? Like you've made up your mind about that job offer."

The second he says it, she knows it's true. She talked herself out of it almost as soon as Veronica laid all her cards on the table. She just didn't turn it down flat at the time because, well, Ves.

"Dad, do I have a few minutes before we eat? I want to send an email really quick."

"Sure, honey."

So while her dad flips more pancakes and listens to her mom sharing the Goa group chat's latest gossip, Elisha tugs out her laptop and starts to type.

To: Fox, Veronica
From: Rowe, Elisha

Dear Veronica,

I hope this email finds you well. Having had some time to think about your generous offer, I've reached a decision. It may not come as a surprise to you that, with genuine regret, I have to decline.

I know you won't agree with my reasons, but as someone who just struck out on her own, I also know that you admire women who take their own initiative. I believe that if I seek magic, I can find it. And I think there's nowhere in the world that's ready to be found more than Piney Peaks. As my former mentor, I hope one day you'll see what I can do and be proud of however far I get in my hometown.

Wishing you a happy New Year!

Elisha Rowe (she/her)

Film & Digital Media Liaison
Piney Peaks Chamber of Commerce

CHAPTER FORTY-NINE

Ves

Ves doesn't have an Ebenezer Scrooge epiphany moment that magically and irrevocably changes him overnight. Rather, it happens over many small moments, over time. But they all include one person, and she doesn't haunt him so much as make him whole.

December 31st, 11:55 PM

> Ves: Happy New Year's Eve [sends picture of himself, Arun, and Cade in suits]

Elisha: HAPPY NYE!!!

Elisha: How is the Iyers' party?

> Ves: They've gone all out. It's even bigger than last year's. [sends picture of the room]

Elisha: WOW so fancy fancy

Ves: I'd trade it for Piney Peaks.

Elisha: Yeah no

Elisha: If you think Mistletoe Miscreants are bad, wait for the NYE Midnight Miscreants

Ves: Tell them you're spoken for.

Elisha: I think I've learned my lesson about claiming nonexistent boyfriends haha

Ves: He could exist.

Elisha: Ves

Ves: I'm just saying.

Elisha: Don't JUST SAY

Elisha: Of course it's you I want to be kissing tonight

Elisha: Not just tonight

Elisha: Every night

Elisha: Whenever I wanted

Elisha: I'm not kissing anyone else tonight,
just fyi

Ves: Good. Me neither.

Ves never imagined a day would come when he'd say this, but he's finally found the girl who consumes his every thought. It's only when he's without her that he becomes acutely aware of how different *he* is, how much he's changed from the man who arrived in Piney Peaks so sure of everything he knew nothing about.

It's only when he's not talking to Elisha that his life goes by in slow motion, everything sluggish and fuzzy.

He hates it.

For the first time in his life, his heart is arguing with his head, refusing to accept anything less than what will make him incandescently happy.

CHAPTER FIFTY

Elisha

Elisha thinks that in a perfect world, she would never have made the mistake of falling for Ves. Of tricking herself into thinking that once she'd had a taste, she could say goodbye to him like they'd never been together at all. Of thinking she was capable of something fleeting instead of forever.

But no sooner does the thought cross her mind than she yanks it back. Maybe there is a world out there in which she sticks to the terms she'd outlined—*a little holiday romance, just casual, no strings attached*—but it's not this one.

January 3rd, 2:05 PM

Ves: How was your flight?

> Elisha: Just landed and can't wait to catch
> some zzz's bc it's so impossible on the
> plane. I hateeeee long flights, I'm so stiff.
> Food was blah, but the in-flight movies

were good. Saw the newest *Banshee of the Baskervilles* movie!

Ves: I enjoyed it, too. Finally got around to watching *The Holiday*, by the way.

Elisha: You get the Jude Law thing now?

Ves: I preferred the Jack Black storyline.

Elisha: There you go being unpredictable again!!!

Ves: It's called having taste 💁

Elisha: You've never used a sassy emoji before 👀

Ves: I'm growing as a person 😏

Elisha: Wait, what time is it for you?

Elisha: My phone already switched me to local time

Elisha: OMG WTF VES IT IS THE MIDDLE OF THE NIGHT FOR YOU, GO TO SLEEP

Elisha: WAIT HOW DID YOU EVEN KNOW WHEN I LANDED

Elisha: ???

Ves: You told me what flight you were on, so I looked it up and tracked the flight plan.

Elisha: HA HA, NO REALLY

Ves: I assure you, it's perfectly normal and publicly available online.

Elisha: How are you real?

Ves: I'm sorry. Should I not have?

Elisha: No, it's sweet. But now I feel bad you were probably worried I could crash in the Atlantic or whatever haha

Elisha: Now go to sleep xxxxx

Elisha: You're not the elf and the three socks anymore btw

Elisha: You haven't been for a long time actually

Ves: What's my new emoji?

Elisha: [sends screenshot]

Ves: A scarf, my name, and a flan?

>Elisha: The flan is standing in for bebinca.
>Too cheesy?

Ves: No, it's perfect.

Elisha's heart gives a giddy backflip, then sinks to the bottom of her stomach. Not for the first time, she has to wonder whether she was too hasty in not even trying a long-distance relationship with Ves. Isn't that already kind of what they're doing?

Somehow, without even intending to, they've slipped into an easy friendship and flirtation. Sure, their timing doesn't always align, and yes, she misses the hell out of him, but . . . he messaged her as soon as she landed. He tracked her flight, a thing she didn't even know existed but was positive no other guy had ever done for her.

Lana would call him a simp, for sure, but all Elisha wants to call him is *hers*.

CHAPTER FIFTY-ONE

Ves

Ves counts down the days and knows she'll be returning home soon. *Home.* It's taken him a while to come to terms with it, but he knows now: New York isn't his home. Not anymore. It's just the place where he lives. For now.

January 10th, 8:32 PM

> Ves: I know you won't see this until you wake up, but I thought you'd get a kick of this. [sends picture of a restaurant sign]

Elisha: No worries, I'm up! The waves and the birds ease me into it haha

Elisha: OMG is that a RAT on the sign

> Ves: I'm out with the boys for Cade's birthday. Arun swears it's the best

Brazilian steakhouse ever. Since you've
been making me jealous with all the pics of
the Goan food you've been eating, figured
I'd return the favor. Not sure how the rat is
relevant, but it made me think of you.

Elisha: You sweet-talker youuuuu

Elisha: I mean, on the other hand lol, I'm glad
you're thinking of me?

Elisha: The name is Tuco-Tuco? What does
that mean?

Ves: No idea.

Elisha: LMAO VES DID YOU GOOGLE THE
MEANING

Ves: I'm going to guess that you did?

Elisha: [sends screenshot]

Ves: You're kidding me.

Elisha: I never kid about something as
serious as rodent-named restaurants.

Ves: Even when I'm not in Piney Peaks, I
can't escape from it.

Ves: Stoats, mice, chinchillas, and now
tuco-tuco.

Elisha: Again, technically a stoat is a
weasel . . .

This exchange never fails to make him laugh, no matter how
many times he rereads it, until he's sure of one thing beyond all
doubt: he is absolutely, totally, and completely in love with her.

CHAPTER FIFTY-TWO

Elisha

After their two-week vacation in Goa, the Rowe family returns home to Piney Peaks. Elisha yawns around her thermos of hazelnut coffee, brewed hot at the Chocolate Mouse, and crosses the street to survey what's happening at the diner, where the first scene is being filmed. The street is cordoned off, but there are enough people milling around hoping to catch a peek of the leads.

Just like the original *Sleighbells*, all the extras and minor speaking roles will be locals, to everyone's delight. And no one is more excited than Grandpa Dave, personally requested by Damian to play a townsperson after he heard about the revamped sleigh. Even Noelle the Clydesdale plays a part in pulling the sleigh, dubbed by Damian as the most photogenic horse in the stables thanks to Elisha's pictures.

"How are you not jet-lagged?" asks Mia, who's been running point in Elisha's stead. Around a mouthful of Pop-Tart, she adds, "If *I* got back in the middle of the night I wouldn't be working today."

"Oh, I'm not officially back yet. But it's January fifteenth! The first day of filming! I'm probably not going to last the whole day, but of course I had to visit the set." Elisha glances at the diner. Cameras, cords, and production lighting are everywhere, but she doesn't see Heather or Nathan, who were supposed to have flown out over the weekend, or the up-and-comer leads playing their grandkids and respective love interests. "Uh, Mia. Fill me in, what's going on? Where's the cast?"

"The leads are still in their trailers and apparently some of the extras are sick, so Damian's trying to wrangle replacements."

No sooner is the sentence out before the man himself appears, looking relieved beyond measure to see her. "Elisha, I didn't think you'd be here today."

"I wouldn't miss this for the world. I hear you've had some trouble with the extras? Is there anything I can do to help?"

He scrutinizes her, then snatches the coffee from her hands and passes to Mia. "Yes, actually. How would you like to be one?"

"But I'm not an—" Her yelp trails off as he herds her toward the entrance of the diner.

Elisha is all too aware of the flight fatigue that even her morning skincare couldn't quite cover. She presses the heel of her palms into her eyes, willing away the dryness and the start of a headache. "Damian, really, you don't want me, I promise. You don't know this about me, but I was replaced as Tree #3 in my first-grade play! There's a reason I'm strictly behind-the-scenes only! I am literally the worst person for this!"

"Nonsense. Now, I won't hear another word about it. You are the perfect person." His face breaks into a smile. "It's good to have you back, Elisha."

Elisha sighs and gives up, sinking into the red-plastic booth. The other extras semi-perk up when Damian says they won't have to wait much longer, which makes her wonder exactly how much earlier they got here. Someone plonks down a mug of coffee in front of her, along with instructions to not actually drink it because it's already cold and this scene may need a few takes to get right.

"I thought this would be way more fun," Becca says with a sigh, twirling her hair. She's in the booth opposite Elisha with the people playing her family: a hot older DILF-type fondly watching his two little boys play on their Nintendo Switches.

At the table between them, Riley nods in agreement. He's here with his parents, and all three of them look bored as hell. Adhira's at work, but her husband, Sam Ambani, a stay-at-home dad, is there with their toddler daughter, Taj, who's determinedly clutching crayons and focusing on her coloring book. He catches Elisha's eye and sighs with exaggerated boredom that sets everyone off in laughter.

The minutes slowly tick by. Every few seconds Elisha's eyes flutter shut and her neck droops, but she catches herself in time. Maybe she should have slept in after all, but she felt guilty doing so when her parents were opening the Chocolate Mouse first thing.

She stares down at the cold mug, half tempted to risk taking a sip. God, she wishes she had her own thermos back. Hot coffee would wake her up for sure.

Someone abruptly slides into the other side of the booth. Her head jerks. "I wasn't sleeping!"

Mia snorts. "Uh-huh. Change of plans, Sleeping Beauty."

Elisha brightens. "You mean I get to leave? I mean, oh darn." She tries to look suitably disappointed.

"Very believable," says Riley, straight-faced. "I can see why they picked you to be an extra."

"Watch it or I'll stage a coup at the next trivia night," says Elisha. "I'd be an *awesome* captain."

"Do you need a second-in-command?" Mia asks with a wink. "I've wanted to oust him forever."

"Fuck you guys," he grumbles.

Sam blinks. "Adhira never said trivia was so cutthroat. I've really been missing out."

Mia gestures for Elisha to get up and follow her. "So," she says, keeping her voice low as they exit the diner, "little problem."

"Okay, that's something you never want to hear on day one of a new project."

"There's some problem in the Enchanted Forest, and Damian needs you to get up there and deal with it. You walked here, right? Here, take my car." Mia presses the keys into Elisha's hand.

"Wait, but what's the problem, exactly? Hey! You don't need to push me!" Elisha protests.

"He wants you there *now*."

"I didn't think the forest scene was on today's call sheet! What's going on with the diner?"

Mia doesn't let them break stride. "Damian knows what he's doing."

"Of course, but—"

"Elisha, he said now!"

Which is how, ten minutes later, Elisha finds herself about a mile into the forest, bypassing the general park for the pull-out where white traffic cones are marked with signs for *Sleighbells* use.

After spending the drive over panicking about everything that could have possibly gone wrong despite all their best planning, she was expecting chaos. Actors losing their shit all over the place, Damian threatening someone over the phone in a booming voice, the wail of an ambulance, maybe even a lurky photographer stuck up a tree in hopes of a salacious photo or two.

Instead, what she finds makes zero sense in the slightest—nobody else is here.

"Great," Elisha mutters, scanning the scraggly canopy of birches and pine overhead. "I'm a woman alone in the forest. That's not creepy at all."

She's about to call Damian for some idea of what has actually gone wrong and what he needs from her, when she hears the faint tinkling of . . . sleigh bells?

The sound drifts from far away, too distant to pinpoint exactly, and then it's everywhere, all at once, surrounding her.

Her grandpa's gleaming red sleigh is gliding determinedly toward her, pulled by Noelle. Sunlight dapples through the trees, basking the driver in a spectacular gold. Gilting the tips of his platinum hair, peeking over the broadness of his shoulders. Elisha doesn't dare blink in case he slips away.

"Ves?" Her heart stutters as he comes to a stop in front of her.

"Whoa," he says to the horse, relaxing his grip on the reins.

"What are you doing here?"

"I got here just a little while ago. I told Damian I needed to talk to you, and I tried to get on to the set, but he said he'd do me one better." He holds out his hand. "You deserve the magic, Elisha."

She lets him help her into the sleigh. "So there's no disaster I need to mitigate? No impending crisis?"

His mouth twitches into a slightly remorseful smile. "Sorry about the pretext. Didn't need much convincing for Dave to help me hitch Noelle to the sleigh, or for Mia to get you here."

She gapes. "Everything I said about you being predictable? Scratch that. But also, why? And how?"

"Well, I met a girl," he drawls. "Someone who got me to move out of my comfort zones."

She bats at his hand when he spreads a red plaid blanket over her lap, far more interested in getting answers than getting warm. "No, seriously, Ves. How are you here?"

"I took the bus."

"You took the—" With a disbelieving laugh, she reaches out, grasps the collar of his gray corduroy jacket. "I'm not dreaming."

"I don't want to not have strings with you, Elisha."

"What?"

"I know I gave you a hard time in the beginning, but you were the best welcome committee I could have ever asked for. In fact, I . . ." He visibly swallows. "I'm thinking about staying for a while. Enjoy Piney Peaks's famous hospitality a little longer. Or a lot longer. If I'm . . . if I'm wanted."

For a moment, she's nearly too stunned to speak. In this town decorated in nostalgia, Ves Hollins is real and solid and right in front of her, doing the most romantic thing she's pretty sure either of them has ever done. At least, until she hears what he says next.

"I bought my house back."

Her second *"What?!"* is earsplitting.

"Here," she repeats, just to make sure she has it right. She's so stunned that he manages to snugly tuck the blanket around her waist. "What about New York? What about your home?"

"After I left, I kept waiting for the city to feel like home again. But it wasn't New York that was different, it was me. And I saw myself reflected in the subway windows, in random shop windows on the street, and I'd try to figure out what about me had changed. I used to feel comforted seeing myself, one person among so many others, and I used to think, *There I am. I exist. I'm a person in this world and this city is my home.* But it couldn't be that for me anymore, not now that I met you. Randomly enough, I realized it while I was on my way home from picking up dinner one night and I caught my reflection in the window of a passing bus and it struck me so fucking hard: home is wherever *you* are, Elisha Rowe."

She isn't sure what he sees in her face, but some of the tension eases out of his shoulders.

"You asked me once if I wanted to keep the house," he continues. "I think *everyone's* asked me that, honestly. And I listened with my head instead of my heart when I said no. It's what I've been doing my whole life and I don't want to do that anymore."

His hand drifts to her waist, holding her tight. She thinks he means to kiss her, if that burning ferocity in his eyes is anything to go by, and she eagerly tries to meet his mouth. Then his fingers dig into her hips, and before her brain can catch up with the surprise move, he's hauling her up onto his lap.

Ves's arms wrap snugly around her waist and his mouth presses to hers, lips cold, but the moment they meet hers, she's warm all over. She missed this, missed him, and she wriggles as close to his chest as she can get, drawing every bit of his scalding heat.

He kisses her like it's a *need*, not just a want. With desire and desperation and possessiveness that makes her shiver, thread her fingers into his hair. The hungry, greedy rumble from deep within his chest sends her every thought scattering.

"Ves," she mumbles against his lips. "What are you doing?"

"Kissing you. If you thought I was doing something else, clearly I was doing this wrong."

With one finger, she traces the line of his jaw. "Don't be a smartass."

Noelle whinnies her agreement, tossing her head and stamping her hooves.

"All right." Ves brushes his lips over her temple. "Maybe this is just a holiday romance. Maybe it's a lot more. I don't know which it is, but god do I want to find out. Personally, I know what I prefer." His eyes crinkle at the corner when he smiles. "Damian understood why I needed to get the house back."

Yes, Elisha can see how—of all people—he would.

"What color are your nails in the spring?" he asks.

Bewildered, she blinks at him. "Pink, usually. Blue or white sometimes. Why?"

"No reason." And then he's kissing her again, and she's grabbing at his hair, at his shoulders, at anywhere she can reach.

"Don't do that again," she whispers.

"Do what, my love?"

"Leave," she confesses.

"Elisha, if I'm right about this, I'm not going anywhere ever again."

EPILOGUE

Ves

Next Year, May

Spring in Piney Peaks, Ves discovers, is just as enchanting as winter. Everything is in bloom, his kitchen remodel is finally done, and any second now, Elisha will be back from her work trip. The last week without her has, in a word, sucked.

When the Rowes took their annual holiday vacation to Goa, her absence didn't ache as much as it did last year. Maybe because they FaceTimed every night and she "took" him with her on live video whenever there was something cool she wanted to show him.

Ves had done the same for her when he went to the city for the monthly brother-sister weekends he and Hanna had started ever since he decided to keep Maeve's house. He let her pick whatever she wanted to do together—this time had been a Broadway show and Petrossian for their rich and silky hot chocolate and flaky croissants. Their latest adventure, which Hanna took very seriously, was narrowing down the city's top three hot chocolates. Mission successful, Ves had just returned home to Piney Peaks.

"Honey, I'm home!" Elisha cries dramatically as she enters the living room. Like the kitchen, he's updated it to match his tastes. A neutral palette, gray and cream with the occasional leather accent, and not a floral in sight. Well, except for the white peonies he got to celebrate her return.

"Welcome home, my love."

"Ves, did you really leave the door unlocked?" she asks, incredulous, stepping around Thor and Thorin, who also missed her but won't deign to stop for a hello. "We're a safe town, but still!"

Seeing her again is like seeing the sun after a lifetime spent in gray cloud. Maeve's necklace glints at her throat, and the white sundress she's wearing makes his mouth run dry. He wants to pull the bow straps on each shoulder and let the cotton puddle to the floor.

"Can't have you breaking in again," he says, getting to his feet with a smirk. The banter is their thing, even though he returned her key to her a year ago. He leaves the document open on his laptop; he's just started writing Chapter One of the new fantasy novel Dominique green-lit.

"Mm-hmm, but is it still breaking in if I'm wanted?" she asks, batting her eyes at him.

He thinks he's wanted her from the moment he saw her, even if he wasn't ready to realize it then. "I still can't believe you thought *I* was the thief," he says, amusement quirking his lips. He takes her hand, eyeing the baby-blue nail polish and the white daisies with their perfect yellow circle centers. "Little did I know you'd be the one stealing my heart."

She groans but tugs him closer for a sweet peck on the lips, pulling back before he can deepen it. "Were you working on that line the whole time I was gone?"

He draws back, mock offended. "You mean it didn't work?"

Elisha grins up at him. "Of course it worked. I haven't seen you for a week. You just looking at me with those eyes is enough to 'work.'" She quirks an eyebrow at his laptop. "How's the writing going?"

It had taken him a while to figure out what he wanted to write next, and in the meantime, he'd taken Hero up on her offer to co-write the graphic novel. Arun is *still* crowing over the success of the collab, mostly because when Ves grudgingly admitted what a good idea it was after all, Arun got to deploy an "I told you so."

While Hero finishes up the art, he's moved on to his own new middle-grade series: about a boy new to a magical town, the local girl who takes him under her wing, and the adorable chocolate-brown mouse who accompanies them on their adventures, often sitting snugly in Alycia's pocket or perched on Wesley's shoulder.

"Wesley just met Alycia for the first time," says Ves with a soft smile. "He doesn't know it yet, but his life is never going to be the same again."

Elisha grins ruefully, slinking her arms around his neck until they're pressed flush, chest to thigh. "I still think the names are too on the nose."

He folds her into his arms, heart to heart, as he lets her feel how much he's missed her. Her moss-brown eyes fasten on his, breath coming in short gasps when he grinds against her belly. "Eh, I'm not exactly hiding it. I don't mind if everyone knows that I'm totally and completely in love with you," Ves murmurs.

"You open book, you," she teases, skating her lips along his jaw. "Let's go upstairs?"

"How was your trip?" he asks, pulling her to the stairs, making sure to lock the door on the way. He doesn't want any future in-laws from across the street popping in to visit. They'll see them tonight at dinner, along with Solana and Adam, plus Arun and Cade, who are bringing Hanna with them.

Where, if all goes like he hopes, he and Elisha will have some good news to share with their loved ones. Maybe his relationship with his parents will always be strained, but he knows this to be true: his real family is whatever he decides it is.

"Amazing!" she enthuses, so happy to be home she misses the look of profound love and pride on his face that almost gives him away.

After *Sleighbells*'s runaway success, a few more commercials, and a lineup for the next two years to film Lifetime and Hallmark movies in town, every other small town in Pennsylvania wants to know how she did it and get the benefit of her experience. With Danica's unflinching support and the right words in the right ears, Elisha's been given the task of leading a tri-county pilot program to revitalize the economy and bring new media interest to the region.

She even got to handpick her own team to help her, which means Ves has gotten to know Mia and Riley a lot better in the last few months. He's even gotten the stink eye from Greg a couple of times, which, Ves supposes, officially makes him a local now.

He supposes it was inevitable that Elisha's friends would become his, especially since Came to Sleigh adopted him as their newest trivia team member last January. *And* since Tori started her own team, All the Single Ladies, having a whole rivals-to-lovers competitive thing going on with Riley ever since her divorce.

"Everything you wanted?" asks Ves, unable to stop himself from dropping a kiss on her shoulder and fiddling with the bows. Just one tug is all it would take . . .

She catches his hand. Her ring finger is still empty, but if the next few minutes go the way he hopes, it won't be for long. He thinks about the vintage engagement ring he bought in New York, the one he's been hiding in his sock drawer for months. A heart-shaped ruby surrounded by diamonds. The candy-cane colors caught his eye the first time he saw it, and he knew at once this ring was the one.

"Everything I wanted," Elisha confirms, and then she tugs him down for a kiss, arms wrapping tight around her beau. She pulls back, brown eyes sparkling. "How about you?"

He knows she isn't just talking about work. He plucks at the straps, and by the time they reach their bedroom, the dress is fluttered in a heap halfway up the stairs.

"Everything I ever wanted," says Ves. "Wrapped with a bow."

ACKNOWLEDGMENTS

You snow the drill! It's acknowledgment time!

I'd always wanted to write a Christmas rom-com, especially one with a diverse cast, so I'll never fir-get the email in which the wonderful team at G. P. Putnam's Sons greenlit *Wrapped with a Beau*. (How many puns is too many? Answer: the limit does not exist!!!)

I've been tree-mendously fortunate to work with editor Gabriella Mongelli on three books, and each experience has been better than the last. Like putting up decorations or layering bebinca, this book came together in stages, and as I write this, we're at the final one! That's a wrap! Thank you for supporting the heart and heat of this cozy, charming, nostalgic Christmas story I envisioned. And for your clarity and fielding my occasionally panicked questions and accommodating me when I needed more time. In short, thank you for everything.

As always, my evergreen thanks to my agent, Jessica Watterson, a bastion of relentless passion and positivity. Your support is immeasurable.

Thank you to the entire team at G. P. Putnam's Sons who spruced up my manuscript into this be-yule-tiful book. You're all sleigh-in' it! Every cheery, festive element invites the reader into the story, and for that, cover artist Petra Braun, jacket designer Vi-An Nguyen, and interior designer Katy Riegel have all my thanks. Petra, you've long been an artist I follow, so to have a cover (I so deerly love) illustrated by you is a gift. Thanks also goes to production editor Leah Marsh and copyeditor Amy J. Schneider.

To Emily Leopold in marketing and Kristen Bianco in publicity, I can't begin to express my gratitude for all your hard work in bringing my books to the hands of readers all over the world.

I'm blown away by my fellow authors—who are literal *angels*, by the way—who showed up for *Wrapped with a Beau*. Thank you for being so generous with your time and kind words. Jessica Joyce, Alicia Thompson, Lauren Kung Jessen, Amy E. Reichert, Courtney Kae, Sonya Lalli, Falon Ballard, and Kerry Winfrey, thank you for the present of your presense!

Kate, you were the first person to get excited about the Chocolate Mouse. I hope this book gets you feline festive.

Mom, Dad, thank you for believing in me, never thinking my dreams were too big, and raising me in a house full of books. None of us are bakers, but in every other respect, there's a lot of us in the Rowes. Thank you for Christmas in Nice and for every marché de Noël and all the holly-jolly knickknacks gifted over the years (I agree with Elisha, decorations are not mess!!!). Thanks to Granny for the bebinca.

To all the readers, bookstagrammers, influencers, booksellers, librarians, and everyone else who has spread the word about my books: you are the greatest! I am in awe of your passion and creativity, and so grateful for the tireless enthusiasm with which you support my work.

I think that probably most of us spend our lives chasing, seeking, yearning for that intangible thing called *home*. That might be a place like Piney Peaks, or maybe it's between the pages of a book or in a loved one's embrace. Whatever home is for you, whether a long road has already led you there or you're still on that journey, I hope you discover exactly where you're meant to be. This is, to me, what books and life are all about: coming home.

Thank you for inviting Elisha and Ves and the whole Piney Peaks family into your imaginations and, I hope, your hearts. I hope you fa-la-la-la-la-fall in love with them the way I have.

DISCUSSION GUIDE

1. In the world of *Wrapped with a Beau*, *Sleighbells under Starlight* was a classic Christmas movie. Do you have a favorite holiday movie? If so, which one and why?

2. Right from their first meeting, it's clear that Elisha and Ves are complete opposites. But in what ways might the two be similar to each other? Did you relate to one character more than the other?

3. Why do you think Elisha wants the *Sleighbells* sequel to be so successful? What does that movie mean to her? To Piney Peaks?

4. Ves is at first reluctant to get into the holiday spirit. What changes for him over the course of the novel?

5. Piney Peaks is a picturesque town, perfect for winter festivities. Was there a tradition or activity in the book that was your favorite? Do you have any holiday traditions of your own?

6. Talk about Elisha's and Ves's support systems, whether that be the Rowes, Solana, or Arun and Cade. How do their friends and family influence them?

7. Would you ever want to live in a place like Piney Peaks? Why or why not?

8. Both Elisha and Ves are facing crossroads in their careers and where they choose to call home. Do you ultimately agree with their respective decisions about where to build their lives?

9. What was your favorite holiday pun from the book?

10. What do you think Elisha and Ves's next holiday season together will look like?

ABOUT THE AUTHOR

PHOTOGRAPH OF THE AUTHOR © LILLIE VALE

Lillie Vale is the author of *The Decoy Girlfriend* and *The Shaadi Set-Up*, as well as the young adult novels *Beauty and the Besharam* and *Small Town Hearts*. She writes about secrets and yearning, complicated and ambitious girls who know what they want, the places we call home and people we find our way back to, and the magic we make. Born in Mumbai, she grew up in Mississippi, Texas, and North Dakota, and now lives in an Indiana college town.

VISIT LILLIE VALE ONLINE

lillielabyrinth.com

🐦 LillieLabyrinth

📷 LabyrinthSpine